Desire
Becomes Her

Books by Shirlee Busbee

Scandal Becomes Her

Surrender Becomes Her

Seduction Becomes Her

Passion Becomes Her

Rapture Becomes Her

Whisper to Me of Love

Desire Becomes Her

Desire Becomes Her

SHIRLEE BUSBEE

ZEBRA BOOKS
KENSINGTON PUBLISHING CORP.
www.kensingtonbooks.com

Busbee

ZEBRA BOOKS are published by

Kensington Publishing Corp.
119 West 40th Street
New York, NY 10018

All Kensington titles, imprints, and distributed lines are available at special
quantity discounts for bulk purchases for sales promotion, premiums,
fund-raising, educational, or institutional use.

Special book excerpts or customized printings can also be created to fit spe-
cific needs. For details, write or phone the office of the Kensington Special
Sales Manager: Kensington Publishing Corp., 119 West 40th Street, New
York, NY 10018. Attn. Special Sales Department. Phone: 1-800-221-2647.

Zebra and the Z logo Reg. U.S. Pat. & TM Off.

ISBN-13: 978-1-4201-1844-5
ISBN-10: 1-4201-1844-7

First Zebra Trade Paperback Printing: July 2012
10 9 8 7 6 5 4 3 2 1

Printed in the United States of America

To a pair of dear friends, who, for reasons that escape me ☺,
have left California and moved to Vermont:
JOHN KILLACKEY and LAWRENCE CONNOLLY.
Hey, you guys, we're all laying bets on how soon you,
Raindrop (awesome American Shetland pony), and
Zephyr (equally awesome border collie),
return to Area VII and to all your friends who
really, *really* miss your cheerful faces.

AND

Howard, after forty-nine years (yikes!),
still the love of my life and the best proofreader, bar none!

Prologue

Gillian Dashwood glanced around the dining room in the Duke of Welbourne's palatial hunting lodge in Hampshire and wondered, not for the first time, what she was doing here. Her gaze took in the huge stone fireplace, the bronze silk-hung walls adorned with the glassy-eyed heads of fox, boar and roebuck no doubt killed by his grace, before her eyes considered the guests seated around the long crystal- and silver-laden table.

Gillian recognized several of the men—all friends of her husband, Charles. Lord Padgett, Miles St. John, William Stanton and, not surprising, the duke's youngest son, Lord George Canfield, were seated around the long table. All of them, at one time or another, had been guests in her home, but she couldn't say their presence gave her any comfort. Being friends of her husband, they were all dissolute gamblers and heavy drinkers and beyond presiding over the dining table at her home, she avoided them, retreating upstairs with her companion and cousin, Mrs. Easley, as soon as politeness allowed.

Her gaze happened to meet Canfield's and a chill swept through her. Averting her eyes, her chin lifted. What a detestable creature—staring at her bosom that way.

Once again, she glanced around the table. It wasn't a large party, but that *she* was here was puzzling. From what she could discern, she and Charles were the only married couple in attendance. She'd assumed that the duchess would be attending, as well as the wives of the other gentlemen, but of the duke's wife—or anybody else's *wife*—there was no sign.

Several of the gentlemen, including her host, were married, but all the women present, with the exception of herself, were either widowed or unattached and none with any chaperone in attendance. The ladies, while young and attractive, were not in the first blush of youth either, but it was astonishing that they would be mingling so freely with the gentlemen.

Gillian told herself not to be judgmental, but the bold mannerisms and forward behavior of the women made her uncomfortable. The clinging hands, the too-loud laughter and the assessing, avid eyes . . . And the gowns! Nervously, she glanced down at her own self. Helped by a diamond and topaz brooch she'd used to alter the neckline and a bronze gauze wrap worn like a shawl and crisscrossed in front of the brooch, her breasts were decently covered—even if it didn't prevent Canfield from ogling.

When Charles had presented her with the gown, she'd taken one look at the amber silk confection he'd bought for her to wear tonight and had known immediately that it was far too dashing for her. They'd argued over the gown, Gillian refusing to wear a garment cut so low that the bodice barely covered her nipples. Mrs. Easley agreed with her. Furious, Charles stalked around the room, berating them for being a pair of country mice and unaware of the ways of the world. His words fell on deaf ears. Looking from one set feminine face to the other, shaking a finger at Gillian, he snarled, "By God, you'll not defy me! You *will* wear the gown at Welbourne's party, if I have to put it on you myself," and stormed from the room.

Gillian and Mrs. Easley looked at each other and then at the silk and lace gown spread across Gillian's bed. Fingering the offending neckline, Gillian sighed. "I suppose we can find some way to make it respectable."

Mrs. Easley nodded. Taking the gown from Gillian, she studied it. "Perhaps I can do something with that diamond and topaz brooch he recently bought for you. See here? The brooch is certainly large enough and if we center it and use the clasp to hold the edges of either side . . ."

Between the two of them, they managed to weave the fabric onto the pin of the large brooch and raise the neckline to some degree. The addition of a wide swathe of bronze gauze gave even more concealment.

While he amused himself in London, Charles determined that Gillian should remain home in their pleasant cottage in Surrey, but that didn't mean that she wasn't aware of society ways. Her parents had been members of the gentry and she'd been raised with all the benefits and rules pertaining to proper young ladies; if she'd been so inclined she could boast of titled ancestry a few generations back. Glancing around the table again, she suspected that there was nothing *proper* about this evening.

She looked at her husband seated down a few seats and across from her and frowned. He had been exceptionally kind to her in the time leading up to the duke's dinner party and that alone should have made her suspicious. Once he'd gambled away the respectable fortune she'd brought to the marriage, he'd had little use for her except to run his household and see to it that his friends, like Padgett and Stanton and the others, were made comfortable when staying with them in Surrey.

Her golden-brown eyes resting on Charles's dark face as he beguiled the woman sitting next to him, Gillian could still see signs of the handsome and charming man she had fallen in love with and married nearly nine years ago. He was a month away from his thirty-fifth birthday, and while the ravages of an indulgent and rakish life were increasingly evident, there was no denying that when he entered a room women noticed him.

Watching the woman, a widow, flower under Charles's

warm look, Gillian wanted to warn her not to believe the honeyed words that fell from those chiseled lips and the promise that gleamed in those striking blue eyes. Unable to bear watching him work his charms on yet another foolish woman, her gaze dropped.

Wondering how different her life would have been if she'd listened to her uncle and heeded his words, she sighed. Except for her older half brother, Stanley Ordway, her only other male relative had been her uncle, and since she and Stanley were often at odds with each other, she'd had only her uncle to look to for approval when Charles had asked her to marry him. Uncle Silas had chosen his words with care. Smiling fondly at her, he'd said, "He's a handsome bit of goods, I'll grant you that, but I worry, my dear, that he might make you an *uncomfortable* sort of husband." She'd brushed his comment aside, at eighteen so besotted by Charles Dashwood that no one could have prevented her from marrying him.

Thinking back to that time, she grimaced. The fact that she and Stanley had been in agreement about something should have warned her. Shaking her head, she realized that Stanley's friendship with Charles had been an obvious clue to his nature: her half brother was addicted to all games of chance and his friends were known gamesters. If only—

"Some more wine, my dear," purred a voice in her ear, breaking into her thoughts. "Your glass is nearly empty."

Gillian started and glanced at Lord Winthrop, the gentleman seated next to her. She knew him slightly, he was one of Charles's friends, but she did not like him—or the assessing gleam in his gray eyes. Like the others, Winthrop had visited them a few times in Surrey and he always made her uneasy, staring too long at her bosom, his hands holding hers longer than necessary. She sensed if she were ever foolish enough to be alone with him that he could not be trusted not to make unwanted advances.

Easily a decade or two older than most of Charles's friends

and like her husband and her half brother, Winthrop was a gambler. Unlike Charles and Stanley, he was also wealthy and a close crony of Welbourne's; she suspected it was Charles's association with Winthrop and Canfield that explained their presence here tonight.

Forcing a smile, Gillian replied, "No, thank you."

His eyes traveled over her, lingering on the soft swell of her breasts hidden beneath the bronze gauze, and she flushed and picked up her wineglass. Bringing the glass to her lips, she used her arm to shield herself from his bold gaze.

"It's a warm night . . . surely you don't need that bit of gauzy nonsense hiding your charms," he murmured.

A spurt of temper shot through her, and with ice in her voice, Gillian said, "You are too forward, my lord. I would thank you to keep your opinions to yourself."

He laughed, not at all abashed. "Ah, I like a lady with spirit." When Gillian glared at him, he murmured, "Forgive me, I was too bold, indeed."

Gillian shrugged, wishing he'd turn his attention to his neighbor and leave her alone. Would this interminable meal ever be over?

"You've not attended one of the duke's, ah, parties previously, have you?" asked Winthrop, not the least put off by her manner.

Stiffly, she replied. "No, this is my first time."

He smiled. "Your first time . . . well, let us hope you find it memorable . . . I will certainly do my best to see that it is quite, quite pleasurable for you."

His words and smile only increased her discomfort, and she glanced around for a distraction, but seeing that everyone was busy with their own conversations, she turned back to Winthrop and asked brightly, "Have you attended many of these, these parties?"

"Oh, yes. Frequently. One never knows what . . . *delights* Welbourne will have arranged for us."

Feeling as if they were talking about two different things, Gillian babbled, "And the duchess, does she attend?"

Winthrop threw back his silver-streaked dark head and laughed. "Oh, my sweet, you are adorable. Wherever did Charles find you?"

Her fingers tightened on the wineglass and she decided she *really* didn't like his lordship very much . . . or the duke's party. She wanted to go home. Now.

Perhaps, she thought unhappily, Charles was right and she *was* a country mouse. Certainly this glittering, sophisticated group made her feel out of her league.

As if guessing she was ready to bolt from the room, Winthrop said, "Forgive me—I see that I was too free in my comments. I apologize." When Gillian nodded and kept her gaze averted, he murmured, "Come now, I've apologized. Won't you relent, fair lady, and favor me with some conversation?"

"I doubt my conversation would interest you," she muttered.

"How do you know unless you try me?"

She glanced sharply at him, wondering if there was a double meaning behind his words, but there was only polite inquiry on his face.

"Let us see, what topic would you like to discuss?" he asked. "Fashion? The latest gossip circling the *ton?* Or are you a bluestocking and prefer to talk about books and music? Ah, perhaps, the plight of poor King Louis and his beautiful queen, Marie Antoinette?"

Seated on Gillian's other side and hearing Winthrop's question, a florid-faced gentleman, one of the few men present with powdered hair, exclaimed, "Indeed, the situation in France should concern us all." He looked around the table. "Everyone knows that since Mirabeau's death in April the French assembly has been in utter disarray—why, even the royal family tried to flee the country. It is a shame they were caught before they could escape." Shaking his head gloomily, he added, "You mark my words, there are dangerous days ahead."

A blond-haired beauty nearby leaned forward and murmured, "Poor Marie Antoinette! Imagine being dragged back to Paris like a common criminal. Shameful!"

"At least the king and queen are still alive," said another gentleman. "Not like several other unfortunates. It's no wonder that London is being flooded with aristocratic émigrés. No one knows what will happen next."

Winthrop yawned. "Dear me, I feel as if I have wandered into the House of Lords." Plaintively he asked, "*Must* we discuss politics?"

The gentleman on Gillian's other side flushed, but a ripple of laughter went around the table and the situation in France was dropped.

A gentlemen on the other side of the table asked, "Speaking of tragedies, has anyone heard anything new about the widowed Mrs. Soule?"

"Wasn't it shocking?" exclaimed one of the women. "You'd have expected it in London, but who'd have thought such a thing would occur here in the tranquility of the country."

"Yes, it was shocking," agreed Miles St. John.

An awkward silence fell, everyone suddenly remembering that one of the latest on-dits had been that St. John had been snared at last and that an engagement had been in the offing.

Self-consciously St. John cleared his throat and murmured, "Elizabeth was a dear friend. As many of you know I often escorted her around London." His handsome mouth thinned. "It's appalling to think that someone broke into her home and murdered her in her bed and if I ever . . ." He broke off, flashed a wry smile and said, "Forgive me. I allow my emotions to run away with me."

Not at all happy to be usurped by a rehashing of the tragic event that had ignited the neighborhood two months ago, Winthrop murmured, "First politics and now something that would provide the plot of a Minerva Press Novel." Sending a pained look around the table, he asked, "Must we discuss these things?"

Charles laughed and said, "Come now, Winthrop, you like gossip as well as the rest of us."

"Yes, but not," he said, "when I am in the presence of a beautiful lady like your wife."

"Point taken," Charles murmured and turned his attention back to the lady next to him.

Smiling at Gillian, Winthrop murmured, "Ah, and now where were we? Was I admiring your eyes? Or perhaps, it was that delicious mouth of yours?"

"Actually," she said with a bite, "*you* were the one who introduced the topic of King Louis and Queen Marie Antoinette."

He shuddered. "How gauche of me." His gaze moved over her, lingering once again on the swell of her breasts. "I would much rather dwell on your beautiful self."

Wishing this interminable evening would end and that Lord Winthrop would turn his attention elsewhere, she dredged up a smile and replied, "Surely, talking about oneself is as boring as politics."

"Not when someone is as lovely as you are, my sweet."

Gillian never took credit for the beauty that fate had bestowed upon her. Without being vain, she knew she was beautiful, her mirror as well as many admirers had told her so, and at twenty-seven she was at the height of her stunning loveliness, but Winthrop's comments increased her discomfort. She wasn't *un*accustomed to compliments—during her sole Season in London she had been much sought after, not only her tidy fortune drawing the gentlemen to her, but her smiling golden-brown eyes, sable locks and ethereal form adding to the appeal. There had been much chagrin amongst the gentlemen of the *ton* when her fancy had settled on Charles Dashwood.

She'd taken pains with her appearance tonight—not wishing to appear a frump in front of Charles's friends—as much to avoid another heated argument as any other reason. She knew the gown complemented her slender body, and the handiwork of Nan Burton, her longtime maid, was not to be discounted. Earlier this evening, lips pursed, Nan had arranged the lustrous dark brown locks into ringlets that framed her face and brushed a bit of rice powder across her face and rubbed a tiny amount of rouge into her cheeks.

Stepping back to admire her work, Nan said, "It's a pity that the wearing of patches has gone out of style because I think a tiny patch near the corner of your lips would be perfect." Tucking in one wayward ringlet near Gillian's ear, she added, "But I'm happy that powdering the hair has gone out of fashion except for a few diehards." Smiling fondly at her mistress, Nan said, "I must say, Madame, that I have not seen you in such looks in a long time."

Rising to her feet from behind the dressing table, Gillian had shaken out the folds of the amber silk and lace gown and smiling asked, "Does that mean I go around looking dowdy?"

Nan laughed and shook her head. "As if you could! Garbed in rags you'd turn the head of any man without ice water in his veins. Now go on with you and join the guests and have a jolly good time."

Nan's remark, while meant to cheer her up, only reminded Gillian that she was married to a man who did indeed have ice water in his veins, but she quickly pushed that thought away. Winthrop's determined flirting and compliments should have made her feel attractive, but they had the opposite effect and she sighed, wishing that she was at home reading quietly in the front parlor with Mrs. Easley.

Hearing her sigh, Winthrop said, "I see that my much vaunted charm is having no effect on you. Tell me, lovely lady, is it just me or men in general?"

Gillian flushed. Forcing a smile, she looked at her companion and murmured, "I apologize, my lord. I'm afraid that I am not used to hearing such extravagant compliments."

"Oh no," he said, "don't go all starchy and formal on me now. I much preferred the shy rose." His gaze caressed her. "I wonder if you'll be so charmingly shy in the morning?"

She looked sharply at him, but he only smiled and, apparently having grown bored, began to work his wiles on the young woman seated on the other side of him. Grateful Winthrop's attention was fixed elsewhere, she finished the meal in relative comfort.

As the hour grew later, some of the gentlemen, Charles, Welbourne, Padgett, Canfield and Winthrop amongst them, disappeared into the nether regions of the house to drink and gamble, leaving the other guests to fend for themselves. Deserted among strangers in the gilt and cream salon where the other guests had assembled after dinner, Gillian tried her best to mingle, but the ladies were far more interested in the gentlemen than in talking to her, and the gentlemen . . . After repulsing a drunken viscount's attempts to kiss her for the third time, Gillian fled.

Entering her bedroom, she leaned back against the door and took her first easy breath since she had descended the stairs that evening. She might be somewhat naïve and out of the social whirl, but only a fool wouldn't have realized that this party was one that no respectable woman would have attended. What in the world had Charles been thinking bringing her to such an affair? Did he value her so little? Or was it his way of punishing her for refusing to play hostess to just the sort of party that was taking place downstairs at this very minute?

Angry and puzzled, she walked across the room and sat down at her dressing table. Staring at herself in the mirror, Gillian considered ringing for Nan, but decided against it. Nan would be agog to hear about the party and at the moment, she wasn't up to relating an expurgated version of the evening. Morning would be soon enough and perhaps by then, she thought wearily, she would have made sense of the evening.

After removing the scant makeup she had worn, she undid Nan's carefully arranged ringlets and brushed her hair until it fell in gleaming dark waves around her shoulders. Standing up, she kicked off her satin slippers and began struggling with the fastenings at the back of her gown. Her fingers fumbling with the ties and hooks, she crossed to the huge bed with its gold and rose velvet bed curtains; her nightgown and robe lay spread out across the mattress where Nan had left them for her. After several frustrating minutes, the last hook came undone and the gown finally slid to her feet. With corsets and stays no longer in fashion, Gillian was left wearing only a delicate lawn chemise and a linen petticoat trimmed in lace, and it took her only a second to be rid of them.

Her fingers had just closed around the finely embroidered nightgown when she heard a sound. Whirling around, she clutched the flimsy garment to her breast and stared in horror as Winthrop, just as if he had every right, entered her room.

His eyes assessing the charms barely concealed by the nightgown she held tightly against her body, he strolled toward her. "Charles said that you were beautiful," he drawled, "but he failed to mention precisely *how* beautiful."

"C-C-Charles? My h-h-husband?" she stammered stupidly. "What are you talking about? Are you mad? Charles will kill you if he finds you here! You must leave! Immediately!"

Winthrop laughed. "What an innocent you are! Who do you think sent me here?" Approaching her, he ran a caressing finger across her shoulder and down her arm. "So shy. Charles said that you might be recalcitrant at first, but that it was worth the effort to make you biddable."

Embarrassingly conscious of her near-naked state, the nightgown fisted in her hand providing little cover, Gillian stared at him openmouthed, unable to believe what she was hearing. Charles knew he was here? Had, if she understood him correctly, sent him here.

Equally frightened and furious by the implication, her eyes narrowed and she said, "Let me understand you: my husband, Charles, sent you to me? To make me biddable?"

Liking the silken feel of her skin beneath his fingers, hunger rushed through Winthrop. He was hard and ready for her, but the glitter in her eyes gave him pause. With one sweet pink-tipped breast peeking out from behind her nightgown and an enticing glimpse of the thick patch of curls nestled between her legs, she was everything Charles had claimed, but the expression in those long-lashed jeweled eyes . . . He had understood from Charles that she had agreed to their bargain and that she was willing, if reluctant. The woman before him did not look the least willing, and she confirmed his impression by violently shoving away his wandering hand.

"How dare you!" she exclaimed, her voice shaking with rage. "I don't know what my husband has told you, but there has obviously been a mistake."

Winthrop frowned. "Charles didn't mention the vowels? Or our bargain?"

"What bargain?" she demanded, clutching the nightgown even tighter to her body.

He studied her, his frown growing, passion dying. "Your husband," he began, "owes me a great deal of money." For a moment his gaze skimmed over her near-nakedness. "And he knows that I have long, ah, admired you. He suggested a trade. He gets his vowels returned and I get a night with you."

Gillian blanched. "He g-g-gave me to you?" she whispered, revulsion in every syllable. "For the night . . . in return for his vowels?"

He nodded, looking unhappy. "It was my understanding that you knew and were willing."

Whatever vestige of affection she might have held for her

husband died in that moment, but beneath the hurt, the grievous wound to her heart and pride, she was aware of a glorious sense of freedom seeping through her. By his own doing Charles had freed her from their travesty of a marriage. But first, she thought, her jaw clenching, she had to deal with Winthrop. . . .

Winthrop was a strong man, and Gillian knew that in any contest of strength he could overpower her. Finding her unwilling, and unused to being thwarted, rape was not out of the question. . . . Hiding her fears, she held her nightgown like a steel shield against her body and regarded him. He did not, she decided, look like a man with rape on his mind.

Winthrop had few scruples, but he was sober enough to balk at outright rape. And it was clear from her reaction, and the set of her jaw, that rape was the only way he would have the lady in his bed tonight.

"There seems to have been a misunderstanding," he muttered.

"Indeed," she said, icily polite, "that does appear to be the case." Not giving an inch, she glared at him, her eyes glittering. "And since there does seem to have been a 'misunderstanding,' I suggest that you leave my room immediately."

His gaze slipped down her body and he sighed. "You would have been worth every penny."

"No doubt," she snapped. "But I believe I asked you to leave. *Now.*"

Winthrop held up his hands. "Very well." He bowed, turned on his heel and disappeared through the connecting door.

Fearful he might change his mind, Gillian flew across the room to lock the door only to discover that there was no key in the lock. Heart banging in her breast, fighting back sobs of fright and fury, she raced back across the room to the bell rope that would summon Nan and yanked frantically on it.

Remaining here for the night was out of the question, and

with shaking fingers, she scrambled back into her chemise and petticoat. Her gaze fell upon the amber silk and lace gown and she shuddered. Charles had bought the gown for her . . . for her to whore for him. Another shudder racked her. She'd rather die than wear that hateful garment again, and she hurried to the big mahogany wardrobe where Nan had hung the clothes she had brought with her.

Her hand found the fawn and gold traveling gown she'd planned to wear for the journey home. She had just managed to drag it on and was fighting with the fastenings when a sleepy-eyed Nan stumbled into the room.

Astonished to find her mistress dressing to travel, she gasped, "Madame! What are you doing?"

An unnatural brightness in her topaz eyes, Gillian said, "*We* are leaving immediately! Send a message to the stables for our coach and driver and tell them to be at the front door within fifteen minutes."

"Fifteen minutes! Madame, it's the middle of the night! Everyone is asleep and will have to be awakened—and fifteen minutes is hardly enough time for the horses to be harnessed. Besides, I cannot pack your things in that time, let alone my own," protested Nan.

"I don't care what time of night it is," Gillian said, thoughts of Winthrop returning adding a hysterical edge to her voice. "I will not remain in this house one minute longer than necessary." More calmly, she added, "Worry about your own things then and as for mine . . ." She glanced at the amber silk and lace gown with revulsion. "Leave everything here, it matters little to me—I intend to be gone from this house just as soon as possible."

Perplexed by her mistress's actions, but seeing that there was no dissuading her, Nan made a face and said, "Very well, but first let me help you finish dressing."

A moment later, with Nan gone to get her own things and to send a servant to the stables for the coach, Gillian struggled with her hair. Her fingers shook and the gleaming strands kept slipping from her grasp, but she finally managed to push the thick mass into a haphazard bun at the back of her neck.

Feeling more in control of the situation, Gillian took a deep breath. Nan was packing. The coach had been sent for. That left Charles . . . A steely gleam in her eyes, her jaw rigid, she marched from the room, intent upon finding her husband.

Unaware of the events that had taken place upstairs, as Gillian left her room in search of him, Charles was feeling rather smug and satisfied as he lolled back in the mulberry velvet chair and regarded the angry gentleman across from him. The gaming room was deserted except for the two men—the other male guests having abandoned the appeal of the cards and dice and sought out the charms of their various mistresses. Most of the candles had burned out and only a few gutted in their holders, leaving the room filled with shadows.

"Give it to me," demanded the gentleman across the green baize-covered table from Charles.

Charles took a sip of his brandy and, carefully setting down the snifter, smiled at the younger man. Shaking his head, he said, "No. I'm sorry—you were the one who risked it on a throw of the dice. It's mine now."

"But I told you, it was only until I could raise the funds to redeem it," the other man protested. "I have the money now and to, to compensate you for waiting for your money, I've offered you more than the original debt." Accusingly he stared at Charles. "You promised I would have it back."

"Well, yes, I know," Charles admitted, "but, you see, you offered such an, er, generous amount for its return that it made me wonder if it would be unwise of me to let it go."

The other man surged to his feet, sending his chair tipping

over backward. Fists clenched, a dangerous cast to his face, he growled, "You're a fool if you don't give it back to me."

Charles shrugged. "Perhaps, but all that needs concern you is the fact that at the moment I have no intention of giving it back." Speculatively, he eyed the man. "I wonder why you are so desperate to get it back and what it is really worth to you."

"No more than I've already offered," the gentleman snapped.

Smiling, Charles shook his head. "Oh, I think you'll go higher. It's obviously worth a great deal more to you than the sum you offered me."

Infuriated, the other man leaned forward and snarled, "Give it back to me, you bastard!"

"Temper, temper," Charles taunted, toying with the younger man like a cat with a mouse. It was a mistake.

With a cry of rage, the young man tossed the table between them aside and launched himself upon Charles. "Give it back to me!" he cried. "Give it back!"

Charles sought to throw off his attacker, but caught by surprise, his opponent bore him to the floor. Hitting with a thud and more annoyed than hurt, Charles didn't realize his danger. It was only when he saw the dagger that suddenly appeared in the other man's hand that he realized he'd pushed his luck too far.

Shaken from his complacency by the sight of the dagger, Charles defended himself savagely, and locked in a mortal battle, the two men rolled and tumbled across the floor, sending tables, chairs, cards, dice, snifters flying. Against an enraged, armed attacker, Charles had no chance. The dagger rose and fell and Charles knew a moment of panicked disbelief as the blade sank deep into his chest. By God! He's actually killed me, was his last thought.

Breathing heavily, Charles's attacker rose to his feet. Stunned by what he had done, he stared at the body lying on the floor amidst the scattered cards and dice and overturned furniture. He swallowed. He hadn't meant to kill him. He'd only come for what was his. It was Dashwood's own bloody fault, he told himself, vindicating his actions.

His thoughts raced as he stared at the body on the floor in front of him. His jaw clenched. What was done was done— and now to retrieve the cause of it all.

Dropping down on one knee he systematically searched Charles's body. Not finding what he was looking for, he cursed and stood up. What had the bastard done with it?

The sound of an opening door sent him leaping into a shadowy corner. He must not be discovered here with a dead body on the floor!

Startled by the sight that met her gaze, Gillian paused on the threshold. In the faint glow of the candlelight, she saw the overturned tables, the complete disarray of the room. "Charles! What is going on in here?" she demanded, taking a few cautious steps into the room. Thinking her husband must be hiding in the shadows, she snapped, "Oh, stop it! I know you're here, the butler told me so."

Silence met her words. In no mood to play hide-and-seek, she said, "Very well! Hide like the coward you are, but know this! You . . ." Something on the floor, sticking out from behind one of the overturned tables, caught her eye and she froze. Peering through the shadows she made out what looked like a boot. . . .

Mouth dry, her heart thudding, she stepped nearer for a closer look. She recognized the man lying so still and lifeless amidst the wreckage of the room. Charles! With a cry she sank to the floor next to the body.

In shocked disbelief she stared at him. It was Charles. And he was dead.

Frightened now, averting her eyes from the bloodstains on his embroidered waistcoat, she staggered to her feet. Help. She needed help.

Gillian spun around, looking for the bell rope to summon assistance. She never saw the man who crept from the shadows and struck her a vicious blow to the temple with the handle of his dagger. Light exploded behind her eyes, and she dropped to the floor beside the body of her dead husband.

Chapter 1

When the news that Marie Antoinette, the imprisoned queen of France, had been executed on the 16th of October of 1793 reached England, it hit Luc Joslyn hard. It wasn't that he was an admirer of the queen or that he felt any loyalty to France, but for her to die under the blade of the guillotine seemed a terrible end for the woman who had ruled over the glittering court at Versailles. Of the poor dauphin and, since his father's execution in January, titular king of France, there was little word.

Not for the first time, Luc blessed his own timely escape from France and his unorthodox arrival in England in February. He'd known it was a fool's errand, but ignoring all advice to the contrary, he'd sailed to France from America the previous fall, determined to find if any of his mother's family had survived the savage upheaval that was taking place in the land of his birth. Despite a careful, diligent search, he'd found no trace of his mother's family, and it was only by a stroke of luck that he had not died in France himself.

A crooked smile curled the corners of his mouth. Thank *le bon Dieu* for Emily's smugglers.

Seated at a table in a quiet corner of The Ram's Head tavern, Luc brooded over Marie Antoinette's fate until his attention was caught by a pair of gentlemen playing cards at a nearby table. Through hooded eyes Luc watched Jeffery Townsend lead Lord Broadfoot's youngest whelp, Harlan, down the path to perdition. In the brief time he watched the pair, by his reckoning Jeffery had won over four thousand pounds from Harlan, and Luc, familiar with the Broadfoot family through his half brother, Viscount Joslyn, knew that Harlan couldn't sustain those kinds of losses. A fashionable family could live for a year on six thousand pounds, and while Lord Broadfoot was known to be warm in the pocket, it was unlikely he would look with favor at his youngest son throwing away a small fortune in one night of gaming.

Convinced that Jeffery was cheating and glad of the distraction from his bleak thoughts, Luc paid close attention to the flash of the cards, but he had yet to catch him at it. His azure eyes narrowed as Jeffery quickly won another hand and he decided that he really didn't like Jeffery Townsend very much—even if he was the local squire and they were related by marriage.

Staring at his sister-in-law's cousin as Jeffery ordered another round of undoubtedly smuggled French brandy and suggested another game to his companion, Luc shook his head. *Zut!* How Emily, as warm and charming a young woman as one could find, could be related to an egg-sucking weasel like Jeffery puzzled him. Oh, there was a superficial physical resemblance, the Townsend cousins were blond and tall, but while Emily was as true and honest as the finest English steel, Jeffery . . .

Luc's mouth thinned as the two men rose from their table and walked, in Harlan's case unsteadily, in the direction of the private gaming rooms at the side of the tavern. The boy was foxed, and Luc had been aware of the liberal supply of liquor Jeffery had kept coming to their table since he had been watching them.

It wasn't his responsibility to guide the steps of a green boy, Luc admitted, but neither could he sit by and allow Harlan to be plucked naked by the likes of Jeffery Townsend. Unless he missed his guess, once Jeffery had Harlan in one of those private rooms, Harlan would be lucky to stagger home with his boots. Sighing, he rose to his feet.

For many reasons, Luc wouldn't normally be found in the environs of The Ram's Head, and before he had taken more than two steps, one of those reasons stepped directly in his path. He groaned inwardly. Bandying words with Will Nolles, the proprietor and owner of The Ram's Head, was as appealing to him as dancing nude with a copperhead.

Nolles was a diminutive man, his build slender, and wearing a close-fitting dark green jacket, a wide white cravat tied in a bow adorning his throat and striped hose on his legs, his leaning toward dandyism was obvious. His pale green eyes glinting in the smoky candlelight of the inn, Nolles blocked Luc's path. "I couldn't believe my ears," Nolles murmured, "when one of the barmaids came into my office and told me that you were here tonight." His eyes as unblinking as a snake's, he asked, "I don't believe I've seen a Joslyn in my humble tavern in . . . months. How is it that we're honored with your presence tonight?"

Luc regarded him, deciding his next move. On the surface, Nolles was an honest tavern owner, but he made his profits, rather large profits, as the leader of a gang of smugglers— Luc had already spotted several known members of the gang scattered about the room. With good reason, none of them had any love for the Joslyns, and Luc was quite certain that there wasn't one of them who wouldn't enjoy putting a knife between his ribs.

Earlier in the year, Barnaby, Luc's half brother, had cost the smugglers a fortune by capturing the huge cache of smuggled goods they'd been hiding in the tunnels beneath Windmere, the ancestral home of the Joslyn family. Not only was the contraband turned over to the Revenuers, access to the tunnels had been destroyed. If Barnaby could have brought Nolles to the hangman's noose he would have, but during the confrontation in the old barn, Nolles had managed to slip free.

The discovery of the contraband had been a nine-day's-wonder, and no one had acted more astonished than Nolles. Publicly, all was polite, but Luc knew that the intervening months had done nothing to lessen the desire for revenge that burned in the breast of Nolles and his gang, and he winced. He could almost hear Lamb's voice in his ear berating him for sticking his head in the lion's mouth.

Standing six feet four and with the muscle to match his imposing height, Luc wasn't the least intimidated by the situation, but conscious that every minute he delayed allowed Jeffery to dip deeper into Harlan's purse, Luc decided to forego the pleasure of inciting a brawl and shrugged. "I felt like a change of pace," he answered with barely a trace of a French accent in his voice. One sleek black brow rose. "Any objections?"

Nolles spread his hands. "Of course not." He smiled tightly. "The Ram's Head is a public tavern after all, open to one and all."

"*Precisement,*" Luc said, noting out of the corner of his eye which room Jeffery ushered Harlan. "And now if you will excuse me . . . ?"

Nolles half-bowed and moved out of his way.

Feeling Nolles's gaze on his back like the kiss of a blade, Luc walked toward the door through which Jeffery and Harlan had just disappeared. Reaching the door, he didn't knock; he simply opened the door as if he was expected and entered the room.

It was a pleasant room. A small fire crackled on the brick hearth, keeping the faint chill of the October night at bay, and pairs of candles burned in pewter sconces placed around the room. Beneath a window that faced the front of the tavern was a carved oak lowboy, decanters filled with spirits and glasses neatly set in the middle. On the opposite side of the room, flanked by two brown leather chairs, squatted a small chest, the top littered with several packs of cards, dice and other items used for gaming. In the middle of the room was a large, green baize-covered table; a half-dozen wooden armchairs with padded leather seats were placed around the table.

Harlan was slumped in one of the chairs on the far side of the table, and Jeffery, in the act of tenderly pressing a snifter of brandy into Harlan's hand, glanced up at Luc's entrance. Recognizing Luc, annoyance on his handsome features, Jeffery said, "This is a private room."

Luc smiled, and there were those who would have warned Jeffery not to be misled by that particular smile. "Come now, *mon ami*," Luc said, "we are practically cousins. Surely you cannot object to my joining you."

Harlan stared happily at him. "It's Luc Joslyn. I like Luc. Luc's a friend of m'family," he said, smiling beatifically at Jeffery. When Jeffery remained unmoved, Harlan added, "He's Joslyn's half brother. Half French, you know. Your cousin Emily married him." He giggled. "Married Barnaby, not Luc."

"I'm aware of that," Jeffery muttered.

Harlan frowned, seeking a thought. "Older than Barnaby. Would have been the viscount," he said finally, "but born on the wrong side of the blanket."

Gritting his teeth, Jeffery said, "I'm quite familiar with Luc's antecedents."

Harlan reared back in the chair and stared at him in astonishment. "You know Luc? His half brother is Lord Joslyn."

"I know that," Jeffery said tersely. "Lord Joslyn married my cousin, remember?"

Harlan nodded cheerfully. "Married your cousin, Emily." He looked at Luc. "I like you. M'father likes you, too." He thought a moment. "My brother, Miles, likes you, too. Says even if your mother was French that you're a good 'un."

"Yes, yes," Jeffery snapped. "Everybody likes Luc." A wheedling note in his voice, he said, "But I don't think we'd like him joining us, do you?"

That Harlan was cup-shot and in no condition to be gambling was obvious, but he was an amiable, well-brought-up young man, and even as drunk as he was, it would never have crossed his mind to deny another gentlemen his company. "I like Luc. No reason he shouldn't join us." A huge yawn overtook Harlan and he added sleepily, "Think I'll nap. Change my luck."

Before Jeffery could argue with him, Harlan's head dropped to his chest and to Luc's relief, he passed out. Harlan was safe from Jeffery for tonight.

Strolling over to the small chest, Luc picked up several pairs of dice. Taking a chair across from Harlan, he placed the majority of the dice to one side, keeping one pair. Tossing the dice with a careless ease that spoke of experience, he smiled at Jeffery and said, "Hazard? Shall we toss a few? I understand from your cousin that you are a great gambler."

Jeffery hesitated. Passed out, Harlan was of no further use to him tonight, and while he had a pocket plump with Harlan's vowels, the gambler in him wasn't ready to walk away and end the evening so tamely—not when there was a bigger prize to be won. In the seven or eight months that Luc had been on British soil, his reputation, earned in the gaming hells in London, for winning all games of chance, was well established. Besting Lucifer, so called because no one denied that Luc had the devil's own luck, had become the goal of many a foolish young man . . . and some older, wiser gentlemen who should have known better.

Jeffery considered himself an expert gamester, and the thought of beating Lucifer was an exciting one, but he was wary. He had confidence in his own skills, but he couldn't dismiss Luc's reputation. Dare he try his hand?

From beneath lowered lids, Luc watched Jeffery struggle with prudence and temptation, betting that temptation would win. Jeffery was, after all, a gambler, and he smiled to himself when Jeffery shrugged and said, "Why not? The evening is young yet."

Luc kept a cool head when gambling, eschewing, except for an occasional glass of wine, any liquor. He ascribed that one trait to his phenomenal luck, that and an instinctive skill with the cards and knowing when to call it quits. Jeffery appeared not to have learned that lesson.

Luc was correct. Jeffery was unlucky and threw crabs again and again while Luc knicked it every time the dice were in his hands. After several tosses of the dice, instead of realizing that luck did not favor him tonight, in a bid to recover his losses, Jeffery kept raising the stakes. Luc did not stop him until boredom set in and, perhaps, a touch of compassion. From Emily he knew that Jeffery had been draining The Birches, the family estate, for years to support his gaming and that if Jeffery did not change his ways, he would lose everything. Luc was a calculated gambler, but he wanted no man's ruination on his conscience, even a weasel like Jeffery, and after a few hours, he ended the game. Rising from the table, Luc had not only Harlan's vowels in front of him, but he had vowels from Jeffery in the amount of two thousand pounds.

His face tight, Jeffery rose from the table and after giving Luc a curt nod barged from the room. Alone with Harlan, Luc shook him awake. Harlan started when Luc said gently, "Come, *mon ami,* I think it is home for you."

Harlan smiled angelically at him. "Luc. I like you. M'father likes you. Miles does, too."

Luc laughed. "*Bon!* Now let me stay in everyone's good graces and get you to your horse."

Harlan glanced around and, spying the dice on the table, he blinked. "Did we gamble?"

Luc nodded. "*Mais oui!* And the Lady Luck, she was with you. You won your vowels back."

Harlan's blue eyes opened very wide. "I did?" he asked, astonished.

Luc smiled and waved the vowels in front of Harlan's face.

"Indeed, you did. Now before the night is much older, I suggest we go home."

Harlan nodded and said confidingly to Luc, "I'm foxed, you know."

Even after his nap, Harlan was quite inebriated, but Luc managed to get him into his greatcoat and maneuvered the staggering young man out of the tavern. Outside in the chilly October night, with no little exertion, Luc hoisted him onto his horse and stuffed the vowels into one pocket of Harlan's greatcoat. When he was certain that Harlan was alert enough not to fall off, he mounted his own horse and, holding the reins to Harlan's horse, began the journey to the Broadfoot estate, Broad View.

By the time they reached the tall iron gates that marked the entrance to the driveway to the house, Luc was more than ready to be relieved of his drunken charge. The journey to Broad View was necessarily slow, and only Luc's quick action had prevented Harlan from falling off his horse numerous times. If Harlan wasn't on the verge of taking a bad spill, he was telling Luc how much he liked him, how much every member of his family liked him and singing at the top of his lungs every ribald ditty he'd ever learned.

A pair of torches burned on either side of a pair of double doors of the mansion, and while Harlan continued to sway and sing, Luc dismounted in front of the brick and stone mansion. Immediately one of the doors opened and Miles stepped out onto the terrace in front of the house.

Miles was an older version of Harlan, a little taller and broader of shoulder, but with the same blue eyes and light brown hair. Smiling, Miles shook his head as he walked toward Luc. "Chirping merry, is he?"

"I'm afraid so."

"When I heard the racket, I assumed as much." Miles hesitated. "Was he at The Ram's Head again?"

Luc nodded. "Gaming with Jeffery Townsend."

Miles's pleasant features stiffened. "Devil take it! Father is going to disown him if he's lost to that rakeshame again."

"You have nothing to worry about tonight. . . . Harlan showed great skill at Hazard and was able to recover all of his losses and, I think, a few thousand pounds from Monsieur Townsend. You'll find the proof in the pocket of his greatcoat."

Miles's eyes narrowed. "Really."

Luc nodded again. "Indeed, I was there and saw the whole thing."

"And did Harlan display this, er, great skill before or after he was fuddled?"

"During. I believe the liquor allowed him to toss aside his inhibitions and simply throw by instinct," Luc replied with a straight face.

"Really," Miles repeated, the dryness of his tone obvious.

"Truly," Luc said. "And now if you will excuse me, I must be on my way."

Mounting his horse, Luc tipped his head to Miles and swung the animal around. *"Bon soir,"* Luc called over his shoulder as he kicked his horse into motion and the darkness swallowed him up.

Leaving the gates of Broad View behind him, Luc turned his horse in the direction of Windmere. Long after midnight, the night was increasingly chilly and Luc thought he caught the scent of rain in the air: he would be glad to reach Windmere and his bed.

There was no moon, but familiar with the road and the trustworthiness of his mount, he kept his horse at a brisk trot. Rounding a bend in the road, his horse snorted and shied. A short distance ahead, in the light from its lamps, Luc could make out the shape of a wrecked vehicle. The phaeton sat at a drunken angle, the right wheels lodged in the ditch next to the road.

Approaching nearer, in the shifting fingers of light, Luc

recognized the pair of blaze-faced chestnuts that looked at him with perked ears. The horses belonged to Silas Ordway and unless he missed his guess, so did the vehicle. A quick glance at the scarlet striping on the wheels and body of the phaeton confirmed it.

Alarmed, Luc halted his horse and leaped to the ground. There was nothing to tell him how long ago the wreck had occurred, but Luc knew that the old man would not have left his prized chestnuts standing at the side of the road unattended.

"Silas!" he called out as he walked up to the phaeton. To his alarm, Silas answered him from the ground on the other side of the vehicle.

"Luc? Is that you, lad?"

The old man's voice was weak, and ignoring the jolt of anxiety he felt, Luc said, "*Oui!* Let me secure the horses and I shall be with you in a moment."

After tying his horse to a nearby sapling and doing the same with the chestnuts, Luc hurried around to the other side of the phaeton. He found Silas half-lying, half-sitting in the bottom of the ditch, his right arm cradled next to his frail body.

"*Mon Dieu!* What happened?"

In the pale light of the carriage lamps, Silas grimaced. "Some fool came racing up behind me and crowded me off the road. Clipped my wheels and tipped me into the ditch as pretty as you please." Forcing a smile, he added, "Damn fool thing to have done at my age, but I suspect I've broken my arm."

Luc carefully shifted the old man, but at Silas's swift intake of breath, he stopped. Glancing down at him, Luc asked, "How bad is it?"

"Not so bad that I intend to lie here all night," Silas replied testily. Scowling at Luc, he muttered, "Get me out of here, lad. I ain't made of crystal—I can stand some jostling— just get it over with."

"Let's do something about that arm first," Luc said. From beneath his greatcoat, he tugged his cravat free and used the wide strip of linen to anchor Silas's arm to the elder man's body. Satisfied the arm was secured, in one easy movement, Luc picked up Silas as if the old man were a doll and, carrying him in his arms, clambered from the ditch.

Luc glanced around, seeking a safe place to deposit his burden. In the dim light from the carriage lamps, except for the stand of trees where he had tied the horses, only darkness met his eye.

Aware of Luc's dilemma, Silas said, "Put me down, lad. I ain't a swooning damsel from a Gothick novel." Dryly, he added, "My arm is broken, not my leg."

Setting Silas down gently, Luc waited until the old man was steady on his feet before saying, "Let's see if I can free the phaeton before anything else."

Silas nodded and Luc walked over to the chestnuts. It was tricky, but the animals were powerful and well trained, and with a minimum of anxiety, under Luc's guidance, the phaeton's wheels were freed from the ditch as the vehicle lurched fully onto the road.

Approaching the side of the vehicle, Silas said, "Help me up—I can handle the reins while you tie your horse to the back of the phaeton."

Luc hesitated and Silas said, "Luc, I know my animals. These horses have been mine since birth. They're good, steady boys. They won't run away with me—they'll stand here steady as rocks until they're asked to do something else."

Trusting Silas's word, Luc jumped down from the phaeton. A few minutes later, Luc had the old man settled in the phaeton and his own horse tied to the back of the vehicle. Climbing into the vehicle, he took the reins from Silas's hand.

Noting the lines of pain around Silas's mouth and the paleness of his complexion, Luc asked again, "How bad is it?"

Silas dredged up a smile. "Not as bad as the time I was

silly enough to fight a duel and get myself shot in the shoulder for my efforts. Now, if you please, get me to High Tower before I shame myself by fainting."

Luc grinned and gently set the chestnuts into motion. He'd met Silas in April and, astonishing both of them and everyone who knew them, a friendship had grown between the two vastly different men.

Luc had liked the elfin old gentleman the moment he'd been introduced to him by his cousin, Simon Joslyn. They'd met in one of the fashionable gaming hells in London and within a matter of days, this past Season, it hadn't been unusual to find Ordway leaning on Luc's arm as the older man showed him around the city and introduced him to various members of the *ton*.

They made a strange pair, the tall young man with questionable antecedents and the wizened old gentleman. There were a few raised eyebrows, but by the time the Season ended in June and the *ton* dispersed to their country estates, the friendship between the two men was taken for granted.

Silas's country estate, High Tower, was situated not far from Windmere, where Luc was staying, and over the summer the friendship between the two men had continued to prosper and grow. The old man was reclusive, but Luc was often at High Tower, dining and playing cards with Silas until the morning hours, when he would return to Windmere.

The phaeton was well sprung, and the ride to High Tower passed without incident. A lone torch flickered near the door of the house, and slowly halting the horses underneath the small portico that had been added in the last century to the half-timbered Tudor manor house, Luc said, "If you'll hold the horses, sir, I'll rouse the house."

Silas grunted. "If someone isn't at the front door within the next five minutes, I pay them too much."

The words had hardly left his mouth before the stout oak door was opened and Silas's butler, Meacham, poked his head out. Seeing Luc at the reins and spying the swathe of material wrapped around his employer, his eyes widened.

Rushing outside, Meacham cried, "Master! What has happened?"

"Nothing that a visit from the bone-setter won't take care of," Silas said. "Now don't just stand there gawking at me like I'm a freak at a fair. Help me down."

Since Meacham was of Silas's generation and not much larger than his employer, Luc interceded and said, "Allow me, sir."

Not giving Silas a chance to reply, in one easy motion, Luc lifted the old man down from the vehicle and gently deposited him on his feet.

"Much obliged to you, lad," Silas said. "Don't like to think how long I would have lain there if you hadn't happened along. Indebted to you. Won't forget it."

"Think nothing of it, sir," Luc replied. Offering his arm, he said, "Let's get you inside and out of this chill weather."

After a sleepy footman was sent to bring the physician posthaste and a pair of stable boys had led the chestnuts away, with Silas leaning heavily on his arm and Meacham following anxiously on their heels, Luc escorted the old gentleman upstairs to his rooms.

Aided by Meacham and Silas's valet, Brownell, Luc's cravat was carefully removed. There was no hope of saving Silas's upper garments, and the sleeves of his greatcoat and jacket had to be cut open to free him from his clothes. Despite their gentleness, by the time the ordeal was over, his face white and drawn, Silas was slumped exhausted in a dark green damask chair by the fire in his room. His broken arm was once again secured against his body, this time by a wide strip of clean cloth provided by Meacham.

Not liking Silas's color, Luc quietly ordered Meacham to bring them some brandy. Within minutes Meacham returned with a decanter of brandy and a pair of snifters on a silver tray: an envelope lay to one side of the tray. After Silas had taken a few sips of the brandy, Luc was satisfied to see some color return to the old man's face. Feeling superfluous now that the immediate crisis was over, he set down his own snifter and murmured, "Well, sir, now that you are safely settled here at home, I shall be on my way."

Silas nodded. "I cannot thank you enough, lad. If you hadn't come along . . ."

"You would have managed," Luc returned lightly. "As you said, your arm was broken, not your leg."

Silas gave a bark of laughter. "If I'd been thirty years younger, perhaps. If not for you, I suspect it would have been morning before some farmer discovered me lying cold and shivering in that ditch." His expression grew somber. "It's a bitter night out there. I might have died."

To distract him, Luc indicated the envelope on the tray. "Is that a letter for you?" he asked.

Noting the envelope for the first time, Silas scowled. "Probably from that rascally nephew of mine—wanting me to pull him from the River Tick again."

Luc knew all about Stanley Ordway, and he agreed with Silas's assessment. The younger Ordway was on friendly terms with Jeffery Townsend and appeared to be of the same ilk.

Luc picked up the envelope and, noting the feminine hand-writing, grinned. "Perhaps not. Perhaps it is from the so charming Widow Dobson, who pursued you so assiduously in London."

Silas snorted. "Spare me that. I've escaped the parson's mousetrap this long; I ain't about to let a silly pea goose like Kitty Dobson leg-shackle me. Hand it here."

Luc handed him the envelope, noting the expression of pleasure that crossed Silas's face as he recognized the hand-writing. "It's from m'niece, Gillian, and she's a far different kettle of fish than Stanley," he said, glancing at Luc. Opening the envelope, Silas extracted the single sheet of paper and quickly read the contents. A smile spread across his face.

"Good news, sir?" Luc asked.

Silas put the note and envelope down on the table beside him and nodded. A sly expression crossed his wrinkled features. "Just what I've been hoping for."

Chapter 2

Arriving at Windmere, Luc left his horse at the stables and walked swiftly to the Dower House, where he had been living off and on these past months. Approaching the impressive house, he sighed. Living at the Dower House had been an acceptable solution when he had arrived in England within days of Emily and Barnaby's marriage, penniless and barely alive in the bargain. Presently, however, he was fully recovered from his infected wound, gained while escaping from a French prison, and with help from Lady Luck and some gentlemen who should have known better, no longer penniless—far from it.

When he had returned from London at the end of the Season in late June and suggested to Barnaby that he take a pair of rooms at Mrs. Gilbert's inn, The Crown, both Barnaby and Emily had been hurt and adamantly opposed to the very idea.

His black eyes glittering like chips of obsidian, Barnaby growled, "You're my brother! I have a bloody house sitting empty. . . ." He'd paused and muttered, "God's wounds! I have a half-dozen houses at my disposal, and you want to live in rented rooms at an inn?" His harshly handsome face annoyed, he demanded, "Are you deliberately insulting me, or is it just that your wits have gone wandering?"

The two half brothers bore little resemblance to each

other. Their height and black hair were the most obvious paternal traits they shared. Barnaby took after his mother, his swarthy skin and black eyes coming down to him from the Cherokee ancestry in her background. Ironically, Luc, the illegitimate brother, looked like the Joslyns, having been blessed with the azure eyes and patrician features of his father's family. While Barnaby looked like a tough brawler, with the size and muscle to match, Luc appeared every inch the aristocrat, from his elegant lean form to the haughty nose and beautifully chiseled mouth. Barnaby was generally reputed to be the steadfast one, while Luc lived a reckless, vagabond life, earning his keep at the gaming tables—much to Barnaby's irritation. Barnaby had attempted to share their father's estate with Luc, but Luc had inherited the stiff-necked pride of the Joslyns and would have none of it. As he had snarled at Barnaby, "If our sire didn't see fit to name me in his will, I sure as the devil don't intend to take your charity!" It was an old argument between them, and the years had not lessened the intensity of it.

Luc would have dug his heels in about removing to The Crown if Emily, her lovely face anxious at the discord between the two brothers, hadn't stepped in. "Please, Luc," she said, "won't you allow your brother to share some of his good fortune with you? Windmere, the title, none of it comes directly from your father." She grimaced. "Well, I suppose it could be argued that if not for your father being who he was, Barnaby wouldn't have inherited the title and Windmere, but my point is that he didn't inherit it from your father. He inherited from his great-uncle." She smiled warmly at him and asked gently, "How would you feel if positions were reversed? Won't you allow him to help you just a little . . . or is your pride too great?"

Luc looked down at her, thinking idly that pregnancy agreed with her. The baby wasn't due until late December, early January, and there was a certain roundness to her figure and the unmistakable glow that pregnant women exuded. At this moment, he wished he didn't like her so much or that she wasn't such a clever minx. She'd put forth the one argument that left him with no defense.

Giving in gracefully, he'd flashed her that grin known to cause many a woman the most delightful heart palpitations and murmured, "To please you, Lady Joslyn, I will accept your husband's kind offer."

She'd grinned back at him. "Emily, if you please. Every time someone calls me Lady Joslyn, I find myself looking about for the viscountess, forgetting that *I* am the viscountess."

"And a very pretty viscountess you are at that," said Barnaby, the love he felt for her open and obvious. She smiled at him, her gray eyes reflecting back her deep love for him.

The matter had been settled, but as he slipped into the Dower House this October night, he knew that wounding Barnaby's or Emily's feelings or not, he was going to have to find his own place. Gliding up the curving staircase to his bedroom, he sighed again. The Dower House was simply too big, too grand for someone like him.

At least, he thought with a smile, he had managed to rid himself of all the servants Barnaby had thought were necessary for his comfort. Walker, Mrs. Spalding, Jane and Sally, once Emily's staff at The Birches, all now worked at Windmere for Barnaby and Emily. Walker had replaced the nefarious butler, Peckham, who had been hand-in-glove with Nolles, and Mrs. Spalding had taken over the duties of her sister, Mrs. Eason, the cook, after Mrs. Eason had decided, with a generous pension from Barnaby, to retire near her daughter in Brighton. Of the original servants he'd started out with only Alice, once a scullery maid, but now cook and housekeeper, and young Hinton, ably filling in as valet and butler, remained. Despite the size of the residence, since Luc only used a few rooms in the house, the three of them muddled along together just fine.

Reaching his suite of rooms, he noted with approval that Hinton had left a pair of candles burning for him on the mantle of the brick fireplace. A small fire glowed on the hearth and kept the October chill from the room. In the flickering light of the fire and candles, Luc quickly undressed.

After blowing out the candles, naked as the day he was born, he slid under the pile of blankets and quilts, sighing with pleasure when his feet touched the warmed brick Alice had provided for him. Used to being on his own, except when at home in Virginia at the family plantation, Green Hill, he'd grown accustomed to the niceties provided by Alice and Hinton. He'd decided several weeks ago that when he left the Dower House, he would take them with him. Thanks to the foolishness of several gentlemen, some well-known peers amongst them, his pockets were full and he'd even invested a handsome amount in the funds. He grinned. *Nom de nom!* He was *almost* respectable.

Though the hour was late, sleep eluded him, and in the faint light provided by the dying fire, Luc stared at the shadows sliding around lazily overhead in the canopy. It had been an interesting night. Young Harlan would wake up with an aching head and no doubt befuddlement at his luck. His mouth twisted. Making an enemy of Jeffery Townsend hadn't been wise, but he didn't much give a damn about how Emily's cousin felt about him.

Silas's injury troubled him, and if he could discover who had ditched the old man, he'd enjoy having a word with whoever had forced his friend into the ditch and left him lying there injured without a backward glance. Inquiries in the village might give him a clue.

Luc frowned, thinking about the note from Silas's niece. Until tonight he hadn't been aware that Silas had a niece, but if she was anything like the old man's nephew, her note didn't bode well for Silas. Silas had never so much as mentioned a niece before now, so it was obvious the woman took little interest in her uncle. So why was she writing him now? He hoped that Silas's initial pleasure in hearing from her didn't cause the old man heartache down the road.

A yawn overtook him. Have to talk to Emily and Cornelia, he thought as he drifted off to sleep. They will know something of this mysterious niece.

Striding into the breakfast room at Windmere the next morning, Luc was pleased that he had caught Emily and Cornelia there lingering over their coffee. Both ladies were delighted to see him, and after helping himself to a plate of rare sirloin, coddled eggs, a small bowl of applesauce rich with cinnamon and several yeasty, raisin-studded warm rolls, he joined the ladies.

Though it was still two months or better before the baby was expected, Emily's pregnancy was advancing nicely, her rounded belly and fuller breasts now very evident. This rainy, cool morning, her silvery-fair hair was caught up in a chignon at the back of her head, and wearing a blue woolen gown, she looked very appealing as she smiled up at him. Barnaby, Luc thought affectionately and with no envy, was a lucky man. And so was he, he reminded himself, to have him for a brother.

Seated across from Emily, sending him a smile as welcoming as a spring day, sat Cornelia. Cornelia, he decided, looked particularly fetching today in a rosebud-pink gown embellished with cream lace. Emily's great-aunt had celebrated her ninetieth birthday in August, but the lively sparkle in the hazel eyes belied her age, and except for a few curls near her cheeks and a fringe across her brow, she wore her gray hair swept back. The style revealed the elegant bones that had made her a stunningly attractive woman in her youth, and the chiseled cheeks and jaw still served her well, as did those large, penetrating eyes. Tall for a woman of her generation, her spine was as ramrod straight as a maid of twenty; Cornelia's one concession to age was her carved walnut walking stick. Luc grinned. She could, when necessary, wield that cane with great skill.

Seating himself next to Cornelia, Luc asked, "And where is my brother this morning?" Smiling from one woman to the other, he murmured, "His obvious desertion of two such winsome ladies makes me wonder if we are even related."

Cornelia chuckled and tapped him smartly on the arm. "Doing it up too brown, you young scamp. My mirror doesn't lie, and I haven't been winsome for fifty years or more."

Luc lifted the wrinkled hand that rested on his arm. Dropping a kiss on the back of it, he said, "I beg to differ, Madame— your mirror *does* lie, and if not for the scandal it would cause, I would steal you away from Windmere in a heartbeat."

Looking pleased, Cornelia said, "Now if I *were* fifty years younger, I might just let you do it."

Grinning at her, Luc replied, "Madame, you could not stop me."

Emily cleared her throat. Sending Luc a mocking glance, she said, "If you're through trying to seduce my aunt, perhaps you would like to know where your brother has gone."

"Ah, *oui,* I did ask after him, didn't I?"

"He has gone with Worley to inspect one of the old barns on the farm leased by Farmer Calkin," Emily said. "According to Calkin, that storm we had last week damaged the roof so badly that only an entirely new roof will make it weather-tight. Since Calkin is known to be a complainer, Barnaby decided to see for himself just how badly damaged the roof is before he approves the expenditure. It could merely need patching."

Luc glanced outside at the rain pelting the windows. "Not a day I would have chosen to go out riding with my bailiff."

"Barnaby is not a man to be put off by a little wet weather—or a task that needs doing," she said with a smile.

Luc agreed with her. Barnaby took his duties as landowner

seriously, whether it was overseeing a vast estate like Windmere or the plantation in Virginia. For a moment Luc wondered if he'd be as good an overlord, then shrugged the idea away. Far better that he be footloose and unhampered by responsibilities or dependents. He told himself he liked his life the way it was and wasn't cut out to be a landowner—great or small.

Yet the thought nagged that he might not do too badly. From the age of twelve, when he'd arrived at Green Hill in Virginia, he'd helped work the land and in his aimless wanderings, when the cards had failed him, he'd hired himself out as a simple laborer or whatever job he could find to keep his belly full. He didn't envy Barnaby his lands or fortune or wife, but it occurred to him that sinking down roots and owning his own land and house might not be the prison he had always viewed it. Was it possible that he was mellowing with age? *Zut!* He hoped not.

Frowning, he picked at his sirloin, and noting his expression, Emily asked, "Is something wrong? Has something happened?"

Luc shook his head. "*Non.* I am fine." Plunging right into his story, he added, "Unfortunately, I cannot say the same for my friend Ordway. Someone ran his phaeton off the road last night and left him lying in a ditch with a broken arm."

Both ladies were horrified, full of queries about Mr. Ordway, and Luc said hastily, "Do not be anxious! I came along not long after the accident occurred and was able to get him safely to High Tower. I stayed until after his arm was set and he was comfortably settled in his bed and had swallowed a dose of laudanum."

"Thank goodness you found him when you did," Emily said warmly.

Cornelia said with her usual tartness, "Perhaps there is something to be said for your late nights."

Luc laughed. "In this case, yes. But tell me, if you please, what do you know of Silas's niece?"

The two women exchanged glances.

"Which one?" asked Cornelia. "He has two, Mrs. Easley and Mrs. Dashwood."

"I do not know her surname, but I believe her given name is 'Gillian.'"

"That would be Gillian Dashwood, his younger niece. Mrs. Easley is the older one," Cornelia said. Looking carefully at Luc, she asked, "Why do you want to know about Mrs. Dashwood?"

Luc had not missed the exchange of glances or the hint of disapproval in Cornelia's voice. "Why do I have the impression that you do not approve of this Mrs. Gillian Dashwood?"

Cornelia made a face. "There is no way to wrap it in clean linen: her husband, Charles Dashwood, was murdered two years ago this past August and there is the strong suspicion that she did it."

Emily leaned forward, saying quickly, "It is all gossip, you understand. She was never arrested by the authorities, but many people think she murdered him."

"She wasn't arrested only because they could not find the weapon that had been used to stab her husband to death," Cornelia added grimly. Looking at Luc, she added, "She was found sitting beside his body, bleeding from her temple. It's generally believed that she and her husband had a vicious fight and that Dashwood struck her just before she stabbed him. Caused a terrible scandal." An expression of distaste crossed Cornelia's face. "Happened at the Duke of Welbourne's hunting lodge in Hampshire—at one of his notorious romps. Aside from being suspected of her husband's death, it certainly makes one wonder about Mrs. Dashwood's morals that she was even attending such a disgraceful affair. The parties hosted by Welbourne at his lodge are legendary for their depravity and disgraceful antics—no *respectable* woman, or at least none who care about their reputations, would dare be found in the vicinity of that sort of gathering."

"*Mon Dieu!*" exclaimed Luc. "No wonder Silas has not mentioned her to me before now. Poor fellow."

Cornelia shrugged. "I'll agree between that rascally nephew of his and Mrs. Dashwood that your friend has not been blessed with relatives of noble character. Not so surprising I suppose, since they are half brother and sister. Ordway's older brother was a widower with a child, Stanley, when he married Mrs. Dashwood's mother. It's a pity that the pair of them have brought your friend nothing but trouble." She hesitated, then added not unkindly, "Perhaps he is reaping what he has sown."

Luc looked at her sharply. "What do you mean?"

She sighed. "The circumstances surrounding Ordway's possession of High Tower caused a scandal at the time—especially what happened afterward."

Looking startled, Emily said, "I've never heard anything about him other than he likes his own company and doesn't care much for country society. I think I can count on one hand the affairs where I have seen him." She smiled at Luc. "He seems a nice man."

"He is," said Luc firmly, thinking over Ordway's kindness to him in London.

"I'm not saying that he isn't a perfectly acceptable gentleman," Cornelia admitted. "Just that . . ." She glanced at Emily. "The reason you've probably never heard about it is because it happened forty years or more—long before your birth. After this length of time, few people remember the old scandal."

"What scandal?" Luc demanded.

"First I have to tell you about the former owners of High Tower," Cornelia said. "Forty years or so ago, High Tower belonged to the Bramhall family and had for several generations. The family was respected and held in high regard in the area. At the time, Robert Bramhall, an only child himself, and his wife, Mary, owned High Tower. They were childless for many years, and all of us were delighted when long after everyone had given up hope, Mary gave birth to a son, Edward. Robert was overjoyed, as was Mary." Her lips tightened. "Unfortunately, they indulged him excessively, and Edward grew up spoiled and headstrong—a wild boy, dashing from one scrape to the next. By the time he was twenty-two years old, both his parents were dead and he found himself in control of a fortune and master of High Tower." She sighed. "He turned a deaf ear to all who tried to guide him—he drank and gambled recklessly. Four or five years later, one night in London he sat down to gamble with Silas Ordway. By the time the evening ended, Ordway owned High Tower—everything. Edward was left as close to penniless as makes no never mind."

Luc shifted uncomfortably. What happened was lamentable, but having won some high stakes himself and aware that sizable estates *did* change hands on the turn of a card, he didn't see that Ordway could be blamed for Bramhall's foolishness. Play or pay was always the rule when one sat down to gamble.

"And this is the scandal? That Ordway won High Tower from Bramhall?" Luc asked. "Ordway cannot be blamed for winning." Defensively, he added, "It was not Ordway's fault that this Edward was a fool."

Cornelia nodded. "You're right, of course. That High Tower was lost through Edward's stupidity surprised no one: it was expected he'd do something like that one day. What no one expected was that he'd kill himself by leaping from the tower that gave High Tower its name on the day Ordway came to take possession."

Emily gasped, her hand to her mouth.

Luc reared back, shocked. "*Mon Dieu!* What a terrible thing."

"It was, indeed, a terrible thing," Cornelia agreed. "Edward's loss of High Tower was a scandal to be sure, but it wouldn't be the first time a foolish young man had lost the family home at the gaming tables, but when he killed himself and in such a ghastly manner . . ." She shrugged. "Well, you can imagine. And while it wasn't Ordway's fault, there were those in the neighborhood who blamed him for Bramhall's death, and some of them think Ordway deserves his niece and nephew."

"Do you?" Luc growled.

Cornelia shook her head. "No. When you've lived as long as I have, you realize that some people cannot be helped; that they are going to the devil one way or another. I believe that Edward was just such a person. If Ordway hadn't won High Tower, it would have been someone else."

Cornelia's words didn't erase the unpleasant taste in his mouth, and having lost his appetite, Luc pushed away his plate, thinking he might never be able to face rare sirloin again. Or sit down at a gaming table. He grimaced. Now who was being foolish? He made his living gambling.

"Why did you want to know about Gillian Dashwood?" Emily asked, thinking to interject a different topic into the gloomy silence that had fallen.

"There was a note from her to Silas when we arrived at High Tower last night," Luc answered, glad of the distraction.

"Hmmm. I wonder why she wrote to him," Cornelia mused. "The last we heard she was living somewhere in Surrey with Mrs. Easley."

"The other niece?" Luc asked.

Cornelia nodded. "Yes. Sophia Easley must be over thirty years old now, and as I recall, her husband was much older, a gamester, not unlike Bramhall, or Charles Dashwood for that matter. At any rate Mr. Easley left her destitute. Fortunately, Mrs. Dashwood was in a position to offer her a home." Cornelia thought a moment. "Although, I'm sure," she added, "that Silas would have taken her in and provided for her if Mrs. Dashwood had not." She looked thoughtful. "I imagine that Stanley and the two nieces will inherit High Tower when he dies."

Was it possible, Luc wondered cynically, that Mrs. Dash-wood's note to Silas was in anticipation of the day she would inherit? Was she trying to turn the old man up sweet to in-sure that she *did* inherit? Disliking the Widow Dashwood more and more, after a few more minutes, Luc took his leave.

The light rain turned in a full-blown storm, and staring out the window of the library at the Dower House that after-noon, Luc decided to postpone the trip to visit Silas that he had been considering. Tomorrow would be soon enough to check on Silas . . . and mayhap get a better lay of the land in regard to Mrs. Dashwood.

It was late Sunday afternoon before the rain turned to showers, and in deference to the weather, he chose to drive his phaeton, purchased this summer after a particularly prof-itable night of gaming. Shortly afterward, he'd bought a pair of blacks from Barnaby; both horses noted for not possessing even one white hair in their glossy coats. Barnaby had laughed when Luc had chosen them.

"Somehow I'm not surprised that you want those two," Barnaby had said. When Luc had looked at him, he'd ex-plained, "I've heard the pair of them described as black as the devil . . . appropriate, don't you think, for Lucifer to drive?"

Not displeased in the least, Luc promptly dubbed them Devil and Demon. Azure eyes dancing, he'd said, "They'll only add to my reputation." When Barnaby had looked skeptical, he added, "What gamester alive could resist gam-ing with a man who drives horses black as midnight named Devil and Demon and whose skilful gambling has earned him the name Lucifer?" He'd laughed aloud. "*Mon Dieu!* I could not."

Luc's pleasure in Devil and Demon had not dimmed in the months since he'd purchased them, and as the two magnifi-cent animals powered through the muddy roads between Windmere and High Tower, he grinned and congratulated him-self again on his selection. As High Tower came into view, his grin faded and he could not prevent his gaze from going to the high-turreted tower that had given the estate its name . . . and from which the luckless Edward had thrown himself.

He had never paid attention to the tower that adjoined the manor, but this afternoon he studied it with new eyes. Built in Norman times, the stone and brick tower soared four stories into the air, and staring up at the massive structure, he shook his head. He could not help imagining Edward's leap from the top of the tower. *Sacristi!* To choose such a manner to die!

As he passed in front of the tower, he found himself staring down at the cobblestones in front of the tower as if he might still see signs of Edward's blood. Annoyed with himself, he pushed aside his maudlin thoughts, and once under the protection of the portico, handed the reins to the stable boy who came running up to meet him.

Meacham answered his rap on the door. A broad smile creased his wrinkled face. "Mister Luc!" he said. "Mister Ordway was about to send a note to you asking you to dine tonight." The faded blue eyes full of pleasure, he added, "We've had an exciting morning, and your arrival will only add to Mr. Ordway's pleasure."

Taking Luc's greatcoat, brushed beaver hat and leather gloves, he said, "Go ahead—you know the way. Mr. Ordway and the others are in the front salon."

Luc's brow flew up. "Others?"

Meacham smiled. "Yes, but I'll not be stealing Mr. Ordway's thunder. Go. Go. You'll see for yourself. Mr. Ordway is over the moon at their arrival."

The "others" could be visitors from the neighborhood, but he doubted it. Using the same perspicaciousness that he brought to the gaming table, Luc was certain he knew the identity of Silas's guests. His jaw tightened, and with a determined stride, he headed down the hall toward the front salon.

Luc entered the salon and wasn't in the least surprised to

see two women seated on the cream- and russet-figured satin sofa near the fire. His broken arm swathed in a black silk sling, Silas was enthroned in one of a pair of high-backed green velvet chairs directly across from them. A tray of refreshments sat on a low table between the chairs and sofa. It was a warm, cozy scene, the doting family gathered near the fire, but Luc's gaze was hard and assessing as he studied the women.

One of the women was a handsome female with a Junoesque build and red hair, in her early thirties. Luc thought she must be the eldest niece, Mrs. Easley, and after a lightning assessment, his gaze passed onto the other woman, sitting next to her.

Gillian Dashwood wasn't what he expected. A tawny-eyed sprite was his first thought. Small and slimly formed, even with her dark brown hair scraped back into as severe a bun as he'd ever seen, he admitted reluctantly, Gillian Dashwood possessed one of the most enchanting faces he'd ever seen. The hairstyle only emphasized the cat-shaped eyes fringed with heavy black lashes, straight little nose and the surprisingly firm jaw. Stubborn, he decided, eyeing that jaw. If her jaw, and chin for that matter, bespoke stubbornness, that full, rosy mouth was another matter. . . . Passionate, Luc thought speculatively, a tingle of lust making itself felt in a certain part of his anatomy. A fetching little baggage, he concluded, one that looked nothing like a murderess—which made her all the more dangerous.

"Luc!" Silas cried, delighted, jerking Luc from his study of Mrs. Dashwood. "What a happy coincidence that you have come to visit this afternoon." Smiling as Luc advanced toward him, he added, "I was on the point of sending you a note, asking you to dine tonight."

Smiling down at his friend, Luc said, "So Meacham informs me."

"He didn't ruin my surprise, did he?" Silas asked anxiously.

Luc shook his head. "Not if you mean, did he tell me the name of your two lovely guests?" he replied, with a smile in the direction of the two women.

"Excellent! And now before someone *does* spoil my surprise, let me introduce you to my nieces, Mrs. Sophia Easley and Mrs. Gillian Dashwood." His affection open and obvious, he added, "My dears, this is my good friend Luc Joslyn."

Luc acknowledged the two women with a bow and a polite greeting. Smiling with sardonic pleasure, he noticed that Mrs. Dashwood didn't seem any more thrilled to meet him than he was to meet her, her reply so cool it bordered on rudeness. Introductions completed, Silas beamed at the room in general. "They've come to stay for an extended visit. Isn't it grand?"

Chapter 3

Gillian disliked Luc Joslyn on sight—not impressed by the tall, broad-shouldered form or the striking azure eyes set in the darkly handsome face. Having already formed a bad opinion of him, the sudden kick in her pulse when he bent over her hand and pressed a polite kiss on the back of it stunned her. Aghast at her reaction to him, she disliked him more heartily. Worse, with his black hair, blue eyes and height, he reminded her far too vividly of her murdered husband for her to feel anything but antipathy.

From her uncle's letters over the summer and his frequent references to his new friend, she knew a great deal about him—and little of it put him in a good light. She not only mistrusted his motives for befriending an elderly man, a man old enough to be his grandfather, but she viewed him with a strong dose of contempt for his predilection for the gaming table—all of which Silas had happily related in his letters.

Smiling at both ladies, referring to Silas's comment about the length of their stay, Luc said, "Ah, this is to be a long visit with your uncle then?"

"Yes," answered Gillian, not liking the speculation she glimpsed in his eyes. His gaze did not leave her face, and feeling more was required of her, she said, "It is a trip that has been put off for far too long."

Mrs. Easley smiled at Silas. "The timing turns out to be

most fortunate though," she said in a calm manner. "We will be here when Uncle needs us most and we will be able to provide him with company during his convalescence."

Luc's eyes had not moved from Gillian's face, but he nodded. "*Bon!* I'm sure he will be happy to have his family around him." He grinned at Silas and, looking back at Gillian, murmured, "Your presence will lessen the demands on my pocketbook—he is a fierce gambler and with nothing else to provide a distraction, I fear he will beggar me."

Silas laughed. "What flummery! *I* am not called 'Lucifer' for my devilish luck at the gaming tables." Smiling at Gillian he said, "He's a modest lad. Believe me, he is a far better gambler than I ever was on my best days, and the Lord knows that they are behind me."

A gambler, she thought bitterly, just like Charles—and like Charles, using his charm to disarm and take advantage of the unwary. Only Luc Joslyn, instead of preying on silly, young women, as Charles had done, had set his sights on a lonely old man. Guilt smote her. It was her fault that Uncle Silas appeared to be alone, with no one around who cared about him or who would question this sudden friendship. Though she and Sophia regularly exchanged letters with their uncle, they had not been frequent visitors to High Tower.

We should have realized that letters, she scolded herself, no matter how frequent or how warm and affectionate, were not enough and that Uncle Silas needed his family around him. If only, she thought, I had swallowed my pride and given in to his many requests for Sophia and me to come for an indefinite visit. But she had not, and her only consolation at the moment was that they were here at last. She glanced at Joslyn from beneath her lashes, her heart sinking at the easy familiarity between the two men—that and her uncle's obvious fondness of the younger man. Her lip curled. "Lucifer" had probably seen the old man as easy prey. And that, she vowed, was about to change.

Keeping up a polite façade Gillian smiled and nodded at

the right places, but as the evening progressed, behind her smiles she considered how best to oust such a charming, dangerous predator as Luc Joslyn from her uncle's affections. Silas was a sophisticated man, a man of the world, not easily duped, and she wondered how Joslyn, with his obviously practiced charm and guileful smiles, had slipped beneath her uncle's guard and insinuated himself into the old man's affections.

Gillian sighed. The situation was complicated and there was no denying that *her* motives would be questioned. The odds were that her arrival on Silas's doorstep after all this time would cause talk and that many members of the *ton* would view her visit in the worst possible light. The gossip, she admitted with an ache, would only add to her already scandalous reputation. Not only was she labeled a murderess, but now she could add fortune hunter to her title as well, and nothing, she thought fiercely, in either case, could be further from the truth.

As his only relatives besides her half brother, Stanley, it was likely that she and Mrs. Easley would be named in their uncle's will, but the two women had always agreed that it was Silas's fortune to dispose of however he saw fit. Her gaze fell on Luc's handsome face and her lips thinned. Uncle could leave his entire estate to a home for calico cats for all she cared, but she wasn't going to stand by and watch him be taken advantage of by someone like Luc Joslyn.

A pang knifed through her. The last thing she wanted was to cause Silas pain. It was clear, whatever plan she concocted to break Joslyn's hold over her uncle, it had to be done in such a manner as to cause Silas as little disillusionment and disappointment as possible.

Watching as Silas's face lit up at something Luc said, beneath the table her hand formed a fist. Oh, Uncle! she almost cried aloud. Don't you see him for what he is? Can't you see that he is a wicked predator with you as his intended prey?

Gillian's hostile regard hadn't escaped Luc's notice, but her attitude didn't surprise him: he had already come to some conclusions of his own about her. Like hers of him, none of them reflected well on her. He'd not missed the flash of antipathy in her eyes when they'd met: from the beginning the dark-haired sprite had not been happy to find him on such friendly terms with Silas. All through the evening, he'd noted her covert study of him. Her sly scrutiny had nothing to do with finding him attractive, he admitted wryly, and everything to do with trying to find a weakness in an enemy. No, the lady was definitely not happy at his presence here tonight, and since he'd been on his best behavior he could only think of one reason why she viewed him so adversely: he was competition.

Luc nearly laughed aloud. Did the sprite really think she could best him? His relationship with Silas was based on simple liking and respect, but if Gillian Dashwood wished to ascribe evil intentions to his friendship with her uncle, so be it. His expression giving no clue to his thoughts, he considered the situation. Silas was an old man and possessed a comfortable fortune and a fine home. . . . Perhaps *she* had designs upon her uncle's wealth and assumed that he did, too? Certain he had hit upon the reason for both her dislike of him and the unexpected visit, he nodded to himself. *Naturellement!* There could be no other explanation. His eyes narrowed, studying the trim form and enchanting face. If Madame Dashwood was up to something, it might be diverting, he decided, to overset whatever plans she had for her uncle.

Anticipation licked along Luc's veins. Crossing swords with a suspected murderess would prove amusing and break the boredom of a long winter. His gaze traveled over that lush mouth and surprisingly generous bosom for one so slender and that earlier tingle in his groin reasserted itself. Hmmm. It might also prove exceedingly enjoyable in the bargain.

Dinner behind them, Luc did not linger, but as he prepared to depart, he said, "When the weather clears, since your uncle will be unable to do so, may I have the pleasure of escorting you ladies for a ride around the neighborhood?"

Before Gillian could refuse, Silas exclaimed, "Excellent suggestion, my boy."

"Of course, if you would like to accompany us," Luc said slowly, "we could take your barouche and those grays you're so proud of and go for a drive instead."

Silas shook his head and indicated his broken arm. "Thank you, no. Until the bone knits, the ride home in my phaeton the other night was enough jostling for me." Slyly he added, "I'll admit it's a tempting idea, though—you'd get to see my grays in action."

Luc smiled and shook his head. "I'm not in the market for a team—no matter how well matched." When Silas would have pressed the issue, Luc held up a hand, saying, "Buying those four horses of yours would also entail my purchasing a proper vehicle for them to pull." He gave a theatrical shudder. "Tooling around in a barouche such as yours would make me feel like a settled family man."

"You may find yourself a settled family man one of these days," Silas observed and at Luc's skeptical look, added, "If you are not careful, you'll end up a crusty old bachelor like myself."

Bowing in the direction of the two ladies, Luc quipped, "But if I have two such lovely young women as your nieces to tend me in my old age, who is to say it would be such a terrible fate?"

"Coming it too strong, my boy," Silas said, smiling. "But enough of this wrangling—the ladies will expect you on the first fine day to squire them around the neighborhood. And as is befitting a man of my age, I'll remain home by the fire sipping hot punch until you return."

Gillian leaned forward and protested, "But, Uncle, we

wouldn't enjoy ourselves knowing you were here at the house by yourself while we were gallivanting about the neighborhood."

"The lady has a point, sir," Luc murmured. "Perhaps the ride should be postponed until you can accompany us."

"Nonsense!" said Silas forthrightly. Bending an affectionate look on Gillian, he added, "How do you think I will feel, knowing you are denying yourself a pleasure to sit by an old man? No. I insist that you go. It will only be for a few hours, and it will be good for you to get out of the house for a while."

Her reluctance obvious, Gillian gave in. "If it is your wish, Uncle," she said with a decided lack of enthusiasm.

Silas beamed. To Luc he said, "We'll expect you the first fine day."

Entering the Dower House forty-five minutes later, Luc walked into the library, and despite the hour, approaching eleven o'clock, discovered he had guests. His half brother, Barnaby, and their uncle, Lamb, like Luc born on the wrong side of the blanket, were seated in a pair of high-backed fawn mohair chairs arranged near the fireplace. Partially filled snifters of brandy rested on the green-veined marble-topped table situated between the two chairs. A low fire burned on the stone hearth and cast dancing shadows into the room; the only other light came from a pair of candles on the mantel.

Luc grimaced, having a fair idea for their visit. Ignoring them, he stalked to the long mahogany lowboy that, these days, held an array of Baccarat decanters filled with various spirits and glasses and, selecting a snifter, poured some brandy from one of the decanters. Looking over his shoulders at the other two, he asked, "Refills?"

Both men nodded and once Luc had added to their snifters and returned the decanter to the lowboy, he picked up his snifter and sprawled on the green and cream damask sofa across from them. After taking a swallow of his brandy, he looked at Barnaby and said wearily, "I suppose this is about my visit to The Ram's Head."

"Christ! What were you thinking?" burst out Lamb. "Or were you, as usual, *not* thinking? Didn't you stop to think that Nolles could have had you knocked in the head by one of his gang and had your body thrown over the cliffs into the sea with no one the wiser?"

Not recognizing the anxiety beneath Lamb's words, Luc's lips tightened. "If that happened, at least you'd have the satisfaction of knowing I lived down to your low expectations for me."

Lamb smothered a curse. To Barnaby he growled, "You talk to him. He'll listen to you."

Barnaby sighed. It seemed that from the moment twelve-year-old Luc had stepped foot on Green Hill after his mother died and had met fourteen-year-old Lamb, they'd been at each other's throats—when they didn't have each other's back. At ten Barnaby had been the youngest, but right from the beginning he'd been cast in the role of peacemaker, continually running interference between the two older, strong-willed men. The three of them shared a bond of blood and an affection that was as powerful as it was unshakeable—even if Lamb and Luc would rather have their tongues torn out than admit to the steadfast tie that bound them all together.

Picking his words with care, Barnaby said, "Lamb has a point. If he got the chance, Nolles wouldn't hesitate to kill you."

Grudgingly Luc admitted, "Though it pains me, I'll concede that our dear uncle has the right of it this time. I *wasn't* thinking when I decided to visit The Ram's Head." He stared down at the amber liquid in his snifter. "I wasn't in the mood for the cheerfulness of The Crown and Mrs. Gilbert and her lovely daughters. Perhaps I was even looking for trouble, something to distract me. The queen's death . . ." He tossed down a swallow of brandy. "It won't happen again."

Lamb grumbled, "Let us hope so." But there was no heat in his voice.

"Who told you I was there?" asked Luc with a lifted brow, glancing at Barnaby.

Barnaby smiled. "Lord Broadfoot, for one. He came by this evening while you were gone to thank you for saving Harlan's hide."

Luc looked innocent. "I beg your pardon? I had nothing to do with it. I merely saw that young Harlan arrived safely home."

Lamb snorted, but the azure eyes so like Luc's held amused affection. "You want us to believe that Broadfoot's whelp, drunk as a wheelbarrow, was able to best a hardened gambler like Jeffery at Hazard?"

"But it must be true," Luc protested, his expression guileless. "How else could Harlan arrive home with his own vowels . . . and a few from Jeffery in his pockets?"

Lamb grinned at him. "Don't try to bamboozle me, my clever buck."

"How much did you take Jeffery for?" asked Barnaby.

Luc shrugged. "I cannot remember. Enough to make it painful for him and perhaps make him think twice before preying on fledglings."

"Did you see Lieutenant Deering when you were at Nolles's place?" Barnaby asked, swirling his brandy around in his snifter.

"*Non,*" said Luc, looking surprised. "Was our favorite riding officer there?"

Barnaby nodded. "Yes, he was." He smiled. "Broadfoot wasn't the first to tell me of your visit to The Ram's Head. I met Deering on the road yesterday afternoon returning from my visit to Farmer Calkin."

"Ah, yes, the damaged barn roof," Luc murmured. "How did that go?"

"Well, for once Calkin had a legitimate complaint. The roof is beyond repair." Barnaby sent Luc a level look. "But you will not distract me from my meeting with Deering." He swallowed some brandy and said, "It appears that Nolles and his gang have reorganized after the blow we gave them in February. Deering says that during the last month or so, there has been an increase in the smuggling activity in the area—rumor has it that Nolles has a new financier."

"Another one such as Cousin Thomas?" asked Luc, referring to their cousin killed by his brother, Mathew, back in February.

"That I don't know, but most likely," Barnaby answered. "He can't prove it, but Deering doesn't feel that Nolles is putting up the money for the runs to France. He suspects that Nolles has made contact with a wealthy landowner in the neighborhood or, and this is Deering's best guess, someone in London is financing the smuggling—as Thomas did."

"One hopes that this new investor is *not* another relative of ours," Luc muttered.

"I doubt that Mathew has the stomach for *any* connection with smugglers—killing Thomas devastated him and discovering his brother was financing the Nolles's gang did nothing to ease his anguish. I think we can eliminate Mathew, don't you?"

Luc made a face and nodded.

Lamb spoke up, saying, "And can you imagine Simon doing such a thing?"

Thinking of affable, charming Simon, the youngest of the English Joslyn brothers, Luc shook his head. "*Non!* Simon and Thomas may have been at daggers drawing, but his grief was deep over his death."

"Simon's mourning is more, I think," observed Lamb, "for the pain and guilt that Mathew suffered than for Thomas's death."

The other two men nodded.

Discovering that Thomas Joslyn had been the shadowy figure behind the handsome sums of money that had filtered through Nolles's fingers on their way to France to buy shipload after shipload of contraband goods for sale in England had stunned the entire family, but Mathew most of all. Already reeling from the horrific knowledge that he had shot and killed his own brother, the discovery of Thomas's unthinkable alliance with a vicious gang of smugglers had only added to the guilt and horror that consumed Mathew.

"Has he stirred from Monks Abbey yet?" asked Luc, mentioning Mathew's estate some distance away.

Barnaby shook his head. "Simon is worried about him. Says he locks himself in his rooms at night and drinks himself into a stupor."

Thinking of the staid and proper Mathew drinking himself into a stupor, Luc frowned. "We shall have to do something about that. It was an appalling situation, but he's had enough time to lick his wounds and realize that none of it was his fault."

"I agree," said Barnaby.

Glancing at Barnaby, Lamb said, "You'll have to do something very un-viscount-like and annoy him enough to bring him posthaste to the steps of Windmere." Lamb half-smiled. "Once we have him here, we'll figure out a way to shake him from the worst of his grief. Simon will help."

Luc grinned. "I'm sure that I can think of something for Barnaby to do that will upset Cousin Mathew enough to wrest him out from behind the walls of Monks Abbey."

"Of that, I have little doubt," said Lamb flatly. "No matter where you are, you have a decided knack for being at the center of most upsets."

Luc scowled at him. "And would you expect any less of me?"

Barnaby sighed. He loved the pair of them, but Christ! Sometimes it was hard not to give in to temptation and knock their heads together.

To Luc's disgust the inclement weather—showers and drizzle—stayed around for a while and it was Wednesday before the proposed ride with Silas's nieces could be undertaken. The drizzle had slackened the previous morning and the moment the sun came out, Luc sent over one of Barnaby's footmen with a note to Silas, making the arrangements for the ride.

The sun a pale orb in a cloudless blue sky, Luc set out for High Tower astride a bay gelding with two hind socks. Anticipating the prospect of crossing swords with Mrs. Dashwood, the ride seemed shorter than usual and soon enough his horse was trotting up the driveway leading to Silas's house. As the house and tower came into view, his gaze locked on the turreted tower from which Edward Bramhall had thrown himself decades ago. Did Bramhall's ghost haunt Silas's dreams during the darkest hour of the night, he wondered, or did his friend never give the unfortunate young man's fate any thought at all?

Pushing aside useless speculation, Luc dismounted, and after handing the reins of his horse to the stable boy who ran up to meet him, he walked to the front door. He'd hardly taken his hand from the black iron knocker before the oak door swung open and Meacham ushered him inside.

Giving Meacham his curly-brim beaver hat and York tan gloves, he asked, "How is your master doing this afternoon?"

Meacham's eyes held satisfaction. "He's in high gig, sir—as pleased as if he was going to go with you." A smile flitted across his face. "I'll warn you, though—he's not given up on trying to sell you those grays of his."

Luc laughed. "He can try, Meacham. He can try."

The remnant of Luc's amusement was still evident on his face when he strolled into the front salon where Silas, Mrs. Dashwood and Mrs. Easley waited for him. The ladies were again seated on the cream and russet sofa and Silas was in the high-backed chair across from them.

Greetings exchanged, after a few minutes' conversation,

Silas asked, "Would you care for some refreshment before you leave?"

Luc shook his head. "No, thank you, sir." He glanced at the window. "The days are short and it is already gone one o'clock. If we are to take advantage of the best part of the day, we should be on our way."

Silas agreed, and promising to have some hot punch waiting for them when they returned, he urged them on their way.

The day was pleasant for late October and, despite feeling guilty at leaving Uncle Silas behind, Gillian was delighted to be outside in the thin sunshine. For just a while, seated upon one of her uncle's magnificent horses, the sun warm on her face, a faint sea breeze caressing her cheeks, all the pain and disagreeableness of the past two years vanished. As High Tower fell behind, she reveled in the pleasure of the moment and her spirits lifted. She slanted Luc a glance. Enduring his company, she decided, was a small price to pay.

They rode abreast down the road with Luc between the two women and a groom riding a respectful distance behind the trio. Mindful of his feminine charges, Luc kept the horses at a sedate pace and resigned himself to plodding along. He didn't mind their slow progress—an ambling walk allowed conversation and gave him an opportunity to determine if his suspicions about Mrs. Dashwood were correct.

After they had ridden a few miles, Mrs. Dashwood asked, "Mr. Joslyn, since the road doesn't appear too muddy, would you mind if we picked up the pace?" She flashed a smile at her cousin. "Sophia and I love a good gallop."

"As you wish," Luc replied, taken aback by the sheer charm of the smile she had given her cousin.

The words had barely left his lips before Gillian and Sophia, using their heels, urged their mounts forward. In an instant the horses transitioned from a walk into a trot and seconds later settled into a smooth gallop. Luc and the groom had no choice but to harry after the two women as they sped down the country road.

Both ladies were, Luc observed as he pounded down the road behind them, intrepid riders, easily controlling their horses and their bodies moving as one with their mounts. This was no race and after a few minutes Luc and the groom caught up with the galloping pair. Aware they were on an unfamiliar public road, the two women didn't keep the horses at a gallop for long and eventually they brought their animals back to a trot and then a brisk walk.

Her face glowing, tendrils of sable hair escaping from beneath her green hat with its saucy pheasant feather, Gillian glanced at her cousin and exclaimed, "Oh, Sophy, wasn't that wonderful? I had forgotten the joy of a good horse beneath you."

Sophia, looking as delighted as Gillian, nodded. "It was indeed! Most exhilarating. There is nothing like a ride on an excellent horse to bring a smile to your face and ease your mind." To Luc, Sophia said, "We are indebted to you, Mr. Joslyn. It was most kind and thoughtful of you to suggest a ride."

"It is my pleasure," Luc replied, tearing his gaze from Gillian's vivid face. *Mon Dieu!* The sprite was enchanting. Conniving, too, if his suspicions for her arrival at High Tower were correct. And dangerous, he reminded himself, thinking of her murdered husband.

Irritated for reasons he couldn't explain, he said briskly, "I am new to the neighborhood and your uncle would be able to show you more of the area, but if you like I can show you one or two of our more well-known landmarks."

Gillian said, "It is the ride we are enjoying, Mr. Joslyn— not so much the destination. Lead on, if you please."

They continued on the main road for some miles, Luc indicating the location of various places known to him as they rode. Turning off the public road a short while later and leav-

ing it behind, Luc guided them across the undulating, green
velvet chalkland spread out in all directions around them. As
they rode, he said, "This is very different from fields and
woodlands of Virginia, but it has a beauty that takes one's
breath away, *oui?*"

Gillian nodded absently, her gaze on the grazing fat, gray-
and brown-faced Sussex sheep. She spied the occasional cow
or horse; now and then smoke rising into the air from behind
the low hills hinted at a dwelling, but none came into view.

Topping a hill, Luc brought their horses to a halt. "The
Cuckmere Valley," he said simply.

An exceptional view spread out in all directions and
Gillian's breath caught in pleasure. Like a lazy snake, the
Cuckmere River flowed through the broad valley below them
toward the sea; uneven banks of trees and shrubs strung here
and there evidence of the narrow creeks that meandered
through the rolling, green countryside. A glimpse of the glinting blue waters of the Channel could be seen through a break
in the rising cliffs in the distance.

Leaning toward Gillian, his lips inches from her ear, Luc
pointed and said, "You see the opening in the distance with
the sea beyond it? That wide stretch of beach is Cuckmere
Haven and is a favorite landing spot for some of our local
smugglers."

Gillian nodded, aware of a sudden kick in her pulse at his
nearness. "Uncle mentioned at dinner the other night," she
said, turning her head away from Luc's disturbing closeness,
"that smugglers are very active around here."

"That's true," Luc said, smiling at her withdrawal. Was it
mere dislike that caused her reaction, or was the lady as
aware of him as he was of her? He preferred to think the latter. Straightening, he added, "The worst of the gangs are led
by Will Nolles, the owner of the tavern named The Ram's
Head."

"But if his identity is known," interjected Sophia from his
other side, "why is he allowed to continue his activities?"

"The smugglers are a close-knit community and most people in the area are either smugglers themselves, or they have family that plies the trade, or they benefit in some way from the smugglers' activities," he answered, glancing at Sophia. "Besides that, Nolles's gang is a powerful one and he and his men are greatly feared. You'll not find many who are willing to go against them."

When both ladies looked uneasy, Luc cursed his unruly tongue and apologized. "Forgive me! I did not mean to frighten you. There *are* smugglers about, but you have nothing to fear from them. They have no wish to bring attention to themselves and generally go about their business with no one the wiser." He grinned. "Usually the only sign of their passing is a cask or two of fine French brandy left in one's stable or barn."

Sophia chuckled and murmured, "You mean like the brandy Uncle drank last night?"

Blue eyes dancing, Luc nodded. "*Exactement!* And enough of this talk about smugglers and contraband—I am forgetting my role as guide." Waving a hand in the direction of Cuckmere Haven, he said, "Those chalk cliffs you see before you are the Seven Sisters; the tallest of them rises five hundred feet above the Channel." His grin deepened. "And that, Madame Easley, is the extent of my knowledge of the area."

He looked far too attractive, Gillian thought as she watched Sophia respond to his charm. It irritated her that she had noticed the russet color of his coat intensified the azure hue of his already striking eyes and that the excellent fit of his buckskin breeches kept drawing her gaze to the smooth muscles of his thighs. And we won't even mention, she scolded, the way his coat displays his shoulders and arms or how handsome he looks on horseback. She jerked her eyes away and stared straight ahead, but a few minutes later they strayed back to his tall form. Broad shoulders and strong arms, she admitted, with a quiver down low in her body.

Annoyed with herself, Gillian said sharply, "Uncle said that the nearest village is Broadhaven. Is it nearby?"

"Not far," Luc replied, wondering at the note in her voice. More dislike? Surely the lady was not jealous of his attention to her cousin? "Broadhaven," he added cheerfully, pleased at the idea she might be jealous, "is beyond that rise just below us." He looked at Gillian with a cocked brow. "Would you like to ride through the village?"

Displeased that she had allowed her annoyance with herself to color her words, Gillian forced a smile and replied, "Perhaps not today. I just wondered where it was."

"Well, I, for one, am ready to head back to High Tower," said Sophia. "This has been most enjoyable, but the breeze is no longer as pleasant as it was when we began our ride, and unless I miss my guess, the temperature is falling. If we tarry much longer, we'll be chilled to the bone by the time we arrive home."

Aware of the creeping coolness in the air and the cutting edge to the breeze, Gillian agreed. "You're absolutely right," she said. "We should be going back. We've left Uncle alone long enough as it is."

"As you wish, ladies," Luc said gallantly and swung his horse around.

Sophia had been right. The air was distinctly chilly by the time they arrived at High Tower. With the groom holding the reins of the horses, Luc first lifted Mrs. Easley down from her horse before turning to Gillian to help her dismount. His hands around her slim waist, his eyes met hers and for a moment time stood still.

Gillian's breath stopped as she looked into those azure eyes. She could feel the warmth and strength of his hands through the heavy velvet material of her riding habit, and a mixture of pleasure and wariness churned through her.

Their gazes clung and Luc's hands tightened around her waist, the urge to pull her from her horse and into his arms overpowering. His eyes fell to her lips and desire coiled within him. Would that tempting mouth taste as sweet as it looked? And how would that slender body feel pressed next to his?

"Ah, there you are," drawled a voice from the direction of the house. "We wondered when you would return. Uncle has been most anxious."

The spell broken, Luc politely lifted Gillian down from her horse. The moment her feet touched the ground, his hands fell away and he put several feet between them.

Looking at the speaker, his brow cocked. Stanley Ordway. Now why wasn't he surprised? It would appear that the vultures were gathering around his friend. An unpleasant smile curved his mouth. Whatever nefarious plans Mrs. Dashwood and her half brother had for his friend Silas, he certainly intended to disrupt. His eyes slid over Gillian. And he would take pleasure in doing so.

Chapter 4

Gillian's heart sank at the sight of her half brother standing on the steps of the house, his lips curled in that derisive smile that always nettled her and brought out the worst in her. The surge of vexation she felt didn't surprise her— even as very young children, the two of them rubbed each other the wrong way and time had changed little. In her opinion, from a scornful boy, he'd grown into a condescending coxcomb.

Oblivious to Luc, she stalked toward her half brother. Stopping at the bottom step, her eyes hard on Stanley's face, she demanded, "Did Uncle know you were coming? Or have you, as usual, simply inflicted yourself on him when you've fallen into dun territory?"

Stanley's face darkened. "I see that you are as rude and impolite as ever." He looked at Mrs. Easley, who walked up to stand beside Gillian. "And I suppose you'll take her side— just as you've always done."

"Perhaps I take her side," Mrs. Easley said coolly, "because she is usually in the right. Gillian asked a reasonable question: did our uncle know you were coming?"

Scowling at the two women, he snapped, "I hardly need an invitation to visit my uncle."

"That's true," Gillian agreed. "But could you tell me why you come to visit him only when you need money?"

"What about you?" Stanley shot back. "Don't tell me you're here because of the great affection you bear him—you haven't stepped foot in this place for years, and before that, you weren't here more than two or three times." He smirked. "So tell me, why are *you* here?"

"Whatever her reasons, she is here now," Luc interposed smoothly, "and that is all that need concern you." Placing a hand beneath each woman's arm and ushering them forward, he smiled at Stanley. "Now if you'll excuse us—there's a chill in the air, and if you wish to continue this, ah, discussion, I'm sure that the ladies would prefer to do so in more comfortable surroundings."

Mrs. Easley glanced at Luc and chuckled. "A man with common sense—how rare."

Luc laughed and urged the ladies forward, leaving Stanley no choice but to follow. Inside the house, the women disappeared upstairs to change out of their riding habits and boots; Meacham whisked away Luc's hat and gloves before showing him and Stanley into the front salon.

A fire burned on the hearth, and the scent of mulled wine wafted in the air. A slender young man, garbed in a blue jacket trimmed in black braid and gray pantaloons, a pewter mug in one hand, lounged near the fire, and Silas sat enthroned in his usual chair. On the low table in front of Silas reposed a silver tray heaped with various items and refreshments.

Silas greeted Luc with a smile, but Luc sensed that it was forced. Smiling down at his friend, Luc said, "I have returned the ladies safely. They are presently changing before joining us."

"Good! Good!" Silas indicated the young man by the fire. "Think you met Welbourne's youngest son, Lord George Canfield, during the Season in London." At Luc's nod, he added, "He is a great friend of my nephew's."

Acknowledging Canfield with a slight bow, he said, "How do you do?"

"Fine, thank you," said Lord George Canfield, his nostrils quivering as if he smelled offal.

When Canfield offered nothing more, Luc murmured, "I'm doing well. Thank you for asking."

Canfield's lips tightened. After a second, Luc turned away and winked at Silas. Canfield's reception, though he acknowledged a slight sting, amused him, and heaven knew this wasn't the first time he'd been snubbed. He'd already come into contact with other members of the *ton* who felt that their consequence was so high that rubbing shoulders with the bastard half brother of Viscount Joslyn was beneath them. But not so far beneath them, Luc thought, that they weren't willing to gamble with him. Canfield had done so and rose from the gaming table after a night of cards with Luc, several thousand pounds lighter in the pocket. But Luc had been aware of Lord George Canfield for another reason—Canfield, along with Lord Padgett, had been cronies of Thomas Joslyn. A connection between Thomas's friends and Nolles's gang had never been discovered, but Luc, Barnaby and Lamb had wondered if other seemingly respectable gentlemen might have been seduced by the easy money to be made. Hence, Luc had cast a speculative eye upon them from the moment they had been introduced, but he'd seen nothing to raise his suspicions, except Canfield was here now. . . . Interesting.

Indicating the chair next to him, Silas said to Luc, "Sit here and tell me about the ride. Where did you go?"

"I showed them the Seven Sisters, Cuckmere Haven and the general location of the village," Luc answered, sitting down next to Silas. "There was no time to explore the village—the hour was growing late and I wished to have them home before dusk."

"Capital!" A sly gleam in his eyes, Silas said, "They're both excellent riders, are they not?"

Luc grinned at him. "Indeed."

Waving a hand in the direction of the refreshments, Silas said, "Help yourself to some mulled wine Meacham just brought in a few minutes ago. Pour me a mug while you're at it."

Luc leaned forward and ladled some of the wine from the big silver bowl set in the center of the tray into a mug for Silas and, after handing it to Silas, helped himself. Settling back into his chair, Luc stretched his long legs out in front of him and breathed in the scent of cinnamon and lemons before taking a swallow of the warm wine. Heady flavor caressed his tongue and he relaxed as the warmth of the mulled wine spread through his body. *"Bon!"* he said. Smiling at Silas, he asked, "Do you think that Meacham would share the recipe with me?"

Silas chuckled. "There's not many he would but I think he'd be pleased to give it to you."

"You appear to be quite at home," Stanley observed. "How often do you visit my uncle?"

"As often as I ask him to," said Silas, sending Stanley a sharp glance from beneath his brows. "And I fail to see that it's any business of yours."

Stanley flushed. "I would remind you, Uncle, that you are no longer a young man, and though it pains me to say so, there *are* people who take advantage of the elderly." Silas sucked in an outraged breath but Stanley pushed on doggedly, "I would be remiss in my duty as your nephew if I didn't question your sudden friendship with a stranger." He glanced at Luc. "Of course, I mean you no insult, but I'm sure you understand my position. I am only looking out for my uncle's welfare."

"I ain't in my dotage!" snarled Silas, the knuckles of the hand holding his mug of mulled wine gleaming white. "Furthermore, I don't need you or anyone else to look out for my welfare." His eyes narrowed. "You've just insulted a guest in *my* house. I've a good mind to send you and that namby-pamby friend of yours packing."

The double doors opened at that moment, and the ladies walked into the room. Neither woman could pretend not to notice the charged atmosphere, and Gillian's eyes flashed instantly to her uncle. One look at his face told her that he was agitated and she had little doubt of the cause: Stanley.

Gillian rushed to her uncle's side and placed one hand protectively on Silas's shoulder. Glaring at Stanley, she demanded, "What have you done to upset him this time?"

Luc admired the picture she made with the sable hair swept back, her cheeks flushed as rosy as the elegant woolen gown she was wearing and her eyes flashing with golden fire. He considered the slim, white hand on Silas's shoulder and her aggressive stance. A lioness on guard, he thought. But to what end? Challenging Stanley for the bone Silas represented? Or was she as concerned for her uncle as she appeared?

"All I did," muttered Stanley, not looking at anyone in the room, "was inquire how often Mr. Joslyn came to visit."

"That was just before he informed your uncle of the treacherous people who prey on the elderly . . . strangers such as myself," Luc interposed helpfully.

Gillian paid him no attention. "And what business of yours is it," she asked Stanley, "how frequently Mr. Joslyn comes to call? Surely it is up to our uncle whom he invites to *his* house and how often?"

"That's my gel!" chortled Silas, his good humor restored.

Thinking this was as good a time as any, Luc rose to his feet and, setting down his mug, said, "I must be on my way." He bowed toward the ladies and murmured, "Thank you for a most enjoyable ride. Perhaps you'll give me the pleasure of escorting you again around the neighborhood in the near future." He grinned. "Especially now that I know what intrepid riders you are." Amidst protest from Silas and Mrs. Easley, Luc prepared to leave. He noted that Gillian and the other two gentlemen didn't add their voices to the others.

Before he could make good his escape, Silas demanded that he come to dine with them on Friday evening. When Luc hesitated, Silas added coaxingly, "Meacham will prepare more mulled wine . . . and have the recipe for you. I'll ask Cook to serve some of those buttered lobsters you complimented her on a few weeks ago."

Luc laughed. "It would be rude of me to refuse such a tempting invitation. I shall see you then, sir."

Gillian didn't know whether to be relieved or disappointed when Luc Joslyn left. His presence provided a counterpoint to Stanley and Lord George Canfield, but he was also a problem she didn't need to deal with right now. She sighed. Stanley and Canfield provided enough trouble for her without adding the distracting Mr. Luc Joslyn to it.

Taking the chair Luc had just vacated, she studied her half brother. Tall and slimly built, his tawny hair was worn without powder and, except for a few locks on the side, tied into a queue. Stanley was a handsome young man, she admitted, but there was nothing remarkable about him. His complexion was pale, his eyes brown, and he was correctly garbed in a long-tailed blue coat, buff pantaloons and black boots.

Stanley generally avoided the country, and she wasn't aware that he was particularly fond of their uncle. Yet here he was. The reason wasn't hard to guess: money. But why, she mused, as she took a cup of tea from Mrs. Easley, had Stanley brought along Canfield? Her gaze shifted to Canfield, who, from the way he was staring at them, appeared to be fascinated by his boots.

Canfield, like Stanley, had been a crony of her late husband, and like Stanley and Charles, he was addicted to all games of chance; she had never cared much for his company. She took a sip of her tea. Of course, she thought dryly, she could say that of nearly every one of Charles's friends.

Canfield's eyes lifted suddenly and he looked straight at

her. He smiled and something in that knowing smile infuriated her. Her chin lifted and her eyes glittered with temper as
she met his stare. She'd be damned if she'd let a wastrel like
Canfield intimidate her. She had done nothing wrong, no
matter what the wags claimed, nor how much was whispered
behind her back. She had *not* murdered her husband!

But something in Canfield's pale blue eyes made her un-
easy. He looked as if he knew a secret. She stiffened. Surely
he could not know of Charles's despicable bargain with Lord
Winthrop? It was impossible! No one knew except Charles,
Lord Winthrop and herself . . . unless, she thought sickly,
Winthrop had bragged to his friends. . . .

Even more determined to hold her own across the short
distance that separated them, Gillian's eyes clashed with
Canfield's, and when he dropped his gaze a long moment
later, one of her hands had curled into a tight fist and she discovered she had been holding her breath. Letting her breath
out slowly, she forced her fisted hand to relax and kept her
eyes lowered, her thoughts unpleasant and chaotic.

She considered the terrible possibility that Canfield knew
of Charles's bargain with Winthrop, and it was several minutes before she could tear her mind away from that dark place.
Forcing herself to concentrate on the conversation going on
around her, she wasn't surprised that Stanley had once again
brought up the subject of Luc Joslyn.

"I do not mean to harp, Uncle, but do you think it wise to
foster a friendship with Mr. Joslyn?" Stanley asked. "I mean,
I realize that his half brother is a viscount, but need I remind
you that Luc Joslyn is illegitimate?"

"There are many within the *ton* who refuse to acknowl-
edge him," drawled Canfield.

"Well, I ain't among them," snapped Silas. "Luc Joslyn's a
fine man, and I'm proud to call him a friend." His gaze
sharpened on Canfield. "I seem to remember that you didn't
have any problem sitting down with him and losing several

thousand pounds to him in May." He smiled with his teeth. "Perhaps that is why you were rude to him."

Canfield flushed. "I didn't see any reason to encourage his pretensions."

"Pretensions!" hooted Silas, enjoying himself now. "I fail to see how returning a civil reply would encourage anyone's pretensions."

"May I remind you that Lord George Canfield is the son of a duke and that he is my guest," said Stanley stiffly.

"Remind me all you want," Silas said. "It's my house and I can speak my mind if I want to. If your fine friend don't like it, Broadhaven sports two inns—he can put up there and take you along with him."

Before the exchange devolved into a shouting match, Meacham opened one of the double doors and announced: "Dinner is served."

"I don't know when I've ever spent a more diverting evening," Sophia observed to Gillian a few hours later. "Although I could have died of mortification with the way Stanley and Canfield treated Mr. Joslyn. It was most ill-bred of them."

In her nightgown and robe, Sophia was seated in a yellow-and-blue-striped satin chair in the small sitting room that divided her bedroom from Gillian's. Curled up on the blue damask sofa across from Mrs. Easley, Gillian was also garbed for bed and the two women were enjoying a cup of hot chocolate before retiring for the night.

Gillian nodded. "Stanley was certainly trying to assert himself, wasn't he?"

"Yes, he was, but Uncle pinned his ears back very nicely. If he's wise and wishes to remain at High Tower, your half brother will take care not to irritate Uncle Silas too much."

Gillian smiled. "I agree. Uncle was in high fettle tonight, wasn't he?"

"Indeed, he was. I'm surprised that Stanley and his lordship didn't pack their bags and ride off with their tails between their legs." Sophia shook her head. "If it had been anyone else, I'd have died of shame at Uncle's antics, but since it was Stanley. . . ."

Both women giggled.

Sobering, Gillian asked, "Why do you think that Stanley is so determined to stay at High Tower?"

"Money!"

"Most likely, but why drag Canfield along?"

Sophia pursed her lips. "You know my friend, Mrs. Barbara Lawrence, who lives in London?" At Gillian's nod, she went on, "I received a letter from her a few weeks ago and she mentioned that one of the topics of conversation during the recent Little Season was the Duke of Welbourne's displeasure with his youngest son." She shook her head. "It seems that Canfield is too wild and dissolute even for his grace and Welbourne had threatened to disown him. Mayhap he has and Canfield is living off his friends for the time being."

Eyes wide, Gillian asked, "Did Mrs. Lawrence know what Canfield had done to cause his father's ire?"

Sophia shook her head. "Barbara alluded to something involving a young lady, but she didn't elaborate."

Gillian looked thoughtful. The news that Canfield's problems involved a woman didn't surprise her. In the years following Charles's death and that terrible night at Welbourne's lodge, she'd learned a great deal about the Duke of Welbourne. He was notorious for debauchery and the "parties" at his lodge. She shuddered. If only she had known!

"It must be very bad if his grace has disowned him," she said finally.

"I agree. My best guess is that Canfield went beyond the pale and seduced a young lady from amongst the *ton*. Welbourne's predilection for wenching and whoring is legendary, but if he has any virtue at all, it is that he limits his licentious behavior to women with, ah, a certain reputation. Even he would balk at ruining a respectable lady from amongst the *ton.*"

"Do you think so?" Gillian asked with a raised brow. After what she had observed that night at Welbourne's lodge, in her opinion there was nothing too low for Welbourne and his circle of friends—especially his friend Lord Winthrop.

Sophia shrugged. "Welbourne treads a fine line, but to my knowledge he has never crossed it. There are many things the members of the *ton* would be willing to overlook, but the seduction of a young lady from their ranks isn't one of them."

"Well, if Canfield was foolish enough to do so," commented Gillian, "the unnamed lady, if there actually *is* a lady, must not come from a family with any influence, else the scandal would have spread faster than the wind."

"I suspect you're right." Sophia bent a look upon Gillian. "And you, my dear, be very careful around Canfield. I mislike him and I don't trust him—even when I'm looking at him."

"You have nothing to fear. He makes my flesh creep and I intend to avoid him like the plague."

Despite her good intentions, Gillian was not able to avoid Canfield. Late the next afternoon, Sophia had gone ahead and Gillian had remained behind for a few minutes' conversation with her uncle before going upstairs to join Sophia and change for the evening. She had just shut the door of the salon and was heading for the stairs when Canfield waylaid her.

He stepped out of the alcove near the base of the stairs and said, "A word with you, Madame?"

Gillian didn't like the expression in those blue eyes, and a feather of unease brushed her neck. Canfield had obviously been waiting for her.

Wanting to get away from him, never breaking stride, she continued toward the stairs, asking sharply as she passed him, "What?"

His hand on her arm startled her and her step faltered. His grip tightened and in one easy motion, he halted her progress and pulled her into the alcove.

Smirking at her, he murmured, "Just a private word with you, if you please."

"And if it doesn't please me?" she demanded, her eyes shimmering with anger.

"I don't think you understand the situation, and I should warn you—annoy me and you'll regret it."

"I beg your pardon?" Twitching her arm from his grasp and taking a step away from him, she added, "I'm afraid that you have a mistakenly high opinion of yourself—I don't care one whit whether you are annoyed or not. And if you dare touch me again, my uncle will hear of it—right after I box your ears." Her chin lifted. "And now if you'll excuse me, I'll be on my way."

The smirk wiped from his lips, he grabbed her arm again and pulled her next to him. His face inches from hers, he growled, "I wouldn't act so haughty if I were you, my pet. I know things about you that I don't think you'd like made public—such as what you were wearing"—an ugly smile curved his mouth—"or *not* wearing when Winthrop entered your room that night at my father's hunting lodge."

Gillian froze. Her eyes searched his and what she saw there chilled her. She swallowed and tried to brazen it out. "I'm afraid I don't know what you're talking about."

"Then I'll tell you," he said, aroused by the quickly suppressed fear he glimpsed in her eyes. "I know of the bargain your husband made with Winthrop."

Devastated, for a moment she couldn't think beyond the awful knowledge that someone else was aware of Charles's shameful agreement with Lord Winthrop. Discovering that

Canfield knew what had gone on in that bedroom between her and Winthrop left her shaken and questioning if she'd ever be able to put the events of that night behind her. How many others, she wondered, feeling ill, knew of Charles's perfidy and her humiliation? How many others thought her a slut, an easy woman willing to be handed over to any man her husband chose like a piece of booty, as well as a murderess?

She'd always hoped that someday Charles's murderer would be unmasked and that her reputation could be redeemed. At least, I wouldn't be called a murderess anymore, she thought numbly. Her presence that night at one of Welbourne's gatherings might never be explained away, but she had comforted herself with the belief that the trade Charles had made with Winthrop would never come to light. Canfield had just shattered that belief. And how many more gentlemen, she wondered miserably, were familiar with Charles's infamous bargain?

"Not so proud now, are you?" Canfield gloated.

Unwilling to let him know how devastated she was, Gillian met his eyes steadily. "Why, yes, I believe I am," Gillian said. "I have done nothing to be ashamed of. And now, if you will excuse me . . ."

His mouth thinned. "Don't be a fool!" He leaned even nearer. "No one needs to know . . . if you are nice to me."

She drew back as if confronted by a demon. Contempt in her gaze, she said, "You are a guest in my uncle's home. I will be polite to you—provided you give me no cause to act otherwise."

He shook her. "Don't you understand: I *know*."

Telling herself that she dared not weaken, dared not let him gain any advantage, in a calm voice that would have done Sophia proud, she said, "I don't know what you think you know, but it does not concern me."

"You think so? I have your husband's vowels." At the dawning horror in her face, he went on silkily, "I won them from Winthrop a few weeks ago in London before he left for his estates for the winter."

"You're lying," Gillian managed from a mouth gone dry.

"Oh, it's true," Canfield said smugly. "He may have been drunk when we met, but Winthrop regaled me with the entire tale. It was folly on his part, but the old fool kept Charles's vowels as souvenirs of a bad bargain and a lost opportunity. His only regret was that he hadn't forced you to honor your husband's debt." His eyes skimmed down to her bosom. "When the moment comes, and it won't be far off, I'll not make the same mistake."

Gillian fought to escape, but his hand gripped her arm tighter, his fingers digging into her flesh. "I expect you to be *very* nice and accommodating to me," he said, ignoring her struggles, "or else I'll just have to take that pitiful cottage you and your cousin live in to cover the debts." His eyes cold, he said, "I can take everything you own—even the clothes on your back. So keep that in mind when I have you in my bed."

Rage and terror gave her strength, and she tore her arm from his grasp. Breathing heavy, her eyes as cold as his, she snarled, "And I'll see you in hell first!"

Picking up the skirts of her gown, she dashed from the alcove and fled upstairs. Reaching her rooms, she ran inside, slamming the door to the sitting room behind her. Heart banging, gasping for breath, she leaned back against the door, her eyes closed.

Having heard the door slam, Sophia hurried into the sitting room wearing a hastily donned dressing gown, followed by Nan Burton. Sophia took one look at Gillian's white face and rushed to her.

Sophia's expression concerned, she laid a gentle hand on Gillian's arm and asked, "My dear! Is it Uncle Silas? Has something happened?"

Gillian gave a vehement shake of her head. "No. Uncle is fine."

Relieved, Sophia asked, "If all is well with our uncle, what is it that has you looking so miserable and unhappy?"

The tears she had held back in front of Canfield leaked down Gillian's cheeks and she choked back a sob. Opening her eyes, she looked into her cousin's face and cried, "Oh Sophy! My life is over! We are ruined."

Sophia smiled. "I hardly think so. Now come over here, sit down and tell me all about it."

"Would you like a nice cup of tea?" asked Nan anxiously. She hadn't seen her mistress so distraught since the night Charles Dashwood had been murdered, and she'd hoped never to see that expression on Gillian's face again.

"That's an excellent notion, Nan. Please see to it," Sophia said, urging Gillian to take a seat on the sofa. As Nan vanished from the room, Sophia sat down beside Gillian. Taking both of Gillian's hands in hers and rubbing them, she commanded, "Now tell me what happened."

Gillian fought for control of her emotions, and once she was certain she wouldn't burst into tears, she muttered, "It is Canfield." Her face full of misery, she cried, "Oh Sophy, he knows *everything!*"

Not by a flicker of an eyelash did Sophia show her own distress. Her voice as calm and comforting as always, she asked, "Are you certain, my dear? He is an unpleasant young man, but not I think stupid. He might just be guessing."

Gillian swallowed what felt like sand in her throat. "I'm certain. He caught me just as I was coming upstairs and dragged me into that little alcove." A shudder racked her at the memory. "He told me that he had won Charles's vowels from Winthrop a few weeks ago." Her mouth twisted. "His lordship was drunk and told him everything."

"I see," Sophia commented evenly, hiding her turmoil. "And what does he propose to do with the vowels? You have nothing. The only thing of value you were able to save from the debacle following Charles's death was our small cottage—" The expression on Gillian's face told her everything she needed to know. "Ah, of course. The nasty little maggot threatened to take the cottage away to cover Charles's debts if you don't allow him . . . certain liberties."

Her dark head bent, Gillian said thickly, "He wants me in his bed, where I am to be 'nice and accommodating' to him, or else he'll throw us out onto the streets."

Sophia searched for words of comfort, wondering if she'd go to hell for despising a dead man and wanting to get her hands around Canfield's neck. There was no question of Gillian submitting to Canfield's demands, and if Gillian thought about it for a moment, she'd realize that Canfield had no power over them. Even if Canfield carried out his threat, they would certainly lose the cottage, but Uncle Silas would be delighted if they lived with him—he'd mentioned it in his letters in the past and he'd already made it clear during their visit that he'd like their stay to become permanent.

Lifting Gillian's chin up, Sophia smiled at her. "Well, I think this is a tempest in a teapot. I'll miss our little cottage to be sure, but I'm positive that Uncle would have room for Matilda, the cow, and can even find a place for Angel, the sow." She looked thoughtful. "I wonder, should we bring the chickens?"

Brushing away signs of tears, Gillian swallowed a bubble of laughter. "Oh Sophy! What would I do without you? You make everything seem so simple."

"That's because it usually is, my dear." Rising to her feet, she said, "Now Nan should be back with that tea any minute. We'll speak no further on this matter for the time being, but I suggest we have a talk with Uncle Silas after dinner tonight and apprise him of the situation."

Gillian looked away. "If only there was some other way . . ."

"There isn't," Sophia answered crisply. "Unless, of course, you'd like becoming Canfield's mistress."

Gillian stared at her in horror and Sophia smiled. "I didn't think so. We'll talk to Uncle after dinner."

A flush staining her cheeks, Gillian asked in a small voice, "Do we have to tell him everything?"

"Yes, my dear, I'm afraid we do."

Chapter 5

Gillian and Sophia decided that a note to their uncle requesting a secret meeting with him tonight after he retired to his rooms would be the easiest arrangement. Gillian gave the note to Meacham and begged him to deliver it to her uncle before Silas went downstairs for dinner.

"And Meacham," she said as she pressed the note into his hand, "please do not let Stanley or Lord George Canfield see you giving this to my uncle."

Meacham studied her strained face a moment before nodding and saying, "The master is currently in his dressing room—I shall deliver it to him immediately . . . and wait for any reply."

"Oh Meacham, thank you!"

While Sophia placidly plied her needle on a piece of embroidery, Gillian paced the confines of the sitting room waiting for Meacham's return. Fortunately for the state of the blue and cream rug beneath her feet, Meacham was not gone more than ten minutes.

At the knock on the door, Gillian leaped across the room to answer it. Seeing Meacham standing there, she dragged him inside the room and shut the door. "No one saw you?" she asked.

"No one, Madame," he said. A look of distaste flitted across his face. "I believe the two, er, gentlemen are in their own rooms dressing for dinner." He handed her a small, folded piece of paper. "Here is your reply."

"Thank you."

Meacham hesitated and Gillian looked at him. "Yes? What is it?"

He cleared his throat, his cheeks reddening. "It isn't my place to speak out," he mumbled, "but should you need help of *any* sort, do not hesitate to call upon me. It would be my pleasure to serve you and Mrs. Easley however I may."

Gillian flashed him such a dazzling smile that he blinked. "Oh Meacham! Thank you. You do not know how much we appreciate your support."

Blushing right up to the top of his bald head, Meacham bowed. "Thank *you*, Madame," he managed and strode from the room.

Gillian opened the note and read the few lines. She hadn't expected that Uncle Silas would deny them a meeting, but relief washed through her when she read his reply.

"Uncle has agreed to meet us after dinner—once he escapes from Stanley and Canfield," she said to Sophia. "He suggests that after we've eaten, we retire upstairs as soon as politeness allows. When it's time, Meacham will come for us and take us to his rooms."

The hour was late when the two women, escorted by Meacham, slipped into Silas's rooms. The evening seemed interminable, and only the wink Silas had given her when she'd entered the salon where they gathered before adjourning to the dining room enabled Gillian to act normally. It helped that Stanley was on his best behavior, determined to redeem himself in his uncle's books—and when Stanley wished, he could be quite charming. Beyond taking an insulting scan of her body through his quizzing glass when he first spied her, Canfield behaved himself. Somehow Gillian managed to act civilly to him, but the unladylike desire to land him a facer was never far away.

Dinner behind them, not wishing to arouse suspicion, Gillian and Sophia, as was custom, left the gentlemen to their wines and removed to the salon for tea and cakes. The gentlemen joined them before long and shortly afterward, the ladies retired to their rooms.

Gillian had thought of nothing but the coming meeting with her uncle, and she couldn't deny a growing reluctance to confess all to him as Sophia insisted. Every instinct rebelled at involving someone else in the situation, and she wished for the time and the wisdom to think of another way of dealing with Canfield. Embarrassment cascaded through her. She felt such a whining little fool running to her uncle for help, but at present, there didn't seem to be another solution. Her lips thinned. Unless, as Sophia had suggested, she reminded herself, she wanted to become Canfield's mistress. Her stomach roiled. No! Never that. But did she have to tell her uncle everything? Could she hold some of it back?

"Couldn't we just tell him that we've decided to accept his offer of a home?" Gillian asked abruptly. "Does he have to know . . . everything?"

Sophia was quiet for second. Then, her eyes meeting Gillian's, she said, "Yes, I suppose we could keep quiet, but is that the wisest course? Whether you tell Uncle the truth or not, we'll lose our home; Canfield will still hold the vowels and he will still be able to gossip about Charles's bargain with Winthrop— even if he can't force you into his bed. If Uncle knows the entire story, he may be able to prevent Canfield from besmirching your reputation more than it already is. At the least he'd be warned and braced for the scandal that could erupt."

Gillian bit her lip. "I feel such a mewling weakling. He is an old man—he doesn't need this kind of problem."

"Have you considered what could happen if you don't tell him and Canfield gossips about the vowels and the bargain your husband made with Winthrop?" asked Sophia. "I repeat—if our uncle is to welcome us into his home, he needs to know the truth. He should have the choice of accepting us into his home, knowing a terrible scandal may follow us, or of turning his back on us, now before anything happens. To act otherwise would be dishonorable and unfair."

Sophia's words hit home. It would be cowardly—and dishonorable, Gillian admitted, not to let Uncle Silas know of the scandal he might be facing. She had no choice. She had to tell him. And pray God, he didn't toss them out of the house.

It seemed like hours before Meacham scratched on the door to the sitting room and a moment later whisked them down the long hall and into their uncle's rooms. Silas was seated in the green damask chair by the fire. He'd removed the tobacco brown jacket he'd worn to dinner, but his broken arm remained swathed in the silk sling and his feet, shod in slippers, were resting on a footstool.

A tray of refreshments had been placed on the mahogany chest that sat against the far wall, and indicating the tray, Silas said to Meacham, "After you serve the ladies, you may leave us. I'll ring you when it's time to escort them back to their rooms. And remember, no one must know that they are here with me." Meacham smiled. "There is no one to see—as soon as you came upstairs the gentlemen left for The Ram's Head looking for livelier company. I do not think they will return for several hours."

Silas nodded, pleased. "Good. Good."

Both ladies declined refreshments and after Meacham had poured Silas a snifter of brandy, he bowed and departed.

Gillian and Sophia sat together on the cordovan leather sofa across from Silas and he regarded them with affection. He thought they made a pretty picture, Gillian glowing in a gown of amber sarcenet and Sophia serene in a garment of blue with a silk fichu several shades lighter than her gown. Noting the tense way Gillian sat on the sofa, the fingers of both of her hands clenched together, he said gently, "Now why don't you tell me what has you in such a fret and why we are skulking around like a trio of conspirators."

Even though she had known this moment was coming, Gillian didn't know where to begin. She rarely spoke of the night Charles had died and then only to Sophia. Despite the passage of time, beyond the horror of her husband's murder, she writhed with shame every time she thought of that confrontation with Lord Winthrop. A shudder traveled down her spine when she recalled the look in Winthrop's eyes as he stared at her body and she dreaded having to speak of that night again. Charles's bargain certainly wasn't something she had ever wanted to discuss with her uncle and yet she knew she must. . . . But dear God! It was difficult. She looked helplessly at Sophia.

Sophia patted Gillian's clenched fingers and smiled at her. "I know it is hard, but Uncle needs to know everything. Start at the beginning—the night when Charles was murdered."

Silas stiffened. He'd known that his nieces must have something of importance to discuss with him and that the matter was urgent, else they would not be meeting tonight in this clandestine manner, but that the matter harked back to Charles Dashwood's murder hadn't crossed his mind.

Leaning forward, he said, "Tell me, my dear." He sent Gillian a singularly sweet smile. "I promise that I shall not be shocked."

Taking in a deep breath, Gillian said, "You must understand that I had no idea of the sort of party I was attending at Welbourne's hunting lodge."

"I never imagined that you did. Nor have I ever thought for a second that you had anything to do with Charles's death." Sadness crossed his wrinkled face. "I should have done more to stop you from marrying him. . . . I blame myself for what happened. I was aware that he was not a . . . good man, and I can never forgive myself for not speaking out more strongly. Just look at what you've had to endure because of my silence!"

"Oh, Uncle!" cried Gillian, slipping from the sofa to kneel near his chair. "It was all my fault—I was silly and determined to marry him—you could not have stopped me." Her fingers gripping the hand of his good arm where it lay on the arm of the chair, she said, "I am the only one who bears any blame for the foolish choice I made."

He raised his hand and brushed back a tendril of dark hair that dangled against her cheek. "Since we disagree on that, shall we settle on sharing the blame?"

She blinked back tears and smiled shakily. "If you wish."

"Well, now that we have that out of the way, suppose you tell me what this is all about."

A pair of pewter candelabrum on the mantel provided the only light, and the room was quiet except for the pop and crackle of the fire as Gillian sought to find the words. It was an ugly story she had to tell, and fearing to see the affection in Silas's gaze turn into disgust, she turned her head away. Her cheek resting against his leg, the skirts of her gown spread out like an amber cloud around her and her eyes fixed on the fire, she began to speak about that night. Lost in relating the events, she was hardly aware of Silas's hand caressing her dark hair.

The first part was easy, but humiliation and shame seared through her again when she told of Lord Winthrop's entrance into her bedroom and her throat closed up, her voice dying away.

After allowing her brief pause, Silas said quietly, "Go on, my child. Do not falter now."

Her voice not much above a whisper, Gillian continued, stopping only at the part when she discovered Charles's body lying on the floor and she suffered the blow to her head. Silas was silent for a moment after her voice died away. He'd said he wouldn't be shocked, but he was—not by any action of

Gillian's, but that Charles had been so vile! Guilt smote him. Good God! Charles had been a despicable creature, a man who had thought so little of his wife that he had expected her to whore for him—and I let her marry him, he thought bitterly. His eyes dwelled on her dark head resting confidingly against his leg. She has much, he decided, to forgive me for.

"I suspected that Charles wouldn't make you a good husband, but I never envisioned he would sink to such depths," Silas said unhappily. "It is a good thing that he is no longer alive, fouling the air with his breath." He waited a second before adding gently, "But the tale doesn't end there, does it, my dear?"

Still not looking at him, Gillian shook her head. In many ways, now came the most difficult part. She and Sophia had discussed Silas's reaction and tried to gauge how he would react when he learned of Canfield's threat. As children, they'd heard tales of the duels Silas had fought when a young man and the fear that he might feel compelled to call out Canfield could not be dismissed. Gillian had never thought she'd be grateful for his broken arm, but she was—it might be the only thing that prevented him from challenging Canfield.

"Winthrop kept the vowels and a few weeks ago, he lost them to Canfield," she said baldly. She swallowed. "Unless I become his mistress, Canfield has threatened to take our cottage to cover the vowels."

"Ah, I see," said Silas, a note in his voice that made Gillian turn and look at him.

"You won't do anything foolish, will you?" she asked anxiously, not liking the expression in his eyes or the set of his mouth.

"Of course, he won't," said Sophia with great calm. "His arm is broken—he can hardly challenge Canfield to a duel in this condition." She smiled serenely at Silas, who scowled at her. "And by the time your arm is healed and you *could* challenge him, this situation will be resolved."

"And how do you figure that, my gel?" demanded Silas, not at all pleased that Sophia was right.

"Because I suspect by the time your arm is healed that Lord George Canfield will have realized that if he opens his mouth about Charles's bargain with Winthrop, it will not reflect well on him. Unless he wishes to appear a blackguard himself, he'll keep his tongue behind his teeth."

"You could be right," Silas agreed, "but I mislike letting the rascally scoundrel escape without retribution."

"I doubt that he will," Sophia said. "His kind almost always comes to a bad end."

Silas didn't disagree and if he had his way, that bad end would come sooner than later. . . . Staring down at Gillian, who still looked at him anxiously, he smiled. "Let him have your cottage, my dear—you know that it is my dearest wish that you and Sophy live here with me."

"But what about the scandal, if Canfield gossips?" Gillian asked tightly. "Are you sure that you want us living here when the *ton* might be abuzz about me and what a wicked woman I am? A murderess and now a strumpet?"

"Without question!" Silas declared roundly. "As for the *ton*—it has been a long time, my child, since I have worried about the *ton*. Let them gossip! While their tongues wag, we shall be here snug as bugs in a rug. What do we care?" He smiled at her. "I am an old man. And I would far rather spend my last days having my two favorite nieces brightening my days than to be parading up and down Pall Mall." Gillian choked back tears. "Oh, Uncle Silas! We are your *only* nieces."

He beamed at her. "Yes. And isn't it lucky? We have no one else to worry about except ourselves."

It was nearly an hour later before Meacham came to escort the ladies back to their rooms. Much had been discussed and decided in that hour. Silas would make the announcement that Gillian and Sophia would be living permanently with him at High Tower sometime tomorrow evening when Luc Joslyn came to dine.

Rubbing his hands together, Silas said with glee, "I can hardly wait to see the expression on Canfield's face. Stanley will most likely get his nose out of joint at the news, but with Luc present, he should behave himself."

"Or not," interposed Sophia. "He and Canfield were both rude to Mr. Joslyn, and there was no need for Stanley to air our private affairs in front of him. What Mr. Joslyn must think of us I dare not guess."

Silas waved a dismissing hand. "Don't you worry about Luc. He can handle a lot worse than what Stanley and Canfield can throw his way."

The final decision had been the disposal of the cottage where the two ladies had lived. On the morrow Silas would send several servants to Gillian's cottage to pack and bring all of hers and Sophia's belongings back to High Tower. The cow, the pig and even the chickens didn't give Silas pause: they all could go to the estate farm.

Following Meacham down the hall, Gillian admitted that while it wasn't very nice of her, she couldn't deny a sense of satisfaction knowing that by the time Canfield initiated his threat to take the cottage to cover Charles's vowels, he'd find nothing but an empty building. Her eyes glittered. Now if the cottage would only burn to the ground . . . It was a wicked thought and she was ashamed of herself . . . but not, she admitted wryly, as much as she should have been.

Through the neighborhood grapevine, Luc heard of Stanley and Canfield's Thursday night visit to The Ram's Head the next afternoon. Bored and restless, he'd ridden into Broadhaven to while away a few hours at The Crown, the only other tavern in the village, before returning home to dress for dinner at High Tower.

Run by Mrs. Gilbert, a widow, and her five daughters, The Crown was as different from The Ram's Head as chalk is to cheese. Older and less flamboyant, Mrs. Gilbert's establishment was smaller, more intimate than Nolles's place—and with none of the loud, rough crowd one would find at The Ram's Head. Primarily the haunt of hardworking, honest fishermen, laborers and farmers and their families, The Crown had a comfortable, settled charm—like a favorite pair of slippers. Since Barnaby arrived in the area and his preference for The Crown became known, the clientele had changed slightly. Lord Broadfoot and a few other members of the local gentry wandered in these days to enjoy a tankard of ale or a snifter of brandy in Mrs. Gilbert's establishment.

In the main room of the tavern, the oak beams in the ceiling were black with age and crisp lace curtains hung at the windows. The furnishings were rustic, the sturdy oak tables showing the nicks and dings of age; the planked floor gleamed with a patina only obtained by the passage of decades. Nose-twitching scents floated in the air—fresh baked bread and simmering meat mingled with the smell of lemon punch, ale and spirits, and the fire burning in the big brick fireplace welcomed one to come and sit and share a pint or two with friends.

Entering the tavern, Luc wasn't surprised to find the tavern nearly empty at this time of day. Farmers were still busy in the fields and the fishermen hadn't yet docked their boats with, hopefully, a hold full of fish.

At Luc's entrance, the young woman behind the long counter at the rear of the room looked up from wiping the gleaming wooden surface of the bar. A smile burst across her pretty face and, stuffing the rag underneath the counter, and with the skirts of her brown woolen gown flying, she rushed up to Luc.

"Master Luc!" Mary Gilbert cried, blue eyes full of delight, dark curls bouncing around her shoulders. "You just sit right over there by the fire and let me go tell Ma that you are here." Wiping her hands on her big white apron, she added, "She was just saying the other night that we haven't seen you in a while."

Mary Gilbert was the youngest of the five Gilbert daughters and looked very much like her sisters. All had their mother's lively blue eyes and dark brown hair, though Mrs. Gilbert's was liberally sprinkled with gray these days. Watching Mary bustle away, Luc grinned, thinking that the whole family was as appealing and as hard to resist as a basket of big-eyed kittens.

Following Mary's directions, he settled himself at a table near the fireplace and stretched his legs toward the fire. Glancing around the room, he noted three men he recognized as day laborers nursing their mugs of ale at a table underneath one of the lace-curtained windows and nodded at a pair of retired fishermen he knew seated a few tables away.

Her cheeks pink, blue eyes bright and her gray-streaked hair pulled back into a bun, Mrs. Gilbert sailed into the room and, spying Luc, hustled over to join him.

Plump as a pouter pigeon, her features pleasant and cheerful, Mrs. Gilbert looked nothing like a smuggler, Luc mused, his lips twitching.

Yet it was true. Until a short while ago, Mrs. Gilbert, her five daughters, Jeb Brown, a local fisherman, and Luc's own sister-in-law, Emily, now the Lady Joslyn, along with a few others, had been exactly that: a gang of smugglers. Luc owed his own arrival in England to Emily and Jeb and their smuggling activities. Jeb had been making a run to France and at Emily's request had been on the lookout for Lord Joslyn's half brother. Jeb had found him, ill and weak from an infection from a bullet, concealed in a brothel. Luc often wondered what his fate would have been if Jeb hadn't so providentially shown up in Calais and wafted him to England.

His eyes hardened. It was only luck that he hadn't been

killed when Jeb and his men had made a landing that night near Cuckmere Haven and members of Nolles's gang had attacked them. Jeb and his men had been roughed up, their contraband stolen, but no one had been killed. If for nothing else, Luc thought, he owed Nolles for that near miss.

"Now why do you look like that, young man?" Mrs. Gilbert demanded, seating herself across from him.

"I was thinking," Luc admitted, "how much better the world would be if Nolles was no longer in it."

Mrs. Gilbert nodded. "Now *that* I can't disagree with!" Mrs. Gilbert had her own reasons for feeling as she did about Will Nolles. Her husband had been murdered after visiting The Ram's Head one night, and though it could not be proved, the general belief was that Nolles had ordered Mr. Gilbert killed, hoping to eliminate the competition The Crown provided.

Mr. Gilbert's death had been a blow, and Mrs. Gilbert and her daughters struggled to keep the tavern going, until Emily, in desperate straits because of her cousin's spendthrift habits, had come up with the outrageous idea of repairing their fortunes by smuggling. With five daughters to provide for and faced with losing the tavern, Mrs. Gilbert had been the first member of what had become a small group of village investors that profited from Emily's idea.

Smuggling might be illegal but it was the only thing that had saved some of the inhabitants of the neighborhood from losing everything they owned. It was also, Luc conceded, a way of life in these parts. Finding anyone not connected to the smuggling trade in some manner would be nearly impossible whether it was the relatives of the farmer whose horses were "borrowed" or the day laborers that helped move the contraband, all benefited from the trade. It wasn't so surprising that Emily had turned to smuggling as a way of saving herself and the others.

Of course, Luc thought with smile, Barnaby hadn't wanted

his viscountess to continue as the head of a gang of smugglers, and since he married Emily, Barnaby had been busy concocting ways for everyone to earn a guinea or two. An *honest* guinea.

"What do you want to drink?" Mrs. Gilbert asked, breaking into his thoughts.

"This time of day—a tankard of ale, I think."

Mrs. Gilbert waved over Mary, and once she had given Mary Luc's order, she turned back to him. "I heard that you were escorting Mr. Ordway's nieces around the other day," she said. "You should have stopped—the day was chilly as I recall and I'd baked a nice Cheshire pork pie. It would have been my pleasure to serve the ladies in one of the private rooms and allow them to warm up near the fire before riding back to High Tower."

Luc grinned at her. "You just want to be the first to meet them."

She smiled. "I'm sure they would find The Crown more to their liking than Nolles's place—even if Ordway's nephew and his friend prefer The Ram's Head." At the sharpening interest in Luc's gaze, she added, "One of my regulars happened to stop in there last night and saw the pair of them sitting at a table with Townsend and Nolles." Slyly, she added, "I also heard that you were there last Friday night—watching Harlan Broadfoot gamble with the squire." When Luc remained silent, she went on, "Now if *you* gambled with the squire that might explain why he has been whining to Nolles all week about his losses . . . to young Broadfoot."

Luc shook his head as Mary came up and set down his tankard of ale. "*Diantre!*" he exclaimed, amused and annoyed at the same time. "Does nothing happen in the neighborhood that you don't hear about?"

Mary giggled and shook her head. "Now, Mister Luc, you know that you can't hide anything from Ma. There's some in the village that think she's a witch." She dimpled. "A *good* witch."

"I run a tavern—people talk," Mrs. Gilbert said, her blue eyes amused.

Someone called Mary's name and she danced away to answer the call. Mrs. Gilbert watched her daughter's slender form a moment before looking back at Luc. "Heard, too, that you were the one who found Silas Ordway that same night and rescued him from the ditch."

"After I'd taken young Harlan home—drunk as a wheelbarrow."

"I heard about that, too . . . and what a wonderful run of luck he had pitted against the squire," she retorted, disbelief in her tone.

"*Oui*—it was quite remarkable," Luc said, his expression guileless. "I was amazed at the boy's skill."

Mrs. Gilbert shook her head and laughed. "You're a very good liar."

Luc looked modest and Mrs. Gilbert chuckled. "Very well, since you won't tell me what really happened, tell me about Mr. Ordway's nieces." Thoughtfully, she added, "Odd that they should show up now for a visit, when to my knowledge it's been years since they were last here. And now his nephew has also shown up on his doorstep—practically on their heels. Interesting, don't you think?"

"My dear Madame, surely you do not expect me to gossip about my betters?" Luc teased.

Mrs. Gilbert snorted. "I doubt that you consider anyone your 'better.' "

"That's true," Luc agreed. He was fond of Mrs. Gilbert, but he didn't want to talk about Silas's nieces with her, and if it had been anyone else but Mrs. Gilbert, he'd have frozen her with a look. Yet because of his fondness for her, for her whole family, he didn't want to snub her either.

Mrs. Gilbert occupied a unique position within the American Joslyn circle, and none of them considered her merely a tavern keeper. Her connection with the Townsend family was long and close—she had been Emily's wet nurse, and Emily and Cornelia held her in great affection. The smuggling scheme had deepened the bond between the women, and from the moment Barnaby had awakened in The Crown's best bedroom, after nearly drowning in the Channel, he'd found himself in close association with Mrs. Gilbert. She knew, Luc thought with a smile, where all the family skeletons were buried. But that doesn't mean, he admitted, that I intend to gossip about Gillian and Sophia with her. Now Stanley . . .

"Did you hear anything else about Stanley Ordway's visit to The Ram's Head?" Luc asked abruptly.

Mrs. Gilbert shook her head. "Why are you so interested?" she asked.

It was his turn to shrug. "Idle curiosity."

She didn't believe him, but since she knew nothing else, she changed the subject, asking after Emily and Cornelia. After a few minutes of conversation, she rose from the table. Pausing for a moment before leaving, she looked down at him and said, "I don't know why you were at The Ram's Head talking to Nolles the other night, but I would remind you to step carefully around him."

"Please, *non*, not you, too," Luc said disgustedly. "I've already heard the lecture from both Lamb and Barnaby about how foolish I was."

She bent near him, her eyes serious. "Luc, Nolles is a killer—no one knows it better than I. He hates Barnaby for what happened earlier this year and don't think for a moment that because he's made no move against any of you so far that he won't do so when the mood strikes him. And it will. I don't think he's bold enough to go after Barnaby or Emily, but hurting you, or even killing you, would please him enormously because he knows how much pain it would cause your brother. Stay away from him."

"I don't fear Nolles, *ma belle*. What would you have me do? Hide?"

Her expression troubled, she muttered, "Just stay away from him. Don't bring yourself to his attention."

Luc rode away from The Crown mulling over what he had learned. That Townsend had been whining to Nolles about the losses he'd sustained Friday night wasn't surprising, nor was the news of Stanley and Canfield's visit to Nolles's place. Knowing their propensity for heavy drinking, wenching and all games of chance, he knew that High Tower wouldn't provide the pair of them with the excitement and entertainment they craved. His lips quirked. And The Crown was far too respectable and staid to appeal to two gentlemen who considered themselves bucks of the first head. Yes, he thought, they would blend right in with the rough crowd, profligate gamblers and drunken revelers found at The Ram's Head.

Turning his horse onto the drive that led to the Windmere and the Dower House, he considered Mrs. Gilbert's warning about Nolles. Luc didn't dismiss her words or take them lightly. Nolles *was* dangerous, and it was only a matter of time until the poisonous little viper struck, Luc admitted.

There had never been any question that sooner or later, Nolles would seek revenge against Barnaby, and it was curious that he hadn't done so as yet. Luc frowned. And Mrs. Gilbert was right that Nolles wouldn't go after Barnaby directly. Even Nolles, he thought, wasn't brazen and foolish enough to kill someone of Barnaby's standing. . . . But there were other targets. Himself for one. Lamb for another. So what, he wondered, was Nolles waiting for?

He turned the question over in his mind as he mounted the steps to the Dower House, but coming to no conclusion, he put the problem away for the time being. He had something far more enjoyable to contemplate—dinner at High Tower with his friend . . . and crossing swords with a woman who stirred his blood and piqued his interest.

It was only after bathing and dressing, as he prepared to leave for High Tower, that Luc admitted that he was looking forward to seeing Gillian Dashwood with far more anticipation than he liked. And reminding himself that she was a murderess and most likely preying on the affection of an old man for her own ends did little to dampen his appetite for her company. She was, he decided, as dangerous as Nolles—perhaps even more so. A grin flashed across his dark face. But so am I, he thought, so am I. . . .

Chapter 6

Luc may have been looking forward to dining at High Tower that evening, but the idea of sitting down at a table with Canfield and Luc Joslyn filled Gillian with anything but pleasure. Stanley was endurable, but having to be polite to that reprehensible Canfield galled her. As for Luc Joslyn . . .

Her physical awareness of him troubled her. Even if she was inclined toward dalliance, which she was *not!* her present circumstances made flirtation with any man impossible . . . and unwise. Besides, she reminded herself, I don't even like him—even if he is the most attractive man I've met in ages. Or noticed, she thought unhappily.

No, she wasn't looking forward to the evening, and the knowledge that Silas was going to announce that she and Sophia would be making High Tower their home only added to her anxiety. Her brother's displeasure at the news was to be expected, and she was positive, like Luc Joslyn, he would attribute the basest of motives to her actions. She didn't care what either one of them thought about her, or at least not a great deal, so she could dismiss their reactions, but she was uneasy about how Canfield would take Silas's announcement. Her finding refuge with her uncle would strip away his biggest weapon against her and he wouldn't, she suspected, take it well. As the dinner hour approached, her stomach was in knots and her nerves stretched thin.

Not wishing to spend any more time than necessary with the gentlemen, she convinced Sophia to delay their appearance downstairs. Consequently, when the ladies entered the salon, it was to find the gentlemen already assembled and waiting for them.

The four men were scattered around the room, Silas in his usual chair, Stanley and Canfield off to one side, Luc standing next to the fireplace, one arm resting on the mantel. At their entrance the gentlemen looked over at them.

Canfield lifted his quizzing glass and leisurely inspected Gillian, and she stiffened with resentment. It took enormous willpower for her not to march up to him and slap the quizzing glass right out of his hand.

Regal in a gown of straw-colored crepe with bronze embroidery, Gillian brushed passed Stanley and Canfield with the faintest acknowledgment and walked directly toward her uncle. Reaching Silas, she gave him a warm smile. "Have we kept you waiting?"

Silas twinkled up at her and, taking her cold hand in his, gave it an encouraging squeeze. "Not long, my dear." He glanced at Sophia as she joined them, approving of her buff glazed chintz gown, a fringed shawl in shades of cream and rose draped around her shoulders. Glancing from one niece to the other, he added, "Far be it from me to object to waiting for such a pair of beautiful women."

Gillian's cheeks pinkened and she murmured, "And you are a terrible flirt."

"Not terrible," said Sophia, giving Silas a tap on his good arm with her painted fan, "practiced."

While Sophia and Silas chatted, against her will, Gillian's eyes slid in Luc's direction and her heart stuttered in her chest when she realized that he was staring at her. Her cheeks even pinker, she dropped her gaze, but the picture of masculine beauty he presented as he stood tall and lean by the fireplace could not be erased from her brain.

Oh why, she asked herself bitterly, did she find him so appealing? He was a notorious *gambler* for heaven's sake! And illegitimate in the bargain, she reminded herself. He was the *last* man she should find attractive. But thinking of those broad shoulders encased in a burgundy silk jacket trimmed with silver thread, and the long legs sheathed in dove-gray breeches, her breath quickened and a flush that had nothing to do with embarrassment spread through her body.

Ignoring all the reasons why she shouldn't, she risked another glance in his direction and nearly stamped her foot in vexation to find him still staring at her, a smile on that mocking mouth. He had no right, she decided resentfully, to be so distracting. His eyes holding hers, Luc cocked an inquiring brow and, her face flaming, she averted her eyes, but the memory of that mobile mouth remained—as did the glitter in the azure eyes. Ruffled, she fixed her attention on her uncle, determined to keep her wayward gaze away from Luc Joslyn.

Luc knew women. Until he'd been shipped off to Virginia to his father's home, except for an uncle and a male cousin, he'd grown up in a household of women. His mother and her widowed sisters and her sister-in-law and their daughters had doted on him, perhaps, trying to make up for disapproval shown by his *oncle* and his *cousine* Jereme. From that bevy of smiling, petal-skinned, loving females, Luc had learned much about women . . . such as when a woman was interested in a man. . . .

The sprite tries to hide it, Luc thought, intrigued, but she is not indifferent to me. *Non,* not indifferent, but she is not very happy about it. He knew precisely how she felt. Since she'd entered the room, he'd been unable to tear his eyes away from her. She drew him like a moth to the flame and it irritated him. But there was something about the way she moved, the sweet swell of her breasts peeking from beneath the crepe bodice and the flow of the material across her thighs . . . *Juste ciel!* he thought disgustedly. Whether she killed her husband or not, whether she was scheming to take advantage of Silas, he wanted her out of that charming gown and naked in his arms . . . and before long, he swore, he'd have her there, too.

Forcing a certain part of his anatomy to behave, he stared at the flames in the fireplace. A harmless seduction was one thing, but falling under the spell of a murderess had no part in his plans. Unfortunately, whenever she was near he tended to forget precisely who she was and what she was up to and would think more of her curvaceous little body and how much he wanted to taste that tempting mouth.

Leaving Gillian talking to Silas, Sophia walked over to Luc and, smiling at him, said, "It is delightful to see you again, Mr. Joslyn."

"It is my pleasure, Madame. It is kind of you and your uncle to invite me to dinner."

"It's small thanks for rescuing my uncle the night he broke his arm and for you being so considerate in taking my cousin and me for a ride on Wednesday."

"You have nothing to thank me for—even if Silas wasn't my friend, I would have lent him assistance. I wouldn't have left anyone at the side of the road with a broken arm." He smiled. "As for the ride—I enjoyed it."

Stanley walked up to them, and after complimenting his cousin on her looks, he turned his attention to Luc. Clearing his throat, he said, "I couldn't help overhearing your conversation as I approached. . . . I apologize for not thanking you the other day for coming to my uncle's aid. I am indebted to you. It might have been much more serious for Uncle if you had not arrived when you did. You have my gratitude."

"You're welcome. I only did what anyone else would have done. You owe me nothing." After the initial reception he'd been given by Stanley on Wednesday, the other man's friendliness was unexpected and his thanks seemed sincere, but he couldn't help wondering what Stanley was up to. Disarming him? But to what end?

Sophia looked approvingly at her cousin. "I must say, Stanley, you surprised me. First you actually gave me a compliment and then you were polite to Mr. Joslyn. It was most gentlemanly of you."

Stanley flushed and fidgeted. "I know that I don't always live up to everyone's expectations, but I ain't a barbarian and I'm as fond of our uncle as anyone." His flush deepened. "Even though you and Gillian think I only see him as a pile of money bags."

"I never doubted your affection for him," Sophia said calmly. "But I do question your affinity for his, ah, money bags."

Stanley scowled at her, but before he could reply, Meacham entered the room and announced that dinner was served.

There was a flurry of movement as the group prepared to leave the room. Despite his broken arm, Silas insisted upon escorting Sophia, and Stanley offered his arm to Gillian, leaving Canfield and Luc to follow them as they exited the salon.

Following Silas and Sophia as they walked down the hall toward the dining room, Stanley said to Gillian, "I must say that you are in good looks tonight—told Sophia the same thing." He smiled. "The country air must agree with both of you."

Gillian looked at him warily. "Are you being nice to me?" she asked with a raised brow. "I don't believe you've ever complimented me before—on anything. Generally all you do is complain about me and what I'm doing or not doing."

"Don't you think it's time we put away our childish rivalry? We're not children anymore, Gilly," Stanley said, using his pet name for her from childhood. "We don't have to live in each other's pocket, but I would remind you that we are a very small family and it wouldn't be a bad thing if we treated each other with respect and politeness—if not affection."

The use of his childhood name for her touched Gillian,

and she reminded herself that he hadn't *always* been a pompous little beast. If she tried, she could dredge up some pleasant memories from when they were children. She sent him a glance from beneath her lashes. Was it possible he was sincere? Perhaps he wanted to bridge the chasm between them? Cautiously, she asked, "Are you serious?"

He nodded. "I know we haven't always gotten along, but we're both adults now," he said. "Our uncle is old, one day it will just be the three of us—you, me and Sophia." To her astonishment, he looked wistful. "It would be nice if we could be around each other without daggers drawing."

Silas and Sophia turned into the dining room and as Gillian and Stanley entered the room behind them, Gillian asked, "Are you suggesting a truce?"

"A truce would be a start."

She smiled uncertainly at him, not quite believing in this change of heart, but willing to try, she answered, "Very well then, a truce."

Dinner went well. It wasn't until the dessert course had been cleared and the ladies prepared to rise from the table and retire to the salon for tea and coffee that Silas tapped his wineglass, capturing everyone's attention.

Looking around the rectangular linen-draped table, he said, "I have an announcement to make tonight that gives me special pleasure. After a discussion with them on Thursday, a momentous decision was made: my two dear nieces will be living permanently at High Tower with me." He beamed around the table. "It has long been my wish that they live with me, and they have finally taken pity on an old man and relented and agreed to share my home. I couldn't be happier."

The announcement didn't surprise Luc; he'd already suspected that Gillian had been maneuvering for such an outcome, but he was a little surprised that Sophia was going along with it. Yet thinking it over, knowing that she was a widowed lady and dependent, if Emily and Cornelia were correct, on Gillian, he concluded that Sophia hadn't had much of choice. Stanley looked poleaxed, but it was Canfield's reaction that caught his attention. Now why, he wondered, watching the flash of rage that crossed Canfield's face, should Lord George Canfield find that news so infuriating?

Whatever his private feelings, Stanley rose to the occasion. Rising to his feet and lifting his wineglass, he said, "A toast. A toast to my sister and cousin and congratulations on their move to High Tower."

The toast drunk, Stanley reseated himself and, looking across the table where Gillian was seated, asked politely, "How soon will you make the move?"

"It's already made," said Silas with satisfaction. "Several of my servants left yesterday for Surrey to pack up their things." He grinned at Gillian. "Even the cow, Matilda, and the pig, Angel, will be finding a new home at High Tower."

The announcement made, the ladies escaped to the salon. Too nervous to relax, Gillian paced the floor, and watching as Sophia prosaically poured herself a cup of tea, she demanded, "Aren't you the least worried about Canfield?" Her face clouded. "And Stanley?" She sank down on the sofa next to Sophia. "Oh, Sophy!" she cried, "Stanley was actually *nice* to me tonight as we went into dinner. He appeared to want for us to become, if not friends, at least friendly. After Uncle's announcement, he's going to be most upset and I can't blame him." She wrung her hands. "I feel terrible. He seemed sincere—he even called me Gilly, and he's not done that in *ages*. We agreed to a truce and I was hopeful. . . ." She made a face. "Now I wouldn't blame him if he thinks me the most deceitful creature in nature."

"He was nice to me, too," Sophia replied. "Polite to Mr. Joslyn, also." Stirring some sugar into her tea, she said, "Based on his manner this evening, it would seem as if he's trying to change his ways." She took a sip of her tea, and putting down the bone-china cup, she added, "I'm sure you're right about his reaction to Uncle's announcement, though—he can't but believe that we've been conniving behind his back—worming our way into Uncle's good graces." She sighed. "What a shame, if it's genuine, that his change of heart had to happen just now."

Gillian frowned. "You don't believe he really wants to mend our relationship?"

"I don't know, my dear. It is entirely possible he is sincere. Stanley wasn't a bad child—spoiled and petted and jealous of you, yes, he was all of that, but don't forget there was a kindness about him—when he wasn't being a wretched little monster." Sophia looked thoughtful, "On the other hand . . . he is here with Lord George Canfield and we know what Canfield is! Most likely Stanley is here to beg Uncle to cover his gambling debts, so it *is* possible that his hand of friendship is a ruse."

"You don't think he knows what Canfield is about?" Gillian asked, horrified. "And that his apparent about-face is all part of a plot?"

Sophia shook her head. "No. Your half brother may be overbearing and love the gaming tables far too much for his own good, but I cannot believe that he would be part of Canfield's scheme." Sophia picked up her cup of tea. "In fact, I think if he knew what Canfield planned, he'd turf him out of the house and challenge him to a duel."

She looked at Gillian. "While he doesn't always treat you with the consideration and affection he should, I'm positive he would be offended by anybody *else* behaving badly toward you. In fact, though they were friends," she said slowly, "I'm certain if he'd known of Charles's bargain with Winthrop he'd have prevented you from going to Welbourne's hunting lodge for the dreadful party and that he'd have called Charles out."

Gillian thought about it and decided that Sophia was correct. Stanley did have scruples of a sort, and like Sophia, she believed that he would have stepped in if he'd had any inkling what was in the offing the night of Welbourne's party.

"Do you think we should tell him what Canfield is about?" Gillian asked.

Over the rim of her teacup Sophia regarded her. "Only if you *want* him to challenge Canfield. Unlike Uncle, Stanley does not have a broken arm."

"Of course, you're right," Gillian admitted, sitting down on the sofa next to Sophia. "I just hadn't gotten that far in my thoughts." She smiled crookedly. "I'm still trying to deal with Stanley being nice."

Sophia chuckled. "I suspect now that the cat is out of the bag about our living with Uncle, we won't have to worry about that any longer."

The double doors opened and the gentlemen came into the room. Silas made for his usual chair and the other three men scattered themselves around the room. Luc took up his former position by the fireplace; Stanley sat in the matching chair next to his uncle, and Canfield lounged on the arm of the sofa next to where Gillian was sitting, his upper body near crowding hers.

His eyes narrowed, Luc observed Canfield's territorial position just beyond Gillian's left shoulder, not liking the surge of possessiveness that powered through him. He'd known many women, but jealousy was an emotion he'd never experienced. He wasn't convinced that what he was feeling was jealousy, but he knew he didn't like it—or Canfield's proximity to Gillian.

Luc had certain rules when it came to women, and he had yet to meet a woman who could cause him to deviate from his own principles. No virgins. No married women, and no flirtatious coquettes who delighted in pitting one man against another. And he *never* poached on another man's preserves. His attitude was simple: the world was full of beautiful, amiable women and with a shrug, he'd move on.

Gillian presented a problem for him: he didn't think he was ready to move on just yet. . . . He wanted the sprite. Badly. His gaze fell upon Canfield and the sudden overpowering desire to pick up Lord George Canfield by the scruff of his neck and goosestep him out of the front doors of High Tower surprised Luc. He scowled. His reaction was understandable—he didn't like the man, but he was *not,* he reminded himself, jealous!

Gillian was acutely conscious of Canfield's presence crowding her and she held her body as far away from him as she could. Using the excuse of pouring more tea, she slid nearer Sophy and away from Canfield.

Luc noted the action. The sprite, it appeared, had no interest in encouraging Canfield, and unless he missed his guess, she wanted nothing to do with the man. Deciding it was his duty to rescue her, Luc strolled over to where Gillian sat.

Smiling down at the two women, Luc said, "It is a pleasant evening. Would you two lovely ladies care for a stroll in the gardens?"

No more than Luc had Sophia liked Canfield's choice of a seat and she responded immediately. "What an excellent idea!" Glancing across at Stanley and Silas, she said, "What do you gentlemen think? A leisurely after-dinner walk sounds like just the thing."

Like Sophia and Luc, Silas hadn't been happy about Canfield's proximity to Gillian and spiking any plans Canfield might have had to cut her out from the others, he said, "Not for me I'm afraid, but Stanley, you go ahead." He smiled wolfishly at Canfield. "Canfield can stay and keep me company."

Canfield had no choice but to remain behind with his host, and he watched in impotent fury as Luc, with Gillian's hand on his arm, and Sophia and Stanley disappeared between the French doors that opened onto the side garden.

It was a pleasant night and though the garden was no longer at its height, there were a few roses still in bloom and most of the shrubbery had not yet lost all its leaves. The four-some spread out, but they did not stray from the stone paths and the faint light spilling from the house.

Gillian was very aware of Luc's lean, masculine body moving fluidly beside hers as they wandered down one of the many paths. Beneath her fingers she was conscious of the muscles in his arm and she wondered what it would feel like to have those strong arms enfold her in an embrace. A pleasurable little shudder went through her at the idea. She risked a glance up at the chiseled mouth, and at the thought of having those lips pressed against hers, heat bloomed low in her belly.

It had been a long time since she had felt desire, but she recognized the emotion lazily coiling through her. Desire. Why, I want him, she admitted incredulously. Her pulse jumped at the admittance, but she didn't deny it. She wanted Luc Joslyn.

A virgin when she had married Charles, her husband had been the only man she had known, and during the first years of their marriage, Charles had been an attentive, exciting lover. He had delighted in her small, generously formed body and had taught her the physical pleasures that could be shared between a man and a woman. In love with him, Gillian had reveled in her husband's lovemaking, but as the years had passed and the estrangement between them grew, Charles's visits to her room became less frequent. Toward the end, she banished him entirely from her bed, and though there were nights she tossed feverishly and burned for his lovemaking, she never regretted her decision.

Aware of Luc in ways she had nearly forgotten, her skin felt hot, tight and to her horror, the image of them entwined naked slid through her mind and her nipples suddenly hardened beneath the soft material of her gown. The idea of being naked in his arms and knowing the demand of that beautiful mouth would not go away and her breathing escalated. Feverish with desire, Gillian kept her gaze fixed on the path, afraid if she looked at him he would glimpse what she was feeling. If he touched me . . .

"The top of your head is very pretty," Luc said, breaking into her thoughts, "but I would much prefer to see your lovely face."

At his words, she became aware of their surroundings. They were in a small, darkened nook, Stanley and Sophia were nowhere in sight and she made the mistake of looking up at him.

His face was deep in shadow, but even with her eyes closed she would have been able to see his dangerously appealing features, the aristocratic nose, the high cheekbones and that sculpted mouth. Her gaze fastened on his lips and she could not look away.

Luc muttered something and then she was in his arms, his mouth feasting on hers. His arms locked her next to his body, the thrust of his rigid member unmistakably pressing into her soft flesh.

Gillian moaned at the sensation of that hard, knowing mouth taking hers, and when he parted her lips and his tongue plunged inside to explore and take, she welcomed him. Gripped by desire, her arms closed around his neck and her small body pressing ardently against his, she wallowed in the sensations shooting through her.

Even when his hand fastened on her breast and those long, elegant fingers began to knead and caress, Gillian made no move to escape. She could not. She was burning up with desire, mindless with need, and if Luc had thrown her down on the ground and taken her then and there, she would not have denied him.

It was the sound of Stanley and Sophia's approach that brought them both to reality with all the finesse of being doused with a bucket of icy water. Tearing her mouth from his, her arms dropped from his neck and Gillian sprang away from him as if stung. Luc swore violently under his breath—

with what breath he had and hoped to hell the darkness would hide his aggressively rampant state. Another minute and he'd have had that enticing little body crushed against a tree, her skirts up and his aching staff buried deep within her.

Grabbing her hand, Luc jerked her from the darkened nook and onto the path where the shadows were not so dark. A lightning glance told him he had not damaged her gown or hair. Satisfied there was no outward sign of that frantic embrace, he placed her hand on his arm and said, "This doesn't end here." A carnal smile curved his lower lip. "The next time I have you in my arms, *chere,* and it will be soon, we will finish what we started. Now come, we must meet your cousin and brother with innocent faces."

Gillian stiffened at the confidence in his words. What had just happened between them, she tried to convince herself, even as her body throbbed for his touch, had to have been an aberration. No man, not even Charles, had made her feel so wanton, so full of mindless need that she wouldn't, *couldn't* have stopped him from taking her there in that little nook. She was a respectable widow, for heaven's sake! Not some female of easy virtue who coupled with any attractive man she met.

Her fingers once again on his arm, as they walked toward the sound of Stanley and Sophia's voices, Gillian fought for composure. Knowing they would come upon Stanley and Sophia at any second, she forced herself to banish those breathless moments in the nook . . . and vowed to stay as far away from Luc Joslyn as possible. Her jaw set. She had no intention of allowing this, this *madness* to continue.

They rounded a curve and found Stanley and Sophia walking in their direction.

Taking the offense, Luc said gaily, "Ah, there you are! Where did you disappear to? We have been looking everywhere for you."

Sophia chuckled. "We didn't disappear, but we thought that

you had." Sophia's gaze ran over the pair of them. There was nothing outward that she could put her finger on, but there was something. . . . Hmmm.

"As I recall," Stanley said, taking Luc's words at face value, "the gardens are laid out in a bit of maze. It's not surprising that we lost sight of each other traipsing through them in near darkness."

"Unless you care to walk further," Luc murmured, "I suggest we return to the house."

"Yes," agreed Sophia. "I think we've left Uncle with Canfield long enough."

Shortly after returning to the salon, Luc took his leave and moments after he'd departed, Gillian and Sophia bid the gentlemen good night and headed toward their rooms. Entering the sitting room they shared, hoping to postpone any questions, Gillian asked, "Did Stanley say anything to you about Uncle's announcement?"

"He astonished me," confessed Sophia. "I was certain he'd start complaining the instant we were alone, but all he did was mutter that he was surprised by our decision to live at High Tower permanently and considering Uncle's age, perhaps it was a good idea."

"He didn't accuse me, us of being underhanded?"

Sophia shook her head. "I was prepared for that, but he was perfectly polite. If I didn't know better I'd swear he was sickening with something."

Seating herself on the sofa, Gillian said, "I wonder if we have wronged him. Not that he hasn't run to Uncle in the past every time he's been badly dipped, but that doesn't mean he isn't fond of him."

Sophia joined her on the couch and sliding off her black satin slippers, she said, "I'm sure he is fond of Uncle . . . and of course, his money, but it's possible he's finally grown up. We'll see." Her laughing eyes met Gillian's. "Now are you going to tell me what you and Mr. Joslyn were *really* doing in the dark by yourselves?"

With only a sliver of moonlight to guide him, Luc rode home. His mind was only half on the road, his thoughts on the past evening . . . and the interlude with Gillian Dashwood in the nook. Just the memory of her intoxicating mouth beneath his aroused him and he moved uncomfortably in the saddle. *Mon Dieu!* The sprite had powers he had never suspected. With one passionate kiss she had brought him to his knees, and he was uneasily aware that nothing would stop him from having her in his arms again.

He smiled in the darkness, his teeth flashing white. In his arms and naked, with no possibility of interruption until he had slaked himself on that sweet feminine body. Which might take awhile, he admitted, thinking of her generous breasts. . . . The impertinent rod between his thighs painfully erect, he decided that if he didn't want to injure himself, he'd do well to think of something else besides the little widow. His attention reluctantly shifted to Silas's announcement and Canfield.

Canfield had been furious at the news that the women would not be returning to Surrey. Why? What did it matter to Canfield where they lived? Luc thought about it. If Gillian and Sophia returned to Surrey, it would be, from what Luc understood, a small household of women: just the two ladies and a few female servants. In a situation like that, with Stanley presumably going back to London and Silas at High Tower, the women would have no one to prevent an unscrupulous individual, like Canfield, he mused, from taking advantage of the lack of male protection. . . . Silas was no stalwart warrior, but he had several brawny young men on his staff and only a fool would attempt any sort of ugly mischief while the women were at High Tower.

So Canfield was up to no good and he needed the women in a situation where he could control events. Luc concluded that Gillian had to be the object of whatever plans Canfield had—Sophia was a handsome woman, but Gillian . . . A surge of desire coursed through him. *Oui!* Canfield wanted Gillian.

There could be other explanations, but remembering Canfield's position on the sofa next to Gillian, he thought the best explanation for Canfield's displeasure at Silas's announcement was that it upset some sort of scheme the other man had involving Gillian. For a moment, he wondered if his own interest in the young lady wasn't coloring his thoughts—because he wanted her, he assumed that Canfield did, too.

Luc shook his head. No. Gillian might send his blood raging through his veins, clouding his brain, but away from her, his brain worked as excellently as it always had. Canfield wanted Gillian. But the lady wanted nothing to do with Canfield, he reminded himself, clearly recalling the stiffness of her body and the quick way she had moved away from the other man. . . .

His horse snorted and shied, disrupting Luc's introspection. Ever alert for danger, he pulled lightly on the reins, halting the horse, and glanced around for the cause of his mount's reaction. They were stopped in the middle of a curve in the narrow, meandering road. The landscape was open meadows and rolling chalk hills, but he'd been traveling along a road adjacent to a creek and with the edges of the creek crowded with willows, beech trees and shrubby bushes, his view was obscured.

The scant moonlight increased his inability to pierce the darkness, but as his horse continued to fidget and snort, he listened intently. No foreign sound carried in the night air, and deciding it was either the scent of a badger or a hunting fox that had disturbed his horse, Luc tapped his heels to the animal's sleek sides.

As the horse stepped forward, there was a shout from the vicinity of the creek. "Get him, boys!"

At the shout and the rustling, crackling sound of bodies breaking through the brush, the horse reared. Struggling to control his mount, Luc had no time to reach for the pistols he carried in the pockets of his greatcoat. In seconds, he was surrounded by the group of men who scrambled from concealment amongst the shrubs and trees that lined the creek. It was too dark to count the constantly shifting forms in the darkness, but he knew there were several.

The reins were snatched from him and rough hands dragged him from the saddle. Luc fought with all the skill he'd learned in dark alleys and gambling dens that few gentlemen had ever seen, but there were too many of them and he was overpowered. But not, he thought with fierce satisfaction, tasting blood in his mouth, without inflicting some painful damage to his captors.

"Bloody hell!" swore one of the men holding his right arm. "I think he's broken one of me ribs. No one said he'd be any trouble."

From Luc's left, the other man snarled, "Oh, stop your complaining! I've got a split lip and I ain't whining, but sweet Jesus! He's got a sweet pair of fists."

"That's enough from the pair of you," ordered a third man, coming to stand in front of Luc.

It was too dark to see their faces, but having grappled with them, Luc knew they were big, burly men and that there were at least four of them—these three and the man holding his horse. Yet even as that thought crossed his mind, he sensed the presence of a fifth person standing a short distance away.

The first vicious punch to Luc's stomach banished any of his concern about a fifth person. Held prisoner by the two men on either side of him, he could not fight back and could only endure the savage beating that followed. The fellow knew what he was about, and by the time Luc slumped, barely conscious, between his two captors, he ached in every bone and knew that on the morrow—if he survived until tomorrow—there wasn't going to be a part of his body that wasn't bruised and bloody.

The man brought his right arm back, ready to begin anew when the fifth person ordered, "Enough. Drop him."

Luc crashed to the ground in a bloody heap, aware only of how much he hurt. From his position in the shadows, Nolles minced over and surveyed Luc's sprawled form with satisfaction. "And now a little something from me," he purred. Taking careful aim, he landed a vicious kick to Luc's head.

Pain rocketed through him and Luc knew no more.

Chapter 7

When Luc woke several hours later, he was in his bed at the Dower House, his body one long, exquisite ache. Grateful to be alive, he glanced around the familiar room, not surprised to see Lamb seated in a chair near the bed; on a bedside table reposed a pewter tray holding what he guessed was food and drink.

Luc wasn't surprised to find Lamb keeping watch over him, and wryly he admitted that while he and Lamb were often at loggerheads, Lamb was always there to nurse him through his latest mishap. His lips twisted. And give him a tongue lashing in the bargain.

From the sunlight dancing around the room, Luc deduced he'd been unconscious for quite a while. "How did I get here?" he croaked.

Lamb started and leaped up. Looming over Luc, he stared down at him, infuriated again at the damage done to him and the fright he'd felt when Luc's body had arrived at Windmere in the back of a farmer's cart just after dawn. "Farmer Fenwick was on his way to market when he found you unconscious in the road about a mile from the turnoff to Windmere."

Luc started to nod, but at the blinding pain in his head, he halted that movement. "Thank God for Farmer Fenwick," he managed. "How long was I out?"

"It's not yet nine o'clock—do you remember the time when you were attacked?"

Luc concentrated, trying to recall the exact sequence of events of the previous evening. Dinner at High Tower. He hadn't stayed late and he'd almost made it to Windmere before he'd been attacked. Frowning, he said, "It had to have been around eleven or eleven thirty."

"So you've been unconscious about ten hours." His voice noncommittal, Lamb added, "That must have been a pretty good knock on the head."

"Wasn't a knock . . . Nolles kicked me in the head."

Lamb's gaze narrowed and something dark and ugly moved in his azure eyes. "Nolles? You're certain?"

"As certain as I can be—I didn't actually see him, it was dark and I was barely conscious when he kicked me. But I'd swear it was his voice I heard." His gaze met Lamb's. "I know you're convinced that I leap from the frying pan into the fire at will, but I can think of no one else in the area who would have reason to assault me."

Lamb didn't rise to the bait and fortunately for the harmony between them, Barnaby entered the room before further words were exchanged.

Pausing just inside the threshold, Barnaby glanced from one man to the other, relieved that they hadn't yet started needling each other. Walking to Luc's bedside, he stared down at his half brother and shook his head. "Tell me," he said with a twisted smile, "do you go looking for trouble or does it just find you?"

Luc risked a grin and winced when his split lip made itself felt. "In this case," he said, "I plead innocent. I was riding home after dinner at High Tower and minding my own business."

Lamb snorted. Looking at Barnaby, Lamb said, "He thinks it was Nolles, and I'm inclined to agree with him."

Pulling up a chair, Barnaby sat down by the bed, wondering how many times in the past this sort of scene had played out. It was a familiar scenario—Luc hurt, Lamb looking to murder someone, with Luc usually second on his list right behind the person who had caused Luc's injuries, and himself in the position of peacemaker and anxious brother. Not, he reminded himself, that Lamb wasn't anxious—Lamb just didn't like being anxious about either one of his nephews.

Watching Lamb gently lift Luc up and help him drink a sip or two of warm chicken broth from a cup, he almost smiled. The biggest of the three American Joslyns, while Lamb's features marked him as a member of the Joslyn family, the crisp curl of his black hair and the dark gold of his complexion hinted at an African ancestry in his bloodline. Lamb was a magnificently built man, strong and powerful, a fierce warrior when needed, yet he could be, Barnaby admitted, one of the gentlest men he knew.

Settling Luc back against the pillow, Lamb ordered, "Now tell us what happened."

The tale didn't take long, and when Luc finished speaking, his black eyes furious, Barnaby growled, "That sounds like something Nolles would do."

"Things have been quiet since Nolles and his gang were rousted from that old barn of Barnaby's last March," said Lamb, glaring at Luc. "You know that Nolles has just been waiting for a chance to get back at Barnaby, and what do you do, but bring yourself to his attention by traipsing into The Ram's Head the other night."

"As Nolles himself reminded me, it's a public place," Luc said mildly. Before Lamb could take exception, he added, "And I agree with you that Nolles has been biding his time before trying to cause trouble for Barnaby, but I have a hunch there was more to my beating than *just* sending a message to Barnaby."

"What do you mean?" Barnaby asked.

Luc grimaced. "Not to offend you, but this might not be about you. . . . Mrs. Gilbert mentioned that one of her regulars was at The Ram's Head and overheard Townsend whining to Nolles about Townsend's, ah, misfortune the night I was there. It's possible that Townsend set Nolles on me."

"Thereby allowing Nolles to kill two birds with one stone. Do a favor for a friend and thumb his nose at me," Barnaby said, nodding. "It would explain the timing of the attack."

"I agree," said Lamb, returning to his seat on the other side of Luc's bed. He looked at Barnaby. "Nolles is a separate problem, but sooner than later, you're going to have do something about Townsend."

Barnaby pulled on his ear. "He's Emily's cousin, and while he is a poor excuse for one, he *is* the squire," he reminded Lamb. "So far as we know, he's done nothing illegal, and though we suspect it, we have no proof he was behind the attack on Luc. Besides which he owns and lives in Emily's family home, The Birches—I can hardly turf him out of his own house, and even if he is the cause of your attack, I would mislike killing him."

Almost as one, Luc and Lamb said, "I wouldn't." They grinned at each other, for the one moment in perfect harmony with each other.

Barnaby shook his head. "No. I'd like Cousin Jeffery gone, as in out of our lives, but," he said with a warning look at first Luc then Lamb, "*not* dead. I'm afraid we'll have to think of another way to be rid of him."

Luc shrugged and groaned as bruised muscles screamed in protest. "Vermin is vermin, Barnaby," he said as the pain ebbed. "Just like Nolles, he's a rat and should be exterminated."

"But not by us," Barnaby retorted. "And presently, we have no way of going after Nolles either." He looked disgusted. "As much as it goes against the grain, we'll have to turn the other cheek with Nolles and hope that an opportunity to catch him out arises . . . soon." He paused, thinking. "Knowing Jeffery and Nolles, if Jeffery is aligned with Nolles," he said after a few seconds, "I'll wager it won't be very long before Jeffery is no longer useful to Nolles and Nolles takes care of Jeffery for us. Perhaps luck will be on our side and they'll take care of each other." He sighed and shook his head. "But as long as Jeffery has something Nolles finds useful—such as The Birches, I don't think we'll see a falling-out."

Luc's gaze sharpened. "You think Jeffery is allowing Nolles to use The Birches to hide contraband?"

"I suspect so," Barnaby admitted. "Nolles has to be stockpiling his smuggled goods somewhere, and with The Birches conveniently near at hand, I think the odds are better than even that he's using the place—with Jeffery's blessing. From the gossip I've heard from Lord Broadfoot and Sir Michael and a few others, Jeffery's mostly to be found at The Ram's Head . . . which leaves The Birches deserted and available for other uses." Dryly, he added, "Jeffery is usually in one of the private rooms gambling—and from what I hear, gaming deep."

"The man is nearly bankrupt yet he is always to be found at The Ram's Head . . . gambling," Luc murmured. "I wonder if Nolles is staking him and taking a cut of his winnings? It would explain why Nolles came after me." Despite his painful lip, he half-smiled. "If Nolles is staking him, it wasn't only Jeffery's money, I, er, Harlan won on Friday night, but Nolles's as well."

The three men considered Luc's words, Lamb saying after a moment, "It fits. If Nolles is staking Townsend, he wouldn't take kindly to the trouncing"—his lips twitched—"Harlan gave Townsend the other night."

"So what do we do next?" Luc asked, looking from one man to the other.

"For now, nothing," Barnaby said, rising to his feet. "I am preparing to leave for London on Monday." When both men looked at him, he added, "Lawyers and matters to do with the estate. I'd hoped for a brief trip, but Emily and Cornelia have taxed me with all sorts of items that they insist *must* be purchased before the baby arrives." He smiled ruefully. "If I am fortunate, I will be home in less than a fortnight." He eyed Luc's swollen, purpling face and shaking his head, said, "You took quite a beating last night—it'll be awhile before you can show that handsome face of yours in public."

"So what explanation are we going to give for Luc's sudden seclusion?" asked Lamb.

"As much as it wounds my pride," Luc muttered, "the best excuse would be that I took a spill from my horse last night." He grimaced. "People will think I was foxed, but a fall, especially if I sprained my ankle rather badly when I landed and am unable to walk on it . . ."

Barnaby nodded. "Yes, that should do it. A fall would explain the bruising." He glanced at Luc, his eyes amused. "You did fall on your face, after all, but perhaps, instead of a sprained ankle, is it possible that your horse kicked you in the head and while you were unconscious stepped on your ankle? That would explain why you were lying in the middle of the road unconscious."

Luc made a face. "I'll never live it down, but it would just about cover the situation." He eyed Barnaby. "You're a very good liar."

Barnaby bowed. "One does try to rise to the occasion."

Barnaby might have been willing to wait to go after Nolles, but Lamb had other ideas. Concealed in the shadows outside The Ram's Head, like a tiger waiting for prey, Lamb bided his time. No one knew where he was or what he planned and that suited him fine. Barnaby would have tried to talk him out of it and Luc . . . Rage roiled through him when he thought of Luc's battered face and body, and his jaw bunched. Luc, he reminded himself, was in no condition to argue about anything.

Even though he allowed Barnaby to think the matter was settled, Lamb couldn't shrug off the attack on Luc. And that was why on the night following Luc's brutal beating, he was loitering, hidden, next to Nolles's inn. Whatever Barnaby thought, Nolles needed a lesson . . . a warning.

Patiently Lamb waited in the darkness, knowing that eventually Nolles would leave his establishment and walk the few steps to the large house Nolles owned adjacent to the inn. In the time that Lamb had been stationed in the narrow alley between the two buildings, the noise from The Ram's Head had diminished and he watched from his place of concealment as the place had emptied out. It had been several minutes since the last drunken reveler staggered home and the tired barmaids trudged away. He spied Townsend as the squire stumbled to his horse, and after several tries, managed to hoist himself into the saddle and disappeared in the darkness.

Lamb manfully suppressed the urge to reach out, jerk Townsend into the alley and give him a taste of what Luc had suffered. I should have killed the bastard when I had the chance, he thought, remembering that night in the barn of the deserted farmhouse when Townsend's friend, Ainsworth, had held Emily captive. His lips twisted with distaste. Emily's cousin had been such a miserable weakling that neither he nor Barnaby could bring themselves to kill him. Townsend's turn will come soon enough, he promised himself.

A sound alerted him to the approach of another person and he tensed. When Nolles's small stature appeared framed in the opening to the alley, fast as lightning, Lamb reached out with one big hand, fastened it into the collar of Nolles's jacket and effortlessly plucked him off his feet and into the darkness. Nolles's startled scream was closed off by Lamb's other hand clamping over his mouth.

"Quiet, little man," Lamb murmured. "We don't want anyone else at our party, do we?"

Shifting his grasp from the back to the front of Nolles's jacket, Lamb slammed him up against the wall of The Ram's Head. Nolles fought to free himself, but despite his violent thrashing, Lamb easily avoided his flailing arms and kept Nolles pressed against the wall of the inn, his feet dangling inches from the ground.

Impatiently Lamb shook him like a cat with a mouse and said, "Stop it. A few minutes more of this and you'll annoy me." His hand closed around Nolles's throat, and bringing his face closer to Nolles's, he said gently, "And you really don't want me any more annoyed with you than I already am, do you?"

There was something about that gentle tone that froze Nolles where he was and his frantic struggles ceased.

"That's better," said Lamb, removing his other hand from Nolles's mouth. As Nolles opened his mouth to shout, Lamb placed a silencing finger against Nolles's lips and warned, "Scream and I'm very much afraid that I'll have to hurt you . . . badly. And believe me, I'd enjoy doing it."

Except for the sliver of moonlight, the night was dark, and here in the narrow alley there was nearly total blackness. Nolles peered through the heavy shadows, but he could not make out any features—but from the ease with which he had been taken, he sensed a big man. A very big, very dangerous man. The man's size and cultured tones gave him a clue to the identity of his captor, that and the knowledge that the Joslyns were the only men who would dare lay a hand on him.

"You're Lamb, Joslyn's man," he blurted.

"More importantly," said Lamb, "I am Luc Joslyn's uncle . . . and I don't take kindly to little snakes like you thinking you can attack him—any Joslyn—and not expect punishment."

Nolles swallowed, enraged, but also fearful of the powerful hand around his throat. "W-w-what are you going to do?" Blustering, he said, "You'll hang if you murder me."

Lamb laughed. "Little man, I have no intention of murdering you." With his free hand, he brought forth the knife he carried and laid it tenderly against Nolles's cheek. "I'm giving you a warning this time," he said, and in one quick motion, sliced a long furrow on one side of Nolles's face.

Nolles screamed and struggled.

"Oh hush," murmured Lamb. "It's enough to scar but it

won't kill you. It will, however, be a reminder. . . ." Lamb
bent nearer and in a voice that filled Nolles with terror, he
promised, "Touch anyone of my blood again, anyone who
bears the Joslyn name, and next time . . . next time I *will* kill
you."

Lamb stepped back and, removing his hand from around
Nolles's neck, let him drop to the ground. Leaving Nolles
slumped on the ground holding his face and sobbing, Lamb
melted into the darkness.

Gillian and Sophia heard the news of Luc's accident on
Sunday when they attended church with Silas. Mindful not to
cause his master any discomfort, Silas's coachman drove the
lumbering barouche to the village church and the footman
who had accompanied them tenderly wafted Silas from the
carriage. The Ordways arrived with only minutes to spare,
and it wasn't until after services that there was time for any
conversation. People spilled out of the church into the fall
sunshine, a few neighbors and friends lingering to inquire
after Silas's injury.

Vicar Smythe and his wife, Penelope, strolled up to Silas,
Gillian and Sophy where they waited for several carts and
gigs to leave and make room for the big barouche in front of
the church. After satisfying himself that Silas was healing
nicely, the vicar turned a friendly smile toward Gillian and
Sophy and said, "You must be Mr. Ordway's nieces. He has
spoken very fondly of you from time to time. It is good that
you have come to visit him."

Introductions were made and Gillian braced herself for the
air of disapproval that usually descended once her name was
mentioned, but the vicar continued to smile at her in a
friendly fashion. Red-haired, freckle-faced Penelope, married
to the vicar for nearly thirty years, stepped forward and, her
brown eyes kind, said, "It is a pleasure to finally meet you.
Will you be staying long?" She chuckled. "I hope so—I am
head of several different committees but all are aimed at im-

proving the plight of our poor and destitute, so if you'll be here for any length of time be prepared to be asked to join one."

"Well, then, you'll be glad to know that they have both agreed to live permanently with me," Silas said, a wide smile on his lips.

"Excellent!" said Penelope. To Gillian and Sophy she said, "I warned you—expect me to call next week and beg you to serve on my favorite committee." With a mischievous smile, she added, "All the ladies will be most jealous that I am the first to call upon you—and if I may, add you to the Committee for the Improvement of Young Women in Broadhaven. It is rewarding work and will allow you to meet several notables in the neighborhood—the Viscountess Joslyn and her great-aunt, Mrs. Cornelia Townsend, are two of its most active members. You'll find both of them delightful." She tapped her upper lip. "Although it might be awhile before the viscountess joined us—she is expecting her first child before the end of the year."

The vicar, laughing at his wife's volubility, interposed, "My dear, I think you are overwhelming them." He looked to Gillian and Sophy and said, "For now, let a simple and heart-felt welcome to our neighborhood suffice."

"Oh, of course." Penelope smiled at both women. "Welcome—we look forward to knowing you better."

"T-t-hank you," stammered Gillian, taken aback as much by Penelope's talkativeness as her open friendliness. Perhaps the vicar and his wife didn't know who she was?

Before more was said, following the lead of the vicar and his wife, a few members of the local gentry wandered over and greeted Silas and were introduced to Gillian and Sophy. Not to be left out, Lord Broadfoot, his wife and Sir Michael and his wife strolled over and were introduced.

"Good to see you about," boomed Broadfoot to Silas once the introductions were completed and greetings exchanged.

"Heard about your accident. Did you ever learn who ditched you?"

Silas shook his head. "No."

"It is a good thing that Mr. Joslyn came along when he did," exclaimed Lady Broadfoot. "It would have been just awful if you'd had to lie there all night."

"Shame what happened to Joslyn on Friday night, isn't it?" said Sir Michael.

"Something happened to Luc?" asked Silas, perplexed. "He dined at High Tower that night and he was fine when he rode away."

"It must have happened on his way home from your place then—he took a nasty spill from his horse," said Sir Michael. "Word is that the breath was knocked from him, and before he could get out of the way, the animal kicked him in the head and stepped on his ankle—almost broke it."

The news of Luc's mishap shocked the Ordways. Gillian paled and a gasp of distress escaped her; Sophy and Silas were stunned. "Why, that's terrible!" Silas exclaimed. Turning to his nieces, he said, "We must go and see him before going home and assure ourselves of his health."

Gillian applauded her uncle's sentiments, astonished at how desperately she wanted, *needed* to see Luc Joslyn and find out for herself the extent of his injuries. "Oh, I agree, Uncle," she declared earnestly. "That's a splendid idea."

Sophy nodded. "Indeed, we must call upon him. Mr. Joslyn has been very kind to us during the short time we have been here. It is only proper."

Lord Broadfoot shook his head. "Won't do you any good. Lord Joslyn's man, Lamb, will only turn you away. My son Harlan and I tried to see him yesterday afternoon as soon as we heard the news, but Lamb told us that it would be a few weeks before Mr. Luc Joslyn would be receiving visitors. Makes me wonder if he isn't more banged up than they've let on."

Broadfoot's words struck panic in Gillian's heart. Oh, please, no, she prayed. Please, dear God, do not allow him to be seriously hurt. Shocked at the depth of emotion that welled up inside of her at the idea of Luc lying injured and helpless, she stared hard at the ground. I don't even like him, she told herself. Naturally, she would feel sorry for anyone who had suffered an accident, but she shouldn't be *this* anxious about the state of his health. Her lips tightened. Especially after the shameful liberties he took on Friday night, she reminded herself, closing her mind to the pleasure she'd experienced in his arms.

Concerned, Silas said, "I don't like the sound of that. Still, I think we'll try our luck."

Gillian could have kissed him for his persistence.

Bidding everyone good day, once they were settled in the barouche, Silas having given the coachman his orders, they set off for the Dower House at Windmere. Arriving at their destination, Silas suggested that the ladies wait in the barouche until they were assured of seeing Luc, and aided by the footman, he descended the barouche and approached the house. Lamb answered the door and allowed Silas inside, but in the handsome foyer of the Dower House, Lamb explained politely to Silas that Master Luc was presently unable to see *any* visitors.

"Oh, don't be ridiculous," Silas fumed, not pleased at being denied. "Go tell him that it is Silas Ordway who has come to call. I am a close friend of his." He waved the black silk sling that encased his broken arm. "Luc rescued me when I broke my arm—the least I can do is wish him well."

Patiently, Lamb replied, "I understand, sir, but I have my orders from Lord Joslyn himself—his brother is not to receive any guests at this time. He fears it will exhaust Master Luc." He smiled sympathetically. "Perhaps his lordship will feel differently in a week or so."

From his diminutive height Silas eyed Lamb. "It was only

a fall from a horse," he said. "Unless, of course, there's something you're not telling me. . . ."

Bending forward confidingly, a devilish gleam in the azure eyes that Luc would have recognized, Lamb murmured, "It is his pride, sir—when Master Luc was pitched off his horse, his face took the brunt of the fall. Between both his eyes being blackened and extensive bruising, his face is enough to frighten the village children. He'd prefer no one see him at this time."

"Well, bless my soul," Silas said, chuckling. "Luc never struck me as vain, but I understand—a pair of black eyes can be a ghastly sight." He hesitated. "How bad was it?"

"As bad a fall I've ever seen," Lamb admitted. "Let me assure you that he didn't break any bones and will recover with no lasting effects, but it will be a few weeks before he will be himself again."

Resigned to being turned away, Silas said, "You'll tell him that I called?"

Lamb bowed. "With pleasure, sir." His thoughts already on Luc's reaction when his nephew learned that it was vanity that kept him secluded, Lamb bit back a grin. Do the scamp a world of good to lose his temper, he concluded—and at least for a while, Luc would have something else to think about other than his aches and pains.

Once Silas was shown to the door, an anticipatory grin on his face, Lamb bounded up the stairs, heading for Luc's bedroom.

No more than Silas was Gillian happy with being denied the opportunity to ascertain for herself the extent of Luc's injuries, but Silas's report of no broken bones, and the only signs of his accident being a pair of black eyes and bruising, relieved the worst of her anxiety. Still she wondered about the accident. From what she had observed the day they went riding, Luc was an excellent horseman and it seemed odd that he'd been thrown from his horse. Deciding that his horse must have spooked at some night hunting animal and caught him off guard, she let the matter go. He would recover and that was the main thing. As for that torrid embrace in the garden on Friday night, she refused, as she had done since it had happened, to think about it. She was not some silly country maid to have her head turned by a handsome rake!

Arriving back at High Tower, Meacham informed Silas that his nephew and Lord George Canfield had gone to the village looking for amusement, but would return home in time for dinner. Aided by Silas and Sophy, Gillian had been able to avoid Canfield, and the news that he was out of the house caused all three of them to relax and enjoy the light repast that awaited them in the morning room. The meal done, they all retired to their rooms, Silas to snooze for an hour or so by the fire and Gillian and Sophia to change from their church finery into simpler clothing before entertaining themselves. Their gowns changed, the two women met in the shared sitting room. While Sophia concentrated on a piece of embroidery, Gillian sat at the cherry wood desk in front of a window overlooking the side of the house writing to the various tradesmen and friends in Surrey, informing them of the change of residence and giving hers and Sophia's new address.

It was a quiet, pleasant Sunday afternoon, but as the time for Stanley's and Canfield's return neared, Gillian felt herself tensing. Though Canfield had made no overt moves toward her, she didn't delude herself into believing he would give up and retreat. He could take her cottage and the three acres that went with it as partial payment for Charles's vowels, she reminded herself, but it was no longer a weapon against her: she and Sophia were safe at High Tower.

Her greatest fear now was that Canfield would reveal Charles's bargain with Lord Winthrop. She sighed. No matter which way one looked at the situation, she did not fare well. Many would believe that she had agreed to the bargain and willingly whored for her husband; others would point out that if she had refused, it increased the odds that, incensed, she had confronted her husband and murdered him.

Preparing to join Sophy and go downstairs for dinner, she wondered if it even mattered what people labeled her. Nearly everyone already thought her a murderess, she admitted bitterly, so what did it matter if they added whore to the title?

It didn't comfort her much but she reminded herself that at least Silas knew what he might be in for if Canfield did spread the ugly story of Charles's agreement with Winthrop. She sighed again. No one connected to the story came out looking very good, but she would bear the worst of it. Charles was dead. Winthrop was a man and a well-known member of the *ton*. Canfield's father was a duke, for heaven's sake—his part in spreading the gossip would be swept under the carpet. No, she would be the one pointed out and gossiped about.

Thinking back to this morning and the friendliness shown her by the vicar and his wife, her heart ached. She didn't want them to look at her with disgust or turn away when they saw her. She wanted, she realized, almost desperately, to be on that committee with the vicar's wife. She wanted to be part of this community, and the last thing she wanted was to bring scandal and shame to her uncle's doorstep. And what about Stanley? They might never be close, but at the moment she was optimistic that they could have a warmer relationship than they had had in the past. She snorted. If Canfield talked she could put paid to that idea. Stanley would wash his hands of her.

Dinner was an uncomfortable meal. Oblivious to the undercurrents, Stanley surprised Gillian by proving to be charming company and had saved dinner from being a disaster with amusing tales of London.

"Thank heaven for Stanley," remarked Sophia as she sat down on the sofa in the salon, the ladies having left the gentlemen in the dining room to enjoy their liquors.

Gillian nodded. "If not for him, it would have been a terrible meal. I never thought I'd be grateful to Stanley, but after tonight I certainly am." Biting her lower lip, she added, "I mislike Canfield's silence. I cannot believe that he will simply go away."

"No, I agree." Sophia frowned. "I didn't like the way he looked at you when he thought no one was looking. I fear you've made an enemy there, and while he may want you in his bed, I suspect that since he has been thwarted he'll seek some sort of revenge against you."

"I know," replied Gillian. "And as long as he holds those vowels . . ." Her lips twisted. "Between Canfield and Winthrop my reputation is in their hands."

"I wouldn't worry about Winthrop," Sophia said in her brisk manner. "Even if he was foxed, I'm astonished he admitted to the bargain at all—especially that he didn't get what he wanted. I'm certain if Canfield does expose the whole despicable affair, to save his own reputation, Winthrop will deny everything."

Sophia's words cheered Gillian until she remembered the vowels themselves. Gloomily she pointed out, "The vowels will lend credence to the story."

"Oh, pooh!" said Sophia with a wave of her hand. "All Canfield really has is a drunken reprobate's claims and a dead man's vowels. He'd be a fool and would only arouse disgust in any sensible person if he started spreading gossip about an supposed event that occurred two years ago."

Gillian started, her eyes widening. "I never thought of it that way."

"Not," warned Sophia, "that it wouldn't be uncomfortable for you, us, but it wouldn't be the utter disaster you think." She smiled at Gillian. "Stop looking at Canfield as an ogre with great power. He's not. He's a nasty little worm who wants treading on and nothing more."

Taking heart from sensible Sophia's words, Gillian was able to get through the remainder of the evening with a measure of poise that not even Canfield's presence could dent. Sophia was right, she reminded herself, crawling into bed a few hours later.

Canfield was a threat to her reputation and happiness, but not the inevitable, devastating one she imagined. No, she thought, staring into the enveloping darkness of her bedroom, Canfield was a problem but a more potent threat to her well-being lay in the formidable masculine appeal of Luc Joslyn.

Heat washed over her, and her breath quickened as the memory of his mouth, hard and hungry on hers, sped through her mind. Even now, just thinking of those stunning moments in his arms, her lower body softened and she shifted restlessly, desire flooding through her, her arms aching to touch him, her body throbbing for the sensation of his driving into hers.

Fighting back the needs clawing through her, with her fist in her mouth, Gillian bit back a frustrated sob. She was *not,* she swore vehemently, going to lose her head over Luc Joslyn— no matter how much he stirred her. I've had enough scandal to last me a lifetime, she reminded herself, and rushing willy-nilly into a passionate affair with someone like Luc Joslyn wasn't going to happen. It was just as well, she decided, that his tempting presence would not be haunting High Tower for a while. His smiling face, the brilliant azure eyes laughing at her, wafted hazily through her brain, and against her will she felt her lips form a welcoming smile. Oh, damn him, she thought helplessly. Damn him. *Damn* him!

Chapter 8

Lamb may have been able to turn others away, but he had no defense against Emily and Cornelia. Within an hour of Silas's departure, looking the Amazon he often called her, Emily brushed right past him with Cornelia by her side—and just as impossible to stop.

He did try. Moving nimbly to the base of the stairs, he stared at the two of them and said, "Ah, I know you want to see him, but even Barnaby thinks it would be better if he were given a few days' rest. It was a nasty fall from his horse."

"Oh, get out of the way, you big lummox, and don't try to bamboozle me with any story of a fall from a horse," snapped Cornelia, giving him a swift whack on his lower leg with her cane for emphasis.

Lamb yelped and yielded the field to the ladies, stepping smartly aside.

Stopping beside him, her gray eyes grave, Emily said, "Don't fret, Lamb—Barnaby told us everything before he left for London."

Lamb scowled at her. "You've bewitched him."

She dimpled, then reached up and kissed him on the cheek. "Yes, I know . . . and you think it's wonderful."

That dragged a laugh out of him. With a grand bow, he murmured, "Right this way, ladies."

Upon entering Luc's room, Emily and Cornelia were horrified by Luc's condition. They rushed to his bedside, their faces reflecting dismay.

"Oh, my dear heaven," Emily cried as she stared at Luc's battered features. "Your poor face."

"You've looked prettier, I'll grant you that," observed Cornelia, her hazel eyes moving hawk-like over him, cataloging every bruise. "My God, boy, what have you done? Riling up Nolles—now that's a fool's errand if ever there was one."

Meekly, Luc replied, "I didn't mean to—and The Ram's Head is a public tavern."

Cornelia snorted. "Humbug!"

"You knew better than to go there," Emily scolded. "Now let's see about putting some of Cornelia's oil of eucalyptus salve on the worst of your bruises. She makes it herself with the oils she has sent to her from London. I promise you it will make you feel better."

Luc enjoyed having Emily and Cornelia cosseting and fussing over him, but as the days passed and he healed, he chafed at the confinement and grew more and more impatient to be out and about. By Wednesday in the middle of the first full week of November, his bruises had faded and his supposedly sprained ankle had healed enough for him to ride into the village with Lamb and enjoy a tankard of ale at The Crown.

The two men had barely seated themselves at a table near the brick fireplace before Mrs. Gilbert appeared from the kitchen, alerted to their arrival by her eldest daughter, Faith, who had been working at the long oak counter this time.

Wiping her hands on a big white apron worn over her gown of brown wool grogram, Mrs. Gilbert walked over to their table. After giving Luc a thorough appraisal, she said, "I see that the . . . fall from your horse left you with no ill effects."

Luc grinned. "It was my pride that was most injured." He

shook his head. "I cannot remember the last time a horse has gotten the better of me and sent me flying like that. It must have been bad luck."

"I'm sure that's true," she answered. Her gaze slid to Lamb. "There seems to be a bit of bad luck going around. Gossip has it that Nolles slipped on his way home the very next night and split open his face. . . . I've heard that it looks more like someone took a knife to him than a cut from a fall." When Lamb's expression remained politely interested, after a hard look at him, she added, "He's healing, but they say he'll have a scar."

Luc's eyes narrowed and fastened on Lamb's face. "Is that a fact," he muttered.

"Indeed, it is, but of course, neither one of you would know anything about it, now would you?"

"*Mais non!* How could I?" asked Luc, his gaze still fixed on Lamb. "I was in my bed barely able to move a muscle."

"And I," murmured Lamb, "never left his side."

Mrs. Gilbert looked from one face to the other. She snorted and retorted, "And you can both go teach your granny to suck eggs."

Lamb grinned at her. "As if I would dare."

She half laughed. "Very well. Keep it to yourselves. Now what will you have?"

Twenty minutes later, Luc and Lamb exited the inn and mounted their horses. The moment The Crown disappeared from view, his face grim, Luc looked at Lamb and inquired icily, "You or Barnaby? And don't try to tell me that one of you didn't go after Nolles."

"I did," Lamb admitted with no sign of contrition. He glanced at Luc. "It had to be done, and you were in no condition to teach anyone a lesson."

"Did Barnaby know?"

Lamb looked askance. "The Viscount Joslyn? Now what do you think?"

"You had no right!" Luc exploded. "I was the one attacked. I don't need anyone—especially *you*—to fight my battles. I would have handled Nolles all in good time."

Lamb jerked his horse to a halt and glared at Luc, who had done the same. "A lesson," Lamb said from between gritted teeth, "is better learned if punishment is administered as soon after the offense as possible. There is nothing to stop you from going after Nolles yourself now that you are healed, but he needed to learn that no one strikes at a Joslyn without swift and, I must add, painful retaliation."

Since their attitudes were the same in this instance, Luc throttled back his anger. "It seems we both disagreed with Barnaby this time," he growled, nudging his horse forward again.

Barnaby arrived home from London Wednesday evening, and on Friday morning he heard of Nolles's accident from Lord Broadfoot, who had come to call. Broadfoot was barely out the door before Barnaby requested Lamb's presence in his office. Once Lamb arrived and shut the door behind him, his face grim, Barnaby said, "I thought we decided to let sleeping dogs lie," he said, staring hard at Lamb.

Taking a seat in one of the leather chairs in front of Barnaby's massive oak desk, Lamb shrugged. "You decided. I didn't."

"Damn it, Lamb! Do you think it wasn't difficult for me to stomach what Nolles did to Luc?" Barnaby demanded, the black eyes glittering. "I wanted to kill the bastard!" He sucked in a deep breath, struggling against rage. "And while you may have gained some satisfaction from your actions," he said in a calmer tone, "we're all going to have to suffer the consequences." He leaned forward, his expression intent. "You've made Nolles doubly dangerous to us. If he wanted revenge before, he'll be foaming at the mouth for it now."

Lamb looked up from his contemplation of his boots. "Better we kill him sooner than later."

Barnaby laughed without humor. "Oh, I don't disagree. But I balk at cold-blooded murder."

"But hot-blooded slaughter is acceptable?" Lamb asked with a cocked brow.

Barnaby pointed a warning finger at him. "You know precisely what I mean."

Lamb sighed. "Luc wasn't very happy with me either."

"Only because he'd prefer to teach Nolles a lesson in his own way," Barnaby grumbled, throwing himself down into the chair behind the desk.

Lamb rose to his feet. "Yes, I'm sure he would . . . and I'm sure he will eventually find a way to get his own back. Luc is very good at that. Now is there anything else you need from me?"

Barnaby waved a dismissing hand in his direction. "No. Go annoy someone else."

Both Barnaby and Lamb were correct about Luc. Luc would get his own back from Nolles, and during the time he'd been forced to remain cloistered at the Dower House, that topic had occupied his mind quite a bit . . . as had the delectable Mrs. Gillian Dashwood. Gillian's sweet form had drifted through his dreams and most nights he awakened with his member hard and throbbing and ready to explode—a situation he'd not suffered since he'd been a green youth. There had been the occasional woman he'd bedded while in London, but that had been months ago and he blamed celibacy for his persistent arousal.

Now that he was back to his normal self, he intended to rid himself of both problems. Lying in bed that Friday night, he considered the problems Nolles and Gillian represented and how best to solve them. Neither one was suitable for a straightforward solution, he admitted with a rueful twist to his lips. Gillian was no eager actress or daring widow willing to be bedded at the first opportunity. Widow Gillian might— and the most likely culprit for having murdered her husband—but he doubted she would fall into bed with him. Or would she?

The memory of that embrace in the garden of High Tower burst across his mind, and to his irritation, desire rolled through him. In an instant his staff was swollen and ready between his legs, and knowing sleep was impossible, he swore and, naked, swung out of bed.

Shrugging into the robe lain across a nearby chair, he lit the candle in the brass holder kept on a small table next to his bed and, carrying it, walked into the sitting room attached to his bedchamber. Crossing to the tray of liquors on an oak sideboard, he set down the brass holder and splashed some brandy into a snifter. Not taking time to enjoy the bouquet, he tossed the liquor down.

After pouring more brandy into his snifter, he wandered moodily around the room. It wasn't like him to be so preoccupied with a woman. But Gillian Dashwood was like no other woman he'd ever met. Irritably he admitted she attracted him in a way he'd never experienced. He wanted her, but he'd wanted other women, many women in his life, but not quite the way he wanted Gillian Dashwood. He couldn't explain how his emotions were different with her, and that worried him.

Snifter in hand, he prowled the room, turning the problem over in his mind. Her reputation, the fact that it was believed, but not proven, he reminded himself, that she had murdered her husband, added a cachet of danger to any affair with her. Ruefully he acknowledged his own predilection toward dangerous situations. But danger aside, she was also lovely. Desirable . . . and she didn't approve of him. . . . But then he didn't exactly approve of her either. He wanted her, though, and despite her reputation and her relationship to Silas, he was certain he'd have her. That kiss in the garden told him as much. But when and where, he wondered.

She was no ladybird to be satisfied with a romp in one of the rooms in the nearest tavern. . . . He glanced around the sitting room bathed in the feeble light of the lone candle and grimaced. Bringing her here was out of the question, and the notion of bedding her in Silas's own house simply wasn't to be considered. Now if the weather was warmer, he could arrange a private picnic in a secluded place. . . . Imagining Gillian lying naked on a quilt, her eyes drowsy with desire and her generous breasts and hips dappled by the shade of tree, predictably he was again hot, hard and cursing.

Mon Dieu! He had to stop torturing himself this way. But the lack of any comfortable, discreet place where he could bed Gillian reminded him of a problem he'd put off thinking about these past days: the need to have his own residence and privacy. Tomorrow, he decided. He'd miss having Barnaby, Emily, Cornelia and even Lamb nearby, but even if Gillian was not an issue, it was time—past time—that he stepped away from the haven Barnaby had provided for him.

The prospect of his own home was a novel one for Luc. Though he'd lived at the château of his French relatives from birth until he'd been twelve and had lived at Green Hill for nearly as many years, he'd never felt that either place had been home. He'd been grateful for Barnaby's offer of the Dower House, but it certainly wasn't home. Now that he'd paid Barnaby back with interest the loan Barnaby had given him several months ago and had money invested in the funds, he was in a position to buy his own residence.

He half-smiled. Luc Joslyn, gambler-at-large, property owner—the idea was ludicrous. That he'd settle in England had never crossed his mind. He'd always assumed, at some point in his life, he'd either return to Virginia or would set down roots in France. The recent events in France had removed that option, and while returning to Virginia to live, perhaps not at Green Hill, but someplace nearby was still viable, he doubted, except for a visit, that he'd return to America. Barnaby's inheritance of the title and Windmere had changed the course of all their lives. With Barnaby and Lamb fixed at Windmere, the notion of living in the area held great appeal.

The day would come when Lamb tired of playing Barnaby's manservant, but Luc couldn't conceive of Lamb living far from Barnaby. Lamb would always be nearby. Emotion unexpectedly welled up inside him. Lamb will always be near for both Barnaby and me, he conceded, acknowledging for the first time that aggravating as his uncle could be, Lamb kept a watchful eye over both the Joslyn half brothers. Damn him!

He sipped his brandy. In the interest of making Lamb's task easier, he thought cynically, it was probably fortunate that he'd be living in the area.

Feeling that until he had found a residence of his own, he could do nothing to ease the desire Gillian aroused within him, he put that problem aside for the time being. Telling Barnaby of his decision to start casting about for a suitable place to buy was a step toward solving the entwined problem of Gillian and a place for dalliance, and so for now he could put that problem aside also. His features grim, he considered the problem of Nolles . . . and Townsend.

Luc was convinced that the attack on him originated with Townsend's gaming losses at his hands. If, as was suspected, Nolles was underwriting Townsend's gaming, then both men had a reason to resent what had happened that night with Harlan. His lips curled. Townsend was too cowardly to take action against him, but Nolles . . . Nolles was a different story entirely. Nolles didn't like losing—anything—and violence was his second nature. Luc's hand tightened around his snifter. Giving him a vicious thrashing was exactly the sort of action Nolles would take against someone who had cost him money, and for Nolles there was the added incentive of gouging a finger into Barnaby's eye.

Thoughtfully, Luc wandered around the shadowy room, aided by the flickering light of the lone candle on the sideboard. So how, he wondered, did he handle Nolles? And Townsend?

Townsend, he decided, would be the easiest, and he knew

just the method. Gambling. The squire was a decent gambler, but he wasn't Lucifer, and Luc knew he could ruin him in an evening if he chose. But did he want to? Emily's face floated in front of him and he winced. Townsend was her cousin, and though she loathed the man, how would she feel if her cousin were booted out onto the street with the clothes he wore on his back his only possessions? Luc made a face. Odds were she'd not turn a hair, applaud his actions in fact, but he didn't want to take the chance that his actions might bring her pain. No, for Emily's sake, he couldn't leave the man penniless, but he could take the squire closer to the brink of ruin. . . .

Which would, he decided with a satisfied expression, enrage Nolles—especially since, if gossip was correct, the majority of the money Townsend was risking belonged to Nolles. Luc paused in his meandering about the room. Infuriating Nolles would be simple, but having achieved that goal, what did he do next? It would depend, he concluded, on how Nolles reacted to Townsend's losses. . . .

Nolles was capable of murder, and he had any number of men who would cheerfully dispatch a problem for him. Luc stared at the drop of amber liquid remaining in his snifter. I'd do well, he told himself, to remember that fact.

But thinking back to the night he was attacked brought something sharply in focus for him. Nolles and his men had been waiting for him . . . they'd *known* he would be riding home from High Tower. . . .

He frowned. His dinner at High Tower hadn't been a secret, any number of people had known about it, but how had that news come to Nolles's ear? It was unlikely that his acceptance to dine at High Tower would have been passed on to Nolles by the three or four people at Windmere who had known of his plans for that Friday night. While it was possible that one of the High Tower servants had mentioned the dinner while at Nolles's inn, Luc didn't think that was what happened.

A fragment of the conversation with Mrs. Gilbert came back to him . . . something about Stanley Ordway and Lord George Canfield being seen with Nolles and Townsend. . . . Luc's eyes narrowed. Either one of those two men was the most likely source, but had there been an innocent transference of information during conversation or something more sinister?

Shaking his head, he walked toward the oak sideboard. He could think of no reason why Stanley would want him beaten, but Canfield . . . Canfield didn't like him, but was that dislike strong enough to have him ask Nolles to attack him? And why would Nolles do such a thing for someone he'd just met?

Stopping in front of the sideboard, Luc snorted. Nolles would have leaped at the opportunity to strike at him without any request or prompting from anyone. Setting down the snifter, he headed for his bed. Either Ordway or Canfield had passed on the information, but he had to believe that it had been an innocent act—not some nefarious scheme. But for the time being, he thought, as he climbed into bed, I will take care around both men.

Determined to begin his search for suitable living quarters, the next morning Luc met with Barnaby in his office. Barnaby was behind his desk, Luc taking the leather chair Lamb had occupied the day before.

After Luc explained why he had come to call, there was a brief silence, Barnaby sitting with his fingers steepled in front of him. After a moment, he looked over at Luc and asked, "You're certain this is what you want to do? Buy some property of your own?"

Luc spread his hands deprecatingly. "I can never thank you enough for all you have done for me since I arrived half-dead in England, but don't you think it's time I stepped out from behind your shadow?"

"Damn it, Luc! You have nothing to thank me for," Barnaby growled. "If our father had been a fairer man, we would have shared in his estate, and if you weren't so stiff-necked, you'd have allowed me to split Green Hill with you as I wanted to do. The money I *lent* you was as good as your own." He sighed. "You and Lamb! Both of you as bull-headed a pair as I've ever come across."

"Lamb and I have created quite a dilemma for you, haven't we?" Luc asked, sympathetic, yet amused.

"Yes, you have." Barnaby eyed his older half brother wearily. "How do you think it makes me feel to have been blessed with great fortune, yet the two men I hold dearest to me . . . the two men who have as much right to that same fortune, refuse to allow me to share with them?" His black eyes bleak, he asked in a low tone, "How would you feel if our positions were reversed? Would you be happy knowing that your brother and your uncle had been denied even a portion of their birthright while *all* of it came to you?" Barnaby's fist hit the desk with frustration. "You both were raised as Joslyns. You *are* Joslyns, yet the pair of you allows pride to stand in the way of what is rightfully yours. Lamb plays at being my manservant and you pretend to be a heartless gambler yet nothing is further from the truth. I cannot," he said heavily, "undo what our father did to you or Lamb, but every time you refuse my offer of help you burden me with the guilt of his doing."

Taken aback by the misery in Barnaby's voice, Luc stared dumbstruck at him. If positions were reversed . . . He swallowed with difficulty, aware for the first time of how his refusals wounded his brother. Unable to stare at Barnaby's unhappy face, his gaze dropped. He'd never once thought of Barnaby's feelings; he'd been so involved in flaunting his pride like a priceless golden cloak that the consequences to Barnaby every time he tossed Barnaby's offers back into his face hadn't ever been considered. *Mon Dieu!* What an arrogant, selfish swine I've been.

"Forgive me," begged Luc, his azure eyes full of regret as

his gaze met Barnaby's. "I would never willingly cause you pain and I never meant to hurt you—in any fashion."

Barnaby ran a hand through his black hair. "I know that." He half smiled. "You're a thoughtless bastard, but not a cruel one."

Luc grimaced. "Thank you." He fidgeted in the chair. Reluctantly, he said, "How do you propose we solve this dilemma?"

From under his brows Barnaby regarded him. "Are you serious?"

Luc nodded. "At the moment, yes." He made a face. "Allow me time to think about it and I may change my mind. When it is the only thing you feel you have, pride is a hard thing to discard—even if only for your brother."

Barnaby hesitated, then reached into his desk drawer and removed some papers. He cleared his throat. "There is a small estate, Ramstone Manor, on the eastern edge of the Windmere lands, that came into my hands when I inherited the title. Our great-uncle, the previous viscount, had lent the owner, a Mr. Benton Coulson, a substantial sum of money several years ago that was never repaid. Coulson died without heirs last summer, and the estate, over five hundred acres, which includes a half dozen or so farms, became mine when I took the title." Barnaby pushed the papers toward Luc. "Lord knows that Windmere doesn't need to expand, although I did think about keeping the place for a younger son, but that's decades in the future—*if* I am fortunate to have more than one son. In the meantime, I'm merely a caretaker of the place." He smiled. "I could sell it, but I'd much prefer you as a neighbor than some stranger."

Luc studied him through narrowed eyes. "Tell me," he said, "do you also have a similar property that you're holding until just the right moment for Lamb?"

Barnaby looked guilty. "Lamb will need, want his own place eventually," Barnaby mumbled.

There was a time when Luc would have stormed out of the room, wrapping his pride around him, but he realized that to do so would only wound Barnaby . . . and he'd be cutting off his own nose to spite his face. He thought a moment and then he said slowly, "I will buy it from you."

When Barnaby looked like he'd object, Luc held up a hand and said, "I suspect that the amount I can pay you will be woefully less than the place is actually worth, but at least allow me to salvage some of my pride."

Knowing it was the best he was going to get, Barnaby nodded, thrilled at the outcome. They haggled over the price, and a half hour later a dazed Luc walked out of Barnaby's office, the new owner of Ramstone Manor. I own a house, he thought stunned. A house. And land. And farms. *Sacristi!* I am indeed becoming respectable.

Shaking his head in disgust, he headed for the stables, intending to ride to Ramstone Manor and see what his money had purchased. Next thing you know, he thought irritably, I will want a wife and a nursery. Gillian's face swam in front of him and he cursed. Forcing her image from his mind, he mounted Devil and set off to inspect his new estate, but against his will, his thoughts turned to Gillian and events at High Tower.

Life had followed a predicable course at High Tower during the time of Luc's withdrawal from public. Gillian and Sophia were settling into the house and under different circumstances both ladies would have been delighted with the change in their lives, but Canfield remained an ominous cloud on the horizon.

It wasn't, Gillian decided, that Saturday afternoon as she, Sophy and Silas sat in the November sun in a sheltered part of the garden, that Canfield had made any overt moves toward her; it was simply that he was *there*. And, she admitted, never far from any of their thoughts. She scowled. How much longer would he remain a guest at High Tower?

Almost as if she read her thoughts, Sophia said, "I wonder how long Canfield intends to visit. He and Stanley have been here for over a fortnight. Surely they must be longing for London or thinking of joining one of the hunts—although I must say I will be sorry to see Stanley go—I've enjoyed his company."

Sitting between Gillian and Sophy, Silas grunted. "Been surprised these past weeks by Stanley myself. Boy seems to be taking an interest in the estate—something he's never done before now. When we met with my bailiff the other day, he actually appeared to listen. Even asked a few intelligent questions." Silas looked thoughtful. "Never stayed more than a couple of nights before either. Most of the time, he'd show up on my doorstep with a friend or two, explain his latest shortage of funds, and once I'd given him the money, after a polite interval, off he'd go until the next time he fell into the River Tick." He frowned. "Don't remember Canfield being one of his friends, though. Not even in London. Stanley's friends have always been untried cubs ready for any lark, but there was never any harm in them."

"I agree," said Gillian, nodding. She stared off into space. "Stanley has been . . . different these past weeks. We have frequently been in each other's company of late—but most telling of all—without bickering. I cannot say that we are close, but like Sophia, I have enjoyed being around him." She dimpled. "He even escorted us into the village the other day to buy some lace and thread at the draper's shop and not once did he complain."

"Extraordinary!"

"Yes, it was," said Sophia. "He seems to be taking his role as brother and cousin seriously."

"I wonder," Silas murmured almost to himself, "if that talking-to I had with him in London at the end of the Season about the way I came to own High Tower has anything to do with the changes we see in him."

Both women looked at him. "What do you mean?" asked

Gillian. "How would the way you acquired High Tower affect him?"

Silas looked uncomfortable. Both women waited for his answer and after a few moments, he sighed and said, "It's a sad, unpleasant story—not for the ears of ladies, but since you're living here, better you hear it from me than someone else." He grimaced. "Not that there are many around who remember the tragedy."

"What tragedy?" demanded Gillian.

Silas took in a deep breath and quietly told them of the Bramhall family and Edward Bramhall's suicide from the tower that gave High Tower its name. When he finished speaking, there was silence for several minutes.

"I blame myself," admitted Silas. "I was too pleased with myself by winning such a plum estate that I never thought of Bramhall—or what it would do to him."

"But it wasn't your fault," protested Gillian, while sparing a thought for the tragic Edward Bramhall. "How often have we heard of grander estates and fortunes changing hands at the gaming tables?" Her lips drooped. "I do not hold you responsible, but this is exactly why I hate gambling. Gamblers never think of the pain they cause." Realizing what she had said, she gasped and flashed Silas an unhappy smile. "Oh, Uncle! I am so sorry—and after all you have done for me. I did not mean to offend you."

Silas patted her hand. "You didn't, my dear. I don't disagree with you. Gambling is a wicked vice—but remember that no one forces a gentleman to sit down at that table and throw away a fortune. The harsh truth is that anyone who gambles more than he can afford to lose is a fool."

"Uncle is right," said Sophia in her prosaic manner. "Young Bramhall's suicide was a tragedy, but I suspect that he would have come to a bad end anyway." She looked at Silas. "This is what you told Stanley?"

Silas nodded.

"Then I think you may be right," continued Sophia.

"Stanley is neither stupid nor unintelligent. It may have taken him awhile, but it appears that he's taken your words to heart."

"He hasn't asked for money since he's been here, either," admitted Silas.

Gillian looked stricken. "Oh dear, I feel dreadful. I accused him of that very thing, the first day he arrived. Everything points to him trying to change his ways—right down to his escorting Sophy and me to the village."

"What I can't figure out," said Silas, changing the subject slightly, "is his friendship with a dirty dish like Canfield. Canfield may be Welbourne's son, but his reputation makes his father look like a saint—and we all know that Welbourne was never a saint, not even in his youth."

"Have you noticed," asked Sophia, "that there seems to be an air of constraint between them lately?"

Leaning forward to look at Sophia where she sat on the other side of Silas, Gillian exclaimed, "You've noticed it, too? I thought I was imagining it."

"I've noticed," admitted Silas, moving his broken arm in its sling to a more comfortable position, "but I didn't want to get my hopes up that they've had a falling-out." Silas frowned. "They didn't move in the same circles in London. Canfield and his friends were rowdier, wilder, wealthier and always, as I remember, falling into one scrape after another—unsavory incidents at that."

"I received a letter from a friend of mine, and she says that gossip has it that Welbourne has disowned Canfield," offered Sophia.

Silas waved a hand. "Welbourne has disowned him at least a half-dozen times that I know of—I wouldn't pay much attention to that particular on-dit." He turned over her words in his head for a moment before saying slowly, "But if the gossip is true . . . it could explain Canfield's presence here with Stanley. If Welbourne has turned his back on him, most of the *ton* would follow suit. With many doors closed to him,

Canfield might find it prudent to latch on to someone like Stanley. . . ." Silas shook his head. "Stanley might think he is a man of the world, but truth is, he's a booby when it comes to sizing up people—one of the reasons he ain't a very successful gambler. Chances are, Stanley hasn't heard about Canfield's disgrace and he was flattered to be sought out by a duke's son—never suspecting that Canfield is only using him."

"Yes, that makes sense," Gillian said, frowning.

"I think we'll find out that Canfield invited himself along and that Stanley was too flattered to say no," said Sophia. "Or wonder why Lord George Canfield, with supposedly wealthier, titled gentlemen with grander places vying for his presence, chose to visit High Tower."

Silas nodded. "Perhaps the coolness between them is because Stanley is finally beginning to wonder about that very thing. . . ."

Chapter 9

It may have just been speculation, but Gillian, Sophia and Silas had hit upon the truth. The events leading up to young Bramhall's death as related by his uncle all those months previously *had* shocked Stanley. Fortunes and estates were lost all the time at the gaming tables and more than one ruined gentleman had taken his life after a night of reckless gambling, but Stanley had never known anyone who had done so. He'd heard stories and shrugged them aside as allegorical tales, not to be taken seriously. Until Silas told him the facts of Edward Bramhall's suicide he'd had no inkling that High Tower had come into the family by way of the gaming table—or that a young man had killed himself right in front of his uncle's eyes.

The story of Bramhall's ruin had not immediately caused Stanley to mend his ways, but as the months passed he'd found himself thinking more and more about his frivolous life. After one disastrous night at a gaming hell in June, his uncle's words ringing in his ears, he realized how easily one could go the way of Bramhall. He realized something else: he didn't take as much pleasure in all that London had to offer as he once had—and hadn't for a while.

Even in the midst of the London whirl he was conscious of feeling lonely. He had friends, but friends, he admitted, were not the same as family. It was a bloody shame, Stanley decided, that he and the remaining three members of his family weren't on warmer terms. His thoughts astonished him. Dash it all, he was fond of Uncle Silas—and not just because of the money! And, he admitted, he wished the situation between himself and Gilly and Sophia was more amiable. He grimaced. Or at least amiable. He acknowledged that he was as much at fault as anyone for the situation in the family, and he determined to institute change. By late summer, Stanley didn't know how he would resolve the conflicts with his relatives, but he was committed to finding a way—and spending time at High Tower with his uncle seemed a step in the right direction.

Canfield's advent into his life had thrown him off track and his relatives had been right about that, too. Canfield *had* sought him out, and Stanley, dazzled at being noticed by Welbourne's youngest son, momentarily forgot all his good intentions. Stanley and his friends, while members of the *ton,* were amongst the lesser lights of that glittering assembly. Content within his own circle, it was a feather in Stanley's cap to be seen in the company of Lord George Canfield—despite Canfield's reputation for dissipation.

Waking that Sunday morning at High Tower with an aching head and a roiling stomach, Stanley cursed himself for thinking that being friends with Lord George Canfield was something to be desired. He liked to gamble, but not for the stakes that Canfield did—the story of Bramhall's death a constant reminder to him of the dangers of gambling beyond his means. Stanley liked to drink as much as the next fellow, but he was not the tankard man that Canfield was. He had a healthy appetite for the fairer sex, but he'd never been one for whoring and wenching, and next to gambling for heart-pounding stakes, bedding the nearest attractive woman seemed to be Canfield's favorite pastime.

Beyond the first few evenings, Stanley had not enjoyed himself at The Ram's Head. A polite gentleman and not indifferent to his fellow man, Stanley found Canfield's behavior to others uncomfortable, but it was Canfield's arrogance toward Nolles that alarmed him. Stanley knew of Nolles's reputation, and he feared that Canfield would offend the man and bring trouble down on them.

Most importantly, he'd recently perceived that he disliked the duke's youngest son and wondered why he'd ever been flattered by Canfield's attentions. He'd also made another discovery that surprised him—during these past weeks he'd been happier at High Tower with his uncle and Gillian and Sophia than he had ever been in his life.

Throwing water into his face from the china bowl on the wooden washstand, he stared at his haggard features in the mirror and winced. Uncle Silas, Gilly and Sophy had every right to look at him with disapproval, and he swore that he had spent his last evening frittering away his time at The Ram's Head.

After their late nights at The Ram's Head it was the habit of the two gentlemen to lay abed until the late afternoon, but Stanley broke that routine by forcing himself out of bed well before noon. Once he was dressed for the day, he surprised Silas and the ladies by joining them for a light repast served in the breakfast room.

When he walked into the breakfast room, they all looked at him astonished. He smiled and, approaching the sideboard, poured himself a cup of coffee from the silver pot that sat among the other offerings of food and drink.

Turning back to his relatives sitting at the round table in the center of the room, he said, "Good morning. I trust all is well with everyone."

"Good morning to you," said Silas. "We don't often see you up this early. Is there some reason?"

Stanley flushed. "Er, nothing particular." He cleared his throat and muttered, "It, um, isn't often that we are together as a family, and I, ah, felt that I should spend more time with you."

"What have you done with my brother?" Gillian demanded

wide-eyed. "First you escort us into the village without complaint, and now you actually seek out our company. You must be an imposter."

"Well, he didn't go with us to church this morning," Sophia pointed out, "so perhaps he's not an imposter, but he must not be in his right mind—how else to explain his behavior?"

"He's mad, do you think?" Gillian murmured with a lifted brow.

"Dash it all, that's not amusing," Stanley complained, glaring at both women. "Here I am, trying my best to put out the hand of friendship, and all the pair of you do is slap it aside."

Silas chuckled and said, "Oh, sit down, boy. Can't you tell when you're being teased? May I remind you that we only tease people we like."

Stanley looked nonplussed for a second, and then a tentative smile crossed his face. "That's true, isn't it?" he said as he took a seat next to Gillian.

"Yes, it is," replied his sister, a twinkle in her eyes. "And we are only rude to people we love. Haven't you noticed how excruciatingly polite one is to a person they dislike?"

"Yes, I suppose that's true," Stanley said and something occurred to him. His family had been *very* polite to Canfield and just as rude as ever to him. It shouldn't have, but that knowledge cheered him.

Glancing around the table, he asked, "So what are your plans for this afternoon?"

Silas spoke up. "We have nothing planned. The ladies usually retire to their rooms and amuse themselves while I take the old man's prerogative and nap for a few hours in my room."

Before more was said, Meacham knocked on the door and at Silas's command entered the room. "Mr. Luc Joslyn has come to call," he said, looking at his master.

"Excellent!" exclaimed Silas, brightening. "Show him in."

Stanley frowned. "I wonder if that's wise. I think Mr. Joslyn is far too familiar with you."

"Don't ruin all the progress you've made," Silas warned. "Luc is my friend and I am always happy to see him—and you would do well to remember that."

"I didn't mean to criticize," Stanley muttered, "it is just that . . ."

"Oh hush," said Gillian, hoping no one could hear her galloping heart. Luc Joslyn was here and until this moment, she hadn't realized that she had been counting the days until she would see him again.

A moment later, wearing a dark blue coat with brass buttons and nankeen breeches, Luc strolled into the breakfast room. After greeting everyone and refusing offers of refreshments, he took a seat between Silas and Sophia. Everyone wanted to know how he was doing, and Luc entertained them with a silly, elaborate tale detailing the fall from his horse and his recovery.

Eyeing him, Gillian decided that he'd never looked more handsome as he sat relaxed across the table from her. There was no sign of the injuries he'd suffered, and with his black hair gleaming in the sunlight streaming in from the window and his azure eyes bright and full of amusement, he was the picture of health.

For a second their eyes met and hers dropped, her pulse thudding. I am *not* a green girl to be bowled over by a handsome face, she reminded herself.

The conversation drifted from topic to topic for a few minutes, until Luc said, "I did have a reason for coming to call today." He looked at Silas. "I am still not certain how it came about," he confessed, "but I find myself the owner of an estate: my brother sold me Ramstone Manor. I spent most of yesterday afternoon inspecting the main house and some of the outbuildings, and while I expected nothing less from my brother, I was pleased to find the place in excellent condition." He grinned. "I've already moved in with my two ser-

vants—we spent last night settling into the place." Diffi-
dently, he added, "Since the weather is fine, if it's not too
short of notice, I was wondering if you," he glanced around
the table, "and the others would care to take a drive over and
see my new home this afternoon."

"By Jove! That's wonderful news, boy!" exclaimed Silas.
"Ramstone, as I recall, is a fine estate."

"You're familiar with it?" Luc asked, surprised.

Silas nodded. "Knew Coulson slightly. When his wife was
alive, dined there a few times. I'd heard that he'd died last
summer and that the property had reverted to the Joslyn estate." Silas looked around the table. "Well? How does a ride
in the country sound to you?"

Gillian could have kissed Sophia when her cousin said,
"Why, I think that would be most enjoyable."

Trying to correct any misstep he had made earlier, Stanley
said, "Yes, it sounds like a pleasant way to spend the afternoon." Forcing a smile, he added, "Congratulations. You
must be very happy."

"Thank you. I am . . . I think." Luc grinned. "I had something much smaller and simpler in mind and had not intended to become a landlord." He pulled on his ear. "It will
take some time getting used to."

Silas motioned to Stanley. "Ring for Meacham. Tell him to
have Cannon harness the grays to the barouche and bring
them to the front door."

It wasn't until the ladies had left to put on their pelisses
and bonnets that Stanley remembered Canfield. His face
comical with dismay, he said, "Blast! I must withdraw from
your kind invitation," he said to Luc. When his uncle looked
at him, he muttered, "I cannot go off and leave Canfield behind to fend for himself. He is my guest and it would be
rude."

"Balderdash!" barked Silas. "If he follows his usual pat-
tern, he won't come downstairs until four o'clock or later.

No reason for you to sit around waiting for him to make an appearance. Write him a note and have his man give it to him when he awakes."

Since he very much wanted to see Ramstone Manor, and keep an eye on Luc Joslyn, Stanley agreed with his uncle's suggestion. The note written, he joined the others, like Luc, riding astride, while Silas and the ladies, despite the faint chill, rode in the barouche with the top down.

Ramstone Manor lay about three miles from High Tower as the crow flew, but by the narrow, winding country road it was over six miles. The horses pulled the barouche at an easy pace; Luc and Stanley rode on either side of the vehicle.

Sophia and Gillian insisted upon sitting with their backs to the horses and faced Silas, who sat opposite them. From her position, Gillian had an excellent view of Luc as he talked and laughed with her uncle. The curve of his mouth as he smiled at something her uncle said mesmerized her, and realizing she was staring, she dropped her gaze. It didn't help. The memory of that mouth moving on hers, the taste of him flooded through her, and to her horror, her breasts tingled and her lower body clenched into a hard knot of desire. Unsettled and embarrassed, she said little for the remainder of the drive, keeping her gaze firmly away from the vicinity of Luc Joslyn.

Luc directed them to a tree-lined lane that branched off from the main road and a scant half mile later, the trees stopped and they entered a circular driveway. A house with a three-storied gable on either end sat centered on the arc of the curve on the far side, and flanked by oaks planted over two hundred years ago, the house welcomed them, the sun glinting off the mullioned windows.

In size, Ramstone Manor was comparable to High Tower and had been built in the sixteenth century. The taller gables were constructed of brick and connected by a two-storied wing of plaster; the steep slate roof gave the house a quaint air. A forecourt with low walls enclosed the front and a wide brick walkway planted with roses and lavender led to a fine two-storied porch.

Luc and Stanley dismounted and helped Silas and the ladies from the carriage. A stable boy hastily hired from Barnaby's staff raced around the corner of the house and took charge of the horses. Self-conscious in a way he had not thought possible, Luc escorted Silas and the others up the walkway to a pair of stout oak doors with heavy iron hinges dark with age. As they walked toward the house, he found himself wondering what Gillian thought of the place and realized with shock that while he wanted Silas's opinion, in some indefinable manner, it was her opinion that mattered most. Irritated and just a little alarmed, he picked up his pace. The sprite was affecting him in ways he didn't understand—or like.

They had hardly crossed into the shadows of the porch before Bertram Hinton, formerly one of Barnaby's footman, opened the doors with flourish. Having served first as Luc's valet and these past months as factotum of the small household, he fairly vibrated with pride and eagerness to please. Slender and fair-haired, Bertram hadn't yet seen his twenty-fourth birthday, but with shining blue eyes he saw his future clearly: he was Luc Joslyn's man down to the last breath in his body.

Bowing as if to royalty, Bertram murmured, "Welcome, sir. I have ordered some refreshments for you and your guests to be served in the salon that overlooks the rear garden."

Once everyone had been divested of their outerwear and Bertram had disappeared with those items, Luc led them down a wainscoted hallway to the back of the house. The room he showed them into was cozy with old-fashioned yellow chintz-covered chairs and sofas; a brick fireplace took up one wall, and dispelling the autumn chill that permeated the house, a cheerful fire burned on the hearth. Tall windows overlooked a garden that would be stunning in the spring.

Luc was proud of the efforts of his miniscule staff. Alice,

onetime scullery-maïd at The Birches, Emily's former home, proved that she had learned well while laboring in the kitchens at The Birches under Mrs. Spalding. Hot tea, coffee and a steaming punch awaited Luc's guests, as well as thinly sliced saffron bread, gingerbread cakes and sugar puffs—and to Alice's credit, they were as delicious as anything turned out by Mrs. Spalding herself, now at Windmere. After Bertram had whisked away all signs of their light repast, Luc gave the Ordways a tour of the main floor and the rear garden.

Again it was Gillian's comments Luc waited eagerly to hear. When they had peeked into the library with its blue and fawn rug and comfortable furniture covered in fabric in darker hues of the same color and she exclaimed, "Oh, what a charming room!" delight and pleasure speared through him. As the group walked down one of several winding paths lined with perennials and flowering shrubs, as the others commented on the extent and layout of the garden, Luc found himself waiting for Gillian's opinion. Stopping before a rosebush where one brave pink bloom raised its head, she looked over at him and smiled. "Your garden will make High Tower's head gardener most jealous," she said. "Even now, with nothing at its best, it is enjoyable to wander through, and in the spring and summer, I suspect it will be spectacular."

Ignoring his happiness at her approval, he bowed and murmured, "Come spring, it will be my pleasure to give you . . . and the others a tour."

A faint blush staining her cheeks, Gillian dropped her eyes and stuttered, "Th-th-thank y-y-you." Hastily turning away from the steady gaze of those azure eyes, for the rest of the tour she was quiet and stuck close to her brother. I will not, she told herself severely, lose my head over a pair of broad shoulders and a handsome face.

*   *   *

Canfield was in no danger of losing his head over anything, but he was less than pleased when he descended from the upper reaches of High Tower that afternoon to discover that he had been left to his own devices. Fuming, he stood in the main hallway, wondering why he had ever thought staying at High Tower would be amusing—even if it suited his purposes.

In her letter, Sophia's friend had been right on the mark. Canfield had, indeed, committed a most grievous transgression. Confronted with having seduced and ruined the daughter of a friend of his father's, Canfield refused to marry the girl. "Pay 'em off," he'd drawled to the duke in the library at the family's palatial home. With his father's blue eyes boring into him, he'd squirmed in his chair and muttered, "It was a wager—I won. That's the end of it."

A monumental row followed, and when Canfield slunk away from the family home in late May, it had been with the knowledge that his father, despite being an old roue of the first order, was within a hair's breath of disowning him. He'd angered his father before by his actions, but this time it appeared he had crossed the line.

Whispers and speculation about Canfield's fall from grace spread through the *ton*. Upon his return to London, with the Season still in full swing, it hadn't escaped Canfield's notice, as the days passed, that doors once open to him were closing and that his circle of friends diminished. Only a few knew the truth, and while he smarted under the slowing of invitations and "friends" no longer having time for him, it was the tightened purse strings the duke had imposed that caused him the most heart-burnings. His mouth tightened. The bloody old bastard had chosen the worst possible time to conjure up a conscience.

The profitable association Canfield had shared with Thomas Joslyn had kept a stream of gold flowing into his purse, but Joslyn's death in March had changed everything, and to his dismay, the money dried up and he scrambled to tap back into that golden cascade. It was difficult. He'd only dealt with Joslyn and Joslyn hadn't shared many details with him, but Canfield had been vaguely aware that, like him, Joslyn's friend, Lord Padgett, was an investor in the smuggling activities. Padgett was not part of Canfield's circle, and though they rubbed shoulders at various London affairs, beyond a polite greeting or nod, their lives were separate, Joslyn the only link between them.

When Joslyn died, hungry to keep the money falling into his hands, Canfield discreetly approached Padgett. It was awkward, Padgett pretending not to know what he was talking about, but in the end, while admitting nothing, Padgett did give him a name. Beyond the one name, Edward Dudley, supposedly Joslyn's man in London, Canfield knew nothing. A talk with Dudley had been called for, and wearing his oldest clothes, his hat pulled down low across his face to hide his features, he'd met the man in a disagreeable tavern on the edge of London. There had been an uneasy dance between them, but they'd come to an agreement. Which, Canfield thought sourly, as he stared blankly around the foyer of High Tower, had been working well until the duke had cut off a sizable amount of his funds.

Canfield scowled. He'd already received the year's second payment of his quarterly allowance at the time of the unpleasant scene in the duke's library, and it wasn't until July when he strolled into his bank to make a withdrawal that he discovered his allowance had been slashed to a pittance. Via Dudley, word had reached him not long after that a shipment from the continent had arrived in England and Canfield had been expecting a tidy return on his investment. The pouch of gold, however, that Dudley surreptitiously slid him when they met in a dark corner of the same disagreeable tavern was smaller than usual, and the suspicion that he was being cheated took root. When he complained, Dudley had shrugged.

"Talk to Nolles if you're not happy," Dudley muttered. "He's running the gang these days. You'll find him at The Ram's Head in Broadhaven on the Sussex coast."

Canfield had been careful to keep his identity a secret, and confident that neither Dudley nor this Nolles person had identified him, he decided a trip to Broadhaven was called for. Unwilling to blindly confront the smuggler leader, he'd been casting about for an excuse to visit the region when one night at a gaming hell, he'd overheard Stanley Ordway talking about leaving London to visit at his uncle's home, near the village of Broadhaven. Canfield had struck up an instant acquaintance.

So far, his friendship with Stanley and his arrival at High Tower had served him well. The recent note he'd received from his father had been cool, but there had been the hint of a thaw in the duke's words . . . and a nice draft for a goodly sum had been included. It was only, he thought, a matter of time before he was back in his father's good graces—and the old devil completely loosened the purse strings. As for Nolles . . . he'd moved slowly, wanting to get the lay of the land before revealing himself as the smuggler's London investor: his friendship with Stanley had provided him with excellent cover.

There had been an added benefit of association with Stanley Ordway: Gillian Dashwood. Canfield had long entertained erotic thoughts of Gillian, and finding the lady already at High Tower had seemed a stroke of luck. Except, he thought darkly, things hadn't gone as he'd planned. That a little country mouse, no matter how lovely, had been able to outmaneuver him rankled every time he thought of it. The widow had won this hand, he admitted bitterly, but the game was far from over.

Realizing he'd accomplished all he could at High Tower, and with the money from his father's draft plumping his purse, he was impatient to be gone from the place. Stanley's abandonment of him this afternoon provided him with an excuse to cut his ties, and spinning on his heels, he bounded up the stairs. Finding his valet puttering around the room, he ordered, "Pack everything, Hyde. We're leaving."

Used to his master's moods, Hyde nodded and began to drag out valises from the big wardrobe against the wall. "Are we returning to London, my lord?" he asked.

Canfield shook his head. "Not yet. We'll be staying for a bit longer in the area—at The Ram's Head. I'll meet you there."

Downstairs Canfield rang for Meacham. To the butler, he said, "I am cutting my visit short and my valet and I are removing to The Ram's Head." Plucking a bit of lint from the sleeve of his coat, he added, "Oh, and you can thank that miserable old man you serve for his hospitality."

Meacham bowed. "I shall do so." He smiled with teeth. "Shall I help Hyde pack?"

Canfield glanced sharply at him, but Meacham's face displayed nothing but polite interest. "No, that won't be necessary," Canfield said. "And now, my good man, if you will send someone to the stables and have my horse brought 'round, I'll be off. Hyde knows where to find me."

Congratulating himself on removing to The Ram's Head, Canfield rode away from High Tower. He had matters under control—the widow was still at hand and he could now concentrate on his unfinished business with Nolles.

When the Ordways returned home with Luc that afternoon, the news that Canfield had removed to The Ram's Head was met with varying degrees of delight. Silas, Gillian and Sophy were plainly pleased; Stanley was less obviously so but it was clear that the unexpected departure of his "friend" caused him no pain.

Luc shared their reaction but with reservations. Knowing Canfield's reputation, his presence at Silas's home had raised Luc's eyebrow and he'd wondered what an out-and-out rake was doing buried in the country far from the dens of iniquity the man was known to haunt. It was obvious that Stanley wasn't the hardened rake that comprised Canfield's circle of cronies and that High Tower wasn't the sort of place that Canfield frequented. So why was he here?

Shrugging aside speculation for the time being, after declining an invitation to stay and dine, Luc took his leave of the Ordways. As his horse trotted through the twilight toward Ramstone Manor, his mind wandered to this afternoon. He should have been filled with satisfaction with the results of the Ordways' visit to his home this afternoon, but, he admitted, for a man who had little more than a discreet dalliance in mind, he cared far too much about Gillian Dashwood's reaction to his home.

It shouldn't have mattered whether she approved or liked Ramstone, but in some unsettling way, it did. Enormously. His mouth thinned. And if he'd bought Ramstone with an idea of the place providing a cozy rendezvous with the lady, he'd been badly mistaken. Ramstone Manor was now his *home,* not some snug nest tucked away from prying eyes. *Mon Dieu!* What if his sister-in-law came to call when he was, ah, entertaining Mrs. Dashwood?

Luc was no puritan, but the notion of bedding Gillian at Ramstone didn't set well. Ramstone Manor was respectable. He half-smiled. His plans for the beguiling little widow were not. And then there was her relationship to Silas. Was he really going to bed the niece of his friend?

Luc moved restively in the saddle. Making Gillian his mistress seemed a poor way to pay back Silas's friendship. Yet like a siren, Gillian called to something within him. . . . The memory of the sway of her hips as she'd walked down the garden path, the sparkle in those topaz eyes and the soft curve of her full mouth when she looked at him, swept over him—with predictable results. He was instantly hard and aching with desire. A desire he was furiously aware that he might not be able to satisfy.

Cursing under his breath, he kicked his horse into a gallop. *Diantre!* The sprite had him twisted in knots and had tossed him painfully onto the horns of a dilemma. Was the desire to have her naked beneath him so powerful that he could brush aside the bonds of loyalty and friendship he felt for Silas? And don't forget that she may have murdered her husband, he reminded himself grimly.

Instinct fought against the notion of Gillian being a murderess, but he couldn't ignore it. Her husband had been murdered and she had been found next to his body, the signs of a terrible fight all around them. Luc's desire cooled and his eyes hardened. Perhaps she beguiled her husband also—driven him mad with desire . . . until she'd murdered him.

It was a very unhappy and conflicted man who returned to Ramstone Manor. After complimenting Bertram and Alice on their efforts that afternoon, Luc retreated to the library. The library, he recalled irritably, Gillian had complimented.

Scowling, he walked over to a mahogany lowboy, and from the small tray of liquors and glasses, he picked up a decanter and splashed some brandy into a snifter. Snifter in hand, his handsome face bleak, he stalked around the room.

What was he going to do about Gillian Dashwood? If that kiss they had shared in the gardens of High Tower was anything to go by, she was no stranger to passion. She was also, he reminded himself, taking a swallow of the brandy, no virgin. She'd been married. And widowed. He winced. Her husband murdered—by her hand, some people thought. And then there was Silas. . . .

Moodily he stared down into the amber liquid in his snifter. The wisest course would be to forget about her. Put her from his mind and forget about having that luscious little body writhing under his caresses. His lips twisted. The question was, could he? She was going to be living at High Tower, and every time he called upon Silas he'd see her there. He'd never been good at resisting temptation, and he feared that sooner or later the allure she held for him would prove more than he could withstand. Which left him where?

Wrenching his mind away from Gillian Dashwood, he focused on the room in front of him. He shook his head, amazed. Yesterday he'd thought to buy a small property, a cottage, perhaps with a few acres and today . . . He shook his head again. Today he owned an *estate* with farms and lands under his control! Even more amazingly, unless he was extravagant, he could live in genteel comfort and never gamble again.

Luc prowled the elegant room, trying to make sense of his actions, trying to understand the change in his circumstances. Over the years, he'd frequently won as much or more and had spent it with hardly a thought for the future. But this time, for reasons that bewildered him, he'd been careful with his winnings, actually making investments, and most astonishing of all, he'd bought a home. With the purchase of Ramstone Manor, he became a landowner, a gentleman farmer, with responsibilities and people whose livelihoods were dependent upon the decisions he made. Which was, he conceded unhappily, as far from the footloose, devil-may-care creature he had been such a short time ago as one could get. It was incomprehensible to him.

Throwing himself down on one of the dark blue sofas scattered around the room, he contemplated the small fire burning on the hearth of the gray-veined marble fireplace across from him. *Mon Dieu!* How had this happened? When had he stopped thinking of the next card game and the next throw of the dice? When had the excitement of risking all on the turn of card disappeared? When had his determination to remain unencumbered, able to move on in an instant if the mood struck him, vanished? And what about his scorn for those men who lived predictable, *respectable* lives? When had his scorn changed to envy?

Luc scowled at the fire. It was England, he decided bitterly. From the moment he'd landed on its shores he'd begun to change, began to blend in with the oh, so proper Englishmen. Perhaps even begun to long to be like them? Had Barnaby's marriage and impending parenthood woken within him some long-suppressed yearning? Watching his brother handle the reins of Windmere, had it roused the curiosity to wonder if he would be as good a caretaker of the land and dependents? It was an unsettling thought. But, he admitted, it didn't terrify him, as it once would have.

He smiled. He was looking forward to trying his hand at being a landowner. If Barnaby was to be believed, keeping abreast of all tasks and responsibilities that came with owning an estate of any size was every bit as exciting and demanding as pitting one's wits against Lady Luck.

In five years, Luc thought, amused, if I continue down this path, I shall be plump and respectable, with a wife and a bevy of children tumbling like a litter of puppies around my feet. The picture made him grin. Perhaps not plump, but he could see the rest of it. His smile faded, though, when his imagination placed Gillian's small form in the chair next to him, a gurgling baby on her lap. . . .

He stiffened and glared at the fire. *Sacrebleu!* Marriage to the sprite was out of the question! Slyly another thought intruded. But *why?* She wasn't indifferent to him, and she wasn't so far above him that there would be any objections to the match. Besides, she was of an age and status that she could make her own decisions. Silas would be pleased. And, Luc acknowledged cynically, he wanted her. With an aching need that showed no signs of abating. Would marriage to her be so terrible? It made more sense than the seduction he had in mind.

Marriage, he admitted, aghast at his own thoughts, had much to recommend it. *Mon Dieu!* Was he actually considering marriage . . . to Gillian Dashwood?

Chapter 10

Coming to no conclusions, and not liking the ones that occurred to him, Luc went to bed in a disagreeable mood. After most of a night spent cursing and wrestling the sheets, he woke early the next morning with his mood not much changed.

Since sleep had eluded him for the better part of the night, there was no point in lying abed and grumbling at life in general. He threw back the covers and strode over to the washstand in one corner of the room. After washing in the tepid water poured from the pottery urn that sat next to a plain white bowl on the stand, he studied the contents of the mahogany wardrobe where his clothes had been hung. Used to looking after himself, he had no need to ring for Bertram and, making his selection of buckskin breeches and a brown coat, gathered what else he needed from the nearby bureau.

Once he was garbed for the day, his mood improved, and Luc wandered around his new accommodations taking stock. While he'd given the Ordways a brief tour of the main floor yesterday, beyond Saturday's initial inspection, he hadn't yet explored much beyond his bedroom. Several minutes later Luc decided, though not as lavish or as large as his suite at the Dower House, his new rooms fit him just fine.

The suite was comprised of three rooms, two large bedrooms with a shared sitting room between them. Coulson's widow had taken the family's personal belongings and many of the furnishings with her when she had moved, but the draperies and several rugs had been left behind; all were of good quality and in excellent condition. Though there were gaps in the furnishings, enough furniture remained to make the place habitable, comfortable even.

Increasingly satisfied with his purchase, Luc had just shut the door to his rooms behind him when Bertram, carrying a pewter tray with various items on it, appeared at the end of the hall. As Bertram neared him, the scent of coffee and yeast, cinnamon and warm raisins tickled Luc's nose.

"Sir!" Bertram exclaimed as he hurried to meet him. "I was just on my way to your rooms with some coffee and hot cross buns—Alice just took them from the oven."

Luc smiled at him. "I'm sure they'll taste just as good downstairs as they would have in my rooms."

"Indeed, they will," Bertram agreed. "Where would you like me to serve them?"

"I think that small salon we used yesterday when the Ordways were here will do well for a breakfast room, don't you? Especially," Luc added with a grin, "since, at present, there is no dining room furniture."

Bertram concurred and they adjourned to the newly designated breakfast room.

Luc enjoyed the buns, and as he finished one last cup of coffee, he stared out at the back garden, mulling over his next move. Becoming familiar with his house seemed a priority—that and making a list of the most necessary items that needed to be purchased. He smiled ruefully. It was a blessing that he had a small fortune invested in the funds. Over the coming months, he suspected he was going to need it.

Ringing for Bertram, once that young man arrived, together they began a more thorough exploration of the house. By midafternoon when Luc stopped to enjoy a tankard of ale and some smoked ham, cheese and bread, he was feeling both pleased and overwhelmed.

Ramstone Manor was not huge, but it was a big house, with several of the rooms devoid of anything but the most basic furniture. The small salon where he sat was completely furnished, and he suspected that it had been left so because of the space constraints in the widow's new home. The formal salon at the front of the house and the dining room, however, was empty except for rugs and draperies, and throughout the house, it was obvious that several larger items of furniture had gone with the widow.

By the time he'd returned to the yellow chintz room for his ale and smoked ham, he was thinking wistfully of the tidy set of rooms he'd first envisioned. *Mon Dieu!* The manor house had linen closets that were larger than some rooms he'd called home.

Bertram entered just then. "Sir," he announced grandly, "Lady Joslyn and Mrs. Cornelia Townsend have come to call."

Luc bounded to his feet and hurried forward to greet Emily and Cornelia as they swept into the room. Fond greetings were exchanged, and after determining that the ladies would indeed enjoy some tea and biscuits, Bertram scurried away.

During the past month the mound projecting from beneath the blue woolen gown she was wearing had grown noticeably, and Emily took one of the straight-backed chairs by the windows, seating herself with a sigh; Cornelia settled herself on the chintz sofa. Both ladies looked around with interest.

"What a pleasant room," Emily said approvingly. "When Barnaby told me that he had sold you Ramstone, I expected to find you living with nothing but a straw mattress and a stool."

Cornelia grinned at him. "I see that as usual luck was on your side and that you have done very well for yourself, young man."

Luc bowed. "But what else would you expect from Lucifer?"

Cornelia laughed. "What else, indeed." She looked around again. "Jane Coulson may have been a scatter-brained goose, but she certainly knew how to make a comfortable home. You'll enjoy entertaining guests in this house."

"I already have," Luc admitted, the faintest hint of pink flaring across his cheekbones. "Yesterday I invited Silas Ordway and his nephew and nieces over to take a tour of the place."

"Is that so?" Cornelia murmured, with her eagle eyes noting the change in color. "And what did they think of Ramstone?"

"Naturally they were pleased for me," Luc said. "Silas had dined here a few times when the Coulsons owned the property, so he already knew what to expect. Stanley Ordway and the ladies had only compliments." Unaware of it, Luc smiled reminiscently and added, "Mrs. Dashwood particularly liked the library."

Emily and Cornelia exchanged glances.

"Is that so?" Cornelia drawled, her gaze never moving from his face. "And Mrs. Easley and young Mr. Ordway, what did they think?"

Luc shrugged. "I don't remember—but they were very complimentary, too."

Emily and Cornelia exchanged glances again.

"Well, how nice that your friends liked the place," Cornelia muttered.

Emily winced and gasped just then and moved uncomfortably in her chair. Noting her movement, his face concerned, Luc asked, "Are you in pain?"

Emily smiled at him. "Nothing to worry about—your niece just kicked me with all the force of one of your brother's mules. Or at least it felt that way."

"Are you sure, it is my *niece?*" Luc asked, teasing. "Barnaby swears that you are carrying his heir."

Emily winced again and muttered, "Perhaps you are right—no daughter of mine would abuse her mother in this fashion."

Bertram returned with refreshments and, after serving the ladies, departed. As the door shut behind him, Cornelia observed, "I see that young Hinton is working out well for you."

Luc nodded. "He and Alice are doing a splendid job—considering the added responsibilities are far beyond what either one of them expected."

"Well, that brings us to the reason for our visit," said Emily, her gray eyes twinkling. "We've come to meddle in your household."

A wary expression crossed Luc's face, and both women laughed.

"It isn't that bad," said Cornelia. "And we have your best interests at heart."

"And those are . . . ?"

Briskly, Emily said, "With a place this size you are going to need more staff than Bertram and Alice can provide."

That notion had already occurred to Luc, but added staff wasn't something he was prepared to take on at the moment. He held up a hand. "Ladies, please," he begged. "Do not add to my burdens. I never thought to own a place like Ramstone, and I am still reeling at finding myself the owner of such an estate. Until Saturday, I was a gambler with little on my mind beyond the next card game, the next throw of the dice." He glanced at Emily, only half-teasing when he said, "Your husband has much to answer for. I went to him thinking to buy a cottage and perhaps a few acres"—he waved an arm around—"and you see what he has saddled me with."

"Are you telling me," demanded Cornelia with a raised brow, "that your brother *forced* you to buy Ramstone against your wishes? That he trampled over your wishes and held a sword to your throat until you agreed to purchase this place?"

That dragged a reluctant laugh out of Luc. "No." He glanced from one woman to the other. "I know that you have my best interests at heart, but I am overwhelmed at the moment. Additional staff is the furthest thing from my mind—I haven't yet even met any of my tenants. Alice swears the kitchen pantry echoes when she walks into it, and we won't even talk about the linens, dishes and other pots and pans she is convinced are needed. And Bertram . . . Bertram complains that the butler's pantry is nearly empty, only the stray piece of crystal, china or silverware to be found. Surely those things are more important than more servants?" When both ladies just stared at him, he added hastily, "Besides, I don't have time to interview staff."

"You don't have to," said Emily. "We have that already taken care of." When Luc would have protested, her eyes very big, she begged, "Won't you at least hear what we have to say?"

Luc was no match for the appeal in the gray eyes, and sighing, he said, "Very well. What have the pair of you planned for me?"

By the time Emily and Cornelia finished speaking, Luc could feel himself weakening. Compared to the staff at Windmere, what Emily and Cornelia proposed was modest and all were trusted, former employees who had served the Townsend family or the previous viscount. Modest or not, it still seemed like far more servants than he needed, but Emily assured him, it was the minimum staffing for a gentleman's estate like Ramstone.

"You do see, don't you," Emily asked earnestly, "that you will be helping some loyal, hardworking folk who suffered because of my cousin's mismanagement and Tom Joslyn's activities?" At Luc's reluctant nod, she rushed on, "Bissell is a nice man. You'll like him. He was your great-uncle's butler for years before your cousin replaced him with that horrible Peckham. Bissell's not as young as he once was and the slower pace at Ramstone would be just the thing for him. Besides, he can train Bertram properly." When Luc made a face, she said earnestly, "It may seem overwhelming, but you'll not regret hiring Bissell's niece, Mrs. Marsh, for your house-keeper, and the extra maids will prove vital—Alice cannot do everything. While it may not be apparent at the moment, a gardener and a helper will be necessary—unless of course, you want this place to revert to wilderness." Her face softened. "As for your stables, Hutton is a dear old man—he was the head stableman at The Birches before Jeffery fired him and put Kelsey in his place." Her lips tightened. "Kelsey was a despicable creature."

"You see, my boy," added Cornelia, "you'll be helping yourself, but you'll also be helping to right some wrongs. Hutton's grandsons are good young men and they'll make you excellent stable boys. Hutton and his grandsons served us well before Jeffery sent them packing. Knowing that they have steady employment would mean a great deal to both of us."

Luc held up both hands. "Stop! No more guilt, if you please. I will hire them all." He bent an only half-teasing look on Emily. "And if I go bankrupt, you will have only yourself to blame."

"Oh, balderdash!" Cornelia pronounced. "That's not likely to happen—you're too clever for that. Managed properly, Ramstone will provide you with a handsome living and you'll never have to trust your fate again to the throw of the dice."

"And I can help with the linens and such," Emily said quickly. "There is an excess of such items at Windmere and it will be my pleasure to give them to you." When Luc looked to protest, Cornelia thumped her cane and snapped, "Swallow your pride, boy! Barnaby and Emily haven't the least use of every single one of the dozen or so sets of china at Windmere and half the things in the storerooms. Consider them a welcoming gift."

Knowing he wasn't going to win against such a formidable pair, Luc bowed and gave in. The ladies moved swiftly, and before dark Luc found his house inundated with his new staff and other items Emily and Cornelia had seen fit to send along. Alice was in raptures over the increase in staff and Bertram was reverently following Bissell around and drinking in every word that fell from the older man's lips. Mrs. Marsh had already set the two young housemaids to work polishing and sweeping and the scent of lemon and beeswax drifted pleasantly through the house. When Luc went to bed that night it was with the awareness that he had been swept from firm ground into a whirlpool, but he never doubted that he would find his footing.

Ramstone Manor wasn't much larger than the house at Green Hill; it was certainly smaller than his uncle's château in France where he'd spent his earliest years. It wasn't, Luc reminded himself as he lay abed staring into the darkness, as if he'd been raised in a hovel or had no conception of the running of a gentleman's household and estate. Rejected by his French relatives and sent to Virginia after his mother's death, he in turn had rejected Green Hill and chosen to live by his wits, but the knowledge and experiences of his youth living in the households of wealthy relatives were not forgotten. The life of a gentleman farmer would be second nature to him, and with a little luck, and every man needed luck from time to time, he knew he'd be as good at running Ramstone as he was at the gaming tables.

Luck, however, was not with Canfield that night. He'd had no complaints initially. The removal to The Ram's Head had gone smoothly and he was now ensconced in a handsome pair of rooms upstairs. Hyde was settled in a small room next door.

After a fine meal served in his rooms the previous evening, satisfied with his decisions, Canfield had sauntered downstairs, looking for a pigeon to pluck. It was fox hunting season and many of the local notables had deserted the area to follow the hounds—which made finding gentlemen who suited his purpose difficult for Canfield. Eventually, he'd joined Townsend at one of the tables in the private rooms Nolles set aside for serious gamblers, and more from boredom than any other reason, he'd accepted Townsend's offer of a game. Having played with Townsend both here and in London, Canfield respected Townsend's skills, but he didn't consider him his equal and he looked forward to winning. He was not disappointed, rising in the early morning hours the winner of a handsome sum.

Tonight, however, luck deserted him and watching the pile of coins in front of him disappear at an alarming rate, Canfield's mood was surly. Townsend, who last night could not win a hand, had done nothing but win this evening and Canfield wondered if he'd been set up.

His eyes narrowed, Canfield glanced across the table at Townsend. "Your luck has changed," Canfield growled.

Townsend looked up from his cards. "Indeed, I will not deny it," he murmured. "Tonight Lady Luck is sitting on my knee—just as she was sitting on yours last night." He smiled. "She's a fickle wench."

Canfield didn't disagree, and after a few more losing hands, he threw down his cards and said, "That's it for me."

Townsend shrugged, making no attempt to keep him at the table. Canfield departed, shutting the door behind him with more force than necessary. Townsend grinned. Arrogant bastard.

A few minutes later, the door opened and Nolles slid into the room, the scar given to him by Lamb a scarlet brand across his cheek. His pale eyes on the money in front of Townsend, he said, "It appears that Lord Canfield's run of luck ended."

"Yes, it did," admitted Townsend. He shifted his arm slightly and a card peeked out from the end of his sleeve. "But not," he added, "without some help."

"Do you think he suspects?"

Townsend shook his head. "No, not if I'm careful. But I

won't be able to pull this trick very often. He's a smart player and if he loses too often . . ."

Nolles grunted. Taking a turn around the room, he said, "And everything is well at The Birches?"

Townsend made a face. "If you mean are the goods safely stored, yes." Townsend hesitated. "How soon before you move more of the contraband to London? I mislike having so much on hand."

"Why? Are you expecting someone to come snooping around your cellars?"

"No." Townsend hunched a shoulder. "I know that soon you'll be landing another load and there isn't much more room to store it."

"Let me worry about that. You just keep your mouth shut and discourage visitors."

Townsend nodded unhappily. Clearing his throat, he asked, "What are you going to do about Canfield? You know why he's here, don't you?"

Nolles smiled thinly. "Yes, I know why he's here and at the moment I'm enjoying his antics. He's a fool if he thinks that his attempts to hide his identity from Dudley worked—or that Dudley wouldn't have warned me to expect him. Even if Padgett hadn't already spoken to Dudley about Canfield before allowing them to meet, Dudley would have learned his name within the hour from one of his street urchins."

Nolles sauntered over to the oak sideboard behind Townsend and from a tray of refreshments in the center of the top poured himself a glass of hock. Glass in hand, he took a seat across from Townsend. "How much did he lose tonight?"

Townsend smiled. "Over four thousand pounds."

"At least you've recovered most of what you lost to that blasted Lucifer last month," Nolles commented, wiping the smile from Townsend's lips.

"I did, indeed," Jeffery said tightly. "And Canfield, though he believes otherwise, is no Lucifer. He hasn't the skill or the cool head of that devil."

Nolles stared at his tankard, unconsciously fingering the scar on his cheek. "Which is as well for us," Nolles muttered. Tom should have killed Barnaby Joslyn when he'd had the chance, Nolles thought bitterly—and that bastard Lamb.

"So what are you going to do about Canfield?"

"When he's no longer useful, he'll . . . have a fatal accident." Nolles flashed Townsend a sly look. "A fall over the cliffs like your friend Ainsworth suffered would do nicely, don't you agree?"

Recalling the night months ago when Lord Joslyn had killed Ainsworth and saved Emily from rape, Jeffery's eyes dropped to the table. He shuddered as the memory of riding through the dark with Ainsworth's body strapped to his horse rolled over him. He'd been terrified of discovery during that dreadful ride and had breathed a sigh of relief when he'd thrown the body over the cliffs near the Seven Sisters. No one, he reminded himself, had seen him. Nolles had to be guessing.

Townsend looked directly at Nolles and said, "Yes, a fall from the cliffs would do very well for Lord George Canfield." Brazenly, he added, "I'd recommend someplace near the Seven Sisters."

Nolles's eyes narrowed, not pleased with Townsend's reply. Perhaps the man wasn't the spineless ninny he'd thought. . . . Nolles swallowed some hock before saying, "At least Canfield is providing some profit in the meantime."

Jeffery Townsend had come a long way since the night he had disposed of Ainsworth's body, but he was still squeamish about murder. "Do you think that killing him is the best way? What does he really know?"

Nolles stared at him as if he'd lost his wits. "He knows that Padgett knows Dudley," he said coldly. "And he knows that Dudley is connected to me. Any one of those things would be reason enough to kill him; he knows too much."

"But why not continue to let him invest? His money has been useful—and as long as he gets a return, he's not likely to kill the goose that laid the golden egg."

"If he'd remained content only to provide money and take his profits, I'd agree with you, but he didn't." Nolles scowled. "His lordship is a spoiled, spiteful child, and if it suited him, he'd turn us over to the authorities in a heartbeat." His fingers tightened on his glass. "I was against letting him meet with Dudley, but Padgett thought otherwise." He took an angry breath. "If Canfield had stayed in London, I'd have been happy enough to take his money and pay him something on his 'investment,' but the fool had to come here."

Townsend didn't care overmuch what happened to Canfield, but no matter how far he had fallen, he had an aversion to outright murder and he mumbled, "But as long as he invests—"

Nolles's hand slapped the table. "You forget I met with Padgett in London last week and he confirmed that Canfield doesn't *have* the funds to invest anymore. Canfield is desperate for money—which makes him dangerous—and useless."

"So where did he get the money to lose tonight? And pay lodgings here? If his finances were so desperate, I wouldn't have thought he'd have left High Towers. He was a guest there and it wasn't costing him a penny."

Nolles tossed down the last of his hock. Putting the glass down on the table, he muttered, "Most likely his father has softened toward him and sent him some money."

Townsend leaned forward. "Well then," he said, "isn't that promising? Perhaps before long, he'll be restored to his father's bosom and once again be plump in the pocket—with money to invest."

Nolles flashed him an icy green glance that sent a chill down Townsend's spine. Showing his teeth, Nolles snarled, "I'll not have my fate in the hands of that strutting coxcomb!"

"And, uh, Padgett agrees? The death of a member of the

aristocracy will not go unnoticed. I would think that Padgett would advise against it."

Nolles shook his head, an ugly smile crinkling the scar on his cheek. "The moment he approached Padgett, Canfield signed his death warrant." His voice full of contempt, he asked, "Who do you think told Dudley to feed Canfield my name and location? Killing him was always part of the plan. Of course, Padgett agrees, you hen-hearted looby!"

Townsend flushed to the tips of his ears, and his eyes dropped to hide the rage searing through him. What he wouldn't give to have his hands around Nolles's throat, throttling the life out of the little bastard.

Nolles watched him, and misliking the line of Townsend's mouth, his fingers closed around the small pistol he carried in his vest pocket. He didn't believe that Townsend would attack him, but he admitted that it had been stupid of him to show his scorn so openly. Dealing with Canfield was trouble enough; he didn't need to give Townsend a reason to betray him.

Knowing he had to retrieve the situation, Nolles muttered, "That was uncalled for. I apologize." He forced a smile. "Take an extra hundred pounds from tonight's winnings and put my outburst down to frustration with having to swallow Canfield's arrogance."

His features sullen, Jeffery demanded, "If Padgett wanted him dead, why didn't he have Dudley take care of it in London? Why send him here?"

Wearily, Nolles said, "There are too many eyes in London, too many people we don't own. Dudley could have arranged for Canfield to suffer a fatal knife wound in one of his brothels or in a dark alley, but Padgett thought it, er, prudent to take care of the problem here where we have control of the situation. As he pointed out, there are more places to hide a body where it will never be found. Canfield will simply . . . disappear." He smiled. "No body. No murder. No crime."

When Townsend continued to look unhappy, Nolles sighed and muttered, "If you don't like it, you can discuss it with Padgett yourself—he'll be here before long."

Startled, Townsend jerked in his seat. "Why?"

Nolles's lips tightened. "Because he wants to see for himself *precisely* how well your place fits our needs."

Townsend looked alarmed. "You don't think he's unhappy with our arrangement, do you?"

"No. No, nothing like that," Nolles said quickly, trying to calm the other man. "Padgett is not as familiar as Joslyn was with the way things are run, and he decided that it might be wise to see the entire operation before he invests more money."

The conversation continued for a few minutes longer, but Nolles was aware that when Townsend finally rose and left, the other man was not completely mollified. His face hard, Nolles stared at the door through which Townsend had disappeared.

The squire, he decided grimly, could become a problem . . . much like Canfield, but he'd worry about that later. A second disappearance or murder too soon after the first was bound to ignite the neighborhood and bring attention where he least wanted it, and he had Lord Joslyn to thank for it.

The events of that night back in March had been as devastating as unexpected, and thinking over the days and weeks that had followed Thomas Joslyn's death and the confiscation of the contraband hidden in the tunnels beneath Windmere, his face twisted into a mask of hate. Lord Joslyn and his brother and that wretched Lamb had cost him a great deal, and he swore that soon, they'd suffer retribution—even if Padgett advised against it.

Nolles stared moodily at his glass, thinking of Lord Padgett. Padgett and another friend of Tom Joslyn's, Stanton, had been involved in the smuggling scheme right from the beginning, and while Stanton remained in the background, Padgett quickly bridged the chasm created by Tom's death. Even with Padgett taking over, it had taken them months to recover from the loss of all goods confiscated from Windmere's tunnels, but once Nolles had brought Townsend into the fold and with the access to the cellars of The Birches, they'd progressed.

Padgett was no Tom Joslyn, but he and Padgett rubbed along together well enough, Nolles conceded. Still, they had disagreements—putting Canfield in touch with Dudley and from Dudley to him was only one of them. He sighed. At least Padgett realized that Canfield had to be eliminated, but despite what he'd told Townsend, he'd have preferred it be done in London. With the deaths of Tom Joslyn and the Windmere butler, Peckham, back in March and the discovery of the contraband, there'd been enough upheaval in the area. Lying low seemed wise, but no matter how Padgett felt about it, Canfield had to die. He was trouble. As were the Joslyns . . . His fingers strayed to the still-tender scar on his cheek. *I should have kicked Luc Joslyn to death when I had the chance,* he thought sourly, *and damn the consequences.*

When he'd learned by accident from Canfield and the younger Ordway that Luc would be dining at High Tower, it had seemed a perfect opportunity to strike at the Joslyn family. There was only one route Luc would take home afterward and that made it child's play to lie in wait for him. Remembering the orgasmic rush that flooded through him when his boot had smashed into Luc's head, he decided that he didn't regret his actions and given the chance he'd do it all over again. *My mistake,* he admitted, *was in being overconfident and thinking that it would be Luc Joslyn who would come looking for my blood.*

He'd known that attacking the viscount's half brother would have repercussions, but he hadn't expected such a swift reaction or for the trouble to arrive in the form of John Lamb. He wouldn't make that mistake again. He touched the scar. And he was going to take great pleasure, very great pleasure in killing Lamb.

Nolles stood up. But before he could turn his attention to the vexing John Lamb, there was the disposal of Canfield. . . . Hmm, now how, he wondered as he strolled out to join the patrons of his tavern, shall I do it? A slit throat? Or should I just shoot him? Hide the body or leave it to be discovered? He sighed. So many decisions . . .

Chapter 11

It wasn't until Tuesday morning, after Barnaby had left the morning room, that Emily and Cornelia turned their full attention to Mrs. Dashwood and the role she might or might not play in Luc's affections. They had touched on the visit by Gillian Dashwood and her family on the drive home from Ramstone the previous day, but busy setting the events in motion that would insure Luc's new home was staffed and his larders filled, they hadn't been able to consider all the implications.

After breakfasting with Emily and Cornelia, Barnaby departed for Eastbourne to inspect a new yacht, intending to be gone for the day. The door had hardly closed behind him before Emily set down her cup and asked, "What are we going to do about that woman? I fear that Luc may be falling under her spell." She shuddered. "Good heavens—she murdered her husband. Has he lost his head? Doesn't he see the danger?"

Cornelia looked thoughtful. "He may be fascinated by the woman, but I don't believe that he has lost his head . . . yet." She sipped her coffee. "But that the Ordway family were his very first guests, and the only comment he can remember about his new home is hers, is telling."

"What are we going to do?"

"I doubt we can do anything—not if Luc's heart is set on her."

Appalled, Emily breathed, "Oh Cornelia, you don't think he would be foolish enough to marry her, do you?"

"When it comes to affairs of the heart, anything is possible, my dear." She smiled at Emily. "Considering the circumstances, who'd have thought that you'd end up married to Barnaby?"

A blush climbed up Emily's cheeks. "That was different! I wasn't accused of murdering anyone."

"Ah, and there you have it—no one has proven that she did murder her husband." She bent a look on Emily. "How do we know that she *did* murder him? Obviously, there wasn't enough evidence for the authorities to arrest her. All we know about the woman is what we've heard from gossip. And you know as well as anyone that most gossip holds only a grain of truth. What if she's innocent? Do we condemn her based on gossip?"

It was Emily's turn to look thoughtful. Picking up her cup, she swallowed some coffee. Over the rim she regarded Cornelia and asked, "Do you think she's innocent?"

"I don't know," Cornelia admitted. "I've never even met the woman. Now Penny Smythe has met her and likes her. She mentioned when she was here last week that she's invited Mrs. Dashwood and her cousin, Mrs. Easley, to serve on several committees. Penny appears to find both women delightful. Which leads me to believe that Mrs. Dashwood must possess great charm."

Emily thought about that for a few minutes. Penelope Smythe was a very good judge of character, and if the vicar's wife liked Gillian Dashwood . . . "Does Mrs. Smythe know about the murder?" Emily asked abruptly.

"I don't know . . . and no, I didn't bring it up."

"Why not, you know that Mrs. Smythe loves gossip."

"Again I don't know and usually I would have shared the

gossip with Penny without another thought, but . . ." She frowned. "I think it is the fact that Luc is so fond of Silas Ordway and that Penny herself had only good things to say about Mrs. Dashwood that kept my lips sealed." Cornelia fiddled with her spoon. Unhappily, she said, "Remember, we don't know that Mrs. Dashwood murdered her husband . . . perhaps the gossip is all wrong. It wouldn't be the first time that an innocent was vilified by half truths or even vicious lies."

Emily nodded slowly. "And we don't know that Luc has anything more than a passing interest in her—we may be running down the road to meet trouble and all for naught."

"Perhaps. But I think we would be wise to meet the lady for ourselves."

Emily perked up. Smiling, she asked, "Shall I have Mrs. Spalding prepare a basket with some of her strawberry preserves and some jars of honey from our hives?"

Cornelia's hazel eyes danced. "Yes, I think it is only fitting that we call upon the newcomers and welcome them to the neighborhood, don't you?" She shook a finger at Emily. "But not too soon. Luc is no fool. He would know what we were up to in a flash. Next week will be soon enough."

Walker tapped on the door and sticking his head into the room, grinning, he said, "Mr. Simon Joslyn is here. Shall I show him in?"

"Without question," Emily answered, smiling. She'd known Simon Joslyn since she'd been a child and Barnaby's youngest cousin had always been a favorite of hers.

Simon strolled into the room a moment later, looking handsome enough to steal the heart of half the women in the British Isles. He had the stamp of the Joslyns about him, from his azure eyes and black hair to the tall, athletic build. There were those who thought his older brother, Mathew, handsomer, but gossip pegged Simon as the Most Handsome Man in England.

His dark blue coat of superfine fit his broad shoulders admirably and his buff breeches displayed a pair of nicely formed masculine legs. With a smile that could cause the most hardened feminine heart to beat faster on his lips, he dropped a familiar kiss on first Cornelia's cheek, then Emily's. Azure eyes striking between black lashes, he followed Cornelia's order to help himself to coffee or what else from the sideboard caught his fancy.

After pouring himself a cup of coffee from the silver pot, he took a seat at the table and grinned at both women. "Now how could his lordship go off and leave a pair of beautiful ladies like you all alone? Surely, he knows that you'd be a tempting armful for any marauder that might wander by?"

"I think you forget that I am increasing," Emily said, grinning back at him.

"Yes, and very nicely, too," Simon murmured outrageously. Both Emily and Cornelia burst out laughing. Cornelia tapped him on the wrist with her spoon. "I see that your behavior has not improved since the last time we saw you." There was no censure in her voice, only fond amusement. "But enough of this nonsense. Why are you here? Will you be staying long?"

"Actually," Simon began, "I won't be staying here at all." At Emily's and Cornelia's look of surprise, he added hastily, "Not that I wouldn't prefer to do so, but I am here with Lord Padgett and William Stanton. Padgett is interested in some horses that Lord Broadfoot has for sale; the three of us are staying at a small property nearby that Stanton inherited recently from his great-grandmother." At Emily's raised brow, he added wryly, "I know, I know. Broadfoot is the last person to buy a horse from, but Padgett is keen on a stallion that Broadfoot wishes to sell. We're to meet with him at Broad View tomorrow afternoon."

Emily frowned. "Padgett and Stanton? I don't believe I've ever heard you mention them before. Are they particular friends of yours?"

Simon made a face and shook his head. "Padgett and Stanton aren't exactly the sort of gentlemen I want to be friends with—or that I'd introduce you to—and let's leave it at that.

I know Padgett, but not well—he was more Tom's friend than mine." He looked thoughtful, saying, "I'll admit the invitation surprised me and initially I declined—I didn't want to leave Mathew alone at Monks Abbey." He grimaced. "But Mathew has been in such a surly mood this past week, I decided I'd better vacate Monks Abbey before one of us tried to kill the other."

Her features concerned, Emily said, "Poor Mathew! I cannot be sorry for Thomas's death, he would have murdered Barnaby and Lamb after all, but I am very sorry that Mathew hasn't come to accept that what happened was not his fault."

Simon nodded, his eyes bleak. "There are days he realizes that, but there are times . . ."

He sighed. "There are times when he is best left alone."

"Hmmm. Aren't Padgett and Stanton also friends with Miles St. John?" Cornelia asked abruptly.

Surprised, Simon said, "Yes. Padgett, Stanton, St. John and, to some extent, Canfield were all members of Tom's London set."

Cornelia had a wide circle of friends that she kept in touch with by letter and hearing those names, she frowned. "Not one of them a person I'd be happy to see cross my threshold," she muttered. "Welbourne's whelp, Canfield, is the worst of the lot—he was at High Tower, but apparently a few days ago he took up residence at The Ram's Head."

"How do you know that?" Emily asked, puzzled.

Cornelia waved a dismissing hand. "Walker was at The Crown last night and Mrs. Gilbert told him. He mentioned it to Agatha and she told me."

"Of course, nothing gets by Mrs. Gilbert," Emily said ruefully. Agatha Colby had been Cornelia's maid for decades, and the relationship between the two was close—anything Agatha knew, Cornelia knew and usually within minutes of Agatha learning of it.

"Well, I can't say that I'm happy to learn that," Simon admitted. "Padgett and Stanton are tolerable, but Canfield . . ." He grinned at Emily. "I may end up begging you for a place to lay my head, after all."

"Serves you right for accepting the invitation in the first place," retorted Cornelia. Frowning, she said, "Padgett's invitation is odd, though. I wonder why he invited you along."

"Apparently, Padgett hasn't ever been personally introduced to Lord Broadfoot, and since it's well known that the Joslyn family and the Broadfoot family are friends and neighbors, Padgett thought that my presence would ease any constraints that might arise between virtual strangers."

Cornelia nodded. "Lord Broadfoot is normally a genial gentleman, but having a stranger like Padgett come on too strong could put his back up. Padgett was wise to invite you along."

For several moments the conversation was general, and having finished his coffee, Simon rose to his feet. "Ladies, I must be off." His eyes danced. "I must go and prevent Padgett from buying a three-legged wonder from Broadfoot. Or is it a wind-broken, tied-at-the-knees pacer?"

"You'll come to dine one night while you're in the area, won't you?" Emily begged.

"Be assured of it," he replied. "Now where can I find Barnaby and Luc? It would be rude of me not to say hello to either one of them."

Simon was disappointed that he had missed Barnaby, but the news that Luc was now the proud owner of Ramstone Manor delighted him. A smile spread across his face. "By Jupiter! This is excellent news." He shook his head. "During the Season, London was all agog at the devilish luck of Lucifer Joslyn. I heard that one member of the peerage who should have known better left vowels lying on the table amounting to over thirty thousand pounds. Looks like Luc is investing his winnings wisely." He laughed. "I suppose next you'll tell me he's hanging out for a wife."

Already on his way out the door, Simon didn't see the look the two ladies exchanged. The door shut behind him and Cornelia said, "Now, where were we?"

Emily grinned. "Planning to call upon Mrs. Dashwood next week."

Unaware of the interest of the ladies of Windmere, Gillian and Sophia were settling in at High Tower. Stanley's determination to put his best foot forward and the absence of Lord George Canfield made the process enjoyable. Of course, Uncle Silas was a dear, and Gillian berated herself daily for not having accepted his many invitations to visit in the years since Charles had been murdered.

She'd had her reservations about living at High Tower—she'd run her household without any male interference of any sort since Charles's death, and she'd feared that living with Uncle Silas might be very different from *visiting* with him. To her gratification, Silas was as kind and considerate as always.

It was difficult for her after being married to Charles not to harbor the suspicion that behind a man's smiling façade a monster hid. Not, she admitted hastily, that she'd worried her uncle would suddenly turn into a tyrant. In fact, he was entirely the opposite, telling both women that since they were the women of the house now, that he was turning over the reins of the household to them. His eyes twinkling, he'd added, "This has been a bachelor household for too long, and while my housekeeper, Mrs. Amerson, has always done an excellent job, I think she'll be happier with a feminine hand at the helm. Meacham, of course, is already at your feet."

And just that easily, Gillian and Sophia found themselves running the household at High Tower. To Gillian's surprise, Stanley made no objections. In fact, there was much about Stanley these days that surprised her.

With Canfield gone, other than a friendly hand or two of cards and a snifter of brandy with Silas, Stanley no longer spent his nights gambling and drinking at the tavern in the village. Even more astonishing, her half brother appeared to be absorbed in learning as much as he could about the running of the estate and lifting that burden from his uncle. Some suspicion and curiosity about his motives remained, but both she and Mrs. Easley thought that his actions were sincere.

Happier than she had been for a very long time, Gillian woke each morning looking forward to the day. It was only her nights that were troublesome—vivid, disturbing dreams of Luc Joslyn brought her awake with her body aching and burning with elemental needs she'd never thought to feel again. Telling herself that she was a fool to give him more than a second's thought did no good, nor no matter how often she scolded herself did it have any effect on those explicit dreams. Night after night, Luc came to her in dreams, his azure eyes glittering with desire and a carnal curve to his lips. Those same lips that in her dreams caressed her cheek before sliding warmly to find her mouth, kissing her deeply with a rough passion that swelled her nipples and sent desire spiraling through her.

After another night spent tossing restlessly in bed, her body desperate to feel one man's touch, she stared grimly at herself in the mirror on Thursday morning. Hardly aware of what she did, Gillian brushed her hair and tied the sable curls at the base of her neck with a bronze-green silk ribbon, her thoughts on those agitating dreams. What was wrong with her? She had no business entertaining lewd dreams about Luc Joslyn. His similarities to her husband should have sent her fleeing, but did they? No. She dreamed of him, dreamed of that sensuous mouth moving over her lips, her throat, her breasts, and she woke longing to feel his naked flesh sliding against hers.

Remnants of those dreams taunting her, Gillian swallowed as she stared into the mirror, painfully aware of the throbbing of her breasts beneath the modest bodice of her cinnamon wool gown and the heavy moisture pooling between her thighs. If dreams affected her thus, she thought acidly, heaven help her if she was ever alone with him again—if he kissed her as he had done that night in the garden, she'd not deny him . . . anything.

She closed her eyes, unable to bear the sight of her own eager half-parted mouth at just the idea of Luc kissing her. I am a respectable woman, she reminded herself fiercely, and no silly virgin to be swept off my feet by an attractive male. Her eyes opened and she made a face in the mirror. She'd already let one man with a handsome face and charming manner dazzle her, and look where that had led; marriage to a man who had gambled away her money and traded her body for his vowels. Thinking of that terrible night, of the look in Winthrop's eyes, she shuddered. No. She'd not be taken in again. She was old enough, she told herself, and wise enough to avoid the dangerous appeal of someone like Luc Joslyn. But if she was, whispered a sly voice, why couldn't she put him out of her mind?

Nan Burton bustled into the room and, seeing Gillian sitting at her dressing table, said, "Mrs. Easley is in the breakfast room and is waiting for you to join her. Shall I tell her you'll be down in a few minutes?"

Gillian rose to her feet and after one critical glance of herself in the mirror shook her head. "That won't be necessary. I'm on my way."

Since Stanley and Silas tended not to be early risers, as often happened, Gillian and Sophia had the breakfast room all to themselves. Helping herself to a cup of coffee, a piece of toast and a small serving of scrambled eggs from the buffet, Gillian took a seat across from Sophia.

There was the normal morning chatter between the two ladies until Sophia said in her usual brisk manner, "I suggest that we go through that last trunk from the cottage this morning, what do you think?"

Over the past few weeks their belongings had been unpacked and put away, but there was one remaining trunk still to be gone through. The majority of the furniture from the cottage held no great sentimental value for either woman and the largest pieces had been left behind, leaving only clothing and personal items to be transported to High Tower.

Since others had overseen the dismantling of the house-hold and the packing of their belongings, the ladies had dis-covered a few things that had been sent along that could just as well been given to the rag man—or thrown away. One day last week, watching Nan shake out the faded and patched blue gown she'd worn to weed the garden, Gillian laughed and said, "Surely that garment could have been left behind? I doubt I would ever wear it again and certainly not here."

"Indeed, and these along with it," said Sophia, viewing with disfavor the old shoes she'd worn to gather eggs from the henhouse. "I'm sure that our uncle will not expect us to pick eggs or pluck weeds from between the vegetables."

Gillian had not been left destitute by Charles's death, but the past two years had not been pleasant. Except for the cot-tage and a small annuity, there had been little else in Charles's estate and Gillian had learned quickly how to make every penny count. There'd not been enough to keep on the staff that Charles had felt was necessary for his consequence, and except for Nan and her two sons, fourteen-year-old James and sixteen-year-old John, all of the other servants had been let go. His horses, vehicles and the London flat had been sold to cover his gambling debts, and there'd barely been enough to cover them. She shuddered. If Winthrop had pre-sented the vowels Charles had given him . . .

Pushing aside the gloomy thought, Gillian glanced around her. It was a charming room in which she sat, the walls cov-ered in gold-flecked cream wallpaper, an oak buffet littered with pewter trays and silver covered dishes was against one wall and a thick wool rug woven in shades of blue, gold and ivory lay upon the floor. She shook her head. While the cot-tage had been a pleasant home for a gentleman of moderate means, it bore little resemblance to the luxury of High Tower, and she found the change in her circumstances breathtaking. Only a few weeks ago she'd been worried about the root vegetables stored in the cellar and if there was enough grain and hay in the barn to feed the chickens, cow and sow over the winter, while today . . . she glanced around the room once more and smiled.

Setting down her cup of coffee, Gillian said ruefully, "Realizing how different our lives are now, I wonder if I shouldn't thank Canfield for trying to blackmail me."

Sophia snorted. "You hardly need to go that far," she said. "All things considered, I suspect that we would have ended up at High Tower even without his machinations, but it most likely wouldn't have happened so swiftly."

"I cannot argue with you about that," Gillian said. "It was always troublesome knowing that Uncle had only servants to look after him—or question his absence. When I think of what could have happened the night Uncle Silas broke his arm if Mr. Joslyn had not come across him, and I see how happy he is that we agreed to live with him, I cannot regret our decision—even if Canfield precipitated it."

Sophia eyed her slyly. "And what of the handsome Mr. Lucian Joslyn? What part does he play in your having no regrets?"

Gillian stared tongue-tied at her cousin. Her cheeks flaming, she finally managed, "Thoughts of Mr. Joslyn never cross my mind."

"What a rapper," said Sophia and when Gillian would protest, she added, "But I won't tease you. After you finish your coffee, let us go see what delights await us in that trunk."

On that same Thursday morning, Simon woke shortly after the conversation between Gillian and Sophia with his mouth tasting like the bottom of a swine pen. He'd had his reservations about accepting Padgett's invitation, and after last night's trip to The Ram's Head, the reasons for his reservations had been confirmed. Padgett and Stanton were definitely not men he wished to call friends. He held the same opinion of that insufferable Canfield, and as for Townsend . . . His lips thinned. Townsend might be Emily's cousin, but the man was a fawning weasel, and if he had to spend another night in the company of any one of those four men, he'd be hanged for murder.

Not eager to rise, he lay there staring into space, his thoughts on the previous day . . . and night. The day had been pleasant enough. The introduction to Broadfoot had gone well. He grinned. And for once his lordship actually had a decent animal for sale. The bay stallion was nearly everything Broadfoot had claimed the horse to be, and a deal was quickly struck. By the time they left Broad View for Stanton's house in the late afternoon, Padgett was the new owner of prancing bay stallion.

And after that I should have bolted for Windmere, Simon reflected sourly. There had been no reason for him to stay another night at Stanton's place or to accompany Padgett and Stanton to The Ram's Head last night, but for reasons that escaped him, he had.

He frowned, thinking about last night. It had been . . . interesting. Not the drinking or the ruinous gambling, he'd seen that in London often enough to be inured to it, but the relationship between the four men . . . and Nolles had caught his attention.

Canfield had been clearly surprised to see Padgett and Stanton, but Simon had the impression that Townsend and Nolles had been expecting the other two men. Now how was it, he wondered as he lay there, that Townsend and Nolles appeared to have been aware of Padgett and Stanton's arrival in the area, but Canfield had not?

His frown deepened. Though Padgett and Nolles acted as if meeting for the first time, Simon couldn't shake the feeling that they knew each other very well, which led him to consider the common denominator between two such divergent individuals: Tom Joslyn.

He didn't like the direction his thoughts were leading him. His brother Tom may have been Nolles's main backer, but that didn't mean that his brother had been the *only* one to press money into Nolles's hand. If he'd had to name one person as Tom's best friend, it would be Padgett. So had Padgett been investing in Tom's smuggling operation? More importantly, had Padgett stepped into Tom's shoes?

Simon's eyes narrowed as he played back in his mind the events of last night. He wasn't much of a gambler, but he'd lay money that Padgett, Stanton, Canfield, Townsend and Nolles were involved in some sort of enterprise that wouldn't bear close scrutiny, and he had a fair notion precisely what that enterprise was: smuggling.

He sighed. Before he'd leaped to any further conclusions, Simon concluded that a conversation with Barnaby was in order. Perhaps Barnaby would laugh at his conclusions, he told himself hopefully, but the prickle at the back of his neck made him doubt it. He sensed trouble.

Swinging his feet over the edge of the bed, Simon moaned as the room spun. Christ! How much had he drunk last night? Far too much, he decided when his head stopped spinning.

Gingerly rising to his feet, Simon walked to the small washstand in the corner and was grateful to find the pitcher held water. Thinking of Stanton's two servants, Mr. and Mrs. Archer, Simon grimaced. Mrs. Archer might be called the housekeeper and Stanton might refer to Mr. Archer as his butler, cum-factotum, but Simon couldn't remember when he'd laid eyes on a more rascally pair.

Pouring water into the stained bowl in the center of the washstand and preparing to shave himself, he thought wistfully of his valet, Leighton. Able to fend for himself, Simon often left Leighton at Monks Abbey, but this was one time he'd have been happy to have his precise valet bustling around the room. Not because he wasn't perfectly capable of shaving and dressing himself, but because Leighton would have seen to it that a pot of hot, strong coffee had greeted him when he woke. If the past few days were anything to go by, he thought, he'd be lucky if there was *any* coffee available when he descended the stairs.

By the time he was dressed in a plum coat and dove-gray breeches, he felt able to face the day. And Padgett and Stanton. He sighed. Closer acquaintance with both men had not endeared them to him and accepting Padgett's invitation had been a mistake, he admitted. Wondering how soon he could politely take his leave, he wandered downstairs.

The house, Woodhurst, that Stanton had inherited from his great-grandmother was a snug little place nestled in the middle of a hundred and twenty acres of woodland that had been planted over a hundred years previously. Once the house had been part of a larger estate, but with each generation more and more of the land had been sold until only the hundred and twenty acres and its woodland remained. The house and land, situated five miles from the village, had been more than adequate for Stanton's great-grandmother, but Simon suspected that Stanton would sell it . . . or gamble it away before too many more months passed.

As he'd guessed, there was no coffee or any sign of the Archers, and he walked out of the cold, empty breakfast room, intent upon getting his horse from the stables at the rear of the house. Hearing footsteps, Simon looked up to see Lord Padgett and Stanton coming down the stairs. Forcing a smile, Simon said, "If you're looking for coffee, there is none."

A big, burly man, with dark, heavy features, Stanton shrugged.

"It doesn't matter," Padgett said as he reached the last stair. "Nolles will have coffee waiting for us."

"After last night, if you don't mind, I'll forego the pleasure of another visit to Nolles's place," Simon said easily.

Padgett's pale blue eyes studied him. "I was surprised when you accompanied us last night—Nolles mentioned that your cousin, the viscount, prefers The Crown. I can't say that you looked like you enjoyed yourself."

Padgett was a tall, slender man with wavy fair hair and chiseled features. Like Stanton, he was in his middle thirties, and like Stanton, the signs of a dissolute life were already evident on his once angelically handsome face.

"I can't say that I did," Simon answered levelly. "Becoming cup shot and losing ridiculous sums of money isn't my idea of a pleasant evening."

"Tom always said that you were too nice in your notions," Padgett drawled.

"I'll take that as a compliment," Simon said without a smile.

"Suit yourself," Padgett returned indifferently.

That he had served his purpose as far as Padgett was concerned didn't escape Simon, and glad there was no longer any reason to pretend an affability he didn't feel, Simon said briskly, "I intend to." Looking at Stanton he added, "Thank you for your hospitality. I shall send a servant over to pack up my things later today and bring them to Windmere."

Stanton waved a dismissing hand.

Minutes later, glad to leave Woodhurst behind, Simon was on his horse and riding toward Windmere. Coffee was foremost in his mind, and after that, a private conversation with Barnaby.

Not in the mood for more unpacking even if it was the last trunk, Gillian lingered over her coffee as long as she could, but soon enough, she had no choice but to push away her cup and say, "Enough for me. Shall we go find that trunk?"

One of the footmen had dragged the trunk in question into the sitting room the two women shared and the efficient Nan was already there. Signs of her industry scattered around the room. A pink woolen shawl that Sophia hadn't worn in years was folded over the arm of a chair, a gray striped velvet pelisse that Gillian had never liked lay nearby and a worn pair of jean half boots she'd forgotten sat on the floor.

Smiling, Nan glanced up from her task and said, "I don't know who packed this trunk, but I fear that most of it should be given to the poor in the village."

Watching as Nan pulled out a ragged yellow parasol and a black silk reticule with a large tear on one side, Gillian said, "And some of it, not even suitable for that."

"I agree," said Sophia, sighing.

It was a large trunk and while they came across a few things to keep, most of the contents were added to the pile for the vicarage for distribution to those in need.

While Gillian and Sophia folded the various items and stacked them on the sofa, Nan continued to dig into the trunk. "Ah, here we have it," Nan said, "the last item." Vexation in her voice, Nan added, "Though how it ended up here I have no idea. It should have been packed with your other gowns."

Gillian glanced over at Nan, and the color drained from her face. Frozen, she stared as Nan continued to shake out the amber silk and lace gown she'd worn that night at the dinner party given by the Duke of Welbourne, the diamond and topaz brooch used to alter the neckline still fixed in place. First Canfield and now this, she thought sickly. Would she ever be able to escape reminders of that terrible night?

Chapter 12

Gillian must have made a sound because Sophia glanced at her. Seeing the expression of horror and revulsion on Gillian's face, Sophia rushed over.

Laying a hand on Gillian's rigid arm, Sophia asked, "What is it, my dear? Why do you look as if you've seen a ghost—or something worse?"

Gillian nodded in Nan's direction and said bitterly, "I have seen something worse—look at what Nan is holding."

There were no secrets between the two cousins, and while Nan might not be privy to what had transpired between Gillian and Lord Winthrop the night Charles had died, Sophia certainly was. Glancing over and seeing the amber silk and lace gown in Nan's hands, Sophia muttered, "Oh my. I thought that wretched garment had been given away ages ago."

Puzzled by Gillian's reaction to the gown and Sophia's comment, Nan asked, "But why would you give away such a lovely and expensive gown?" Defensively, she added, "I know you told me to leave your things behind that horrible night, but I could not bring myself to do so: I packed your belongings and brought them right home with us." When Gillian continued to stare at the gown with revulsion, Nan said, "Very well, I'll see to it that the gown is given away, but what of the brooch? Surely, you mean to keep it?"

Gillian opened her mouth to tell Nan to do whatever she

wanted with the brooch, but a thought occurred to her. She walked across the room and stared at the brooch. While she'd never wanted to see the gown again, the brooch didn't have the same effect on her; it was connected with the horrible events of that night, but the sight of it didn't make her flesh creep. She viewed the brooch as a warning—a symbol not to trust a charming man—even when he presented gifts. Staring at the brooch, she realized that it could serve as a reminder of just how perfidious a man could be. Every time she saw that winking topaz and diamond piece of jewelry, it would be a tangible warning not to trust a beguiling smile and a handsome face.

Luc's lean, dark features flitted through her mind. She fingered the brooch, a wry smile curving her mouth. Did she really think a brooch would protect her from his undeniable pull? It might not, but then again . . .

"Save the brooch," she ordered. "Please put it in my jewelry box. As for the gown—burn it for all I care."

Nan removed the brooch from the gown, saying, "Very well, Madame. I'll put it away on my way downstairs." She looked dubiously at the amber silk and lace gown. "This isn't the sort of garment that would be suitable for one of the housemaids; I'll send it to the vicarage along with everything else."

As Gillian and Sophy were going through the things in the trunk, Simon rode up to the front of Windmere. Shown into the morning room by Walker, he was pleased to find that Barnaby was still there, enjoying a late breakfast with Emily and Cornelia.

"How is it," Barnaby asked, grinning, "that you usually manage to turn up on my doorstep when food is being served?"

Simon grinned back. "Talent," he said, pouring himself a cup of coffee from the large silver coffeepot on the sideboard. The scent of the coffee teased his nostrils and he almost moaned with delight, but his empty stomach rumbled and after placing his cup on the table, he returned to the sideboard. Thick slices of ham beckoned and coddled eggs made his mouth water; the sight of some preserved cherries had him scooping up a spoonful or two of them, along with several of Mrs. Eason's delicate Bath cakes. When he rejoined the others, his plate was heaping. Taking that first, reviving swallow of the rich, dark coffee, he sighed blissfully.

Amused, Barnaby watched him. Knowing from the ladies where Simon was staying, he said, "I take it that the amenities of Stanton's bachelor household do not extend to food or coffee?"

Simon nodded. "Or anything else that charitably could be called comfort. He may refer to the Archers as his servants, but a lazier pair I've not seen—when I've seen them about."

Cornelia's eyes narrowed. "Is she a skinny blond rag of a woman and he's a scrawny fellow with a face only a hangman would love?"

"You know them?" Simon asked, surprised.

"Never met them, but they've been pointed out to me in the village, and Mrs. Gilbert is well acquainted with them. You'd best watch your step," Cornelia warned, "and your friend had better check his plate—they answer to Nolles, and anyone who works for Nolles isn't someone I'd want running tame through my house."

"Must you continue to stay at Stanton's?" Emily asked unhappily, not liking the sound of that. "You know that you are more than welcome to stay here."

Barnaby looked alarmed. "What and decimate my kitchen and larders?" he demanded, his gaze on Simon's plate.

"As long as you provide me with such excellent coffee," Simon returned, smiling, "I shall be a perfect guest and restrain myself from laying waste to your kitchen and larders."

"*Are* you staying with us?" Barnaby asked with a lifted brow.

"If I may?"

"Unless I wish to listen to a scolding wife," Barnaby answered, a lazy smile curving his lips, "I fear I have no choice but to offer you my hospitality."

"Aha!" Simon exclaimed. "Mathew is right, you *do* live under the cat's paw."

"But it is such a dainty little paw, don't you agree?" Barnaby murmured.

Emily snorted. "If your brother thinks that anyone can get Barnaby to do anything he doesn't want to do, he doesn't know him very well."

"Cornelia and Emily mentioned that Mathew is still battling his demons," Barnaby said, all trace of lightness gone. "How bad is it at Monks Abbey?"

Simon hunched a shoulder. "There are days I think he's doing better and then there are days that I know he's gone somewhere black and bleak." He made a face. "And then there are times he's just impossible to be around—snarling and snapping at anyone who crosses his path. I try to be understanding, but I fear I have little patience with him when he's simply looking for someone to start a fight with."

"Mayhap I shall do something outrageous to distract him," Barnaby said, only half-teasing. "He does enjoy lecturing me." As much to himself as anyone else, Barnaby added, "We need to give him a focus for all that rage and despair he's feeling."

Simon started, an idea springing full-blown in his mind. Swallowing a bite of ham and coddled egg, Simon said, "I may know just the thing."

When the ladies pressed to know what Simon referred to, he shook his head and would say nothing more.

"It is most unkind of you to say something like that and then not tell us," Emily complained. "And to think that before I met Barnaby you were always my favorite Joslyn." She bent a severe look upon him. "I suppose once we leave the room, you'll tell Barnaby."

Simon smiled angelically, not to be drawn.

Rising to her feet, Cornelia said to Emily, "Come, my dear, let us leave the gentlemen to their secrets. Don't forget we are to meet with Mrs. Smythe within the hour at the vicarage."

Both men rose as the ladies exited the room. With the women gone, Simon wolfed down his food and in between bites, said, "I wanted to speak with you privately anyway, and what I have to say may provide us with a way to drag Mathew from his lair."

Barnaby regarded Simon thoughtfully. Of the three English Joslyns he'd met when he first arrived in England over a year ago, he'd liked Simon best. The youngest brother, Simon had welcomed him, and with his easy charm and teasing manner, most people found it difficult to dislike Simon. Now Mathew . . .

Barnaby grimaced. He didn't blame Mathew for resenting him. Mathew had grown up believing he would inherit Windmere and the title and fortune that went with the great house. Groomed from childhood to step into the 7th Viscount Joslyn's shoes, Mathew, and everyone else in England, assumed that when his great-uncle died Mathew would be the 8th Viscount Joslyn. To discover after the old viscount's death that the title and everything else went to an American, a plantation owner from Virginia, someone the English branch of the family hadn't even known existed, had been a catastrophic shock for Mathew and his brothers.

Since there had never been any question of him inheriting Windmere or the title, Simon had found it easiest to accept Barnaby as the new viscount, but Mathew and Thomas, understandably, had been resentful of the man they viewed as an interloper. The relationship between Barnaby and Mathew had been strained and chilly, but a fair man, even if it damn near killed him, Mathew swallowed most, not all, of his rancor and unhappiness and attempted to, if not befriend Barnaby, at least not treat him like an enemy.

Thomas had been another case altogether, Barnaby admitted. From all appearances, Thomas had adored Mathew and had taken Barnaby's assumption of the title as a personal insult. Barnaby's possession of Windmere had only added to Thomas's rage at the situation, but they all now knew that there had been another more personal reason that the middle Joslyn brother had not wanted Barnaby living at Windmere: the tunnels beneath Windmere.

Barnaby sighed. Aloud he said, "Who could have guessed that Thomas Joslyn would be the investor and brains behind a gang of smugglers?"

"No one," Simon said simply. "I know Tom's fortune didn't compare to Mathew's or yours, but it was more than sufficient to enable him to live like a gentleman and eventually marry and raise a family in comfort." He shook his head. "I don't suppose we'll ever know why he turned to smuggling with Nolles."

"Sometimes sufficient isn't enough," Barnaby said. "Greed is an ugly vice and when in the grips of it, can turn even an honest, reasonable man into a monster. Perhaps that's what happened to Thomas."

Simon pushed away his empty plate and, standing up, walked to the sideboard. He looked at Barnaby and asked, "Would you like more coffee?" At Barnaby's nod, he carried the silver coffeepot over to the table and, after filling Barnaby's cup, poured himself another cup. Setting the coffeepot down on the table, he reseated himself.

"Tom was greedy—I know that from having grown up with him, but I'll admit I never thought he'd become a smuggler." Simon sipped his coffee. "I wonder if it wasn't simply that the opportunity was there and in the beginning he did it more as a lark and then . . ." He shrugged. "And when he saw how much money could be made . . ."

"I suspect you're right." Barnaby stared at the patch of linen tablecloth in front of him, frowning. "I wish it could have ended differently. I never wanted Thomas dead and certainly not by Mathew's hand."

"It wasn't your fault," Simon said softly. "You didn't ask for Tom to try, more than once, to kill you." Simon looked away and for a long moment there was silence in the room, both men lost in thought.

Before the silence became marked, Simon said, "If you consider it without emotion, Mathew being the one to kill Thomas was probably the best possible outcome of the affair."

"Because if I had been the one to kill him, Mathew would have had an added reason to curse and despise me?"

Simon nodded. "The same holds true if it had been Lamb or Emily who had killed Tom that night." He looked away. "I can't seem to make Mathew understand that he is guilty of nothing or that his actions might have saved lives. If he had not fired when he did, you or Lamb or Emily might have died. And if Tom hadn't died . . ."

"The scandal would have been impossible to suppress."

Simon nodded grimly. "The family could have survived the scandal, although I'm sure there would be people who would have assumed we were all in on it, but Tom's death and your clever story to Lieutenant Deering allowed Tom to be considered a hero and avoided scandal."

"You might ask your brother the next time he's being particularly difficult if he'd rather have had the truth come out," Barnaby said. "Perhaps, when he considers all aspects of what could have happened, he might be able to accept his part in it without feeling such guilt." When Simon looked unconvinced, Barnaby sighed. "Mathew will have to find his own peace—you cannot do it for him. Now what did you want to tell me that you didn't want the ladies to hear?"

Simon shook off his glum thoughts about Mathew and succinctly brought Barnaby current with his observations over the past few days and his suspicions about Nolles and Padgett. It took awhile; Barnaby may have heard the names in passing but he was not familiar with Padgett, Stanton or Canfield or their relationship to Thomas. Simon had to explain who they were and how they related to Thomas. Mention of Nolles narrowed his eyes and by the time Simon ceased speaking, Barnaby was frowning.

"So do you think I have concocted a plot that sounds like something out of a gothic novel or is there merit to my suspicions?" Simon asked.

"Gossip has it that Nolles has increased his smuggling efforts again, and Lamb, Luc and I have suspected for a while now that he found another investor," Barnaby said thoughtfully. "Aware now of Padgett's friendship with Thomas it's a logical jump to assume Padgett is the London investor—most likely along with Stanton and Canfield."

Barnaby tapped a finger on the table, his expression intent. "I wouldn't think," he muttered, "that this quiet corner of Sussex would hold much attraction for a trio of young bloods like Padgett, Stanton and Canfield. . . . I'm surprised they're not in Leicestershire hunting this time of year—or taking part in one of the less, er, staid house parties hosted by libertines like themselves. Just their being here is more than curious." He sighed. "I don't know if it's a good thing or a bad that there seems to be some sort of rift between Canfield and the others. A falling-out between them could work to our advantage, but it could increase the possibility of violence—violence that could harm innocents."

"Violence?" Simon asked uneasily. "You don't really think . . ."

Barnaby shot him a look. "If Nolles is involved, you can bet there'll be violence."

"Perhaps I'm wrong," Simon said, "Maybe Canfield knew the others were coming and I was mistaken in my assumption."

"Do you think so?"

Simon thought back to last night to that moment when Canfield had spied Padgett and Stanton and shook his head. "No," he said. "Canfield had no idea Padgett and Stanton were in the area, but Nolles and Townsend seemed not the least surprised."

"If you're right about that, how interesting that Townsend appears to be in Nolles's confidence," Barnaby muttered. "But not at all astonishing." A bite in his voice, he added, "And I suspect you're right about Townsend, too. I've known for some time that our dear squire is exceedingly friendly with Nolles and that most nights he is to be found at The Ram's Head. With all we know about Nolles it's not a far stretch to think that he is tolerating Townsend and under-writing his gambling for use of The Birches."

"I was half-hoping that you'd laugh me out of the house," Simon admitted.

"Believe me, I would be happier if I could, but while this may all turn out to be useless speculation on our part, with Nolles in the mix and rubbing shoulders with Thomas's friends at The Ram's Head, I doubt that will be the case." Barnaby scratched his chin. "I think our next step will be to apprise Luc and Lamb of the situation. Between the four of us we should be able to discover if we are jumping at shadows or if there is real mischief afoot."

Simon cleared his throat. "Uh, I was thinking that Mathew might be able to, uh, help us. Another pair of hands and eyes and all that."

Barnaby shot him a shrewd look. "Distraction? Instead of brooding over Thomas's death, give him a chance to bring down Nolles?"

"Well, it would give him something else to think about," Simon said. Glumly, he added, "I doubt he'll respond if the information comes from me—he'd most likely toss any letter

from me into the fire." He smiled innocently at Barnaby.
"However, if *you* wrote and invited him to Windmere to help
you with the situation, I'm sure he wouldn't refuse."

Laughing, Barnaby rose to his feet. "Tell me," he said,
"how is it that you are not a member of the Diplomatic
Corps—that was most masterful of you. My compliments—I
almost didn't see it coming. Now let us adjourn to my office
where I shall compose an appropriate letter for your
brother—after I've sent Lamb to Ramstone with a note for
Luc. The sooner they know what is in the wind, the better."

Simon supposed he should have felt guilty for letting Barnaby be the one to write to Mathew, but he knew his brother
well enough to know that in his present mood Matt *would*
have thrown anything from him into the fire.

Less than two hours later, the letter to Mathew at Monks
Abbey was on its way and Lamb had arrived back at Windmere with Luc at his heels. Barnaby could only be grateful
that the ladies were busy at the vicarage for most of the day.
The ladies of his household were far too intelligent for his
liking, and Emily and Cornelia would have been instantly
suspicious when Luc and Lamb disappeared into his office to
join him and Simon for a private meeting. There would have
been questions, questions he wouldn't have wanted to answer. Barnaby smiled. The last thing he needed was a pregnant
Amazon, ably assisted with her cane-wielding great-aunt, demanding to take part in whatever they planned.

Before he'd been dispatched to Ramstone to bring Luc
back, Lamb had been made privy to Simon and Barnaby's
conversation and he'd relayed that information to Luc. Once
the gentlemen were assembled and refreshments served, there
was little time wasted on repeating Simon's observations and
speculations.

Simon found it gratifying and a bit unnerving that the
three American Joslyns accepted his speculations without

question. Only when he learned of Luc's beating at the hands of Nolles's men and Barnaby and Lamb vouched for the fact that Emily's cousin was both weak and perfidious did he understand how his observations tied in to what they already knew.

"Thomas's connection to Padgett, Stanton and Canfield was part of the puzzle that was missing," Barnaby explained. "We still may not have all of the pieces, but we know more than we did before this morning."

"But what can we do about it?" Simon asked. "Everything I've told you is speculative at best. Tom was friends with Padgett, Stanton and Canfield, but that doesn't prove that they're in league with a smuggler. Townsend may be a feckless, despicable man, but that doesn't prove he's part of Nolles's smuggling operation."

"We can confirm one thing," Luc said idly, "and within a day or two." When all three men looked at him, he said, "Townsend is known to be at The Ram's Head most nights. All I have to do is make certain he is and then there is nothing to stop me from making a midnight exploration of the inner reaches of The Birches. I'll either find it's being used to store Nolles's contraband . . . or not."

"Not alone," Lamb growled, giving him a sharp look. "I'll come with you."

Barnaby hesitated. What Luc proposed made sense, but he didn't like it—as much because he wouldn't be part of it as the prospect of danger to the two men he loved most in the world. He should be with them, Barnaby thought grimly. He knew the house better than they did, and with three of them involved, they'd present a better defense should trouble arise. He considered the situation, deciding that it would be possible, after Emily retired for the night, for him to slip out of the house and join the other two. . . .

Luc and Lamb knew that expression on his face and almost as one, they said, "No."

"Why not?" Barnaby asked, taken aback.

"Because," Luc said from between his teeth, "you are the Viscount Joslyn and your wife is pregnant, for God's sake! The last place you need to be found is sneaking around another man's house in the dead of night."

If it was possible for one of his maturity and nature to do so, Barnaby pouted. "I don't see why this damned title means I have to remain out of the action," he complained. A guilty look crossed his face. "Emily's pregnancy is another matter though." Resigned, he admitted, "You're right. In this case, I should remain behind." He pointed a finger at Luc. "But being a viscount and a married man with a child on the way doesn't mean I can't still hold my own against a varmint like Nolles."

"No one believes that," Lamb said. "But it'll be better if Luc and I do this on our own." He grinned. "Just think, if we are caught you can disown us and be as outraged as anyone at our nefarious actions."

"I may anyway," Barnaby growled.

"Then we are agreed?" Luc asked, glancing around at the other three men. "Lamb and I shall, ah, visit The Birches this evening and confirm whether or not the place is being used by Nolles and his gang?"

Simon cleared his throat. "Um, perhaps I should go with you. After all, it's my information that is precipitating your activities."

Luc looked at him. "Have you ever done any house-breaking?"

"Of course not," Simon answered. "Have you?"

Lamb laughed. "You don't want to know. Leave this part of the situation to Luc and me. We know what we're doing."

Barnaby supposed he should be pleased that, for one of a few times he could remember, Luc and Lamb appeared to be in complete harmony with each other. He was, but he was uneasy about what they planned to do—if the place was guarded, they could run afoul of more danger than they were prepared to handle. "Are you certain that the two of you will be enough?" he asked.

"More than enough," Luc replied. He smiled at Barnaby. "What would you have us do? Ride in with a troop of revenuers at our backs? Lamb and I know what we are doing. We will be in and out of there before anyone suspects we are in the area." He looked at Simon. "Would Padgett be suspicious if you appeared at The Ram's Head tonight?"

Simon thought back to the exchange with Padgett and winced. "More than likely. Before we parted I made some comment about being cup shot and losing money not being my idea of a pleasant evening."

"But you didn't say anything like you'd never darken the doors of The Ram's Head again?"

Simon shook his head. "No. Why?"

"It would be good to have someone inside The Ram's Head who could let us know if Townsend is there before we ride to The Birches tonight," Luc said. "And delay his departure if for some reason he decides to leave earlier than usual."

"I can do that," Simon said slowly. He grinned at Barnaby. "No one would find it strange, even if The Ram's Head isn't my first choice of where to spend an evening, that I would prefer its delights to the boredom I'd experience visiting with my stiff-rumped cousin, his pregnant wife and her totty-headed great-aunt."

"I suppose," Barnaby said with a laugh, "that I should be insulted, but in this case, I'll swallow my pride." He glanced to Luc and Lamb, who were smiling. "Do you think it will suffice?"

Luc nodded. "Knowing the reputations of the men involved, yes. Not one of them could imagine a duller way to spend an evening and wouldn't question Simon bolting for The Ram's Head."

Barnaby summoned Walker and if the butler thought it strange to be questioned about the exact location and entrance to the cellars beneath The Birches, beyond a flicker of curiosity in his eyes, he said nothing. Before he left the room, Barnaby said softly, "And, Walker, please don't mention what we just spoke of to *anyone*. Not Mrs. Eason or, God forbid, my wife or her great-aunt." Barnaby sent him a meaningful look. "Lives may depend upon it."

One of Emily's cohorts in the smuggling ring she'd run before her marriage, and well aware of Jeffery Townsend's contemptible nature, Walker had a very good idea why Barnaby had asked the questions he had. Bowing low, Walker murmured, "Not one word, my lord." Reaching the door, Walker looked back and said, "My lord, if *someone* was seeking to enter the house, er, unnoticed, I'd suggest the door on the east side of the building—it isn't as exposed as the kitchen entrance. It opens directly into the pantry and to one's left is the passageway to the cellars."

Barnaby grinned at him. "Thank you, Walker. I'll make certain that *someone* keeps that in mind."

The door shut behind Walker and the gentlemen decided upon a plan. With nothing else to be accomplished at Windmere, Luc rode back to Ramstone. Lamb would join him later, and after dark, they would ride to the village, hide their horses nearby and slip into concealment near the back of The Ram's Head: Lamb knew just the place. Simon would already be inside. If Townsend wasn't there, at eleven o'clock, Simon would leave The Ram's Head and ride away to meet up with Luc and Lamb where they had left their horses tethered. If Townsend *was* there and all appeared normal, Simon would step outside for a breath of air. Before returning inside, when he could clearly be seen by Luc and Lamb in the glow coming from the lights of the inn, he'd take out his watch and glance at the time and then stroll back inside the inn.

Luc and Lamb were hidden in position near The Ram's

Head well before eleven o'clock, and once Simon gave them the signal that Townsend was inside the inn, they slipped to their horses and galloped through the night to The Birches. Except for a fitfully burning torch near the front door, a careful reconnoiter of the grounds revealed no sign of human activity.

Using Walker's advice, they entered the large pantry of The Birches. It was black inside, but flint and a small candle provided a faint light. They glanced around, noting that the door from the kitchen into the pantry was closed. Empty shelves and cupboards, dust and cobwebs revealed that the pantry was seldom used these days. Only at the end of the room where Luc and Lamb stood was it obvious from the shine of the floor that someone, several people, had been making frequent use of the pantry. Over the flickering candle they exchanged glances and moved on to the wide passageway that led to the cellars.

There was a whispered, short, vehement argument over who would go down and who would remain on guard. Luc won. Seconds later, leaving Lamb behind, Luc disappeared down the rough-cut stone steps that led to the bowels of the house.

The extent and size of the cellars of The Birches could not compare to the space the smugglers had used at Windmere, but it was enough to allow Nolles and his crew to store a sizeable amount of contraband. Holding a candle in front of him, Luc hurried down the haphazard row of smuggled goods in the center of the cellar, easily identifying tubs of over-proof brandy, packets of lace and silks and ropes of tobacco. A tidy haul, he decided, heading back toward the stone steps, but not nearly as much as he would have expected to be stored here. If he were a gambler, he thought with a feral grin, he'd wager that Nolles was expecting another shipment. Soon.

Luc didn't linger. The whole point of tonight was to confirm that Townsend was, indeed, allowing Nolles to store contraband at The Birches and he'd done that.

Rejoining Lamb at the top of the steps, he nodded curtly. Lamb cursed beneath his breath, but like Luc saw no point in lingering in the area. Seconds later, the two men exited the pantry entrance and melted into the darkness.

Chapter 13

Barnaby was *not* happy when he heard Luc and Lamb's report. Barnaby left his wife's bed well after midnight and, feeling like a felon, slunk out of the main house to meet with the others at the Dower House. Learning that contraband, obviously with Townsend's cooperation, was being stored in the cellar of Emily's beloved former home enraged him and made him long to get his hands on the squire. Preferably around Townsend's neck. His face hard, he glanced at Lamb and growled, "We should have killed him when we had the chance."

Lamb shrugged. "I agree . . . now."

The hour was past one o'clock, and biting back a yawn, Luc muttered, "At least we know that Townsend is in bed with Nolles and allowing him the use of the cellars at The Birches." Thinking of the contraband he'd seen that night, he added, "It's likely that a shipment will be landed sometime soon."

Barnaby looked at Simon. "Padgett wasn't suspicious when you arrived at The Ram's Head tonight?"

Simon shook his head. "No." He grinned. "In fact, I think I went up in his estimation by complaining about how stultifying it was visiting relatives."

"Do you still believe that he is one of Nolles's London investors?" Luc asked.

"I'm almost positive of it. We were in one of the private rooms, and though he left from time to time to, I assume, to take care of business, Nolles was frequently with us and treated by others, I might add, with an easy familiarity. Townsend's manner is understandable: he lives here and smuggling aside, no doubt, has known Nolles a long time. The others acted as if Nolles was a boon companion." Simon frowned. "It's been my observation that gentlemen like Padgett," he said slowly, "and the others, aren't usually on such intimate terms with the common man, a common man, that until recently, they'd apparently never met. To my knowledge Padgett, Stanton and Canfield are strangers to the area, yet . . ." He shook his head. "I can't explain it, but I'd swear that there's something going on between them and Nolles."

There was more discussion, but little else could be gleaned from the night's discovery and no practical plans to expose Padgett's suspected partnership with Nolles were laid. Mention of Lieutenant Deering was made, but any idea of apprising him of the goods stored at The Birches or that a group of London dandies might be in league with Nolles was rejected. Nolles and the London set could go hang for all Barnaby and the others cared, but Townsend's relationship with Emily made the idea of involving Deering unattractive—for now. Deciding that they could do nothing until the next shipment, and hoping to God they'd be able to disrupt it, the four men parted.

Walking Luc to his horse, Barnaby offered him a bed, but as he swung into the saddle, Luc smiled and said, "Ramstone isn't far and if Emily found me here in the morning she'd start to wonder and before long would be pestering you with questions you'd rather not answer."

Barnaby's servant returned on Sunday with a note from Mathew. Reading between the lines of the curt missive, Barnaby smiled. It didn't matter that his cousin didn't appreciate being summoned to Windmere by veiled insinuations, what mattered was that Mathew planned to arrive tomorrow.

Emily sent him a long look when he mentioned that Mathew would be arriving sometime on Monday afternoon for an indefinite stay. "If he and Simon are at odds," she murmured, "do you think having him here now is such a good idea?"

"Why not?" Barnaby asked innocently. "You know that Simon cannot bear a grudge. I'm certain he will be pleased by his brother's arrival—and perhaps a change of scenery will drive away Mathew's doldrums."

"Of course," Emily said dryly, "allowing him to stay on the estate he once thought to inherit, the site of his brother's death, will cheer him immensely."

"Stranger things have happened," Barnaby muttered and like a man avoiding a dangerous pit, he escaped out of her presence. Dealing with intelligent women, he decided, was a dicey business. He grinned. But not boring.

Emily might have been more suspicious of Mathew's sudden visit if she and Cornelia hadn't been preoccupied with plans to learn more about Mrs. Gillian Dashwood—and Luc's interest in the young widow . . . a young widow who may have murdered her husband. They had their campaign mapped out and were impatiently waiting for Tuesday when a stroke of luck came their way. After church on Sunday, as Emily and Cornelia were waiting for their carriage to be drawn up, the paths of the High Tower group and that of the ladies of Windmere converged.

Cornelia had spotted them right away as they came down the steps of the church and nudged Emily. Before Emily knew what she was about, Cornelia had stepped forward and said to Silas, "Good morning, Mr. Ordway. Lady Joslyn and I were sorry to hear of your accident, but we're pleased to see that you are recovering and able to be out and about." She tipped her head in acknowledgment of the presence of the rest of the family who accompanied their uncle. "You must be quite gratified to have your family visiting."

Silas smiled and nodded. "Thank you, Mrs. Townsend." He glanced with pride and affection at Stanley, Gillian and Sophia clustered around him. "Allow me to introduce my nephew and nieces to you and Lady Joslyn."

The introductions were made and polite chatter ensued. The carriage for the Windmere ladies arrived and good-byes were exchanged, but not before Emily had mentioned that she and Cornelia would like to call and officially welcome the newcomers to the neighborhood. "Tuesday then?" she asked, as her footman opened the door to the carriage.

Aware of the honor of being sought out by Viscountess Joslyn and her formidable great-aunt, Silas accepted straightaway, almost rubbing his hands together in glee as he watched the Windmere carriage roll away. For himself it didn't matter, but to have Stanley, Sophia and Gillian welcomed by members of the leading family in the area thrilled him.

Sophia and Stanley were equally flattered and pleased but while aware of a pleasant flutter at the introduction, Gillian couldn't quell an anxious niggle. Had Lady Joslyn and Mrs. Townsend heard the ugly gossip about her? She wasn't so vain to suppose that all of England had heard of Charles Dashwood's death or that she may have been the one who murdered him, but she knew that at the time she and Charles had been the subject of avid speculation in many circles of the *ton*. Was curiosity about the murder, and her part in it, behind their interest in calling at High Tower?

It wasn't until that evening as they climbed the stairs toward their bedrooms that Gillian was able to voice her concerns to Sophia. Reaching the landing, Gillian said, "May I have a word with you before we retire for the night?"

"Certainly, my dear," Sophia said. "Is something wrong?"

"Not exactly," Gillian muttered and led the way into the sitting room they shared. Shutting the door behind them, she asked, "Do you think that Lady Joslyn and her great-aunt have heard the gossip about me?"

Sophia sent her a look. "Does it matter?"

"Well, of course it does! Especially if their reason for calling here is to ogle the reputed murderess."

"Do you think that is what is behind their proposed visit?" Sophia asked calmly.

Gillian bit her lip. "I don't know. But if they've heard the gossip, and I'll wager they have . . . what other reason could they have for wanting to visit?" She sank onto one of the sofas, her lips set. "I-I-I don't want them coming to stare at me like a two-headed heifer at a fair."

Sophia laughed and sat down next to her. "You hardly resemble a two-headed heifer, poppet." She patted Gillian's hand. "I don't know either of the ladies, but I do know that Mrs. Smythe and everyone that we've met speak highly of them. They are both held in high esteem." Gillian nodded and Sophia went on, "You know how it is in the country— I'm sure that Mrs. Smythe and some of the other ladies have talked about us to them and aroused their interest." Gently, she asked, "Have you considered that all that motives them is simple curiosity? We *are* new to the area, so it's perfectly reasonable that they would like to know us better." She tapped Gillian on the cheek and smiled affectionately at her. "You know, my dear, not everyone listens to gossip or gives it credence. It's very possible they may have heard the gossip but have dismissed it as just that—gossip."

Gillian took a breath, a rueful smile lurking at the corners of her lips. "I am being silly, aren't I? And terribly vain to think that I am the sole reason they are coming to call."

"Oh no," Sophia said. "I do think that you *are* the reason behind their visit."

"But you just said—!"

"That you are the reason they are coming to call," Sophia interrupted serenely. "I didn't say, however, that it was because they think you are a murderess." She paused, looked thoughtful. "Of course, they may think that and simply want to reassure themselves that they are wrong."

"So you think that I am right, after all?" Gillian asked, confused.

Sophia shook her head. "Not if you believe they are coming to, er, ogle you like a two-headed heifer." Sophia laughed at the expression on Gillian's face and, taking pity on her, said, "Luc, my dear. They are coming to see you because of Luc."

Gillian stared openmouthed at her. "But what," she finally managed, "does he have to do with anything?"

Sophia glanced down at folds of her green cashmere gown and smiled. "My guess is that he has said something that gave them the idea that he has more than just a passing interest in you and they want to see for themselves just what sort of woman has caught his fancy." Rising to her feet, Sophia said prosaically, "And, of course to assure themselves that he has not involved himself with a murderess."

After Sophia's startling pronouncements, Gillian did not find sleep easy that night. It was ludicrous, she decided, to think that Luc had any interest in her beyond that of a healthy male for the nearest available female under forty. She snorted. He'd kissed her and she'd responded, but that was all it had been. Then why, asked a sly voice, were her dreams full of him? Why each night did she toss and turn and burn to know the magic of that knowing mouth on hers again and to feel those strong arms tighten around her? Why, that nagging voice asked, was he constantly at the back of her mind?

As for being thought a murderess by Lady Joslyn and her great-aunt, Gillian didn't even want to examine how she felt about that. She already knew. It was humiliating and infuriating. More so because she could say nothing, because no one would ask her outright about her part in her husband's murder and if by chance someone was bold enough to question her, anything she said in her defense was likely to be dismissed as a pack of lies. It was a battle she could not win.

Gillian woke Monday morning cross and out of sorts. Noting that she did not seem her usual agreeable self when they met for breakfast downstairs, Sophia said, "Why don't we take a ride today? The sun is out—at least intermittently—and while there are a few clouds and a bit of a breeze, it is not an *unpleasant* day. What do you say? Shall we have the horses saddled and do some exploring on our own?"

"If you wish," Gillian said indifferently, picking at her eggs and toast.

By the time she'd gone back upstairs and changed her clothes, Gillian's mood lifted somewhat. She glanced at herself in the cheval glass, deciding that despite its age, her decade-old amber velvet riding habit trimmed in black braid did not look too dowdy. She liked the way the jacket nipped in at her waist and the black braid on the cuffs, around the collar and down the front gave the garment a military air. The ruffled linen fall that draped down across her breasts needed something, a pin to keep it from flapping about as she rode, and looking through her jewelry box, her fingers lingered on the topaz and diamond brooch. Why not? It would go well with the riding habit, and reminding herself why she had kept it, hoping it would indeed act as a talisman against the charms of perfidious men, she defiantly fixed it in the middle of the linen fall. After placing a small russet hat with a long feather dyed green on her head, she left her room. Meeting Sophia in the foyer, she was surprised to find Stanley in breeches and boots standing next to Sophia.

He flashed her an uncertain smile. "If you have no objections, I've invited myself along for your ride."

There had been a time Gillian would have taken Stanley's inclusion as just another sign of his overbearing manner, but in light of their changing relationship, she accepted it for what it was: a simple offer of companionship. She smiled at him. "Now why would I refuse the escort of a handsome man?" she teased.

Several minutes later, the cousins were mounted and riding away from High Tower. Enjoying the feel of the fine bay gelding she had chosen to ride today under her and the caress of the breeze on her face, the last of Gillian's doldrums lifted. Smiling over at Sophia, astride a skittish sorrel mare, Gillian said, "You were right. A ride was exactly what I needed."

"It's good for the horses, too," Stanley added. "Uncle says that they need far more exercise than he gives them. More so since he broke his arm."

"Oh, I do so look forward to the day that he can join us. Even though he insisted, I felt guilty leaving him behind," Gillian admitted.

"We won't be gone more than a few hours," Stanley said, "and I suspect that he'll enjoy having his house all to himself."

"I suppose you're right. I hadn't thought about how things changed for him, too, with all of us living under his roof—even if it is a big house."

Sophia nodded. "I agree—we tend to think of how *we* are affected, forgetting the differences our presence in his home make for *him*."

"I think he's happy, though," Gillian said.

Riding abreast, the three cousins continued to discuss their uncle and their pleasure in living at High Tower. Casting Stanley a curious look, Gillian asked, "Will you be returning to London after the first of the year?"

"I don't know," Stanley answered, frowning. "Uncle hasn't said anything definite, but I sense that he would like me to stay and take a more active part in the running of High Tower."

"Do you want to?" asked Sophia, studying him.

"Yes, very much," he admitted. "Not that I would abandon London," he added hastily, "but beyond a few months during the Season, living at High Tower with the pair of you and Uncle Silas holds a great appeal."

"What a bouncer!" teased Gillian, her eyes laughing at him. "You actually want to live with me underfoot all the time?"

He smiled. "It wouldn't be the terrible fate I once thought. What about the pair of you? How would you feel with me living permanently at High Tower?"

Gillian grinned at him. "A few weeks ago, I would have bitten off my tongue before confessing that it wouldn't be *such* a terrible fate."

"I agree," said Sophia bestowing a look of approval on Stanley. "And it would please Uncle Silas—which should be our first objective."

In more charity with each other than at any time in their lives, the cousins continued their ride, conversing with an ease that had long been missing from their relationship.

They'd had no destination in mind when they had ridden away from High Tower, and despite the chilly and increasingly overcast day, they wandered farther afield than planned. They'd been enjoying themselves so much that they weren't aware of the passing time, nor their location, until the breeze became a biting wind and a chill rain began to fall. Halting their horses, they looked at each other in dismay, realizing that their return ride was going to be miserable—especially if the wind and rain continued.

Other than their trips to church and the brief tour that Luc had given them, Gillian and Sophia were not familiar with the area, but Stanley was more acquainted with their surroundings, although at the moment, he hadn't any idea where they were. Increasingly uncomfortable, they rode, and uncertain of their destination, to Stanley's relief, recognizing a few landmarks, he realized that they were not more than a half mile from the village. Hoping the rain would not last for long, they decided to ride on to the village and take refuge at The Crown until the weather cleared.

"Or worsens," said Stanley gloomily, eyeing the darkening sky over the Channel. "We may be in for a nasty blow. I don't think you'll enjoy riding home in the teeth of a storm."

"We won't melt," said Sophia calmly. "But if the weather worsens, I'm sure that we can hire someone from the inn to take a message to High Tower. Uncle will send Cannon with the coach for us. Do not fuss."

Stanley couldn't argue with her logic and a few minutes later, they were pulling their horses to a halt in front of The Crown. Stanley helped both ladies down from their mounts and urged them toward the door. "I'll get you settled in a private room and then see to the horses."

Gillian hadn't realized how cold and damp she'd become until she entered The Crown. Just being out of the wind and rain was a relief, but she almost purred at the wave of warmth that enveloped her as she stepped inside the tavern. A big fire blazed on the hearth, and the pleasing scent of spirits and roasting meat wafted through the air. Her stomach gave an unladylike growl, and she became aware of the fact that her meager breakfast had been hours ago and that she was hungry.

The interior of the inn was neat and tidy: the wide-planked floors gleamed, heavy oak beams dark with age crisscrossed the ceiling and lace curtains draped the windows. The room was nearly empty of customers except for a few farmers and fishermen sitting at a couple of tables near the fire. At the long wooden counter at the other end of the room, talking to the plump older woman and a pair of dark-haired smiling young women stood a tall, broad-shouldered gentleman, his back to the door. At the sound of the opening door, tankard held halfway to his lips, a grin on his face, the gentleman turned to glance at the newcomers.

Gillian's heart fluttered when her eyes met Luc's astonished blue stare.

"Tiens!" Luc exclaimed, and putting down his tankard, his grin gone, he strode across the room to meet them. "Is everything all right?" he asked, his gaze moving from face to face as he came nearer. "Your uncle?"

Already feeling guilty for almost getting them lost, Stanley wasn't happy to see Luc, and he said stiffly, "There is nothing wrong with our uncle. We decided to take a ride, but Uncle

Silas remained at home." Under Luc's steady look, Stanley found himself explaining, "The change in the weather caught us by surprise and we decided to take shelter here to wait and see if the rain lessens enough to allow us to continue home." Stanley glanced around the area, noting the interest their arrival had caused amongst the inhabitants, and clearing his throat he added, "I was hoping to procure a private room for the ladies."

"Of course," Luc said, his warm smile encompassing all three of them. "Mrs. Gilbert will be glad to provide you with one."

Mrs. Gilbert trotted up just then, her blue eyes alert and curious as Stanley made their wants known. A moment later, she ushered them into a pleasant room at the side of the inn. After finding out if the room was satisfactory and inquiring to their wishes for refreshments, she left. A moment later, one of the dark-haired young women who had been talking to Luc at the counter hurried in with a bundle of kindling, flashing them a shy smile before lighting a fire on the hearth of the old brick fireplace. In no time, the fire dispelled the faint chill in the room, and as the first young woman departed, another dark-haired young woman appeared with a tray loaded with refreshments.

Luc accompanied them when Mrs. Gilbert had shown them the room and to Stanley's displeasure seemed disinclined to take himself off. He wasn't certain how the man had done it, but it appeared that the Frenchman was now a member of their party. Listening to the light prattle as Luc charmed and disarmed the ladies Stanley sighed. No doubt the fellow would insist upon escorting them home, where his uncle would fall on Joslyn's neck with delight.

The afternoon was well advanced before the weather cleared somewhat, and although the falling wind still had a bite to it and the smell of rain was in the air, it was decided to make a run for home. And proving Stanley right, Luc joined them.

Mounted on an elegant black, as they trotted away from the inn, Luc observed, "It will be much faster if we cut across the fields than follow the road." He looked at Stanley and said apologetically, "Forgive me! I do not mean to usurp your position. Perhaps you know the shortcut, also?"

Stanley shook his head, admitting reluctantly, "I nearly got us lost as it was." Wryly, he added, "It was only by luck that we ended up at the village."

"Then if you will allow me, I will show you the quickest way to High Tower."

Stanley nodded, wishing the man wasn't so damned charming . . . and likeable.

Luc cast another glance at the threatening sky over the Channel and muttered, "If we are very lucky, my friends, we may make it to your home before the storm breaks."

Luc urged his horse forward and the four of them set off at a brisk walk. They had to traverse the muddy, winding streets of the village first before they could leave the road behind and strike out for open ground, and just as they reached the outskirts they were met by a quartet of approaching horsemen. Luc nearly swore aloud as he recognized the gentlemen: Canfield, Padgett, Stanton and St. John. The Four Horsemen of the Apocalypse would have been a more welcome sight, Luc thought grimly. War, famine, pestilence and death had nothing on these four, although, he admitted, putting St. John in that group wasn't fair. His eyes narrowed. But St. John's presence was . . . interesting.

Of these men, Miles St. John was the only one Luc had any liking for, and if not for the company the man kept, he thought they might have been, if not friends, friendly acquaintances. St. John, while part of Padgett's circle of friends, had always been cordial and polite and held himself at arm's length from some of the greatest excesses of vice practiced by the others. That St. John was here now made him thoughtful. There was sharp intelligence behind those green eyes and Luc knew from experience that St. John was nobody's fool, but those traits could be used for good or evil. . . . Was it possible that St. John was the real power behind Nolles? It was a disturbing idea.

No introductions were necessary, all of the men had all been Charles's friends and Gillian and Sophia had met them previously; Luc knew the gentlemen from his time in London. Stanley had a passing acquaintance with them, and until recently had emulated them, but that was before closer acquaintance with Canfield had shown him the error of his thinking.

Stanley had not seen Canfield since the fellow had departed High Tower, and the stiffness between the two men was noticeable. Luc gave Stanley credit for being polite, but aloof; Stanley clearly wanted nothing to do with Canfield. The reaction of the ladies was precisely the same and Luc's mouth tightened when, not at all rebuffed by his cool reception, Canfield sidled his horse next to Gillian's.

Canfield smiled and leaned over to whisper in her ear. She flushed and glanced away, her gaze meeting Luc's. The uneasiness and revulsion in those lovely eyes was obvious, and Luc reacted without thought, swinging his horse around so sharply that the hip of his horse bumped the shoulder of the mount Canfield was riding. The collision between the two horses nearly unseated Canfield and gave him something to think about other than pressing his attentions where they weren't wanted.

Canfield's horse shied violently and half-reared; it took Canfield a moment to control the plunging animal. By the time he had the horse under control, Luc had inserted his mount between Canfield and Gillian. His face red, Canfield glared at Luc. "Watch where you're going—you damn near caused an accident," he snarled.

"Forgive me," Luc said coolly, "I did not realize you were there."

Embarrassed, Canfield burst out, "Bloody Frenchman! I've a good mind to—"

"Now gentlemen," interrupted St. John smoothly, "let us not squabble in front of the ladies. No one was hurt"—he smiled at Canfield—"except for perhaps your pride. It was an accident." An edge to his voice, he added, "Let it go."

Grumbling, Canfield moved his horse to the edge of the group. The other gentlemen crowded forward to flirt with Gillian and Sophia.

"Such a shame," drawled Padgett, his icy blue eyes lingering on Gillian's bosom, "that you have hidden yourself away in the country since even before dear Charles's death. London is poorer for the lack of your delightful presence."

" 'Tis true," chimed in St. John, his lean face crinkling attractively when he smiled. "This past Season was a dead bore. However, if a pair of such entrancing ladies as yourselves would have graced the soirees and balls . . ."

Sophia laughed. "And you, sir, have kissed the Blarney stone once too often."

Green eyes smiling, St. John clutched his heart. "Nay, beautiful lady, how can you say so? I speak most sincerely. You have wounded me."

Gillian gave an amused snort at the exchange, and St. John's attention swung to her. "Do you doubt my words, fair lady?"

Gillian shook her head. "Oh no, dear sir, it would never do for me to contradict such a gentleman as yourself." The amusement in her eyes belied the demure tone.

St. John studied her for a moment, thinking that she looked quite fetching in her amber velvet riding habit. . . . His gaze sharpened and he said slowly, "That's a lovely brooch you're wearing. A family piece, perhaps?"

Gillian flushed and the amusement died from her eyes. "No. My husband gave it to me shortly before he was . . ." She swallowed. "Before he died."

"Did he now? I wonder where he purchased it."

"Good Gad," drawled Stanton. "Have done, St. John.

Can't you see you've brought up a distressing memory for the lady?"

St. John immediately launched into an apology that Gillian politely brushed aside, and while she was grateful for Stanton's interruption, she shivered when his dark eyes moved over her. Like Padgett, his gaze lingered a little too long here and there, making her feel as if she was half-naked. Canfield continued to ogle her and she was relieved when Luc brought the chance meeting to a close. She liked St. John, but Padgett was irritating, Canfield made her uneasy, and Stanton . . .

Eager to put the gentlemen behind her, Gillian kicked her horse into a gallop and followed closely behind Luc as he led them from the road and into the rolling countryside. Sophia and Stanley were right behind her.

It was a cold unpleasant ride through the falling dusk. Within minutes it began to rain in earnest again and by the time the lights of High Tower appeared, it was a shivering and wet quartet that rode into the courtyard. Luc would have departed at that point, but surprising himself and everyone else, it was Stanley who said earnestly, "Darkness is not far off and with this storm, it would be madness for you not to accept our hospitality. I suggest that you dine with us and if necessary stay the night." He smiled, the first natural smile he'd ever given Luc, and added, "Besides, Uncle Silas would have my head if I allowed you to ride away in this weather."

Luc laughed, thinking that Gillian's brother might have some redeeming qualities after all. "Thank you," Luc said. He cast an eye at the blowing rain and added, "I will accept the chance to warm myself by the fire. If the weather continues as it is, I may have to avail myself of your kind offer of a bed."

Silas was delighted at Luc's arrival with his nephew and nieces, and when Stanley mentioned his offer of a night's hospitality, Silas quickly seconded the idea.

"Of course, you'll stay," Silas said warmly. The matter settled, Silas turned his attention to his nieces. Sophia was her usual handsome self and Gillian looked fetching, her trim figure accented by the military air of her riding habit. Gillian was laughing at something Stanley said, her eyes gleaming almost gold between her dark lashes, her cheeks rosy from the cold, and noting Luc's eyes fixed on her vivid face, he smiled to himself. With the gaze of a connoisseur Silas studied Gillian once more, deciding that the topaz and diamond pin nestled against her bosom was the perfect accent. "That's a pretty bauble you're wearing, my dear," he commented.

Her smile fading, Gillian said, "Thank you. Charles gave it to me." Picking up the skirt of her riding habit she murmured, "And now if you will excuse me, I'll go change."

"That's an excellent idea," said Sophia and followed her from the room.

The two younger gentlemen also departed, Stanley to change for dinner, Luc to be shown to his room for the night. Luc had no other clothes with him, but a robe was quickly found and while he warmed himself in front of the flames on the hearth in his room, his outer clothes were whisked away to be brushed and dried by the fire in the kitchen. When his clothes were returned, Luc redressed and joined Stanley and Silas downstairs minutes ahead of the ladies.

Silas noticed Stanley's change of attitude toward Luc immediately. Throughout the evening, with satisfaction, he watched the interplay between the two younger men, noting that Stanley no longer bristled at every word Luc said and that his manner was more open and friendly. Luc was, of course, Silas thought fondly, his usual entertaining and charming self.

Silas found it a most informative evening. The interplay between Luc and Stanley was not the only thing that caught his attention. Gillian's covert glances at Luc when she thought no one was paying attention inflamed hope in his frail chest—as did the way Luc's gaze strayed repeatedly in her direction. . . . He was an old man, but he remembered well those heady first days of falling in love, the uncertainty, the sudden thrill when eyes met, the anxiety and the urgent yearning that was never far away. He smiled. Unless he missed his guess, Gillian and Luc were a good distance down that rose-laden path.

A match between his younger niece and Luc was Silas's secret and most longed-for desire. The idea hadn't occurred to him full-blown, but as he'd come to like and know Luc, the notion had crossed his mind that it was a pity that Gillian hadn't married someone like his young friend, instead of that bastard Charles.

That thought, once planted in Silas's brain, didn't go away and over the months, the more he'd considered it, the more he thought it was a perfect solution for both Gillian and Luc. Luc, because of his birth, and Gillian because of that blasted scandal, were alike in many respects. Society tolerated them, but Luc would never be welcomed into any of the great families of the *ton* and those same families would be appalled at a marriage between Gillian and one of their members.

Luc's relationship to Viscount Joslyn gave him a position and entry denied many in his situation but it didn't change the fact that he was born a bastard and had made his way in the world by his wits. Silas nodded. Luc had done well and while he might be more acceptable these days as the owner of a fine estate, it was unlikely any of the formidable matrons and high-stomached lords of the *ton* would allow him to marry into *their* families.

No, Luc and Gillian were a perfect match as far as Silas was concerned, and it was apparent, at least to him, that they were very much attracted to one another. Of course there was that troubling scandal and gossip surrounding Gillian, but he suspected that if Luc set his sights on her, his young friend wouldn't let a little thing like murder stand in his way. He grinned. A lesser man, yes, but not Luc. If he loved her, Luc would take her and the devil be damned! Luc would also, Silas decided shrewdly, move heaven and earth to prove her innocence.

Silas's gaze moved to Gillian. Luc would sweep away any obstacles in his path, but the problem, and Silas recognized that there *was* a problem, the problem was going to be his dear niece. His mouth tightened. Damn Charles Dashwood! The bastard had taken an innocent young woman wildly in love with him and twisted and trampled over those tender emotions. Offering her to Winthrop! Beneath the table, Silas's veined hands clenched into fists. By God! Besides any other crimes that could be laid at his feet, for that dastardly act alone Charles wanted killing.

It wasn't surprising that after Charles, Gillian was mistrustful of men and had no desire to remarry—and that scoundrel Canfield, he thought disgustedly, had done nothing to endear the male sex to her. Silas saw the problem clearly. On the surface Charles and Luc were painfully similar, both men being blessed with a quick charm, a handsome face and a clever mind. And both were gamblers. . . . Would Gillian, he wondered, be able to put Charles's cruel and careless indifference behind her and see that beyond generalities, the two men were *nothing* alike? Would she realize that with Luc she'd always be treasured and safe? Or would she allow the past to destroy what might be her only chance for happiness?

Chapter 14

What had been merely unpleasant weather turned into a snarling storm and when he retired around midnight, Luc was lulled to sleep by the sound of rain and wind lashing against the walls of High Tower. Once the storm passed, a few hours before dawn, the absence of sound woke him—that and a particularly vivid dream of Gillian writhing naked beneath him.

His body wound tight, knowing that sleep would prove elusive, Luc cursed, threw back the covers and, reaching for the borrowed robe, slipped into it. The garment fit snug through his broad shoulders, the sleeves stopped above his wrists and the hem hit him above his ankles, but it covered his nakedness. Tying the belt around his waist, he walked over to the dying fire and tossed on a few pieces of wood. Remembering that Meacham had pointed out the decanter of brandy and snifter that had been left for him on a small table near the bed, he walked back and poured himself a snifter.

Spotty moonlight filtered into the room from the French doors that opened onto a narrow balcony, and taking his brandy with him, he opened one of the doors and stepped outside. The night air was cool and damp, but not so cold and wet that it drove him back into the warmth of the bedroom. Clouds scudded across the sky, and with a sea-scented breeze blowing in from the Channel ruffling his black hair,

Luc stood near the stone balustrade that framed the balcony and sipped his brandy.

The trailing clouds obscured the moon, but there was enough light filtering through for Luc to make out shapes and shadows. The balcony on which he stood was one of several at the rear of the house, and he guessed each accessed a bedroom; a five- or six-foot gap between the balconies gave a measure of privacy.

As the minutes passed, the raw need that fueled the most erotic dream he'd ever experienced ebbed—as did his fierce erection—but the image of Gillian's face, flushed with desire, her soft mouth rosy and swollen from his kisses, did not.

This evening, with Gillian unbearably near, had been an exercise in torture, he decided. The candlelight had caressed her pale shoulders rising above the sage-green silk gown she wore, making Luc wonder how sweet her skin would taste at that tempting juncture where her neck and shoulder met, and her scent . . . All throughout the evening, Gillian's perfume, a blend of pinks and peonies, tickled his nose, and erotic images of lying her down naked amidst a garden of summer blooms flooded through his brain. It had indeed been an evening of torture. Torture to sit and smile and act the part of a gentleman when every nerve, every instinct, demanded he snatch the tantalizing sprite from her home and family and, using her body as he willed, ease the hunger that clawed through him. At least, he reminded himself, he'd been able to control that mad impulse. He grimaced. Barely.

He took a slow swallow of his brandy, considering his obsession with Silas's niece. There were two solutions, he finally concluded, and neither one pleased him. He could marry her, take as his wife, a woman suspected of murdering her husband. Or he could take her to bed, seduce the niece of his good friend. *Diantre!* What in hell was he going to do about Gillian Dashwood?

Feeling as near bewitched as he'd ever been in his life, Luc scowled. The honorable thing would be to marry her, he ad-

mitted, but he balked at shackling himself to a woman suspected of murdering her first husband. A question popped
into his mind. If she had murdered her husband, why, he
wondered, had she done so?

An arrested expression on his handsome face, he stared
into the night. Emily and Cornelia had repeated what they
knew of the affair, both admitting that it was only gossip.
Gossip that had credence in fact: Charles Dashwood was
dead and he'd been murdered. But had his wife murdered
him? Was it possible her story of being struck on the head
after finding Dashwood dead was true?

Luc's lips twisted. Ah, Christ! The woman *had* bewitched
him. Here he was making excuses for her, grasping at straws.
Her poor murdered husband had probably made excuses for
her, too, he thought disgustedly, right up until the moment
she'd stuck a knife in his ribs. But that didn't change Luc's
basic problem. He wanted her. And he suspected he was willing to risk his life to have her.

Moodily he stared out into the darkness. There was another solution, he admitted finally; he could simply walk
away from the temptation Gillian presented. Cut the connection to Silas and the inhabitants of High Tower. He scowled.
He had too much fondness for Silas to do that. His friend
would be hurt and wouldn't understand why Luc no longer
came to call.

Lost in his thoughts, he was unaware of the click of a door
as it opened onto the balcony next to his, nor did the movement of a slight figure drifting toward the edge of the balcony
catch his eye. It was the scent . . . the scent of pinks and peonies that broke his concentration.

At the first whiff of that evocative scent, the image of
Gillian as she'd been in his dream, naked and writhing beneath him, leaped into his mind, and he was instantly and in-
furiatingly erect once again. Certain the scent teasing him
was his imagination and proof of how far gone he was, he
snarled, "*Zut!* I am mad."

The feminine gasp from the next balcony spun him in that direction. His breath caught. Standing on the twin to his balcony, wearing a filmy white garment, was Gillian. It was too dark to see her face clearly, but the small form and the cloud of dark hair swirling around the slender shoulders identified her—that and the scent he thought of as hers and hers alone.

Since the moment she'd laid eyes on him at The Crown, Gillian had been painfully aware of Luc Joslyn. She tried to ignore him, tried to ignore the sudden thump in her heart, the leap of her pulse whenever their eyes met, but to no avail. He fascinated her, and though she fought against it, she could not keep her eyes off him. It didn't matter whether it was that lean, dark face, the broad shoulders or the elegantly muscular body—they all held her in thrall. All through the evening she'd endured the forbidden images of his features taut with desire and his beautifully masculine hands fondling her breasts before sliding lower. . . .

Her whole body aroused, her nipples peaking beneath her chemise and gown, heat and moisture pooling between her thighs, she'd bid everyone good night and fled to her rooms. But there had been no escape—he'd come to her in dreams, and when she'd woken with the memory of his mouth on hers and his big body locked with hers, she hadn't been surprised.

What did you expect? she demanded, as she'd left her bed and shrugged into a lacy wrapper. That you'd dream of angels and cherubs after an evening spent being seduced by the mere presence of Luc Joslyn? She snorted. She couldn't even blame him. Not once had he done anything but treat her politely. Damn him!

Knowing that sleep was impossible, and glad that the storm had passed, she pushed open her French doors and stepped out into the night. The breeze cooled her cheeks and ruffled her hair as she walked to the edge of the balcony. Leaning against the stone parapet, she stared blindly into the darkness.

Until he'd spoken, she'd been no more aware of Luc on the next balcony than he had been of her. To find the object of her dreams standing only feet away sent a wave of color flying over her face. Across the space that separated them, she stared at him, her lips half-parted in shock and despair.

Leaving his snifter on the edge of the railing of the balcony, Luc walked the short distance to the gap between the two balconies. Ignoring the surge of heat in his groin at the sight of her, he asked, "Trouble sleeping?"

"Apparently so," she muttered. Jerking her gaze away, she stared into the night, her thoughts scrambling.

"At least the storm has passed," Luc said and cursed his dull tongue. She was lovely in the cloud-dappled moonlight, sable hair loose and tousled, drifting around her shoulders, the diaphanous wrapper rippling in the sea breeze. A sudden gust flattened the garment against her body, revealing every line, every curve of the dainty body that bedeviled him, and Luc's mouth went dry. Hunger slammed through him and he could think of nothing but how much he wanted her.

"Yes, it has," she replied. Against her will, she found herself drifting toward him. Opposite Luc, she halted, the gap and the railing around the balcony the only barrier separating them.

In the shifting moonlight they stared wordlessly at each other, neither one able to form a coherent word or thought. Almost a tangible presence, desire swirled in the air between them, Gillian aware that underneath his robe that he was naked; he just as aware that only the thinnest of garments prevented her from being as bare as she had been in his dream.

The memory of that dream, of her face flushed with desire, blotted out everything in Luc's mind but the need to have her. Heedless of the danger, he bounded to the top of the railing and in one fluid movement leaped the distance that separated them.

Gillian had only a second to step back before he was there

in front of her. The next instant, she was swept into his arms. His mouth came down hard and demanding on hers, and she trembled as she was crushed against that muscular form, her breasts flattened against his chest, her mouth invaded and conquered.

She had no thought of resistance, no thought of denying him. Her arms fastened around his neck, her body pressing closer to his, her tongue meeting and tangling with his. The insistent nudge of his rigid member thrilled her and helplessly she arched against him, aching to know him fully.

Luc's hands dropped to her bottom, and cupping that firm flesh, he lifted and pulled her tighter to him. They swayed together, each movement an agony and a delight. His hands holding her pressed against him, his mouth devoured hers, his tongue thrusting urgently into hers, mimicking the motion of his hips.

This was no gentle seduction and Gillian reveled in it, reveled in the frantic movements of his body, the seeking exploration of his tongue. Already aroused by her dream, his touch was fire to tinder and she was aflame, her fingers tearing at the belt of his robe, the need to feel him inside of her overpowering.

Consumed by the same primitive prompting, Luc lifted her clothing, his hand sliding warmly up one leg until he found the damp heat between her thighs. He explored, his fingers burrowing through the springy mat of hair until he found her silken core. Teasing her, his knuckles brushed against that delicate opening, before slowly, deliberately thrusting a finger into the welcoming heat, her excited moan inciting him. He stroked deeper, harder, and she stiffened and cried low as she convulsed helplessly around his fingers.

The need to find his own satisfaction almost had him lowering her to the floor and fitting his body to hers, but a spark of sanity remained, and aware of their location, he dragged his hand away from her sweet center. Swinging her up into his arms, he carried her through the French doors into the privacy of her bedroom. Gillian made no protest, her kiss as hungry as his, and her tongue, an arrow of fire darting into his mouth, banished all thought but one from his mind: he *must* have her. More by luck than instinct he found the bed in the darkness and, dropping her, followed her down to the mattress.

Clothes were thrown off and in seconds warm, silky feminine flesh was sliding against hot, hair-roughened male skin. She was soft and willing in his embrace, arching up and inviting his caress, her fingers moving through his dark hair down to his shoulders and across his back to his tight backside.

Luc shuddered as she explored the curve and shape of his buttocks, and his mouth dropped to her breast, sucking her nipple. Nuzzling the generous breasts, he muttered, "You taste like peaches—ripe, summer peaches, warm and fragrant and oh, so very sweet." His mouth fastened on her nipple and he bit down gently, sending a spear of pleasure soaring through her and her fingers dug into his buttocks.

"You like that, eh?" he murmured. "What else do you like, *m'amie?*" He shifted slightly, and his hand traveled down to the junction of her thighs. Deliberately, he parted the tight curls, and once again finding the damp silk, he thrust one then two fingers inside of her. The clenching of her body around his fingers and the rising of her hips gave him his answer. His voice thick, he said, "I like it, too. I like tasting you and feeling your readiness for me."

Gripped by a passion she had never felt before, wild to have his body sunk deep within hers, Gillian's hand closed around his thick shaft. "And you," she managed. "You are as ready as I am."

"More," he growled and, in one fluid motion, rolled onto his back, taking her with him. Astride him, his hands on her hips, he slowly lowered her onto his member, groaning at the wet heat that met his invasion.

He was well endowed and Gillian had a momentary qualm at his size, but the hunger to have him, all of him, had her pushing down to meet his upward thrust. She gasped as her body stretched and accepted the broad length of him. Experimentally, she wiggled around, the feel of him buried within her exciting and arousing. Reveling in the sensation of having *him* beneath her, she slowly rocked, hardly moving, each shift of her body sending shocks of pleasure spiraling through her.

Luc bore her teasing movements as long as he could, and when he feared losing control, his hand closed around the back of her neck and he pulled her mouth down to his. Against her lips, he said, "Ride me, *amante*. Ride me hard or slow, but dear God! *Ride me!*"

A husky laugh was her reply, but to his relief, she rose above him and then sweetly slid back down onto his shaft. Her movements were still tantalizingly slow, teasing both of them, building the heat and tension between them.

Luc let her have her way, the pleasure of that tight, hot body locked around him almost more than he could bear, but he didn't want it to end. Not yet. Her soft breasts swayed in front of him and he reared up and, capturing one in his mouth, suckled hungrily on the nipple. She gasped as the heat of his mouth and tongue on her nipples increased the pleasure curling through her, and she moved on him faster, rushing toward the edge. He fought against the demand to join her, and feeling her clench around him, feeling the shudder of release that racked her, he smiled tightly.

Dazed, Gillian slumped down onto his chest, aftershocks of the most powerful pleasure she could ever remember rippling through her. Never, she thought, astonished, not once had she experienced such voluptuous fulfillment with Charles.

Keeping their bodies locked together, Luc flipped her over onto her back, and coherent thought vanished when his mouth came down hard on hers. She was only conscious of him: his taste, his scent and the wondrous feel of his body on hers. He gripped her hips, and holding her to his liking, his big body drove into hers, forcing her higher and higher toward another crest. With each slide, each thrust of Luc's body, the magic between them grew, and this time when she cried out and shattered around him, Luc joined her in the glory, his growl of satisfaction adding to the intensity of the moment for Gillian.

Luc kept their bodies merged, his lips moving lazily across hers, his warm body resting against hers. He'd had many women, enjoyed many women in his lifetime, but none had ever given him such primitive pleasure as he had just experienced in Gillian's arms. Despite having just depleted himself in her, he was conscious of a stirring desire, a fierce prompting to hear again her cries of pleasure, and with her writhing beneath him, once more find that sweet oblivion.

Knowing he needed at least a few minutes to recover, regretfully he disengaged their bodies. But not for long, he thought, conscious of desire stirring beneath the lethargy of utter satisfaction that left him momentarily boneless and sated. No, not for long, he promised, not for long. Lying on his back, he dragged her up beside him on the bed and bit down gently on her ear. "You're a witch," he muttered. "And I very much fear before this night is done, I must have you again."

Delight hummed through her, and feeling more feminine and powerful than she ever had in her life, she wiggled next to him, her thigh flung over his hips, her lips tracing the hard line of his jaw. His frustrated groan pleased her.

Gillian amused herself, her fingers sliding through the curly mat of hair on his broad chest. He was so very different from Charles, she thought, bemused, his chest wider, more muscular and far hairier. She nearly purred as she explored, liking the feel of the coarse hair and the feel of the warm muscles beneath the hair. Finding his nipples, she plucked at them until they were hard buds. As the minutes passed, encouraged by his response, her hand slipped lower and she gasped when she found him hard and ready.

Luc turned in her hold and his mouth caught hers. His teeth worried her bottom lip and his hands closed on her buttocks, jerking her closer to him. "See what you have aroused, Madame?" he breathed against her lips. "And having done so, you must bear the consequences."

This time there was not the frantic need to couple, and they made slow, lazy love to each other, exploring each other, their bodies moving together seamlessly, their mouths locked together. But in the end, blind desire dominated, and they moved together urgently, each desperate to find succor from the hunger that savaged them. Feeling the swell of ecstasy rising within her, Gillian tightened around him, pushing him over the edge. With one last, deep thrust, Luc took her with him and together they found the splendor.

Luc didn't remember falling asleep, but when he woke, sunlight was streaming into the room. Gillian, one rosy-tipped breast pressed against his arm, lay by his side, and mesmerized, he stared down into her sleep-softened features. She has bewitched me, he admitted grimly. How else to explain his actions? His passion for her had compelled him to break the habits of a lifetime, to ignore the respect he had for Silas and to besmirch his own honor.

He rubbed his eyes and sighed. Propping himself up with a pair of pillows, his hands behind his head, he considered the prospect in front of him. It was going to be a long, difficult day, he decided, and his life was never going to be the same. His gaze dropped to Gillian. Nor was hers.

The opening of the bedroom door had him stiffening and he cursed. It was bad enough that he had seduced his friend's niece, but to be found in her bed . . . He closed his eyes. Christ!

"Gillian, my dear, aren't you awake yet this morning?" asked Sophia, walking briskly into the bedroom. "Out of bed with you, sleepyhead. Don't forget that we have a guest staying with us."

Unaware of Sophia's presence, Gillian woke and oblivious to the tall, very masculine body next to her, stretched luxuriously. Her eyes collided with Luc's and with a squeak she sat up, explicit memories of last night flashing through her brain. She couldn't pretend that she hadn't been a willing participant in what had occurred between them, but things done in the dark of night look very different in the searing light of day, and she was filled with embarrassment and just a little appalled at her own actions. Jerking the blankets to cover her nakedness, she glared at him and hissed, "What are you still doing here?"

"What was that, dear?" asked Sophia, coming around the end of the bed.

Sophia halted as if having run into a stone wall, and her lips forming a round O, she stared at the pair in the bed.

Horrified, Gillian scrambled from the bed and searched frantically for her gown and wrapper. Finding the garments on the floor where they had been thrown, she scrambled into them.

Luc remained motionless on the bed, his hands still behind his head, his naked chest rising above the tangle of blankets. His face expressionless, he stared back at Sophia.

Sophia looked at him, and he flinched at the flicker of disappointment in her eyes.

"I'm going to marry her," he growled, wincing at the defensive note in his voice. "I'll speak to Silas this morning."

Sophia nodded. "Yes, I expect that would be best."

"What?" demanded Gillian, looking from one set face to the other. "What are you talking about?"

"Why, only that Mr. Joslyn will do the honorable thing and ask our uncle for your hand in marriage," said Sophia calmly, having recovered her usual aplomb and, now that she'd had a moment to think about it, not entirely displeased with the turn of events. She smiled. "Uncle Silas will be delighted."

"Are you mad?" Gillian asked, aghast. "I'm not marrying anyone." She glanced at Luc, her heart pumping at the knee-weakening sight of that beautiful masculine chest and the intent expression in those azure eyes. Dragging her gaze away from him, she snapped, "And I'm certainly not marrying a gambler!"

Spying his borrowed robe on the floor, she picked it up and threw it at him. "For heaven's sake, put something on."

"Whether I am clothed or naked as the day I was born," Luc said, "it doesn't change anything: we will be married."

Gillian's chin lifted. "I am not," she enunciated from between clenched teeth, "going to marry a man whose reputation at the gaming table has earned him the title of 'Lucifer.'" Bitterly, she added, "I was married to a man who beggared me with his gambling habits. I do not intend to find myself in that position again."

Taking the robe she'd thrown at him, he slipped it on and standing up, finished wrapping it around him and tying the belt at the waist. His face grim, he stalked over to her. In a cold voice, he said, "I was born a bastard and I swore that no child of mine would ever suffer that fate. It is unlikely that I planted a child in you last night, but I am unwilling to take the chance. We will marry."

Gillian started, staring wide-eyed at him. The prospect of a child had not yet occurred to her. For a second an odd sort of joy burst through her, but then common sense asserted itself. It had only been one night, and she reminded herself, she and Charles had been married for nearly nine years and in all that time she had never conceived.

"I think you forget that I may very well be barren," she said quietly. "I was married for several years and there was no child from that marriage."

"It doesn't matter," Luc said, not happy with the jealousy that ripped through him at the reminder that she had once loved another man and had married him. His voice harder than he meant, he said, "Honor demands that I marry you. There are no excuses for what I did last night, and I must make what reparations that I can. Marriage is the first step."

Gillian shook her head. "No. I will not marry you." A stubborn glint in her eyes, she added, "There is nothing you can say that will make me accept you as my husband."

Luc's mouth twisted. "As a lover you have no complaint, but you will not take my name?"

She flushed, memories of the previous night streaking across her mind, but managed to mutter, "There is no need for us to take such a drastic step." She swallowed. What she was about to say went against the grain, went against everything she had tried to be, everything she believed in, but she could see no other way to convince him that marriage wasn't the only option. "There are many widows who have lovers, and the world doesn't expect them to marry the men they take to their beds," she said with an airiness she didn't feel. "This is no different."

Sophia gasped. "*Gillian!* You don't believe that."

"It doesn't matter whether I believe it or not, I am *not* going to marry him," she said. Almost pleading, she added, "It was only one night, Sophy. No one else, except we three, knows what occurred. Surely we can keep it a secret and forget it ever happened?"

"And if you are with child?" Luc asked coolly.

Gillian nearly stamped her foot. "I already told you: based on my previous marriage, it is unlikely."

He strolled up to her. Tipping her face up with one finger, he stared down into her willful features. "You may be willing to take the chance; I am not. I will speak to your uncle."

Before she could say another word, he walked over to the door opening onto the main hallway and stepped out of the room. Through the open doorway, both women heard him say, "Ah, good morning, Meacham. I believe that the ladies will be most grateful for the restorative powers of the tea you bring them."

Gillian moaned and closed her eyes. Her fate was sealed.

* * *

Within the hour, Silas had the facts before him. Leaving a stunned Gillian to partake tea by herself and with a pleased smile on her face, Sophia had immediately sought out her uncle and told him what had transpired; Meacham confirmed the meeting with Luc outside Gillian's rooms. Swearing them both to secrecy, he dismissed Meacham, but signaled for Sophia to remain. He considered the situation while Sophia waited. It was very bad of Luc, and Gillian should have known better, but in the end, he decided that his uppermost emotion was satisfaction.

Gillian's stated refusal to marry Luc worried him, though. "Will the marriage make her unhappy?" he asked Sophia. Uncertainly, he added, "They should marry, and it is my dearest wish that they do so, but I cannot force her to marry him if this marriage will bring her misery. I would not see her married to a man she despises."

Sophia snorted. "She's in love with him, for it is my belief that she never would have allowed him in her bed if she *wasn't* in love with him." Considering the situation, she said, "Marriage to Charles did nothing to make her view the wedded state with anything but revulsion. . . . Charles may have besotted her in the beginning, but his indifference to her and his gambling destroyed her affection for him. And, of course, that despicable bargain with Winthrop did nothing to make her cherish his memory." At Silas's nod of agreement, she went on, "Luc Joslyn may be a gambler, but he is nothing like Charles. . . . She is just being stubborn and allowing the fact that Luc is a gambler to keep her from what I am confident would be a happy marriage."

Silas sighed. "Well, there is nothing I can do about that. Luc is a gambler and a damned good one." He shot Sophia a keen look. "She does remember how I came to own High Tower, doesn't she? Surely, that should be a reminder that not all gamblers are like her husband. Or does she put me in the same category?"

Sophia shook her head, smiling. "She adores you and never gives your gambling a thought. We both agreed that it was a tragedy that the young man who gambled away his inheritance committed suicide, but that wasn't *your* fault." She tapped her lip. "She may be reluctant to marry Luc, but she *did* sleep with him. . . ."

Silas brightened. "Of course, there is that. . . ."

Luc was aware that Sophia and Meacham would have reported to Silas what they had seen, and he couldn't pretend that he wasn't uneasy and a little apprehensive as he knocked on the door to Silas's library an hour later. His cravat felt as if it was choking him, and guilt stabbed at his vitals. He was very conscious of his betrayal of his friend, but was determined to rectify the situation the only way he could.

Silas managed to keep a stern expression on his face as Luc stood before him and pled his case, but inwardly, it was all he could do not to leap up and slap him on the back and congratulate him. Would he have wished the offer for Gillian's hand had come about in a more traditional manner? Certainly, but he wasn't going to repine over the circumstances that saw Gillian married to Luc.

When Luc finished speaking and stood stiffly before him, Silas only tortured him for a few minutes. Unable to hold back the grin that had been threatening to break forth since Luc had entered the room, as it spread across his lined features, Silas exclaimed, "My dear boy! Allow me to be the first to congratulate you."

"It was very bad of me, Silas," Luc admitted. "But I swear to you that I will do right by her, and that as my wife, Gillian will never want or be mistreated." He shook his head. "I have no excuse. It was dishonorable and not the act of a gentleman."

"Oh, pshaw! Don't act so namby-pamby, it don't become you," retorted Silas. "Yours won't be the first marriage that came about because you allowed passion to overcome you."

He waved a teasing finger in front of him. "Now if she'd not been married before and had been a decade younger, I might feel differently about it, but as it is . . ." Silas beamed. "I'm delighted!"

"She doesn't want to marry me," Luc stated baldly.

With Sophia's words ringing in his ears, Silas smiled slyly. "I suspect that she will change her mind after she's had a chance to think about it. I'll talk to her. Make her, ah, see sense."

Having been requested to see Silas in his library, with far more trepidation and embarrassment than Luc, Gillian entered the room. Her uncle was seated behind his ornate walnut desk, and instead of the condemnation and disappointment she expected to see, there was only affection and kindness in his gaze. "Sit down, my child," he said, indicating the brown leather chair next to his desk. The skirts of her mulberry woolen gown fluttered around her feet as she settled into the chair. When she looked shyly at him, he smiled and said, "Now tell me what you want to do about this little difficulty before us."

Gillian had thought of little else since Luc walked out of her room. The idea of marriage to Luc, to anyone, turned her world upside down. She'd never thought to marry again, and if she had, it would have been to some older, staid gentleman—or so she had told herself. She'd never thought to fall in love again, but if she had, she'd have sworn it wouldn't have been with someone like Luc. Yet, she couldn't deny what was in her heart. He'd fascinated her almost from the moment she'd laid eyes on him, and she couldn't pretend that she hadn't been drawn to him or that her pulse didn't jump at the sight of him. She'd tried to resist him, reminding herself that, like Charles, he was a gambler and not to be trusted. To no avail, she thought miserably. Luc Joslyn might not be the man she wanted to fall in love with, but willy-nilly she had. She loved him. Regretfully. Unwillingly. Shamefully so. And she very much feared she'd love him forever.

It would be folly to turn her back on him. Foolish folly to spurn what was offered her. Did she tremble at putting her fate in the hands of a man who placed his faith on the turn of a card? Oh yes, she did. But she also realized that life was a gamble and that if she ventured nothing, she gained nothing. In the time she'd paced in her rooms and considered the situation, she'd concluded unhappily that there was just a bit of a gambler in her. Fate demanded that she marry Luc Joslyn and take her chances.

Head bowed, she said softly, "There appears to be nothing for me to do but marry him." Her gaze met Silas's. "I will accept his hand in marriage."

Silas, of course, couldn't be happier. Once he had her decision, he rang for Meacham and asked his butler to see if Mr. Joslyn would join them. "Oh," he said as Meacham prepared to leave, "and bring some champagne! We have an engagement to celebrate. Mrs. Dashwood and Mr. Joslyn are to be married."

Luc took the news expressionlessly and only he knew of the sudden leap of his heart, the keen edge of anticipation that ripped through him at the knowledge that Gillian had agreed to marry him. There were details to be worked out to be sure, and he didn't pretend that there wouldn't be rough roads ahead, but the fact remained: before many more days passed, Gillian would be his wife.

Chapter 15

The family gathered in Silas's library, and though Sophia acted her part, only Stanley was truly astonished by the news of the engagement. "What? What?" he spluttered. "Gillian and Joslyn? Betrothed? By Jove! How did this come about?" He glanced at Gillian, standing beside Luc, and asked, "Is this some sort of jest?"

"It is no jest," answered Luc. "Your sister has done me the honor of accepting my hand in marriage. We will be married by special license by the end of the week."

As taken aback as Stanley by that news, Gillian shot Luc an astounded look, but before she could speak, Silas chimed in with, "Excellent idea, my boy! Excellent!" Guessing Gillian would object, Silas glanced at her and added innocently, "Unless, of course, my dear, you want a large wedding with all the fuss and furbelows like you had when you married Charles."

It was ham-handed of Silas, but it had the effect he wanted. Gillian's protests died on her lips. The last thing she wanted were reminders of her marriage to Charles. A special license and the deed quickly done had its appeal. If she was doomed, she thought bitterly, to marry Luc Joslyn, she might as well get it over with.

"Upon my soul!" exclaimed Stanley, further rocked back on his heels by this turn of events. "Have you all gone mad?"

Perplexed, he stared at Gillian. "This is extraordinary news. First I hear you are engaged to a man you have hardly known a month, and now I learn that you will be married within a few days."

With her usual calm, Sophia said, "You may not have been aware of what was happening beneath your nose, but Uncle Silas and I have been very aware of Luc's courtship of Gillian and have been anticipating an announcement for several days. As for the special license and the length of time they have known each other . . ." She shrugged. "Fiddle-dee-dee! They're neither in the first blush of youth, and they're old enough to know their own hearts. There is no reason for them to wait and put up with all the nonsense a big wedding would entail." Over her champagne flute she regarded Stanley. "In fact, I think marriage by special license is the best solution. You wouldn't want all the gossip and speculation about Gillian's first husband to arise, now would you?"

Luc hid a grin. Again it was ham-handed, but Sophia had put forth the one argument that would carry weight with Stanley.

Appearing much struck by his cousin's commonsense attitude toward the situation Stanley nodded. "Yes, yes, of course, I see what you mean." Forcing a smile, he raised his flute. "A toast! Let us drink a toast to my dear sister and her husband-to-be."

The toast drunk, not many minutes later the library was empty except for Luc and Silas. Grinning, Silas said, "I think we brushed through that rather well, don't you?"

Luc half-smiled. "As well as could be expected, but I suspect that Stanley is going to want a private word with me."

Silas waved a dismissing hand. "As her brother, you can't blame him, but he's accepted that you're going to marry her and that it will be done by special license." His grin widened. "Gillian accepted the idea of the special license, too."

"With a bit of maneuvering on your part," Luc commented dryly.

"Needs must when the devil drives."

Luc couldn't argue with him about that. The devil was indeed driving them, but he could not regret it. Telling Barnaby and the rest of the family wasn't something he looked forward to, though. Gillian's reputation might cause dissension within his family, but he hoped, after their first astonishment at his news, that it would not cause a fatal breach. If it did, his heart would be torn, but his first loyalty would be to his wife—no matter what the gossips said about her. He would, however, he thought with a grimace, take care that she didn't murder him.

Thinking of the fate of her first husband, he wondered if perhaps he wasn't mad. Why else would he be so determined, and he admitted that he *was* determined, to marry a woman many thought had murdered her husband? Again, the question occurred to him: had she murdered Charles Dashwood? Or was she an innocent condemned by gossip and innuendo? Instinct told him it was the latter, but only a fool would ignore the possibility that his bride-to-bride was a clever murderess. He wished he knew more of the circumstances surrounding Charles Dashwood's death. It was something he would have to look into . . . later.

Luc was persuaded to stay for a light repast before he departed for Ramstone. It can't be said that it was a comfortable setting, and only Silas and Sophia enjoyed themselves. Throughout the meal Stanley sent confused glances between Gillian and Luc, and Gillian looked more like she was on her way to the guillotine than a woman newly engaged. Luc's face betrayed nothing other than polite interest in the proceedings.

They finished eating and Luc was on the point of taking his leave when Meacham entered the room. Meacham bowed and murmured, "Lady Joslyn and her great-aunt have come to call." He cleared his throat. "I put them in the formal salon."

Caught up in the events of the morning, the proposed visit

by Lady Joslyn and Mrs. Townsend had been forgotten, and a dismayed silence met Meacham's announcement. Luc hadn't known about it and the news that Emily and Cornelia were here, now, poleaxed him.

Silas recovered first, and rising to his feet, he said heartily, "Splendid! Their arrival could not have been more fortuitous." Smiling at Gillian and Luc, he urged, "Come! Let us share our good news with them."

Sophia echoed her uncle's sentiments. Standing up and shaking out the skirts of her gown, she said, "This couldn't have worked better, don't you agree?" She beamed at Luc. "Naturally, you'd want to tell your family right away."

"Naturally," Luc murmured. It was his right to marry who and when he pleased, but he hadn't been looking forward to exploding the news of his sudden engagement in the faces of his relatives, especially not Emily and Cornelia. It had been Emily and Cornelia who had related the gossip about Gillian to him, and only a simpleton would expect them to welcome her into the family without reservations. Their approval or lack thereof changed nothing, but . . . He grimaced. The family had to know, and soon, about the changes coming in his life, but he'd have preferred to speak to Barnaby first. Men took such things, he thought wryly, with so much less, ah, *commotion.*

Wishing he were facing a pair of murderous rogues rather than two women held dear to his heart, Luc walked with the others toward the formal salon. Meacham led the procession, Sophia and Silas next, with Luc and Gillian following them and Stanley coming up in the rear. Reaching their destination, Meacham threw open the double doors and waved the family into the salon.

Emily and Cornelia were seated on a rose damask sofa, and as the others entered they looked up expectantly. Luc's eyes narrowed at the faint expression of guilt that flashed across both women's faces when they spied him amongst the Ordways. Now what, he wondered, do they have to feel guilty about?

In the flurry of greetings and initial chatter it soon became apparent to Luc that the female members of his family had been snooping. Amusement flickered through him. Today was certainly going to be a revelation to them.

Allowing Silas to take the lead, beyond dropping a kiss on Cornelia's and Emily's cheeks, Luc stood back and watched the proceedings. Sophia and Emily settled in a pair of cream-and green-striped silk chairs across from Cornelia and Emily. Silas selected a high-backed chair in green velvet situated between the sofa and the pair of striped silk chairs; Stanley stood at one end of the fireplace; Luc, an arm resting on the gold-veined marble mantel, lounged at the other.

Silas waited until Meacham had reappeared with refreshments, and once everyone had been served and the butler departed, he said jovially, "You may wonder at being served champagne punch."

"Yes," said Cornelia, "we consider it a celebratory beverage." Having drawn her own conclusions from Luc's presence, her brow lifted and she asked bluntly, "Are we celebrating something?"

Silas's eyes twinkled. He'd always liked Cornelia Townsend and admired her quick intelligence. No matter what her feelings about Luc's engagement to Gillian might be, she would prove an able ally. "As a matter of fact we are," he said. "Mr. Joslyn has offered for my niece, Mrs. Dashwood, and has been accepted." He beamed. "You could have knocked me over with a feather: we just learned the news ourselves this morning."

Emily's heart sank. Dear, dashing Luc to be married to a suspected murderess! Oh, it was dreadful. And how would Barnaby react when he heard the news? Hiding her dismay and anxiety, she forced a smile. "My, how, how . . . exciting. Just this morning, you say?"

Taking a line from Sophia, Luc said, "I know it comes as a surprise, but Gillian and I know what is in our hearts, and at our age we decided that there was no need for a long courtship."

"Of course," Cornelia agreed, her sharp hazel eyes on Luc. "You're both so long in the tooth that you must not squander a moment."

Luc grinned. "I knew you would understand."

Knowing when the deck was stacked against her and not wishing to start a rumpus, Cornelia snorted and merely said, "Then let us drink a toast to the engaged couple." The toast drunk, her gaze shifted to Gillian. Pretty enough gel, she thought, studying Gillian. A little thing and looks as innocent and demure as a novice nun. Staring at the delicate features, the ethereal frame, Cornelia had trouble picturing Gillian as a murderess. But perhaps the wench was exceedingly clever? Or was she a victim of gossip? Hmmm. There was some sleuthing to be done here, Cornelia decided, and with her far-flung net of friends she was just the woman to do it.

Uncomfortable and not very happy with the situation, but determined not to offend Luc, Emily said brightly to Gillian, "Well, this must be a thrilling time for you. My congratulations to you both. Er, when do you expect the wedding will be?"

Luc's relatives were being polite, but Gillian sensed that neither woman was genuinely pleased with the news that she was to marry Luc. Thinking if positions were reversed that she'd feel much the same, she didn't blame them, but inwardly she quailed.

They had no reason to clasp her to their bosoms with joy, she admitted. They knew little about her. Mostly likely, she thought, wincing, what they did know wasn't flattering. Charles's murder aside, she was a stranger to them, a widow of no particular means or status while Luc's brother was the Viscount Joslyn, the wealthiest and most powerful man in the area. Oh, and don't forget, she reminded herself, that Luc had just purchased a handsome estate and would be considered a handsome catch by many. Suspicion of her motives wasn't surprising, and the idea of telling them that she and Luc would be married by special license only made her heart sink lower. Now, she thought mournfully, she could add fortune hunter to her title of murderess. Filled with misery, cursing the folly of last night, the weakness that had propelled her into Luc's arms, it was all she could do not to leap to her feet and run from the room.

Pride and spirit came to her defense, and meeting Emily's gray gaze, she said, "We had not quite settled the date." She swallowed painfully and added, "L-L-Luc is obtaining a special license, so I expect it will not be many days off."

Cornelia choked on her punch. "A special license?" she croaked.

Even more aware than Gillian that Emily and Cornelia were not overwhelmed with happiness at his engagement, Luc strolled over to stand behind Gillian's chair. His hand resting possessively on Gillian's shoulder, he regarded his female relatives with blue eyes that held a distinct warning. "Yes," he said. "We do not want a long engagement; a special license best suits our needs. I intend to ride to London tomorrow." His eyes dropped to the top of Gillian's sable hair. "My bride-to-be was naturally reluctant, thinking it unseemly to be married in such a manner, but I convinced her that it was perfectly respectable and that there was no reason to wait. I told her that my family would understand and applaud our decision." His eyes lifted and he stared levelly across at Emily and Cornelia, daring them to contradict him.

Cutting through the tension that crept into the room, Silas leaned forward, saying genially, "We thought, perhaps, Saturday? That will give Luc time to ride to London to obtain the license and return. And, of course, time enough for Gillian's things to be transferred to Ramstone. Naturally, we'll have to speak to the vicar to determine if that date will be convenient for him to perform the ceremony, and your wishes as to the date must be taken into account." He smiled. "We want everyone to be satisfied."

"You seem to have the matter well in hand," Cornelia commented, setting down her cup of punch with a snap of the wrist.

The heaviest ground behind them, Silas settled back into his chair. "At the moment it may seem so," he explained, "but you must understand that we are at sixes and sevens here ourselves. The news caught all of us by surprise."

At least that much was the truth, Luc thought ruefully.

Somehow they managed to get through the rest of the visit without any embarrassing or upsetting incidents. Resigned to Luc's marriage, Emily and Cornelia were all that was polite and fell in with the plans put forth by Luc and the others, but it was with relief that they were finally able to take their leave and escape.

But they didn't escape Luc. His announcement that he would accompany them back to Windmere filled both ladies with dismay.

"Oh, that isn't necessary," exclaimed Emily, dying for a private word with Cornelia. "You must have many things to discuss with your bride-to-be." A half smile curving her lips, she said, "We won't tell his lordship. *You* may do that."

"And the sooner I tell him, the better," agreed Luc. He cocked a brow. "Will you deny me your charming company on the ride to Windmere?"

There was nothing for it, but to accept the inevitable. Shortly, his horse tied to the back of the closed carriage that the ladies had taken to High Tower, Luc, Emily and Cornelia departed.

As the coach rattled down the road on its way to Windmere, Luc leaned back against the blue velvet squabs and said, "Well? Out with it! You both look like you're going to burst."

"Oh Luc!" Emily wailed, unable to hide her distress. "Are you very sure that you want to marry her?" Her eyes big with horror, she added in hushed tones, "What if she did, indeed, murder her husband?"

Luc brushed that question aside. "Is that your only objection to her?" he asked, his gaze fixed on both women as they sat across from him in the carriage.

Cornelia's lips thinned. "It's rather a large one, wouldn't you say?"

Luc sighed. "I don't disagree, but you admitted that all you really know about the murder of her first husband is gossip. Perhaps the gossip is wrong."

Neither lady looked totally convinced, but Cornelia shrugged and Emily made a face. Luc leaned forward. "The murder aside, I mean to marry her. Is it going to cause a problem?"

"I am too old and too fond of you to cast you out of my heart because I think your choice of a bride is unwise," Cornelia muttered. "I'll not throw a rub your way, and until she gives me reason to act otherwise, I will treat her with politeness and respect."

Emily nodded. "We love you too much to allow your marriage to come between us." She smiled faintly. "We want you to be happy, and if Gillian Dashwood makes you happy . . ." She swallowed. "Then we will be happy for you."

It was as much, even more than he expected. A crooked smile curved his lips. "Thank you." His expression thoughtful, he admitted, "Considering the gossip that she murdered her first husband, your objections are not without merit, but I am relieved that you are willing to give her a chance."

"Do *you* think she killed her husband?" Emily asked, her gray eyes anxious and curious at the same time.

Luc shrugged. "I have seen nothing that would lead me to believe that she is capable of such an act." He paused, frowning. "It would be understandable if she did murder her husband for her family to close ranks behind her, but I doubt they would seek close association with her. I have not discussed it with Silas, but I do not think he would have such deep affection for her or have her living with him, let alone be so happy about our marriage, if he thought that she had killed her husband. Her cousin, too, appears very loyal to her, and it has been my observation that Mrs. Sophia Easley is an astute and intelligent woman. I do not think she would ally herself with a murderess." He stared out the window at the passing countryside, considering Stanley and the tension he had sensed in the beginning between Gillian and her brother. "I know there was an estrangement between Gillian and her half brother of some sort, perhaps in connection with her husband," he said eventually, "but of late they seemed to have put their differences behind them. I do not think such would be the case if Stanley believed or knew she had killed Charles Dashwood."

"I agree with you," Cornelia murmured. Her eyes bright with challenge, she added, "It is my intention to write to . . . friends to glean what I can about the murder—and Charles Dashwood."

Luc tipped his head in her direction. "I thank you for that, Madame."

"Wait until I hear what my friends have to say," Cornelia commented dryly, "before you thank me. You may not like what I discover."

Upon arrival at Windmere, once the ladies had been shown into the mansion and disappeared upstairs to their rooms, Luc had gone in search of his half brother. He found Barnaby in his study. Waved to a chair by the fire, once Luc was seated comfortably and greetings exchanged, he plunged into the reason for his visit.

Barnaby took the news of Luc's engagement without a blink. The information that Luc would be leaving for London in the morning to obtain a special license and that the wedding was planned for Saturday at High Tower raised an eyebrow, though.

"Special license? And marriage on Saturday?" Barnaby asked carefully from his seat across from Luc. "Not that it's any business of mine, but is there some reason for this haste?"

His long legs stretched out in front of him toward the warmth of the fire, Luc grinned. "You're right it isn't any of your business."

Barnaby grinned back at him. "Well, that certainly puts me in my place." He rubbed his chin. "Gillian Dashwood, hmm. I don't believe I've the pleasure of meeting the young woman. Tell me about her."

There was no reason to prevaricate and every reason to tell Barnaby everything, and without hesitation Luc did so, leaving out only the circumstances that led to the sudden engagement.

When Luc finished speaking, Barnaby studied his half brother for a long, unnerving moment. Having come to some internal decision, Barnaby shrugged. "Far be it from me to give you advice when it comes to matters of the heart." He smiled. "So far I find that marriage agrees amazingly well with me—I trust it will be the same for you."

"No words of warning about the folly of marrying a woman some think murdered her husband?"

"Would you listen?"

Gillian's sweet face, her eyes drowsy with desire, shimmered in front of Luc, and an explosive mixture of lust and tenderness slammed through him. Shaking his head, Luc muttered, "I fear not."

Barnaby chuckled. "If that is the case, then allow me to extend my heartiest congratulations and express the wish that you have a long and happy life together."

"*Merci.*"

There was a tap on the door, and at Barnaby's answer Mathew Joslyn wandered into the study. Expecting to find Barnaby alone, Mathew halted a few steps into the room. "Oh. I beg your pardon, I didn't know that Lucian was here."

The eldest of the English Joslyns, Mathew's resemblance to

Luc was striking, clearly revealing a common ancestor in their background. Both men possessed the tall, athletic bodies, the thickly lashed azure eyes and classically handsome features for which the Joslyn family was famous—as did Simon and Lamb. Barnaby, on the other hand, bore only passing resemblance to the others, having inherited from his part-Cherokee mother her dark complexion and gleaming black eyes. While all of the Joslyns were tall men, Barnaby and Lamb were the tallest, standing half a head above the others and their builds were broader. Luc, Mathew and Simon stood within half an inch of each other, and the Joslyn family features were so strongly stamped on the three of them that strangers might mistake them one for the other. Thomas, Mathew and Simon's dead brother, had borne the same family features.

Watching Mathew and Luc greet each other like cats willing to be friends, but wary, Barnaby smiled. They had all come a long way since he had first arrived in London over a year ago to take the title Mathew had thought was his, and much had happened in that intervening time. Warmth flooded through him when he thought of one of those events—his marriage to Emily. Their child would be born before many more weeks passed, and he was elated and anxious for the arrival of the infant. To hold his child in his arms had become one of his greatest desires.

Luc had not seen Mathew for several months, and he was shocked at the changes he saw. Lean and elegantly muscled like all the Joslyns, Mathew was noticeably thinner and his patrician features more finely drawn, the usually brilliant azure eyes appeared dull, glazed. To Luc, Mathew was a stranger, having only been in his company a few times prior to Thomas's death and since the funeral not at all, but even he could see that the man was greatly changed from his first meeting with him earlier in February. Thomas had died in March.

From comments made by Barnaby and Simon, Luc knew

that Mathew had taken Thomas's death and his part in it hard, but until he'd seen the man, he hadn't realized the depth of Mathew's grief. Luc glanced at Barnaby, thinking of his emotions should something happen to his half brother . . . if *he* brought about his death . . . and his heart clenched with such anguish, his knees nearly buckled. Understanding and sympathy flooded through him, and his thoughts of Mathew were far kinder than they had been in the past. Thomas may have been a villain but Mathew had loved his brother and to have killed him . . .

The initial greetings dispensed with, and hoping to arouse a spark of interest in Mathew, Luc said, "I hope that you will wish me happy. I am to be married on Saturday to Mrs. Gillian Dashwood, Silas Ordway's younger niece."

Mathew forced a smile. "I congratulate you." His voice infused with a heartiness he didn't feel, Mathew added, "I understand that other congratulations are in order also—Barnaby told me of your purchase of Ramstone."

Luc nodded. "Thank you."

Mathew shook his head, a faint smile curving his handsome mouth. "You Americans! You certainly move swiftly. In England only since February and already you have bought an estate and are about to marry. Again my congratulations!" Seating himself in a nearby chair, Mathew said, "Barnaby and I are not the best correspondents, but surely I should have heard word of your engagement. When were the banns called?"

Barnaby looked at Luc with a cocked brow. Luc sighed.

"Ah, there was no calling of the banns," Luc confessed. "We will be married by special license. I leave in the morning for London to obtain it and plan to return on Thursday." The flicker of interest in Mathew's eyes should have pleased him, but he found himself cravenly wishing that some other news had caused it.

"Really," drawled Mathew, his eyes fastened on Luc's face. "How, er, enterprising of you." It was obvious Mathew had questions, but he politely refrained from asking them. He did, however, inquire, "Do you have your introduction to a bishop?" When Luc looked startled, he added, "It's required, you know." At the expression of dismay that crossed both Barnaby's and Luc's faces, he added with a genuine smile, "No, I didn't think so. Have no fear, I know a bishop and I shall be pleased to accompany you to London and introduce you. What time do you plan on leaving in the morning?"

Brushing aside Luc's profuse thanks, Mathew said, "I haven't been to London since . . ." He swallowed. "Since Thomas died. An overnight trip will be just the thing to remind people that I am still alive." To Barnaby, he said, "You don't expect anything to happen with Nolles while we are gone, do you?"

Barnaby shook his head, his face thoughtful. "Beyond some heavy gambling amongst Padgett and the others, Simon said that everything appeared normal at The Ram's Head last night. And Lamb reported no activity at The Birches." He cast a look out the window at the patches of blue sky. "The barometer is holding steady since last night's small storm passed, so a run is unlikely tonight or even tomorrow night." He grinned. "You and Luc should be back in time to join in any excitement that might arise."

Eventually Luc took his leave, and having made arrangements to meet with Mathew early tomorrow for their trip to London, he departed for Ramstone. The door had barely shut behind him before Mathew, staring at Barnaby frowning, asked, "You do know who Gillian Dashwood is, don't you?"

"Luc mentioned the rumors associated with the death of her husband," Barnaby admitted. "He discounts it as just gossip." Barnaby's gaze sharpened. "Do you have something to add?"

Mathew leaned back in his chair and contemplated his gleaming black boots. He scowled. "Devil take it! I mislike sharing scandal broth and I'll confess that all I heard was precisely what you say, gossip." His eyes met Barnaby's. "I do know that Welbourne is an ugly customer and that those parties of his at his lodge are notorious for the excesses committed. No woman with any regard for her reputation would be caught within a mile of the lodge when the duke is hosting a, er, gathering. It's hard to come up with a reasonable excuse for Gillian Dashwood to have been there, but..." He paused, his frown deepening. "Charles was a bad 'un and he circled with a segment of the *ton* not held in the highest esteem. Until her husband's death, I never heard a hint of scandal associated with Gillian Dashwood, but then, I did not listen to half the on-dits flying through the *ton* either."

Barnaby rubbed the side of his jaw. "Luc's determined to marry her and I know my brother—objection or resistance will only make him *more* determined." He smiled. "It's been said more than once that there is a strong suspicion of mule in our background."

Mathew laughed and nodded. "Indeed. I cannot pretend that the trait hasn't made its appearance in our branch of the family either."

Despite having thrown his staff at Ramstone into an excitable state by the announcement of his coming nuptials, Luc rode away the next morning, confident that Bissell, Hinton, Mrs. Marsh and Alice had matters well in hand. When Gillian stepped foot into Ramstone, she would find no complaints.

He'd been a little wary of Mathew's offer of help in securing the special license, and aware that they were virtually strangers, he didn't look forward to the trip to London with much enthusiasm. To his astonishment, Mathew proved an amiable companion, displaying a side of himself that only his brothers and those closest to him ever saw. Behind the cool hauteur Mathew showed the world lurked an intelligent, engaging, considerate man.

Luc wasn't the only gentleman to revise his opinion of the

other. Having thought of Luc as nothing more than a skilled gambler and the black sheep of the American Joslyn family, Mathew discovered that he was wrong. For the first time Mathew glimpsed Luc's effortless charm and found himself relaxing and enjoying Luc's easy manner and amusing tales of life in America. They discussed the war with France and Mathew recognized the keen intelligence behind those azure eyes so like his own. He was intrigued by the insights Luc had gained during his time in France, and much of the ride was spent discussing England's dismal showing in the conflict so far. Both men had a common interest in horses, and Luc confessed that he was considering turning Ramstone into a stud farm. Mathew expressed his liking of this idea. By the time they reached London and the Joslyn town house, where they were staying at Barnaby's invitation, they were quite in charity with each other.

There was only a smattering of the *ton* to be found in London at this time of year, but that suited Mathew's purpose. With Luc as his guest he made an appearance at White's, stilling rumors that he had turned into a hermit. Quite the contrary. Known for his austere manner and his abstentious habits, Mathew's drinking and reckless gambling that night raised more than one eyebrow. By the time he and Luc returned to the town house in the early morning hours, he was thoroughly foxed and had lost over three thousand pounds at the gaming tables. Whether he intended it or not, Mathew could go to bed knowing that there would be no more gossip about "grief-maddened Mathew Joslyn."

Despite his aching head, Mathew arranged Luc's meeting with the bishop. Everything went smoothly, and by early afternoon, the special license tucked into his pocket, Luc and Mathew were riding back to Windmere. It was well after midnight by the time they pulled up in front of Windmere and dismounted. If Barnaby had not yet retired for the night, Luc planned a brief word with him before continuing on his way to Ramstone.

Luc and Mathew found Barnaby, along with Simon and Lamb, in Barnaby's study. One look at the three men's faces told the new arrivals that something had happened . . . and that it was not good.

"What is it?" demanded Mathew.

Barnaby waved a hand toward Simon. "Ask your brother. He arrived not half an hour ago with the news."

Both Luc and Mathew swung their gazes to Simon.

Baldly Simon said, "Canfield is dead."

Chapter 16

"*Mon Dieu!* What happened?" Luc demanded, walking over to where Barnaby, Simon and Lamb were gathered in front of the fire.

Simon stared down into the snifter of brandy he was holding. "I was at The Ram's Head with Padgett, St. John and Stanton a few hours ago, continuing to voice my boredom with Barnaby's stuffiness"—he glanced at Mathew—"and complaining of my brother's arrival, when Townsend, accompanied by Nolles, burst into the private room where we were playing cards." Simon tossed down a swallow of brandy and muttered, "Nolles looked quite cheerful; Townsend white and shaken. It was Nolles who told us that there had been a terrible accident and that Canfield, having imbibed freely while visiting at The Birches, rode too near the edge of the cliffs. According to Nolles, the three of them were on their way to join us at The Ram's Head when it happened." Simon's lips thinned. "Nolles, who did all the talking incidentally, claims that it happened in an instant and that there was nothing they could have done. Canfield's horse apparently bolted and while Canfield was trying to get the animal under control they strayed to the edge of the cliff: the footing crumbled beneath the horse's hooves and Canfield and the horse fell into the sea."

Staring at the bottom of his empty snifter as if the answer

he sought was there, he said heavily, "The body has been re-covered and the constable is already going around shaking his head about the tragic accident."

"Not surprising since Constable Ragland is suspected of being in Nolles's pay," growled Barnaby.

Helping himself and Mathew to a snifter and some brandy, Luc asked, "Now why, I wonder, did they decide to kill Can-field?" Handing a snifter to Mathew, he added, "The murder, even if dressed up as an 'accident,' is dangerous when the vic-tim is the son of a duke—even if only the second son and not the heir."

Leaving his snifter on the mahogany hunt table with brass fittings for the various bottles and decanters, Luc waved the brandy decanter toward the other four men. All four lifted their snifters. After pouring brandy into the other snifters, he set down the decanter and, picking up his snifter, wandered over to stand in front of the fire.

The others, having been joined by Mathew, were scattered in a semicircle around the gray marble fireplace, the fire warm and pleasant against the chill of the November night.

The five men drank their brandy in silence, each contem-plating what Canfield's death might mean.

Lamb, seated to Barnaby's right in one of several tall, winged armchairs upholstered in a gray and green damask, muttered, "I knew I should have been watching that blasted place tonight!" He shot Luc a glance. "I would have been if you hadn't gone haring off to London." Reminded of the rea-son Luc had ridden to London, the azure eyes narrowed and he drawled, "I understand from our mutual relative that con-gratulations are in order."

Luc flushed. "I should have told you myself, but there wasn't time."

"Of course," Lamb murmured, his tone indicating the op-posite.

Luc's mouth tightened, but before Luc and Lamb could fall out, Barnaby said quickly, "Were we wrong about Canfield?

Perhaps he was not part of the smuggling operation after all?"

"Or," Mathew said, "for the first time in his life Nolles is telling the truth and it was an accident." He stared disapprovingly at Barnaby. "Have you forgotten that your wife's cousin was with Nolles and Canfield tonight? I know he doesn't have a good reputation, but do you honestly believe that Townsend would turn a blind eye to murder? Especially the murder of the son of duke?"

Barnaby and Lamb exchanged glances. They knew things about Townsend that the others didn't. Townsend would, indeed, condone murder, as well as abduction and attempted rape, to save his own skin . . . and he had already done so. If not for his timely intervention, Barnaby thought viciously, it wouldn't have been *attempted* rape. If he and Lamb had not arrived when they did that night, Townsend would have stayed cowering in the barn so he wouldn't hear Emily's screams when Ainsworth raped her. His fingers clenched around the fragile stem of the snifter, almost snapping it. We should have killed him that night, he admitted, and not for the first time.

Simon frowned, saying slowly, "From what I've observed, I think that Townsend is too deeply in Nolles's power to do anything but agree with whatever Nolles wants."

"Oh, don't be ridiculous!" snapped Mathew. "I'll grant that you're probably right about Padgett and Stanton being involved with Nolles in some way, but I have trouble believing that Canfield has, had, any part in an illegal operation." Mathew shook his head. "I never liked any of them, and I never understood Tom's affinity for their company." Pain bloomed in the blue eyes, and he said thickly, "I understand it now and I think it is more than reasonable to assume that the three of them, Nolles, Padgett and Stanton, are involved in smuggling, but not Canfield. Good God! The man is, was, the son of a duke, and though he was known for his dissolute ways, I maintain that he would not lower himself to do business with a common smuggler."

Bluntly, Simon said, "Do not forget, that our brother *lowered* himself to do business with Nolles. Do you think that Canfield's ideals were higher than Tom's?"

The stark anguish on Mathew's face had them all looking away. There was a moment of silence and then Mathew said low, "You're absolutely correct. A man with Canfield's reputation probably wouldn't hesitate to join in a lucrative operation like the one Nolles is running here."

"It would be interesting," Lamb said idly, "to know the exact spot where Canfield lost his life."

"Why?" asked Luc, sending him a keen glance.

"Oh, just that earlier this year, I think it was January, Townsend's dear friend Ainsworth came to a nasty end over those same cliffs," Lamb answered. "As I recall they were both foxed when Ainsworth went over the cliffs into the sea. A remarkable coincidence, don't you think, that Townsend should be around the second time when a drunken friend of his, an acquaintance if you will, takes a dive off the cliffs?"

An arrested expression on his handsome face, Mathew said, "I'd forgotten about Ainsworth's accident."

"But why did they kill Canfield?" demanded Simon. "A falling-out amongst thieves?" His expression troubled, he asked no one in particular, "St. John just arrived a few days ago . . . could his appearance have anything to do with Canfield's death?"

"I don't know any of them well, but I've been puzzled by St. John's apparent friendship with the others," Luc admitted. "He always seemed the odd man out to me, but the thought crossed my mind that he could be the leader of the group. Frankly, the others haven't impressed me with their powers of acumen."

Both Mathew and Simon nodded, Mathew saying, "I don't disagree. I've always dismissed Padgett and Stanton as dilettantes, and while St. John does join them from time to time, I do not think of him as being one of their set." He smiled crookedly. "St. John was the only one of Tom's friends who found favor with me." He looked away. "I'd hoped that he would be a good influence on my brother and wean him away from Padgett and the others."

"I think," said Simon carefully, "that you're forgetting that Tom and Nolles already had a partnership. . . . Even someone like Padgett could follow the path that Tom forged."

Mathew nodded, his expression bleak. "I keep forgetting Tom's part in all this."

They speculated on the situation for another hour, before Luc set down his snifter and rose to his feet. "We're going in circles. We can agree that Nolles and Townsend most likely murdered Canfield, or at the least, Townsend went along with the murder, even if he didn't do the deed himself. I think we agree that Padgett, Stanton and Nolles are partners in the smuggling. St. John's the wild card. He may be part of the partnership and he may not. Why Canfield was murdered, or if he was murdered, is open to argument, and based on the facts we have before us, it is unlikely we will come to a conclusion tonight—" He glanced at the ormolu clock on the mantel and, noting the time, corrected, "This morning." Biting back a yawn, he concluded, "Gentlemen, it is late and it has been an eventful few days for me. I am afraid that I must seek my bed." He sent a sleepy-eyed glance around the room. "As you know I am to be married within a day and have much to do to see that all is in readiness for my bride."

Barnaby strolled with him outside where his horse waited. Watching Luc swing into the saddle, Barnaby said, "You could stay the night here, you know."

Luc grinned at him. "Afraid to let me ride home by myself?"

Barnaby sighed. "Perhaps a trifle. What with Canfield's

death, I doubt that Nolles is thinking of wrecking vengeance on any of us right now, but . . ."

Luc's grin faded and he said softly, "But Nolles is going to have to die sooner or later, isn't he?"

Barnaby nodded and stood watching his brother ride away into the night for a long time.

While Luc had been away, the ladies of Windmere and Gillian's family had been busy arranging the wedding. Feeling like an onlooker, Gillian was present during many of the planning sessions, but the whole affair held a dream-like quality to her. She was to be married . . . to Luc Joslyn. How could that be? She barely knew the man. A flush stained her cheeks as memories of the night they had spent together riffled through her brain. Oh, she *knew* him all right, but she didn't *know* him.

Only half-listening to the plans being made for her marriage to Luc, her thoughts drifted. She'd married Charles in a dewy-eyed haze, in love with love, while with Luc . . . Her heart twisted in her chest. Older and wiser than she had been at eighteen when she married Charles, she was conscious that the emotions Luc aroused within her were deeper, stronger and more powerful than anything she had ever felt for Charles. She'd been positive when she married him that Charles had been the love of her life, but she knew differently now. Luc touched her in a way that Charles never had, and that knowledge terrified her. She should be paying attention to the plans being discussed, yet all she could do was wonder about Luc and their future together.

This afternoon, she, Silas and Sophia were visiting at the vicarage with the vicar and his wife, and lost in her own thoughts, Gillian stared down at her clasped hands as the conversation whirled around her. She loved Luc; she could not deny it. And because she loved him, she'd consented to the marriage. Luc desired her, wanted her, and she was aware that her body gave him pleasure, but once passion was slaked, would he come to resent her and the manner of their marriage? Her future would be in his hands . . . would he treat her gently through the years or would she find herself married to another man like Charles? One who valued her not at all? She wondered if Charles had ever loved her or if he hadn't had his eyes on her fortune right from the beginning. She shivered, remembering anew her horror and disgust when Winthrop had revealed how little Charles had valued her and their marriage.

"Are you cold?" asked Penelope kindly, having noted Gillian's shiver. "Shall I send a servant for a wrap for you?"

Gillian forced a smile and shook her head. "That won't be necessary. I'm fine."

They were seated in a charming lived-in room at the front of the vicarage. The chairs and sofas were covered in soft worn yellow chintz: the once brilliant colors of the rug on the floor had faded to shades of antique rose and pale green. Small oak tables were scattered here and there, a basket of knitting spilled onto the floor near one of the chairs, a rag doll lay slumped in the corner of the sofa and a desk littered with papers was against the far wall. Signs of refreshments, tea, coffee and little ginger and lemon cakes, rested on a big pewter tray on a low table in front of where Penelope sat.

Penelope sent her a long look, but then with a smile, she turned back to the conversation at hand, nodding at the vicar's proposal that the marriage take place at the vicarage. Patting Gillian's hand, Penelope said quietly, "Cornelia and I have discussed it and we think this would be best." At Gillian's surprised look, she added, "There will be enough gossip about the suddenness of your marriage as it is; the ceremony being performed here will lend an air of normalcy about the whole affair."

Gillian could only nod, grateful for the kindness and understanding of both the vicar's wife and the formidable Cornelia Townsend. The two older ladies were doing their best to put as respectable face on the situation as they could and her heart warmed.

When Gillian retired to bed that Wednesday night, it was with the knowledge that, except for a few minor details, the arrangements were settled. With Barnaby's approval, Emily and Cornelia were hosting a dinner for the engaged couple on Friday night at Windmere. The vicar's suggestion that the actual marriage ceremony take place at the vicarage at eleven o'clock in the morning on Saturday had met with universal approval by everyone involved. Bursting with pride, Silas announced that a celebration breakfast at High Tower would follow the nuptials.

Except for overseeing the packing and the removal of her things to Ramstone there was little for Gillian to do. Sophia and Silas were as excited as a pair of children at Christmas, both of them beaming at her, as if she'd done something wonderful. Stanley was not as caught up in the excitement as his cousin and uncle, but he did nothing to put a damper on things, although Gillian caught him studying her more than once. Wondering at the purple shadows under my eyes, no doubt, she thought unhappily.

The inhabitants of High Tower, involved in the preparations for the wedding and Gillian's move to Ramstone, didn't learn of Canfield's death until late Friday morning when Luc came to call. Shown into the morning room where the family had been enjoying a late breakfast, Luc showed few signs of his swift trip to London and back.

The azure eyes under the thick black brows were bright and clear, and he had the look of a man who found the world to his liking as he strode into the morning room. Beyond one lightning glance at Gillian, his attention remained on the others.

Gillian's heart leaped at the sight of him, that swift, possessive appraisal thrilling and terrifying her at the same time. She was glad his attention was on the others, for it allowed her to drink in the sight of that tall, muscular body and the darkly handsome features. From beneath lowered lashes, she stared at him, thinking he looked magnificent in a form-fitting dark blue coat with brass buttons, his black hair waving near his temples. Dear God! Tomorrow they would be man and wife.

Even when Luc smiled at Silas and took the seat her uncle indicated, she could not tear her gaze away from him. He mesmerized her. Damn him!

"All went well?" Silas asked.

Luc nodded. "Mathew Joslyn accompanied me to London and smoothed the way. The special license is safely purchased—have no fear of that."

"Well, my boy, you're not the only one who has been busy these past few days," Silas announced gaily. "We have made all the arrangements." Quickly, he related the plans that had been laid.

Luc found nothing to fault. "*Bon!* You have matters well in hand." He glanced at Gillian, catching her staring at him. The quick look away and the flush that stained her cheeks pleased him; the dark smudges under her eyes did not. The lady was not sleeping well and he was certain that their coming nuptials were the reason. He sighed inwardly. Their fate was sealed the moment he had taken her into his arms, carried her into her bedroom and made love to her.

Sophia finding them abed hadn't changed anything: he'd known that marriage would be the result of that night of madness . . . and passion such as he had never known. They would be married tomorrow and there was nothing he could do about it. Stunningly he realized that even if there had been a way not to marry her that he wouldn't have taken it. With no little astonishment, he admitted that he *wanted* to marry her.

The conversation was general for several minutes before Luc begged a private word with Silas. Assuming it had something to do with the business end of the marriage, in particular money, Silas nodded, and a moment later, he and Luc left the others and retired to Silas's study.

Taking a comfortable chair by the fire, Silas said, "You know, of course, that Gillian will not come to you penniless. She doesn't know it yet, but I have settled a nice little sum on her and there is the cottage and three acres she inherited from Charles in Surrey."

Luc didn't care if Gillian came to him naked as the day she was born, but he understood that Silas's pride demanded he provide a dowry for his niece.

"That's very good of you," Luc said. "I have already set up the accounts for her pin money and household expenses."

They came to an understanding, and with that out of the way, Luc introduced the reason he wanted a private word with Silas: Canfield's death. He did not mention that there might be more to Canfield's death than met the eye.

Hearing the news, Silas stared goggle-eyed at him, exclaiming, "Upon my word! This is shocking. Just last night, you say?" He shook his head. "I didn't like that young man and I always suspected he'd come to a bad end." He took in a deep breath. "It isn't very nice to say, but I am glad he was not staying here when it happened. I was most relieved to see the last of that young rakehell and couldn't be happier that whatever friendship existed between him and my nephew had ended." Silas frowned. "He was a stranger to the area, and when he and Stanley had their, er, disagreement, I expected him to head back to London. I cannot imagine what interest our little corner of Sussex held for the likes of him."

Luc shrugged. "London is rather quiet this time of year. Perhaps Canfield was simply rusticating, seeking peace and enjoying a respite from all the hurry and flurry usually to be found in the city."

"At The Ram's Head?" Silas snorted. "If it was a respite he was after, he'd have been better off at Mrs. Gilbert's Crown. Less expensive, better company and without the lure of the deep gaming I've been hearing from Stanley goes on at Nolles's place these days."

Canfield's death worried Silas. Not the young man's death, although he deplored it, but the whereabouts of those blasted vowels of Charles's that Canfield had won from Winthrop. Where were they? he wondered uneasily. It wouldn't do for them to fall into the hands of strangers. Silas moved restively. Once Gillian married Luc those debts became his, and if those damnable vowels surfaced . . .

Silas eyed Luc. Should he warn him? He shied away from that. It wasn't his tale to tell. Yet he was uneasy hiding the existence of those vowels from him. It smacked of dishonesty. His first loyalty, he decided heavily, was to Gillian, but he didn't like the idea of handing her the problem. It was his duty to shield and protect her, but he didn't see how he was going to do that.

Luc noticed his introspection and asked, "Sir? Is something troubling you? Your arm?"

Though he still wore the black sling, he barely paid any heed to his healing arm. The physician had said only yesterday that it wouldn't be long before he could dispense with the sling altogether.

Shaking his head, Silas said, "No, no, the arm is healing fine. I was, ah, just thinking about Canfield's death. It'll come as a shock to my nephew and my nieces."

"Would you like me to tell them?" Luc asked. "It would be best if the news is not delayed. I'm sure by now word has spread through the village."

"Yes, perhaps it would be best if the news came from you. They'll be full of questions and I'd have to defer them to you anyway."

Rejoining the others in the morning room shortly, at a nod from Silas, Luc said gravely, "I'm afraid that I arrived with bad news. I've already told your uncle and we determined that there was nothing to be gained from hiding the truth from you."

Both women stared at him with big eyes and anxious expressions; Stanley regarded him with a frown. Taking a deep breath, Luc said, "It is my unhappy task to inform you that Lord George Canfield died last night in a fall over the cliff near the Seven Sisters."

The ladies gasped, horror on their pretty faces. Stanley stiffened and stared hard at Luc. "An *accident?*" Stanley questioned sharply.

Luc looked at him and nodded. "Yes. He was with Squire Townsend and Mr. Nolles and apparently the three of them had imbibed a bit too freely. Canfield's horse acted up too near the cliff's edge and unfortunately horse and rider went over."

It was very hard for Gillian to work up much sympathy for Canfield, but while she despised him, she hadn't wanted him dead and she said softly, "Oh, what a sad fate. I'm sure his family is devastated."

"To be sure," chimed in Sophia, although she suspected that perhaps only his mother would mourn Canfield's passing. She glanced at Stanley. Her cousin was trying very hard to put a good face on it, but even a fool could see that while he was shocked, Canfield's death didn't affect him.

Unaware of it, Stanley echoed Silas's remark. "I'm sorry to learn of his death, but I can only be glad that he was no longer staying here."

Canfield's death held their attention for a brief time and then the conversation shifted to the dinner at Windmere this evening.

Gillian sent Luc a shy smile and murmured, "Lord and Lady Joslyn and Mrs. Townsend have been most generous in offering to host a dinner for us tonight." A blush stained her cheeks. "They didn't have much time to plan it, but I understand that the response has been gratifying."

Luc laughed, his white teeth flashing in his dark face. "Refuse an invitation to Windmere? No one in the neighborhood would dare—Cornelia would come after them with her cane."

Silas chuckled. "Indeed, her cane is a great incentive to do exactly as she wants."

Luc offered to escort them to Windmere, but Silas waved him away. "Oh, pish-posh! With Stanley and myself at her side, your betrothed is quite safe. There's no reason for you to ride all the way here, then to Windmere and back again before riding to Ramstone. We'll see you there." He winked at Gillian and grinned at Luc. "After eleven o'clock tomorrow morning she will be your responsibility. Until then allow an old man that pleasure."

Gillian's ruffled look made Luc laugh, and after agreeing with Silas, Luc said, "Until this evening then." And departed.

Emily and Cornelia had drawn up their list of dinner guests very carefully. It was not to be a large gathering, but they wanted to ensure that Luc and Gillian suffered as little ostracism as possible that the sudden marriage by special license might cause amongst the local gentry. Lord and Lady Broadfoot could be relied upon to treat the newlyweds with friendliness—Luc's activities with young Harlan that night was not forgotten. Sir Michael and his wife, the parents of Barnaby's house steward and secretary, Tilden, could be counted upon to do whatever they could to smooth the path of Barnaby's half brother and his bride. And, of course, Vicar Smythe and his imperturbable wife, Penelope, would do everything in their power to ensure the gentry welcomed the young couple to their ranks. Naturally, Simon and Mathew would be present and neither Emily nor Cornelia doubted that they would close ranks behind Luc and Gillian.

"At least the numbers are even, if not the sexes," Emily murmured as she went over the guest lists that Friday afternoon.

"Can't be helped. Sixteen for dinner is enough for a 'family' party." She smiled at Emily. "Especially with you looking as if you could go into labor at any moment."

Emily giggled. "I don't look that bad, do I?"

Cornelia stared at her great-niece with deep affection. The pregnancy was well advanced, but except for the impressive mound where her stomach had been, Emily looked as lovely as she ever had. There was sparkle in the gray eyes, her skin glowed and there seemed to be a constant, happy flush to her cheeks. Marriage and pregnancy agreed with her and Cornelia thanked God every day for sending Barnaby into their lives. And Emily, she added with a smile, for having the good sense to fall madly in love with him. It had helped, she thought, that Barnaby had been equally, madly in love with her great-niece.

Thinking of Barnaby and Emily and their happiness, she frowned. She had a soft spot in her heart for the gambler Luc and had suffered some anxious moments since learning he was set on marrying Gillian Dashwood. Hearing he'd bought Ramstone had pleased her and she'd hoped that a suitable wife would appear on his horizon before too long. Her lips twisted. She hadn't expected one to appear within days and Gillian Dashwood didn't precisely fit her idea of "suitable." But Gillian was the woman Luc had chosen, for whatever reasons, and she had her suspicions about *that,* and Cornelia would do her best to accept his choice. All she wanted, she admitted, was for Luc to find the same sort of happiness Barnaby and Emily shared and she wasn't convinced, not yet, that Gillian was going to provide it. Time would tell and by God, she thought, if she makes him miserable . . . Her fingers tightened on her walnut cane and her eyes narrowed. I'll just have to put a spoke in her wheel, she decided, an unholy smile on her face.

"What are you thinking?" Emily demanded, seeing that smile.

"Oh, nothing, nothing in particular," Cornelia replied, her

expression changing in an instant to one of guileless innocence. "Now what do you think of some hothouse lilies for the table tonight?" she asked, distracting Emily.

Gillian had not been looking forward to dining at Windmere. Not only did she shrink from what she feared would be a gauntlet of critical eyes, the news of Canfield's death had shaken her. Like her uncle, once the initial shock of Canfield's demise had passed, her thoughts turned to those damnable, *damnable* vowels.

Even as she bathed and dressed for the evening, her attention was on the whereabouts of Charles's vowels. Had Canfield left them in London? Or had he brought them with him? At this very moment, was someone going through his belongings at The Ram's Head and finding them? Misery balled in her chest at the idea of *another* person laying hands on them. Charles might be dead, but the thousands of pounds those vowels represented were still a debt to be paid.

As the carriage bumped and rattled its way toward Windmere, she only half-listened to the conversation between Silas and the others, her thoughts on those vowels . . . and Luc. The man she was marrying tomorrow. A horrible thought crossed her mind. As her husband, since she did not possess the means to retrieve them, it would fall to Luc to make good on that debt. Compelled by convention to marry her, Luc might now be dunned for payments of her late husband's vowels. She faced a wicked dilemma. Should she tell him? Before they married? Or wait and pray to God the vowels never surfaced? Her lips drooped. The latter was unlikely to happen. The vowels existed, and someone, sooner or later, would find them. What a wretched coil!

Slapping a smile on her face and rousing her failing spirits, Gillian stepped from the coach. Like a soldier girded for battle, she entered Windmere. To her amazement with all the unpleasantness lurking at the back of her mind, Gillian enjoyed the dinner at Windmere and basked in the approval and friendliness being showered upon her. She'd have been an ill-tempered Jade beyond pleasing, she reminded herself, not to have found the evening delightful.

Everything was beautifully prepared, from the white linen expanse of the table, to the exotically scented pink and white lilies and lacy green ferns that graced it. The food was superb, each elegant and delicious dish followed by another more elegant and delicious than the first: Beef à la Royal, buttered lobsters, leg of mutton with cauliflower and spinach, pullets with chestnuts and several side dishes. And the company! These people raising their glasses in toast after toast were aristocrats, the elite of the area, and they had come to honor her and Luc, she thought, flattered and much affected. Something approaching joy bubbled through her, and for just a bit she was able to put away her doubts and forget all the troubles that beset her.

Her eyes bright, a dazzling smile dimpling into view, she pretended that Luc loved her and for a precious few moments convinced herself that their marriage was going to be gloriously happy. Her gaze slid to Luc, and beneath her apricot and champagne silk gown, her heart thumped pleasurably. The candlelight picking out blue glints in his black hair, his teeth flashing in his handsome face when he laughed and wearing a burgundy coat with black lapels, his cravat glistening whitely against the fabric, he looked every maiden's dream.

It was late in the evening when Lord Joslyn put her hand on his arm and murmured, "Allow me to steal you away for a few minutes and show you my conservatory." He smiled. "I'm told that it is superb."

With quaking nerves Gillian allowed Viscount Joslyn to guide her away from the others, knowing it wasn't to see the justly famous Joslyn conservatory that he'd cut her out from the rest. Strolling through the exotic plants—banana trees, orchids and tropical ferns—Barnaby said, "It's all a bit overwhelming, isn't it?"

Gillian peeped up at him. She was aware that he wasn't

talking about his conservatory, but seeing the kindness in his dark eyes, she muttered, "You must think our marriage is rather sudden."

"It is, but nothing my brother does surprises me much." His gaze intent upon her face, he asked bluntly, "Do you love him?"

Caught off guard, the truth popped out before she could stop it. "Yes, I do."

She could be lying, but Barnaby thought not. He'd sprung the question on her deliberately and the look in her eyes and the huskiness of her voice told him as much as her answer. Gillian Dashwood might come with a questionable past, but the only thing that mattered to Barnaby was whether she loved Luc or not. He'd noted the looks she'd lavished on Luc tonight when she thought no one was looking, and he'd been confident her affections were involved, but he'd wanted to hear her say the words and judge for himself her sincerity.

He eyed her critically, thinking that she was a taking little thing. Luc was certainly smitten. Barnaby had reservations about the suddenness of the marriage and Luc's choice, but he was going to have to trust Luc's instincts . . . and his own. From all he'd seen and heard, though she came with some baggage, he decided she might do very well for Luc.

Barnaby patted her hand. "Good! Luc deserves to be loved." He winked at her. "Even if at times he arouses within one the most barbaric and unloving urge to throttle him." Smiling more warmly at her than he had all evening, he added softly, "Welcome to the family, my dear."

Chapter 17

Upon Gillian's return to High Tower, Silas asked for a private word with her. A spurt of unease darted through her as she followed her uncle into his study and took the chair he indicated. Seated behind his desk, the gentle smile he sent her way banished her unease.

"Tomorrow you will marry Luc Joslyn," he began, "and I admit that it is my dearest wish. I am very fond of both of you, and almost from the moment I met him, I thought that he would make you a good husband."

She stared at him in astonishment. "You wanted me to marry him?"

"Indeed. I can think of no other man who would suit you as well."

"But he's a *gambler!* Just like Charles."

"No, my dear, Luc is many things, but he bears no resemblance to your late and, I must confess, unlamented husband." Fixing a stern eye on her, he said, "Luc gambles, but he is not a gambler in the truest sense of the word. I've watched him over the months and I know the difference. His success is proof of what I say. He does not play foxed, or throw good money after bad—especially when the cards run against him. I *have* seen him put a small fortune on the table over the course of an evening when luck was on his side, but

I've never seen him wager more than he can afford to lose. You'll not find *his* vowels scattered all across England."

"And that's supposed to make me feel better?"

"It should. Luc may have his faults, but you need never fear that he will place you in the position that Charles did." His face hardened. "Either leaving you as near to penniless as makes no never mind or expecting you to whore to pay off his debts." His expression softened. "I don't bring this up to distress you, my dear, but to make you understand that we are talking about two entirely different men. If I thought for one moment that Luc would use you badly, scandal be damned, I'd do everything in my power to prevent the marriage."

She stared down at her hands folded in her lap. "Thank you for that," she murmured, comforted by his words. Perhaps Luc wasn't like Charles, but Charles's vowels certainly haunted their prospects for happiness. Meeting her uncle's eyes, she said, "The vowels . . . with Canfield dead, who knows where they may surface."

He sighed, nodding. "We were foolish to think that the problem had gone away simply by your moving in here. The vowels were still out there and we should have done something to wrest them from Canfield's hands."

"Ever since we learned of Canfield's death, those vowels have been on my mind—I don't know what to do," Gillian confessed. "Should I tell Luc? And when? Right before I marry him tomorrow morning? Or right after?" She glanced away. "It is bad enough that I'm marrying him with hardly more than the clothes on my back and under these circumstances, but it seems prodigiously unfair to saddle him with Charles's debts."

"Ah, well, that brings me to the reason I wanted to speak with you tonight." He smiled at her. "You are not going to Luc as poor as you think. I have settled a nice little sum of money on you, and he and I have worked out a satisfactory settlement." At her raised brow, he added hastily, "Yes, yes, I know that as a widow you have the right to make decisions, but Luc was very fair and generous. No matter what happens, you will never find yourself without money again."

Gillian stared at her uncle, her ire dying away. How could she be angry with him? He was being kinder and more generous than she deserved. "You are too good to me and . . . and I appreciate what you are trying to do, but I cannot let you do it."

"You can't stop me, gel. It's already done." He wagged a finger at her. "And I'll hear none of this 'it's unfair to my brother and my cousin.' I'm a wealthy man—wealthier than most people know. I always intended to ensure that you and Sophy, as well as your brother, were well taken care of. Of course, Stanley was always in line to inherit High Tower and I'll not deny that I had my doubts about the boy, but these past weeks have made me see that he's got a good head on his shoulders—when he uses it." He scratched his chin. "His inheritance of High Tower will hopefully be awhile yet, but there's no reason that I can't give the three of you an independence now." When Gillian opened her lips to protest, he glared at her. "It's my money and I'll spend it as I see fit. Better all of you have some enjoyment of my money while I'm alive to see it than wait until I'm cold in the ground." Working himself up into a fine temper, he growled, "And you're a damned ungrateful little wretch if you dare throw my money back in my face. Denying an old man his happiness, why it don't bear thinking about."

Her heart overflowing with love for him, laughing and crying, Gillian rushed over to fling her arms around Silas's neck and press a kiss to his wrinkled cheek. "Oh, Uncle Silas! You are the sweetest, most generous man I know. I'll try not to be an ungrateful little wretch. Thank you."

Mollified, he patted her arm. "Now that's better," he muttered. "And don't you be fretting and thinking I gave you more than the others. I didn't. You've each gotten an equal amount." He gave her a sly look. "Of course, I haven't told them yet. Intend to do that tomorrow afternoon once all the fuss with your wedding and such is behind us, so you keep a closed mouth."

Wiping away her tears, she smiled at him. "It will be our secret."

"Good. You run off to bed now and don't worry about those blasted vowels. If Luc has to buy them up—it'll be my money that does so. You'll have no reason to feel guilty or beholden to him over it."

Gillian didn't think it would be as simple or as easy as Silas made it sound, but her heart and her step were lighter as she sped up the stairs to her room.

As Gillian headed for her room at High Tower, at The Ram's Head, a man was sneaking into Canfield's rooms. He'd hoped to make this search the previous night while the inhabitants at the tavern were excited and agitated about the news of Canfield's death, but an opportunity had not presented itself. He'd fretted all day, afraid someone else would be ahead of him in searching Canfield's things, but Nolles had indicated that Constable Ragland had locked the door and pocketed the keys pending the inquest and the arrival of the family. It had been good news, but he could wait no longer. Making an excuse, he'd slipped away from his friends and disappeared upstairs. As Nolles had said, the door was locked, but he made short work of it and, opening the door, slipped into the room.

Shutting the door behind him, he lit a small candle. He worried that the light could be seen beneath the door, but he'd have to risk it—and hope he'd hear the approach of anyone in time to snuff the candle. One ear cocked for the sound of someone coming up the stairs, he searched through the dead man's belongings. He found little that did him any good until he discovered, hidden behind the lining of a traveling valise, Charles Dashwood's vowels.

Frowning, in the faint light of the candle, he pawed through them, his brain seeking a way to turn these old vowels to his advantage. The bargain made by Charles with Winthrop might not have been common knowledge, but there were a few people who'd been aware of what had been planned the night Charles died. A sneer curved his lips, his teeth gleaming like a wolf's in the candlelight. Charles had made a fatal mistake in thinking he'd be able to bleed him for more money and had died because he'd been a greedy bastard. As for Winthrop, his lordship had been a lecherous, old fool. A woman instead of money? Faugh!

But it wasn't the money the vowels represented that interested him. It was how he could use them. . . .

On a bright and cool Saturday morning in November, Luc Joslyn took Gillian Dashwood as his wife. Everyone agreed that the bride looked lovely in a narrow gown of pale green embroidered muslin and the groom was most handsome garbed in a long-tailed dark blue coat and gray pantaloons. As planned, after the ceremony performed by Vicar Smythe, the entire wedding party removed to High Tower for a celebration breakfast.

The attendees of the dinner the previous night at Windmere were present, in addition to several other notables from the neighborhood. Mrs. Featherstone and three of her daughters fluttered about, Lord Broadfoot's two sons, Miles and Harlan, and the family's two eldest daughters had joined their parents for today's festivities, and Mr. and Mrs. Simon Fulton, wealthy neighbors of Silas's, and their son were amongst the first to offer congratulations. Mr. and Mrs. Nathan Dodd with their two strapping sons, as well as the widower, Lord Blackmore, whose lands bordered Silas on the east, helped swell the ranks of the guests. There were others to be sure, prompted as much by curiosity as goodwill, that helped fill the grand salon at High Tower to nearly overflowing.

Watching the chattering, smiling crowd, Silas felt a surge of gratification. There had been some fear that Canfield's death would cast a pall over the entire wedding, but Canfield was known only by reputation by most in the neighborhood and few were touched by his death. There was the occasional murmur about what a tragedy the young man's death had been, but for today it was shrugged aside and everyone seemed to be enjoying themselves.

His gaze moving from one person to another, Silas was aware that there were those who came only to gather gossip, but all in all he was pleased. He and the Joslyn family had done what they could to dilute the worst of the scandal broth at the sudden and unexpected wedding, and he was satisfied that, except for a few high sticklers, Luc and Gillian would be readily accepted into the ranks of the gentry. He smiled. It helped, he admitted, that Luc's brother was Viscount Joslyn. Few would dare insult the half brother, legitimate or not, of the wealthiest and most powerful man in the neighborhood. Watching Cornelia Townsend holding court in one corner of the grand salon, his smile became a grin. Or offend Cornelia.

The morning sped by for Gillian, and all too soon, for her peace of mind, she was bundled into Luc's carriage and with well wishes ringing in her ears, she and Luc were on their way to Ramstone. She was glad to escape from the strain of constantly smiling and trying to look as if she didn't have a care in the world when she was filled with apprehension and uncertainty, but leaving . . . She swallowed. Leaving High Tower meant she was alone with Luc for the first time since Sophy had discovered them in bed together in her bedroom.

From under her lashes, she studied him, this man she had just married, as he sprawled on the burgundy mohair cushions across from her. His eyes were downcast, as if he was contemplating the floor, and her gaze traveled over the sweep of black hair across his brow, the shadows beneath the elegantly sculpted bones of his cheeks, the hard jaw, and lingered on the soft, sensual curve of his full bottom lip. Heat blossomed low in her body and her nipples swelled as she remembered the feel of that warm mouth on hers, on her breasts, her body. . . .

Appalled at her wanton thoughts, she tore her gaze away and stared unseeing out at the passing countryside for several minutes. The erotic images faded and with them her body's uninhibited response, but just as she congratulated herself on her control, her eyes strayed again to him. He looked so comfortable, so at ease sitting there, damn him! His broad shoulders encased in the dark blue jacket rested lightly against the back of the coach seat, and his long legs were stretched out in the space between them, the gray pantaloons clinging to muscular thighs and calves. With every bounce and lurch of the carriage as it bumped over the rough country road, his body swayed easily, bonelessly. Clearly, he had not a care in the world.

It was unfair, she thought resentfully, that he was as relaxed as a big tomcat dozing in the sun while she was as tense as a vixen chased to earth by a pack of hounds. Of course, *he* hadn't just been torn from his home. His life wasn't now in the hands of a stranger. A stranger, she reflected, who would come to her bed tonight and do with her as he willed. A flush stained her cheeks when she admitted with a tiny thrill of anticipation that welcoming Luc to her bed wasn't going to be a chore. Feeling the budding warmth and dampness between her legs, she forced herself to look out the window of the coach again.

I'm married to a man I love, but one who doesn't love me, she brooded. I don't want to love him, and I can see nothing but misery being married to a man who doesn't love me. She suppressed a sigh. Perhaps it wouldn't be terrible, and it was certainly better than finding herself shackled to a man who revolted her—someone like Canfield or Stanton. She shuddered. Oh yes, marriage to Luc would not be a chore at all when compared to some other men she could name. Her practical side took over. My husband may not love me, but

I'll take my pleasure where I can, she told herself firmly, in my home and in the life I'll make for myself. I'll still have dear Uncle Silas, Sophy and Stanley nearby. And if my uncle is right, even if Luc is a gambler, my life won't be like it was with Charles. I will *make* myself happy even if I have to do it all by myself.

Luc wasn't as relaxed as he looked, and Gillian would have been surprised to learn that only by concentrating fiercely on the floor of the carriage was he able to keep his hands off of her. At the first sight of her coming down the aisle this morning, Luc had felt as if the world had tilted, and feelings, emotions he'd never experienced before ripped through him. She looked so perfect, so lovely in her pale green gown that he wondered that he hadn't realized before that he was in love with her. He loved women, but he was *in* love with Gillian. His mouth went dry at the knowledge that somehow, inexplicably this sprite with the cloud of dark hair and golden-brown eyes held his heart, his happiness in her slim, soft hands.

He'd been knocked flat by that discovery and he'd wandered through the rest of the morning in a fog. It was only as he helped her into the carriage for the ride to Ramstone that the fog vanished. The touch of her hand in his, the knowledge that she was his wife and the awareness that they were all alone when the carriage doors had shut behind them jolted his thoughts in another direction. His blood ran hot in his veins, and a certain part of his anatomy made its presence uncomfortably felt. It took all his willpower not to reach for her, drag her into his arms and taste again that sweet, seductive mouth of hers. He tried to think of a safe topic of conversation, but his usually agile brain was curiously blank, except for thoughts of how swiftly he could have those skirts of hers lifted and himself buried in her silken heat.

When the carriage swung down the lane that led to Ramstone, Luc silently breathed a sigh of relief. At least, he thought, the temptation to ravage her would be behind him for the next several moments.

As relieved as Luc, if for slightly different reasons, Gillian leaned forward in her seat, eager to see Ramstone Manor again. As the coach pulled to a stop in front of the building with its twin gables divided by the plaster wing, her breath caught. It seemed incredible that less than a fortnight ago she'd laid eyes on Ramstone for the first time and now it was her home.

With her hand resting nervously on Luc's arm, she walked up the brick walkway to the house. Inside it was as she remembered, but today they were greeted not by Bertram Hinton, but a small, white-haired man in butler's garb who introduced himself as Bissell; beyond him stood other servants. Fortunately, Luc didn't have a huge staff and the introductions went swiftly.

Her own dear Nan Burton and Nan's sons were already here, and seeing Nan's welcoming face amongst the strangers, some of Gillian's anxiety fled. The house didn't feel quite so alien knowing that Nan and her two sons were nearby.

Shown into her bedroom several minutes later by Luc, Gillian's anxiety returned, her gaze locked on the bed that comprised, other than a slightly faded blue brocade chair, a chest of drawers with a mirror above and a night table, the furnishings of the room. Dragging her eyes away from the bed, she spied some of her personal things arranged on top of the chest of drawers and saw that several of her gowns were hanging on a series of hooks on one wall and that a trunk she recognized as hers had been placed at the foot of the bed. A small woolen rug in shades of cream and blue lay upon the floor, and while the bed had been made, there were no hangings, leaving the bed looking rather lonely and naked. She winced. Why did the word *naked* have to leap to mind at this very moment?

Standing beside her, Luc muttered, "I know it isn't what

you are used to, but there wasn't time to select and buy more furnishings." He smiled crookedly. "For the time being, you'll have to make do with what was left by the previous owner in the house. I'm sure that you'll want to decorate and add items that are to your own taste." He cleared his throat. "In fact, when I was in London I obtained furniture and fabric catalogs and brought them back with me. Within reason, you have *carte blanche.* I've been told that once ordered, especially items in stock, they could be delivered within a week or so." He thought a moment, then added, "It's possible that we could go to London for you to make your selections."

The prospect of a trip to London did not excite her. There were few members of the *ton* in the city this time of year, but she shrank from the thought of facing a new barrage of gossip her sudden marriage would cause . . . and the revival of all the old scandal. Luc watched her with a raised brow and just before the silence became uncomfortable, she muttered, "I'm sure I'll find everything I need in the catalogs you've obtained." More for something to say than anything else, she asked, "Are all the rooms like this?"

Luc laughed. "No, most are completely empty."

"With an entire house of this size to furnish, if I am to stay 'within reason' you shall have to give me a budget."

He named a sum that made her eyes go round. Seeing the expression on her face, he disclosed, "I am not a poor man, and unless you intend to have every chair and table gilded and studded with pearls you should be able to buy what you want with that amount." And bored with the topic of furnishings, the scent of her perfume teasing his nostrils, the warmth of her body and the proximity of a bed all conspiring against him, Luc added testily, "Allow me to show you the rest of the suite." Almost dragging Gillian, he whisked her into the sitting room that divided her own bedroom from his. Giving her barely a chance to glance around at the skeleton furnishings, he pointed to a doorway and said, "My room is over there and since it is the twin of yours, there is no need

for you to see it now." He couldn't help it. His gaze dropped
to her lips and his voice suddenly husky, he said, "You'll see
it soon enough. Often."

Her throat dry, her heart thumping, her eyes dropped from
his dark face and she babbled, "Oh yes, I'm sure that I will
enjoy that."

He knew very well that wasn't what she meant to say, but
her words sent a jangle of lust shooting through him and the
urge to soothe it with her soft, little body was overpowering.
He wasn't, he reminded himself savagely, an animal. He was
a gentleman. He could wait. He took a deep breath, forcing
his unruly body into submission. Somehow he managed not
to pick her up and carry her into that very room and appease
the beast raging within him. "Very good," he managed, "And
now if you will excuse me, I'll send your maid to you and
allow you some privacy." Leaving her to stare openmouthed
after him, he bolted from the room. It was either that, he told
himself grimly, or prove that she'd married a rutting boar.

Nan was full of chatter as she helped Gillian out of her
cherry-red pelisse and hung it on one of the hooks. "Oh,
Madame, isn't this just the loveliest house? And once you
furnish it, why, my heavens, it'll be a show place, won't it?
My boys are over the moon with our little suite of rooms.
They've been down at the stables already and have made
friends with a couple of the boys that work there. Now,
would you like to change clothes or do you want to wait
until later?"

Deciding to change out of her wedding finery, once she was
garbed in a simple gown of lilac muslin, a delicate woolen
shawl woven in shades of cream, lavender and green draped
around her shoulders against the November chill, she was
ready to go downstairs. Precisely what she was going to do
once she reached the bottom of the stairs eluded her. Luc had
not given her any clue about his plans for the rest of the day
or any direction at all. Did she talk to the cook about an

evening meal? Or ask Bissell to give her an extended tour of the house?

Walking down the staircase, resentment bubbled through her. It is our wedding day, she thought. Surely, he doesn't expect me to treat it like any other day. By the time she reached the front foyer, resentment had turned to temper and there was a sparkle in her eye and a nice sweep of pink to her cheeks that could have been mistaken for high spirits, but those who knew her well would not have made that mistake.

Bissell walked into the foyer as she reached the bottom step. "Ah, Madame. I was just coming in search of you. The master asks that you join him in his study at your convenience. Allow me to escort you."

Mollified by the news that Luc hadn't just abandoned her to her own devices, Gillian smiled and said, "Thank you, I'd appreciate that."

Luc's study was across the wide hallway from the pleasant room where she and her family had been served refreshments on her previous visit. Bissell tapped on the door and at Luc's voice, opened it and with a smile ushered her into the room.

It was a large room in which she found herself. Against the far wall, flanked by tall windows, was a brick fireplace with a wide oak mantel, and a brace of windows overlooked the garden at the rear of the house. Faded maroon drapes hung at the windows; a gray and black wool carpet lay on the floor; an oak desk and a pair of leather chairs comprised the furnishings. One chair was behind the desk, the other in front of the fireplace where a fire burned.

At her entrance, Luc stood up from behind the desk. He'd discarded his jacket and his skin looked very dark against the white of his linen shirt. Luc dismissed Bissell and the butler departed, closing the door behind him. Uncertainly, bride and groom faced each other.

Staring at her, Luc's heart quickened. *Mon Dieu!* She was lovely . . . and his. Nervous as he had never been in his life, feeling as if his cravat was strangling him, Luc scrambled for something to say, but his brain was blank. Where, he wondered unhappily, had his reputed ready charm disappeared? He was as tongue-tied as a youth. All he wanted, he realized, was to take her into his arms and lose himself in her soft sweetness.

Gillian was feeling as bemused as Luc. This tall, devastatingly attractive man was now her husband, she had known his intimate touch, felt the power of that big body, yet what did she really know of him? That he was a gambler. That her uncle approved of him. And that he moved her as no other man ever had. It wasn't much upon which to build a life, but it was what fate and her own foolish desire for him had given her.

Luc cleared his throat. "Ah, did your uncle explain to you about the settlements?"

Walking nearer the desk, she nodded. "Yes, he did that last night when we returned from Windmere."

"And the arrangements are satisfactory?" Silently he cursed himself. The last thing he wanted to talk about was money. What he wanted was to taste that tempting mouth again and to hear her soft cries of pleasure when she reached her peak. A shudder racked him at the memory of her naked body quaking under the driving force of his, and desire coiled tight and painful in his loins.

Gillian nodded again. "Yes."

Wrenching his thoughts away from naked twisting bodies, Luc muttered, *"Bon. Bon."* He tugged at his cravat, destroying the precise folds. "Uh, would you like a tour of the house? The last time you were here you barely had a glimpse of it."

She had reached the desk. With only the desk between them, she swore she could feel the warmth of his body, swore she could smell his scent and deep within her heat flared. Her fingers absently trailing over the smooth polished surface, her eyes on his hard mouth, she murmured, "If that is what you want me to do."

His eyes dropped to her fingers caressing the surface of the

desk and imagining them on his body, his chest, his belly . . .
he broke. Muttering a curse under his breath, he was around
the desk in a flash and jerked her into his arms. "No," he
half-snarled, "that isn't what I want you to do. What I
want," he breathed against her lips, "is your mouth on mine
and your body mated with mine."

His lips came down hard on hers, his hunger wild. He
kissed her again and again, each kiss deeper, more intimate
than the one before. Her body was molded against his, her
arms around his neck, and her lips were warm and generous
under his, her tongue meeting, tangling with his.

Her hands slipped to his chest and her fingers parted his
shirt, finding the hard wall of muscle beneath the fabric. She
flexed her fingers against the warm flesh and he groaned
against her lips; his tongue captured hers, pulling it into his
mouth.

Feverish with desire, shaking with it, Luc found her breast
with one hand and his fingers closed over it. Through her
garment he caressed the nipple that pressed against his seeking fingers and the craving to taste it, to curl his tongue around
that sweet nubbin of flesh was overbearing. His lips slid down
her neck, his hands making short work of the bodice of her
gown. When she was bare to the waist, he swung her around
and sat her on the desk.

Startled, Gillian glanced up at him as he loomed before
her. His eyes fixed on hers, he stripped the shirt from his
body and stepped boldly between her thighs. She gasped
when he half-smiled and slowly slid her gown upward, stopping the fabric at the top of her thighs.

"This wasn't the way I planned it," he said huskily, "but I
cannot stop myself." He dropped a kiss on her mouth. "You
make me lose my head. I can think of nothing but the soft-
ness of your body. . . ." His fingers caressed her thigh, climbing until they brushed against the patch of curls between her
legs. "And your heat and dampness and what I feel when I
am inside of you." His lips left hers and his dark head bent,

and with a sigh his mouth traveled from one breast to the other before his teeth and tongue scraped and laved the raspberry dark nipples.

Gillian shivered at the touch of those teeth and tongue, desire flowing hot and wanton through her. She scooted to the edge of the desk where she could push against the rigid evidence of his arousal. Her thighs clamped against his lean hips and she arched up when his fingers found her.

His mouth never leaving her breasts, he parted the curls between her thighs, toying with her, his fingers sliding teasingly over the swollen folds, stroking her, probing, yet not giving her what she wanted. Gillian's arms tightened around him and she rocked against those insidiously exploring fingers, seeking relief from the demands of her own body. Her lips found his ear and she nuzzled the ridges with her tongue; his quickened breathing exciting her.

Aflame, lost in desire, Luc's fingers left off their teasing and two of them sank deep within. Gillian moaned, rising up to meet the invasion, shivering as he worked them within her. Each thrust, each twist of his fingers sending a jolt of desire through her. She ached. She yearned. She needed. Desperately.

But Gillian yearned no more desperately than Luc. He could think of nothing but the sweetness of her breasts, the heat and dampness his fingers found and the maddening feel of her tongue delving into his ear. The soft, unconscious sounds of pleasure she gave, the movements of her sleek little body against his seeking fingers, all heightened his lust for her.

Gillian cried out when his fingers were removed as he dealt with the front of his pantaloons. A second later, he sighed as his organ sprang free, the hot tip brushing against her mound. His mouth came down hard and hungry on hers, his hands fastened around her hips and he lifted her to meet the broad invasion of his heavy phallus. Slowly he pushed into her, groaning at the pleasure of her tight, wet heat fisting around him. Buried in her, he savored the moment; then, unable to stop, he plunged deeper, only to withdraw and plunge again and again into the slick heart of her.

He was big and she wiggled to accommodate his bulk, enjoying every solid inch of him. Her arms closed around him, and kissing him as urgently as he was kissing her, her tongue flicked like fire against his. With her naked breasts crushed against his chest, her body breached by his and her mouth locked with his, Gillian's senses spun out of control. She was helpless against the needy desire that commanded her and she clung to him, reveling in and meeting each hard thrust of his body into hers.

It was a passionate joining that could not last, and all too soon, Gillian felt that rush, that incredibly exquisite burst of sensation that heralded the zenith of pleasure. Her scream was muffled against his lips and she convulsed around him.

A carnal growl ripping from him, Luc pumped into her one last time and let the scarlet tide take him. Racked by waves of pleasure, he slumped against her, so sated he didn't think he'd ever be able to move.

Soon enough the reality of where they were filtered into his brain and reluctantly, he shifted away from her. Still between her splayed thighs, he straightened and deftly arranged himself and fastened the front of his pantaloons.

Lost in a dreamy haze, Gillian was only partially aware of Luc's movements or her own wanton state. The desk was cool and smooth against her back and her thighs dangled over the edge of the desk. Her pink-tipped breasts were naked; the lilac gown was bunched up around her waist and her hair was spread out in a sable cloud across the desk.

His eyes drawn compulsively to her, Luc thought she was the loveliest sight he had ever seen. Powerless to stop himself, he bent forward and dropped a passionate kiss between her thighs.

Gillian sighed and looked at him with eyes cloudy with passion. He moved, his lips gently caressing her tender breasts. Against her breasts, he muttered, "I do not think if I

have you every hour of the day that I shall ever tire of you."
He flicked his tongue over a nipple. "Even now, after what
we just shared, I can feel my desire for you burning within
me." He slid upward, his mouth brushing over hers, the
azure eyes staring deep into hers. "You have bewitched me."

She raised a hand and caressed his dark cheek. Huskily,
she said, "No more than you have me."

Luc laughed, delighted. Straightening, he swung her up
into his arms and strode to the chair before the fire. With her
settled in his lap, he said, "And so, Madame wife, perhaps
our marriage will not be the disaster everyone thinks, *oui?*"

Gillian nestled her head against his shoulder. She was astute enough to know that their lovemaking changed nothing,
but at the moment, she was too satisfied, too comfortable to
worry about any dark clouds that might appear on the horizon. Luc was right. Perhaps this marriage of theirs would not
be a disaster. Perhaps, she thought wistfully, he might even
come to love her. . . .

Chapter 18

The Joslyn party returned to Windmere shortly after Luc and Gillian had departed for Ramstone Manor. Emily was tired, these latter weeks of her pregnancy taking their toll, and having turned ninety in August, Cornelia was no more loathe than Emily to linger, both ladies retiring to their rooms for a brief nap before evening.

With the ladies absent, Barnaby, Mathew and Simon, joined by Lamb, adjourned to Barnaby's study. Once everyone had been served refreshments and had found a comfortable seat, Barnaby raised his glass of hock and said, "A toast to my brother and his bride."

After the toast was drunk, they wasted little time on Luc's marriage, Barnaby asking abruptly, "Has anyone heard when the Coroner's Inquest for Canfield will be held?"

Lamb nodded. "I spoke with Mrs. Gilbert after the wedding this morning. It'll be held Monday morning at The Ram's Head."

"Any question that the verdict will be other than accidental death or by misadventure?" asked Mathew.

"Not according to Mrs. Gilbert," Lamb answered. "It's accepted that the fellow was drunk and that what happened was a tragic accident. With two, er, respectable witnesses and no one to gainsay them, the inquest is a mere formality."

The topic of Canfield was dropped, but more discussion

about Nolles and the others followed. Finishing off his glass of hock, Barnaby said, "At the moment, gentlemen, we are at a standstill. Until there is another shipment, we can do nothing to bring Nolles down. And as long as he is using my wife's former home as a storehouse for his smuggled goods, I am reluctant to go to the authorities with any information or suspicion that we have."

Simon groaned. "Which means," he said bitterly, "that I am condemned to more nights gambling and drinking at The Ram's Head. By Jove, I never thought I'd long for a quiet night by the fire with a book."

"Well, I have a bit of news for you that may indicate that your nights of purgatory may soon be ending," Lamb said with a sly smile.

All three men looked expectantly at him. "I meant to say something earlier," Lamb confessed, "but with the frivolities surrounding the wedding there hasn't been time for a meeting between us and it wasn't of grave importance." His glance swept over the others. "While you fine gentlemen were asleep in your beds last night, I wandered toward The Birches and damn near stumbled over three laden wagons driving away from the place."

"Damn it, Lamb!" Barnaby burst out. "If you'd been discovered, Nolles would have had you killed in an instant. You could have been murdered, your body disposed of, and I'd never know where to find you."

"Point taken," Lamb acknowledged, unfazed. "Do you want to hear what I discovered?"

Barnaby shot him a look. "The wagons," Lamb said, "were headed toward London, and since the place was now deserted, I decided that another reconnoiter of the cellars wouldn't come amiss."

"Naturally, you just had to take another chance at being discovered," Barnaby growled.

Ignoring Barnaby, Lamb said, "Luc reported to us that there was still a nice little haul of goods stored in the cellars, but I found the place nearly empty. It looked as if they were clearing out the last of the goods to make room for another shipment."

"So watching Nolles is even more important now," Barnaby said.

"The moon is on the wane . . . and it's been awhile since we've had a serious storm," added Lamb. "I'll wager that sometime soon, Nolles will be greeting a shipment from France."

Barnaby looked at Simon. "Your presence at The Ram's Head is even more vital than it was."

Simon sighed. "I know. I just wish I found the company more congenial."

"What about St. John?" asked Mathew. "I thought you liked him."

"I do. But while I'd like to, I can't ignore the possibility that he could be involved with Nolles and the smuggling." Simon grimaced. "Linking Padgett, Stanton, Canfield and Nolles together is no stretch, nor is throwing Townsend in with them, but if this is such a clandestine operation, I would think they'd limit the number of people who know the truth."

"Perhaps, assuming that it was Padgett who contacted Nolles, those two are the only ones that know the whole truth—the others just know bits and pieces—or simply benefit from the operation," offered Mathew.

"Canfield obviously knew more than was healthy," observed Barnaby. "His death may have been an unfortunate accident, but you'll never convince me. They killed him for a reason—most likely to shut his mouth before he became dangerous."

Mathew glanced at Barnaby. "How involved do you think Townsend is?"

Barnaby shrugged. "My best guess is that Townsend is merely a tool and that his involvement is recent—within the past six months or less. It's no secret he's run his legs off.

Right now it's to his advantage to let Nolles use him . . . and The Birches. He's benefiting from the association, but I suspect that once Nolles has no use for The Birches—or my wife's cousin, that Jeffery will suffer a fatal accident."

Mathew looked horrified. "You think that Nolles will kill him?"

"Of course he will," snapped Simon. He leaned forward, his eyes locked on his older brother. "We're dealing with men who will murder without a second thought anyone who gets in their way or has served their purpose. I know it's hard for you to hear, but Tom was right in the thick of it." When Mathew looked to protest, he rushed on, "Don't forget he was prepared to murder Barnaby in cold blood and Lamb, too, for that matter." His voice tight, he added, "Tom's friends may have glided elegantly through the *ton* but these men are no *gentlemen*. They're merely murderous rogues garbed in fine clothes."

Stiffly Mathew replied, "I'm aware of that. I am not as blind and naïve as you seem to think I am."

Simon snorted, not convinced. Rising to his feet, he said, "If you'll all excuse me, I'm going to get a few hours of sleep before I ride to The Ram's Head. It may be dawn before I return."

The door barely shut behind Simon before Lamb rose to his feet, saying, "I'm going to ride to The Crown and see what I can glean from the village gossip."

Barnaby sent him a long look. "You seem to be visiting The Crown often these days. Is it just to gather information?" A smile curved his handsome mouth. "Or can it be that one of those delightful daughters of Mrs. Gilbert has caught your eye?"

To Barnaby's astonishment, he detected the faintest hint of red winging across Lamb's cheekbones, before Lamb looked down his nose at him and said regally, "Don't be ridiculous."

Barnaby had spoken in jest, but judging by Lamb's reaction, he wondered if he hadn't hit upon the truth. Lamb in love? And, more astonishingly still, he thought, with one of Mrs. Gilbert's daughters? But which one? Only half-listening to a comment made by Mathew, he decided it would behoove him to pay a visit to The Crown one of these days. Soon. He shook his head. Lamb in love? He grinned. Wait until he told Luc.

When Simon arrived at The Ram's Head, he discovered that the others were there before him, Townsend already drunk: that night and the next three followed the same course as the others. At some point before he left for another night of drinking and gambling, Simon, Mathew and Barnaby would meet and Simon would relate the previous night's occurrences. The reports were boringly similar: drinking and gambling, with little to distinguish one night from the other. On Wednesday evening when Simon walked into Barnaby's study, he discovered that Luc had joined them.

Marriage, Simon thought, appeared to agree with Luc. He'd didn't think he'd ever seen Barnaby's half brother look so carefree . . . or happy. Simon wouldn't say that the other man glowed, but it was obvious that Luc was a contented man.

Luc endured the good-natured teasing about his newly wed state from the others, but eventually, he asked Simon, "And evenings at The Ram's Head? Are they continuing to be the same?"

"There's not much change—just which one gets drunker or loses the most money," Simon answered. He frowned. "And yet . . . I can't put my finger on it, but there's something amiss in the group."

Barnaby looked interested. "What?"

Simon shrugged. "It's hard to describe, but there seems to be a . . . coolness between Townsend and the others." He paused, frowning. "And St. John . . . there's something between him and Stanton. . . . There's always been a coolness between the pair, but I've noticed that St. John studies Stanton, watches him almost as if he's waiting for Stanton to make a mistake . . . or, I don't know. Something."

"Somehow that doesn't surprise me—St. John and Stanton. I've always thought that St. John didn't fit within that set and Stanton is the worst of the lot. As for Townsend . . . if he's been drinking as heavily as you say, perhaps he's even disgusted those hardened rakes," offered Mathew.

"No. It's not Townsend's drinking," said Simon, shaking his head. "They're all heavy drinkers . . . except St. John. It's just that there's a way that Nolles sometimes looks at Townsend . . . and Padgett has been more openly contemptuous of him." He shrugged again. "It's probably nothing—I'm just being overly suspicious."

Barnaby frowned. "The Coroner's Inquest came back on Monday as we expected: accidental death. If Canfield was murdered and Townsend was privy to it, they might feel he has become a liability."

"That's true," agreed Mathew, "but they *are* still using his place to store their smuggled goods. Surely, they still need him?"

"Not according to Lamb," said Simon. "The cellars have been emptied out, remember?"

"Yes, but we believe in anticipation of the arrival of new shipment from France," Mathew reminded them.

"Unless," Luc said quietly, "they've found another place to use. . . ."

"That's occurred to me," Simon said. "And if they have . . . I wouldn't want to be Squire Townsend."

Swinging off his horse and walking into The Ram's Head a few hours later, Simon's thoughts were still on Townsend and the rift he sensed between the squire and the others. Since the hour was still early, not many minutes past ten o'clock, the gentlemen had not yet retired to one of the private rooms for deep gaming and were at their usual table in the main room of the tavern. Of St. John there was no sign. As usual the place was loud and boisterous, full of fishermen, day laborers, farmers, a pair of revenuers and several hard-eyed individuals Simon identified as Nolles's men.

Simon strolled over to where Nolles and the others sat and, pulling up a chair, joined them. Greetings were exchanged, and catching the eye of one of the barmaids as she bustled about, Simon ordered a tankard of ale.

The conversation was general and, sipping his ale, other than a comment about the Coroner's Inquest held two days ago, Simon did more listening than talking. He noticed that the others ignored Townsend, almost as if the squire wasn't there. Not that Townsend had much to offer, Simon reminded himself, but he sensed again that something had changed within the group. Canfield's death could account for it, but he doubted it. And considering that Canfield had died less than a week previously and had supposedly been a friend, no one seemed to be mourning his passing. Except, Simon thought, perhaps, Townsend. . . .

Townsend was unusually silent and his features were pale and haggard with dark circles under his eyes that told of sleepless nights. He appeared mesmerized by the snifter of brandy in front of him, only stirring from his contemplation of the liquor when his snifter was empty and then only to order another one. Not yet drunk, Simon decided, but if he kept it up, it wouldn't be long before the fellow was passed out cold at the table.

When conversation lagged, Simon asked, "Where is St. John? I thought to see him here this evening."

"Said he had a meeting and would join us later," Padgett drawled.

"Most likely with that yellow-haired wench," muttered Stanton.

"Ah, yes, the buxom Mrs. Perryman," murmured Nolles. "She's new to the village. Claims to be a widow, but I have my doubts." A nasty smile curved his lips. "She seems to have made many friends . . . all male."

"Trust St. John to find amusement in this boring, benighted village," said Stanton.

Townsend lifted his head and stared at Stanton. "If you find Broadhaven so boring," he demanded, "why do you stay?"

If a rabbit had charged him, Stanton and the others couldn't have been more surprised. Simon took another, longer look at Townsend. The febrile glitter in Townsend's eyes was unsettling, and unless he missed his guess, Townsend was deliberately provoking Stanton, and provoking Stanton was dangerous. If it came to a duel, Stanton wouldn't hesitate to put a bullet between Townsend's eyes. Uneasily Simon remembered all the talk when Stanton had done just that to a foolish young man a few years ago. If Townsend had a death wish, Stanton would be just the man to grant it . . . Simon started. Was that what had prompted Townsend's comment?

Stanton recovered immediately and sneered, "I forgot, you're the squire here, aren't you? Naturally, you'd not find this boil on the butt of a frog dull."

Townsend straightened. "Do you know," he said, "I believe that you've just insulted me."

"Gentlemen. Gentlemen," soothed Nolles. "Let us not carry this any further." He exchanged a look with Stanton. "You'll have to forgive my friend. He is not himself. Canfield's death was a terrible shock to him. You were not there and cannot know how horrible it was to see a friend lose his life, and then having to relate the whole unfortunate event at the Coroner's Inquest . . ."

"Of course," said Stanton. Forcing an apologetic note into his voice, he said, "I apologize. My remarks were uncalled for."

For a moment, Simon didn't think Townsend would back down. The balance hung by a thread until, his pale green eyes boring into Townsend, Nolles murmured, "It would be foolish, dear Squire, to carry this further. We don't want further violence, now do we?"

Townsend shuddered and shook himself as if coming out of a trance, his gaze dropping to his brandy snifter. "No. No. No more violence."

"Very good," said Nolles. "And now, gentlemen, I have some business to attend to and must leave you for a while. Why don't you retire to one of the private rooms? I'll have a tray of liquors and refreshments sent in for you."

Padgett stood up. "Excellent idea." He glanced at Nolles. "I assume our regular room is ready?"

Nolles bowed. "Indeed. As always."

Padgett strode off, Stanton on his heels. Townsend rose from the table, and walking behind him as he followed Padgett and Stanton, Simon was relieved to see from his movements that Townsend wasn't as fuddled as he feared. Which made, he decided, Townsend's behavior all the more puzzling. Townsend had backed down quick enough, but just the fact that Emily's cousin had spoken to Stanton in such a fashion worried Simon. Mayhap, Townsend *was* drunk, after all.

Simon needn't have feared that Townsend was drunk. As Simon watched him throughout the evening, he noticed that Townsend's drinking slowed. As the evening progressed and the snifter by his elbow remained untouched, Townsend played considerably better than Simon had ever seen him play in the past, and since he was partnered with him against Stanton and Padgett in game after game of Whist, he could only be glad.

Time passed as usual, gambling and drinking, Nolles coming in now and then to see how they were faring and stopping to visit for a few minutes before disappearing back into the main room. After several hours and hands of Whist, during which Simon and Townsend resoundingly bested Padgett and Stanton, the losers wandered out of the room, leaving Simon and Townsend alone.

Simon was thinking of leaving, when Townsend cocked a brow and said, "A game or two of piquet before we call it a night?"

Reluctantly, Simon agreed. He was curious about Townsend's manner this evening and saw no harm in lingering.

The two men began to play and while Simon knew himself to be a good player, he was surprised at Townsend's increasingly erratic play. If Simon hadn't known better, he'd have sworn that Townsend was throwing the game, and yet, just when he was about to accuse Townsend of such, Townsend would suddenly win the trick.

Simon tried to end the evening, aware that Townsend was drinking heavily now that Stanton and Padgett were no longer in the room. Each time he mentioned the lateness of the hour and Townsend's increasing losses, Townsend would insist that they continue playing and allow him a chance to recoup the losses.

Sighing, Simon would agree to another game, hoping that Townsend would win so he could go home and get some sleep. Townsend went down hard in the next round and Simon had had enough.

To his relief, Nolles glided into the room and gave him the excuse he needed to call an end to it.

Standing up and uncomfortably gathering up the pile of money in front of him, Simon said, "Luck is not with you. Let us call it a night."

"Never tell me, that Townsend has lost again?" purred Nolles, with a lifted brow. "Not after sending Stanton and Padgett home with empty purses?"

Townsend took a big swallow of his brandy. "I had help from Simon. With piquet I have only my own skill to rely upon, and as Simon said, luck was not with me." He smiled crookedly. "Perhaps this is the way it should end."

"How melodramatic," said Nolles, an unpleasant note in his voice.

Townsend glanced indifferently in Nolles's direction and shrugged. "My choice." He laughed without humor and sent Nolles a speaking look. "The first choice I've had in many a day."

"You've had too much to drink," said Nolles coolly.

Sprawled in a chair across from Simon, Townsend looked at Simon, and something in that gaze increased Simon's uneasiness. The certainty that he was being manipulated increased, but he couldn't see to what end. It made no sense for Townsend, known to be in desperate financial straits, to deliberately play badly, and yet that's exactly what Simon suspected the man of doing. But why?

Townsend smiled and a chill slid down Simon's spine. There was no humor in that smile and the expression in Townsend's eyes . . . "One cut of the cards," Townsend said, shuffling the cards. "Winner take all."

"Have you gone mad?" Nolles demanded. "You've lost enough tonight."

Townsend waved him aside and his eyes locked on Simon, he repeated, "One cut. Winner take all."

"I do not mean to be indelicate," Simon said gently, "but I believe that I have already won more than you can afford to lose."

Townsend shook his head. He reached inside his waistcoat and brought out an envelope manufactured of heavy paper and tossed it into the middle of the table. The envelope was sealed, but when Simon reached for it, Townsend's hand stopped his.

Staring intently into Simon's eyes, Townsend said, "If I win, I take everything you've won tonight. If you win, you get this." His gaze steadfast, Townsend added, "I would ask one indulgence . . . if you win, you do not open the envelope until you are at Windmere."

"What rubbish!" snapped Nolles, his face tight and frustrated, not liking this at all. "Mr. Joslyn would be a fool to take such a wager."

Ignoring Nolles, Townsend's eyes never wavered from Simon's. "Will you do it? One cut of the cards. Winner take all."

Simon's gaze dropped to the envelope. It wasn't very thick.

Obviously, the envelope wasn't filled with bank notes. He frowned, staring at the envelope. He looked at Townsend again. What sort of game was the man playing? There could be blank sheets of paper in that envelope for all he knew. Why should he risk a small fortune on the turn of one card to find out what was in the envelope? On the other hand . . .

Simon sat down. He stared hard at Townsend. "One cut each. Winner take all."

"And if you win, you wait until you have reached Windmere to open the envelope?"

"Very well," said Simon, wondering which one of them was mad.

Townsend smiled faintly. "Then we are agreed one cut each. Winner take all."

Simon nodded curtly.

Townsend pushed the cards toward the center of the table, leaving them in a tidy stack. "Do you wish to reshuffle?"

Simon shook his head. "Which one of us goes first?"

Townsend glanced up at Nolles. "Shall we allow Nolles to make the choice?"

Simon shrugged.

Nolles laughed angrily. "You're fools, both of you." He shot Townsend a suspicious look before saying, "Mr. Joslyn shall go first."

Simon's fingers closed around the deck and he made his cut. Turning the portion of the deck he held in his hand upright, he saw that he had exposed the nine of hearts. Since the piquet deck consisted of only thirty-two cards, ace through seven, the odds favored Townsend.

Nolles grinned when he saw the nine, realizing the same thing. Almost rubbing his hands together in anticipation of Townsend winning, he eyed the two men.

Looking at the nine, Townsend smiled faintly and made his cut. A seven of clubs.

Townsend sighed, but there was an odd smile on his face, almost, Simon thought, of relief. "Your win, I think."

Nolles cursed, his hands clenching into fists and the look bestowed upon Townsend was lethal. "I trust," he snarled from between bared teeth, "that there is nothing in that envelope that you will have cause to regret, my friend."

Townsend glanced at him, his expression hard to define. "Nothing whatsoever."

Standing, Simon picked up the envelope, and stuffing it inside his vest, he muttered, "Perhaps luck will be with you another night and you can have your revenge of me."

An odd smile curved Townsend's lips and there was a curious light in his eyes. "Perhaps," he returned mildly.

Nolles wasn't happy at the outcome and did his best to delay Simon's departure, pressing another round of drinks on him, but Simon refused. Edging out of the room, Simon was glad that Padgett or Stanton were not present, feeling that if they had been, the likelihood of him walking out of The Ram's Head with that envelope was scant. Striding out the main door, Simon mounted his horse and, with the envelope burning against his chest, rode toward Windmere as if the devil were at his heels. The contents of that envelope worried Nolles. The question that had Simon alert for danger was whether Nolles wanted to know the contents badly enough to send someone after him?

The road to Windmere had never seemed so long, and twice Simon thought he heard the sounds of pursuit and pushed his horse hard. How much of a head start he had he couldn't guess, but if Nolles had sent his henchmen after him, they wouldn't be far behind. Simon was as brave as the next man, but he admitted he was damned happy when he saw the gleam of the lamps of Windmere before him and knew he had reached safety. Fear wasn't something he was familiar with, but he could not deny that fear had been his companion from the moment he'd picked up that blasted envelope of Townsend's.

Luc, too, was aware of fear, but his had nothing to do with the contents of any envelope. His fear had everything to do with the small woman lying asleep in his arms, and it was a fear like nothing he had experienced in his life. The growing realization that his happiness, his reasons for living, his whole world was wrapped up in this bundle of exquisite femininity terrified him.

Propped on one elbow, in the darkness of his bedroom at Ramstone, Luc stared down into her sleeping face. The waxing moon shed scant light, but Luc needed no light to see Gillian's face. Her features were stamped on his brain, as was every tempting line of her seductive little body. After nearly five days of marriage, spent almost exclusively in each other's company, the curve of her lips, the arch of her brows and the shape and color of her eyes were now as familiar to him as his own.

He knew her moods, when she was pleased, annoyed or aroused. His body quickened. Oh yes, he knew how she looked aroused. She fascinated him, from the sparkle that lit the golden-brown eyes to the way she had of tilting her head when she was puzzled or uncertain. Unhappily he admitted that he loved her more than life itself, and yet, beyond knowing he pleased her in bed, he had few clues about the state of her heart and it was driving him mad.

She appeared to be delighted with the house and had been eagerly drawing up lists of furnishings; she had a sure hand with the servants and already he saw the signs of change throughout the house, in the meals that were served. And in his arms she transformed from an industrious wife into a passionate woman whose lightest touch sent his senses stampeding out of control. She was everything he wanted in a wife, a woman. So why, he asked himself, wasn't he deliriously happy? Why was he lying here awake, aware of a gnawing fear?

His gaze swept over her. He could see in his mind the long sweep of her dark lashes lying against her cheeks and the relaxed curve of her mouth, and the need to snatch her into his arms, to crush her to him was nearly overpowering. And there in the blackness of the night he admitted his fear. He feared that she did not love him. She might have a fondness for him. Even affection, but love? The realization tumbled through him that if she did not love him, if in time he could not win her heart, that their life together was doomed and he would be condemned to misery.

Sighing, Luc sank back down, his dark head resting on the pillow beside Gillian's. He loathed this feeling of helplessness, of no longer being in command of his life, of knowing that another held his fate in her slim hands. For a proud man who had always gone his own way, it was galling to find himself in this position. If I am not careful, he thought savagely, like a man besotted, I'll be on my knees begging her to love me. *Zut!*

It was inevitable that his thoughts would turn to her first marriage, wondering if she had loved Charles Dashwood. Wondering if the ghost of Charles Dashwood would stand between them. So far, the subject of her first husband . . . and the manner of his death had not been mentioned. It wasn't, Luc admitted, something one would discuss easily and certainly not within the first few days of a new marriage. His mouth twisted. Their marriage, he reminded himself, had not been her choice. She had been compelled by circumstances to marry him, and like the blade of knife twisting in a wound, the terrible suspicion that she was still in love with her first husband crossed his mind.

Luc snorted. That made no sense, not when she had been all but accused of murdering Charles. But again, as had happened so often lately whenever the question of her guilt in the murder of her first husband arose, he rejected it. Call him a fool blinded by love, but he did not believe that she had murdered anyone. There had to be a logical explanation why she had been at one of Welbourne's notorious parties that night. And as for her murdering her husband . . . Through the darkness his gaze slid to her. Gillian was no murderess. But someone had murdered Charles Dashwood. . . .

Luc's eyes narrowed. Someone had murdered Charles Dashwood. Why?

The gentleman who knew the answer to that question sat alone in his room, staring at the vowels he'd stolen from Canfield's rooms at The Ram's Head. His fingers moved over them, pushing first one then another aside, his thoughts on the night Charles Dashwood had died. It was Dashwood's own bloody fault, he thought viciously. *All he had to do was give me what was mine and that would have ended it.* His lips thinned. *Bastard deserved to die, trying to extort more money from me.*

He closed his eyes, remembering the sensation of the knife sliding into Dashwood's body, and a thrill of pleasure whipped through him. It had been an accident, but by God! He wasn't sorry. If he had any regrets about that night it was for not thinking fast enough and for not placing the knife he'd used to kill Dashwood in Gillian Dashwood's hand after he'd knocked her out. If he had done that, there would never be any more questions about Dashwood's death . . . or Gillian Dashwood's guilt.

His eyes opened, his gaze falling on the scattered vowels. Gillian was a problem, but perhaps the solution lay before him. He considered it. Yes, mayhap, a solution lay before him . . . and if the new Mrs. Joslyn did as he wanted, then he might just let her live. An ugly smile tugged at the corner of his mouth. Then again, perhaps not. . . .

Chapter 19

Leaving his horse at the stables, the hair on the back of his neck prickling, alert even now for an attack, Simon hurried to the main house. It wasn't until he bounded inside the mansion and the door shut behind him that the fear of attack by Nolles's men abated. Taking the envelope out from inside his vest, in the black and white tiled foyer, he stared down at it. Should he wake Barnaby? His lips quirked. If he did and the envelope contained nothing but pieces of foolscap, he was going to feel like a damned dunce.

A yawn overtook him. Christ! It was nearly five o'clock in the morning and he was stupid from lack of sleep. Some coffee wouldn't come amiss, and hoping that someone was stirring in the kitchen, after admitting that he was looking for an excuse to delay opening the damned envelope, he stuffed it back inside his vest and headed in that direction.

Mrs. Spalding, the cook, and a pair of sleepy-eyed scullery maids were busy preparing for the day: a couple of footmen were already seated at a long scrubbed table eating breakfast. The scent of coffee and yeasty bread filled the air, and the welcoming warmth from the massive woodstove and ovens greeted Simon as he stepped into the big kitchen. At the sight of him, as one, the inhabitants stopped what they were doing and gawked at him.

Simon smiled at Mrs. Spalding and asked, "I wonder if I

could have some coffee and perhaps some toast served in the breakfast room as soon as possible?"

"Absolutely," answered Mrs. Spalding, her plump cheeks red from the warmth of the ovens. "I have a nice fresh pot of coffee that just finished perking and some leftover bread from yesterday for toast." Her eyes twinkling, she added, "There are some hot cross buns already in the oven, if you wouldn't mind waiting a few minutes longer for them to finish baking."

His mouth watering, Simon nodded. "Hot cross buns! That sounds wonderful."

Looking at one of the footmen at the table, Mrs. Spalding said, "James, run along and make certain the fire in the breakfast room is lit. We can't have Master Simon taking a chill."

A young man jumped up from the table and, brushing past Simon, disappeared down the hall. Walking more slowly, biting back another yawn, Simon followed him. By the time Simon reached the breakfast room, candles had been lit and a fire roared in the fireplace.

Warming himself against the chill of the November morning, Simon stood with his back to the fire, fighting against the waves of exhaustion rolling over him. He yawned again, wishing for his bed, but the envelope and what it contained kept the seductive call of sleep at bay.

Sighing, Simon once again took the envelope from his vest and stared down at it. When he hadn't been looking over his shoulder expecting Nolles's henchmen to rise up out of the darkness to kill him, curiosity about the contents had bedeviled him. Now that he was safely within the walls of Windmere, there was nothing to stop him from tearing open the envelope and satisfying his curiosity, yet he hesitated. His lips twisted. He was, he admitted, reluctant to find out what Townsend had wagered, but he had a strong suspicion what might lie within the envelope. If he was right ... He swallowed. If he was right, he realized that he'd most likely gambled tonight with a dead man . . . realized brutally that as he stood here looking at the envelope, Townsend was lying somewhere dead.

The arrival of a footman with a tray laden with a coffeepot and several covered dishes distracted him. After the footman deposited the tray and had been dismissed, Simon laid the envelope at the end of the table nearest the fire and, walking to the sideboard, poured a cup of coffee. Sipping the coffee, he examined Mrs. Spalding's additions to his original request. She'd not only frosted the hot cross buns, but under the other covered dishes, he discovered some slices of ham, coddled eggs and a large dish of warm cinnamon-sprinkled applesauce. Absently, his mind on Townsend, Simon served himself and wandered back to the table.

Pushing the envelope aside, he put down his cup and plate and seated himself with his back to the fire. The room was heating nicely, but from the moment he'd agreed to Townsend's wager, he'd not been able to shake the chill that had come over him.

He ate slowly, not tasting the food, his eyes on the envelope. It represented a Pandora's box. There were many things it could hold. A confession to taking part in Canfield's death and/or a recitation of his dealings with Nolles were two things that came to mind. Yet Simon suspected it was neither of those things.

Nolles had been worried, but Simon knew if Nolles had thought for a moment Townsend had put either of those things in the envelope, he'd never gotten out of The Ram's Head with it. Recalling the sound of hoofbeats behind him as he'd ridden home, he was certain that Nolles had sent someone after him. Whether to simply rob him of the envelope or murder him he didn't care to contemplate.

Mrs. Spalding's fine cooking sitting like a bag of sand in his belly, Simon gave up eating and, pushing aside his half-empty plate, picked up the envelope. Oh, stop being such a namby-pamby coward, he chided himself, and open the bloody thing!

Simon took a deep breath and did so. He scanned the two pages and his expression bleak, guilt churning through him, he set down the document. It had been drawn up by an attorney in Brighton and signed by Townsend on Friday morning, just over twenty-four hours after Canfield's death.

The document was simple. The entailment that had seen Townsend inherit his uncle's fortune and estate ended with Townsend, and in his Last Will and Testament, Townsend bequeathed all of his belongings, his entire estate, to Simon Joslyn.

Simon slumped in his chair. He'd suspected it had to have been something like this. The Birches, his lands, even encumbered with debt, were the only things of value that Townsend possessed. He shook his head. Why not simply deliver the document to him at Windmere? Why go to these elaborate lengths? Knowing what he did of the man, Simon concluded that Townsend, a gambler to the end, had simply chosen to stake his life on the turn of a card.

In hindsight it was easy to see how Townsend had manipulated the situation. With the Will drawn and safely in his vest, Townsend must have guessed that time was running out for him and had engineered the sequence of events tonight. St. John's absence had been a stroke of luck. Once Padgett and Stanton had grown tired of losing, which wouldn't have happened if Townsend had been drunk as usual, they'd left—exactly, Simon guessed, what Townsend had been angling and hoping for all night.

With the others gone, it had been simple to lure him into remaining and playing piquet, Simon thought bitterly. All Townsend had to do then was lose until there was nothing but the contents of the envelope to lay on the table. Blast him! Simon swore explosively under his breath, one hand clenching into a fist. *I knew there was something odd about* the way he was playing. The suspicion even crossed my mind that he was losing deliberately, but the bastard was cleverer than I realized and won just enough to allay that idea.

Simon had no trouble guessing the "why" behind Townsend's actions. Canfield was dead, whether accidentally or not, and the inquest was over, Townsend's testimony no longer needed. At present the cellars at The Birches were empty of smuggled goods, and while the arrival of a new shipment from France was expected, Simon surmised that Nolles, in anticipation of getting rid of Townsend, had found a new place to hide the contraband. The inquest behind them, The Birches no longer needed, Townsend became superfluous to Nolles and the others. Knowing the men he was associated with, Townsend knew, or suspected, that before a great deal of time passed that the odds were in favor of him suffering an "accident" much like Canfield's. The moment the inquest ended and the coroner gave his verdict on Monday, Townsend had known that time was running out for him. It wasn't a question of if, but *when* Nolles had him killed.

Simon shook his head. Poor bastard. He looked at the Will. Christ! Why the hell hadn't Townsend come to Barnaby for help? Why did he believe that his death was the only solution?

Barnaby would have to know, he thought heavily, and was conscious of a sneaking feeling of relief that he wouldn't have to be the one to tell Emily. Not that Emily and her cousin had been close, but Townsend *had* been her cousin and they'd known each other since childhood. He wondered if he could turn over Townsend's estate to her. The Birches had been her home. Perhaps, one of her children?

The opening of the door startled him, and he looked up to see Barnaby entering the room. Barnaby was surprised to see him sitting there, but knowing Barnaby rose early, Simon didn't find it strange to see the viscount booted and garbed for the day at this hour of the morning.

Recovering, Barnaby flashed a smile. "Just get in?" he asked, crossing to the sideboard and, taking one of the cups kept there, poured himself some coffee.

"No," Simon answered. "I've been here awhile. Mrs. Spalding was kind enough to cook me something, but I find my appetite is gone."

A note in Simon's voice had Barnaby taking a closer look at him. "What is it?" he asked quietly.

Silently, Simon pushed the Will across the table in Barnaby's direction. Picking it up, Barnaby read the document quickly. Laying it down, Barnaby took a chair and said, "Tell me."

As succinctly as possible, Simon did so. When he finished speaking, Barnaby shook his head and echoed Simon's earlier assessment. "Poor bastard."

The two men sat in silence a moment before Simon asked, "Do you think he's already dead?"

Barnaby shrugged. "Most likely. If Nolles let him leave The Ram's Head alive, he probably killed himself once he arrived home."

Simon nodded. "That's what I was thinking." He sighed. "I guess we'd better ride over there and find out for ourselves."

In the faint light of dawn, The Birches appeared still and deserted. There was no sign of Townsend's horse and they assumed the animal was in the stables, unless Townsend had not returned home. . . . Opening the door, Barnaby and Simon stepped into the house, silence and cold greeting them.

They found Townsend in a small room at the rear of the house. A decanter of brandy sat on the table before him, an empty snifter nearby. Townsend was seated at the table, slumped back in the chair, one hand hanging down by his side, a pistol lying on the floor directly beneath his fingers.

Examining the neat round wound in the temple, Barnaby said, "So did he do it himself, or did Nolles arrange this tidy little scene for us?"

Thinking back over the night, the look in Townsend's eyes, Simon muttered, "My money's on Townsend having done it himself. He knew he didn't have much time before Nolles killed him or had him killed. I'll wager, though, that he had more time than he gave himself. Canfield's death occurred a week ago almost to the day—Nolles would have waited awhile before dispatching him."

"I agree. Nolles may be a snake, but he's a clever snake." Barnaby's jaw clenched, a muscle bunching in his cheek. "I never liked Emily's cousin and I'm not sorry he's dead," he admitted. Sighing, he added, "This is probably for the best, but I wish the coward had helped us catch Nolles before he decided to kill himself."

"Perhaps he was trying to spare the family embarrassment," offered Simon. "If he helped expose Nolles, during any trial his part in Canfield's death and the smuggling would be bound to come out. And if they did murder Canfield, he would have hung right alongside Nolles."

Barnaby shrugged. "It's possible, and if that's the case, it's the only decent thing he ever did." Turning away from the body, Barnaby said, "We'd best notify the constable." His expression bleak, he muttered, "And I have to tell Emily and Cornelia."

Four hours later, the constable notified and their statements taken, the two men rode to Windmere in a misting rain. The day was gray and depressing and Simon thought it appropriate.

Once they were inside and closeted in Barnaby's study, Simon cleared his throat and asked, "Uh, what about the Will? Do you think I should give everything to Emily?"

"No," Barnaby said flatly. "She needs nothing from that bastard."

Looking bewildered, Simon demanded, "What am I to do with it?"

Barnaby thought a moment. "Keep it," he said. His eyes narrowed and he admitted, "It's possible that Townsend was trying to make amends." He studied Simon. "Yes, I think maybe he was. You'll make a fine squire, cousin. And you have the fortune and the ability to turn The Birches into the place it was before Townsend got his hands on it." He frowned. "That may even have been what he had in mind when he drew up that Will."

"Me!" yelped Simon. "What about his brother, Hugh? If not to Emily, shouldn't the estate go to him?"

"Hugh has his own estate, his own fortune, and he's quite happy where he is."

"But there have been Townsends living at The Birches for ages, and a Townsend has been squire for generations," argued Simon, feeling as if he were being swept into a whirlpool.

"And now there won't be," said Barnaby, amused. "There'll be a Joslyn." He grinned. "Squire Joslyn has a nice ring to it, don't you think?"

Simon eyed Barnaby with dislike. "You're happy about all of this."

"If you think about it, it settles several things," Barnaby replied, ticking off the items on his fingers. "Emily's contemptible cousin is dead. There will be no scandal—other than the manner of his death. An honorable man will now be squire. Emily's home will be restored to its former state and I'll have a genial neighbor. Why shouldn't I be happy?"

To Simon's astonishment, Barnaby's assessment proved correct and the family and neighbors, in one way or another, all echoed the viscount's sentiments. Even before Townsend was buried, Simon was startled to hear himself referred to as "the new squire" or "Squire Joslyn."

Simon had expected Emily to have reservations, but once she had dealt with the first shock of Townsend's death, she'd flung her arms around his neck and cried, "Oh Simon! Jeffery was a beast, but in the end he did something good. You will make a *fine* squire, and to know that The Birches is in your hands is more than I could have wished for."

Cornelia, too, had fixed her eagle eyes on him and remarked, "Squire Joslyn, eh? Lord knows you'll be a grand improvement over that rapscallion Jeffery!" She smiled at him. "You might think that your inheritance is more a burden than a prize right now, but once you drop some blunt on it, you'll find that The Birches is a handsome place and quite comfortable." She tapped him on the cheek. "Don't look so uneasy—you'll do well, boy."

Even Mathew seemed pleased about Simon's elevated status in the area. "I'm sorry for the way it came about," Mathew told him, "but it is, I think, a good thing." He half-smiled. "Now when I complain about all the details involved in running an estate, you'll know precisely what I'm talking about."

The affection and respect people in the area held for Emily and Cornelia ensured that Townsend's burial on Monday morning was well attended by the gentry, as well as the common folk. Townsend's mother, Althea, his brother, Hugh, and Anne Townsend, Emily's stepmother, had made the trip from Hugh's home, Parkham House, and stood with other members of the family. Mrs. Gilbert and her daughters were there, as was Nolles, looking suitably saddened, and Padgett, Stanton and St. John also attended. Despite the number of attendees, the manner of Townsend's death and his unpopularity in the neighborhood produced a short service and a quicker burial. The lightly falling rain made no one inclined to linger, and after paying their respects to the family, the crowd quickly dispersed.

Luc and Gillian attended the funeral and afterward, along with the rest of the family and invited friends, drove to Windmere. Except for his mother, few mourned Townsend's passing, but there was no rejoicing and there was a subdued air surrounding the gathering inside the great mansion. No one, other than family, lingered long.

The funeral was Gillian and Luc's first public appearance

since their wedding, and Gillian was guiltily aware of being grateful that everyone's attention was on Townsend's family and not her and Luc. She felt sorry for Mrs. Althea Townsend, but she'd have been a hypocrite if she'd shed any tears. It wasn't, she excused herself, as if she'd known Squire Townsend. She hadn't. Beyond hearing his name mentioned once or twice, she knew nothing of him, and her sympathies were for his mother and Emily and his family. It didn't take her long to realize, except in the case of Townsend's mother, those feelings were misplaced.

After the guests left, Althea, looking worn and sad, disappeared upstairs to her rooms, leaving the other women sitting in a semicircle in front of the fire. The gentlemen were gathered at the other end of the room, talking quietly amongst themselves and drinking hot punch.

Watching Althea leave, Cornelia commented, "Poor woman. He treated her as badly as he did anyone else, but she's suffering."

Sipping a cup of tea, dark-haired, pretty Anne said, "I know. She is such a dear creature and I have tried to comfort her, as best I am able, but it is difficult. I feel sorry for her, but when I think of what he tried to do . . ." She stopped, her pansy-brown eyes filled with remembered horror. "He was a monster! I cannot be sorry he is dead. I just wish dear Althea didn't suffer so."

Emily, looking tired, the bulge under her gown impressive, sat beside Anne. Touching the mound where her child grew, Emily murmured, "She is his mother, and no matter what we think of him, even if he disappointed her and treated her wretchedly, she loved him."

"I know," said Anne, "but knowing the lengths he was prepared to go to get his own way—" She bit her lip. "I cannot be happy over his death, but it is hard to offer kind words about him."

"Then don't," said Cornelia. "Althea is as kindhearted a person as you will find and a shatterbrained little widgeon, but she knows what her son was like. She doesn't expect you to sing his praises. Just comfort her and love her."

Garbed in a dove-gray gown, the neck and sleeves trimmed in Brussels lace, a few sable curls dangling near her cheeks, Gillian sipped tea and listened with growing mystification to the conversation between the other women. If she understood matters correctly, except for his mother, not one of the women here bore the late squire any love. Anne's allusion to "what he tried to do" made her wonder "what" it was he'd tried to do. Emily and Cornelia obviously knew what Anne referred to, but no one seemed inclined to share that knowledge with her.

Having secrets of her own, though curious, Gillian didn't hold it against them for not telling her. The other three women had known each other for years, while she was a newcomer to their circle and family. She felt a trifle left out, it was true, but not enough to dwell on it or feel hurt over it. Everyone, she reminded herself, was entitled to keep some things private. She almost snorted. How virtuous she sounded, when the truth was that she was dying to know more.

Taking her mind off the curious reference, Gillian's eyes sought out Luc, her heart giving that by-now-familiar leap when their eyes met across the room. Luc was standing next to Barnaby, the other men arrayed nearby. Luc was listening to what was being said around him, but his gaze was on her. His eyes slid over her demurely garbed figure and back to her face, a half smile tugging at the corner of his mouth as he stared at her. She flushed and buried her nose in her cup. Drat! Even though there wasn't a part of that long, lean body of his that she wasn't intimately familiar with or a part of her own that he hadn't touched or kissed, with just a look he had the power to fluster her.

It was incredible that they had been married now for over a week. Only partially listening to the conversation between the other women, Anne asking about the preparation for the birth of Emily's child, Gillian let her thoughts drift. These past days of marriage to Luc had been a revelation to her.

When she'd married Charles she'd been madly in love with him and had thought that he loved her; she had been, she'd thought at the time, deliriously happy. Yet, now she wondered about the depth of her feelings for Charles. With age, she'd realized that what she'd felt for Charles had been a girlish emotion—especially when compared to the bone-deep emotion she felt for Luc. Yes, she'd loved Charles, but she had been as much in love with love as *in* love with Charles, and loving Luc as she did, she now knew the difference. That Charles had not loved her and had married her for her fortune, she accepted these days with an equanimity her eighteen-year-old self could not have faced.

She admitted that her time with Luc had been short, but even now she could not envision a morning not waking in his arms. The thought of a day without seeing his beloved face filled her with fear, and the force and depth of the love she felt for him terrified her. She half-smiled and shook her head. Not once had Luc declared that he loved her, but she felt loved. She couldn't explain it. There were none of the flowery compliments that Charles had bestowed upon her in the beginning; yet every time Luc's eyes touched her, she felt as if he caressed her and the sound of his deep voice warmed her, wrapping around her like a rich, ermine cloak. Gillian did not consciously make comparisons between Charles and Luc, and yet she was aware that there was a world of difference between the two men. Silas had been right about that.

Charles had been, she'd thought, an excellent lover; she had enjoyed his lovemaking, but when Luc touched her . . . She sighed dreamily. When Luc touched her, when his mouth claimed hers, when that elegant body of his took hers, she discovered that there was lovemaking and then there was *lovemaking*. . . . Beneath her dove-gray gown her nipples tightened into hard, round little berries, and she was embarrassingly aware of a pleasurable ache and a growing dampness between her thighs. She was, she decided, a lascivious little slut. But only, only for Luc . . .

Over the rim of her cup, she studied him, this tall man she had married. He hadn't said that he loved her, but she sensed that he did. At present, it was unspoken, but it was there in the consideration and generosity he showed her every day. Like a warm, protective cocoon, she felt it in every look he gave her, in his kiss, in his passionate lovemaking, and when he was ready, she was serenely confident, he would give her the one thing she wanted more than she had wanted anything in the world . . . his love. She could be deluding herself, or being arrogant, but she didn't think so. Luc did love her. He just hadn't, she thought with a soft smile, told her yet. But when he did . . . Her heart thudded with anticipation of that magical moment.

"I'm sure this isn't what you thought would be your first public appearance after your marriage, is it?" asked Cornelia, breaking into Gillian's thoughts.

Jerking her mind to the present, Gillian put down her cup and murmured, "No. But tragedies don't, I'm afraid, look at calendars. They happen without warning and with no consideration of the timing."

Emily and Anne had their heads together, lost in a discussion about the coming baby, but Cornelia's attention was fixed on Gillian. "Yes, I imagine you are, more than others, too well aware of the unpredictability of sudden death."

A hollow feeling echoed through Gillian, but she met Cornelia's hazel-eyed gaze. "You are," she said, "referring to my hus—my *first* husband's murder."

"Weren't you?"

Gillian's chin lifted. "As a matter of fact, no. If I can help it, I don't think of that night at all. It was a painful time."

Cornelia's eyes moved intently over her face, studying each feature, and Gillian had the curious feeling that the old woman was coming to some conclusion about her. Gillian stilled, hardly daring to breathe, and just when she thought she could not bear this intense scrutiny one moment longer, Cornelia nodded as if to herself and said, "I'm sure it was. More than anyone could realize. I apologize for bringing up distressing memories."

"Th-th-thank y-y-you," Gillian stammered, feeling she had passed an arduous test.

Cornelia smiled at her, a dazzling smile Gillian had never seen before. Patting her cheek, Cornelia said, "You're a good gel. Luc is to be congratulated." Before Gillian could reply, Cornelia's gaze shifted and she said, "Ah, and here he comes to whisk you away, no doubt, but before he does, if you don't mind I'd like a private word with him."

"Of c-c-course," Gillian managed, still off guard.

Luc had come to fetch Gillian, but upon reaching the ladies, Cornelia stood up and, leaning heavily on her cane, said quietly, "A word with you, young man, before you leave with your charming bride."

If Luc was surprised he didn't show it, but after giving Gillian a reassuring smile, he took the arm Cornelia offered and escorted her from the room, leaving Gillian, Emily and Anne to stare after them.

"Hmm, I wonder what *that* is all about," muttered Emily.

"I think it might be something that Hugh told her," offered Anne.

Gillian could have kissed Emily when, staring hard at Anne, Emily demanded, "What could Hugh have told Cornelia that she has to talk to Luc in private?"

Anne sighed. "He didn't tell me. I just know that he received a letter from Cornelia several days ago and that he has been gone this past week. I think his absence had something to do with Cornelia's letter, but he wouldn't say. In fact, he'd just returned to Parkham when news of Jeffery's death reached us."

"Oh!" Emily said in an odd voice and promptly lost interest in the subject.

Gillian's heart clenched and she thought she'd faint from the pain. In her mind, there was only one reason Cornelia could have for speaking privately with Luc and she didn't doubt for a moment what it was . . . Charles's murder.

Gillian was correct.

Seated in a blue mohair channel-back chair, her hands resting on her cane, Cornelia said bluntly, "I wrote to Hugh and asked him to visit some people for me. I wanted to find out what happened at Welbourne's hunting lodge the night Charles Dashwood was murdered."

Luc stiffened. His face set, he asked, "And did you find out anything interesting?"

"I did and you're not going to like any of it," Cornelia warned. "Worse, it's gossip." She smiled tightly. "But after a visit from Hugh, I don't think that Winthrop will be mentioning it to anyone else." Her eyes narrowed. "Not if he knows what's good for him."

Luc took a step forward, his hand clenched into a fist, a dangerous glitter in the azure eyes. "What," he asked grimly, "did Hugh learn?"

Cornelia told him. When she finished speaking, Luc stared at her, white-faced with fury.

"*Sacristi!* Monstrous! What sort of a *quel salaud* was this Charles Dashwood?" he demanded. "To offer Gillian . . ." His rage overcame him and he could not speak. He took several agitated steps around the room before coming back to stand before Cornelia. Breathing hard, he asked, "And this Winthrop? Where is he? I will kill him myself."

"No, you won't," responded Cornelia calmly. When Luc shot her a look full of fire and fury, she said, "Of course, if you want your wife's name connected to more infamy, by all means, do so. I can give you his direction."

Luc rocked back on his heels as if a bucket of ice water had been thrown in his face. He regained control of himself.

"Yes, of course, you are right." His eyes fastened on hers. "He will say nothing? Ever?"

She smiled. "Not if he wants to live. Hugh made it clear that not only would *you* come after him, but Barnaby as well, and most likely Mathew and Simon, and if they failed to kill him, he would himself."

Luc took another deep breath. "And the vowels? Where are they?"

"That's where it gets interesting. Winthrop claims he lost them to Canfield."

"Canfield! *Mon Dieu!* Canfield is dead. They could be anywhere."

"I'm afraid that much is true, but until they surface . . ."

He eyed Cornelia with hostility. "Do you think she killed him? Offering a night with her for his vowels is not something many women would stomach." Harshly, he said, "It gives her a reason to have killed him."

"It gave her a reason to go looking for him with murder on her mind," Cornelia agreed. When Luc would have argued, she raised a finger and went on, "From others Hugh learned that the room where Charles was found was in shambles. Overturned tables, chairs, etc. It was apparent a violent struggle had taken place. Charles Dashwood was a man about your size—Gillian would never have been able to cause the damage done to that room. Even with rage driving her, Charles could have easily overpowered her, tossed her aside, if you will. The condition of the room, as well as being found unconscious and the lack of a knife or a weapon were the reasons she was never brought to trial." Her eyes met his steadily as she said gently, "To answer your question. No. I do *not* believe that she murdered him. It's my opinion that she is telling the truth and has been unjustly vilified." She smiled at him. "And we're going to do something about that, aren't we?"

Luc smiled dangerously, the azure eyes glinting. "Indeed,

we are, Madame. I shall find this villain and prove my wife's innocence."

Beyond answering her questions in monosyllables, Luc was silent on the drive back to Ramstone, his thoughts clearly somewhere else. Gillian glanced at him several times, uneasy with the grim line of his lips and the rigid cast to his jaw. She desperately wanted to know about the conversation with Cornelia, but coward-like, she could not bring herself to broach the subject. By the time they reached home and he helped her down from the carriage, fear and anxiety were tearing her apart. Cornelia had obviously related something that had disturbed Luc and guiltily she could think of only one event that would cause his reaction: Charles's murder.

With exquisite politeness Luc escorted her inside the house. Leaving her in the foyer, he said, "I have some business to attend. I'll see you later."

Gillian watched his tall form disappear down the hall, wanting to call him back, wanting to scream that no matter what Cornelia had told him, she was innocent. *Innocent!*

The moment was lost, and she was left staring at an empty hallway. Dispiritedly, she climbed the stairs to her rooms. She wanted to believe otherwise, but she could not help but think that the specter of Charles's death was about to destroy her only chance for happiness. What she found waiting for her when she entered her rooms confirmed all her fears and suspicions. . . .

Chapter 20

The envelope was lying in the pewter salver resting on a small table in the sitting room that separated her bedroom from Luc's. Her name was scrawled across the front of it, but Gillian did not recognize the handwriting.

Puzzled, she picked it up and carried it with her into her bedroom, wondering who had written to her. A premonition shivered through her. Whatever the envelope held, it wasn't, she was certain, something good.

Nan Burton was waiting for her in the bedroom, and laying down the envelope for the moment, she allowed Nan to help her undress. Nan was full of a proposed trip to London Luc had suggested only yesterday, and half-listening to her chatter, Gillian stared at the innocuous envelope, trying to figure out who had written her and why.

"Oh, Madame! It will be so exciting," Nan declared, her eyes sparkling as she whisked the dove-gray gown off of Gillian and brought forth an older gown of mulberry wool. "Imagine, the gowns and the furniture you will buy! It will be wonderful to finally have proper wardrobes in which to hang your clothes. Master Luc is being most generous, isn't he? And to think the viscount has offered us his town house to stay in while we are in London." A blissful expression on her face, Nan burbled, "I can tell you I am so over the moon, I can hardly sleep at night. London!"

Her clothing changed and her hair re-combed, Gillian dismissed Nan. Picking up the envelope, she sat on her bed and studied it a moment longer. Taking a deep breath, she carefully opened it. She shook out the folded piece of paper that had been within the envelope. As she did so, another, smaller sheet of paper fell free and floated to the floor.

Reaching down, she picked it up, her heart leaping to her throat when she realized what she held in her hand. One of the vowels Charles had given to Winthrop.

Dazed, she stared at it for a long time, her eyes going over again and again Charles's bold signature. Giving herself a shake and putting the vowel on the bed beside her, she read the note that had been with Charles's vowel.

> *You have something I want, Charles's last*
> *gift to you. As you can see from the gift I*
> *have enclosed, I have something you want.*
> *South of the village, there is an abandoned*
> *fisherman's cottage about a half mile beyond*
> *the fork in the Coast Road. Meet me there*
> *alone Tuesday afternoon at four o'clock. Tell*
> *no one.*

There was no signature. She read and reread the note, an uneasy hope rising in her breast, wanting to believe that she would finally have her hands on Charles's vowels and that Luc would never have to know. . . . Because of Silas's generosity, she breathed easier, knowing that she had the ability to wipe out the debt should the vowels have been presented for payment. The whole notion of Luc knowing about the vowels made her cringe and made her willing to do anything to keep them from him.

Part of her knew she was being foolish, but the vowels were all tied up with Charles's ugly bargain with Winthrop and Charles's murder that night—anything connected to that time filled her with revulsion and fright. Canfield's possession of the vowels had shown her just how dangerous their existence could be, and the knowledge that they now lay in the hands of someone else brought all those emotions roiling back, making her ill and afraid. She stared hard at the note, wanting to believe that an opportunity to finally have the vowels in her own hands lay before her, but she was wary.

Charles's last gift . . . for a second she couldn't think what the writer referred to and she frowned. Charles's last gift to her . . . She stiffened. *The brooch!* The diamond and topaz brooch she'd worn for the first time on the night Charles had been murdered. Now why, she wondered, would someone be willing to trade a small fortune in vowels for a brooch that could be fashioned and bought for considerably less from any knowledgeable jeweler?

Leaving the bed, she ran over and pawed through her clothes until she found the brooch still pinned to her riding habit. Unpinning it, she walked across the room and, reseating herself on the bed, stared at the winking jewels. Careful examination revealed nothing out of the ordinary about the brooch. There was nothing significant about the arrangement of the precious stones that she could see, nor was there, as she half-hoped, some secret compartment that would hold the answer to why it was so important to the writer of the note.

She'd never cared for the brooch, but she could see that it was a handsome piece of jewelry and that most people would find it lovely. It was an expensive piece, but not worth anything near the amount represented by Charles's vowels, so why was someone willing to exchange one for the other? And why be so mysterious about it? Why not simply request an interview with her and offer her the vowels in exchange for the brooch? Why want her to meet alone? And the warning to tell no one disturbed her as nothing else had. It was ominous and told her that this would be no simple exchange. The sensation of danger was overpowering.

Hearing the steps of someone crossing the sitting room,

she leaped up from the bed and looked around for a place to hide the brooch and the other items. Why she felt the need to hide them escaped her. Whatever the reasons, there was no time; she heard Luc's voice calling her name almost at the same instant the door to her bedroom opened. She dropped everything to the floor and slid all the items under the bed with one swipe of her foot.

Gillian couldn't have explained her actions if she'd been placed on the rack. The closest she could come to making any sense of her furtive and out of character reaction was that she was ashamed. Ashamed of everything connected with that night—even if she had been guilty of nothing more than naïveté. Perhaps that was it, she thought as she swung around to face Luc, a smile plastered on her face. She was ashamed that she had ever been that gullible and stupid.

Luc was not gullible or stupid, and one look at Gillian's face told him that something was amiss. She looked guilty, her face pale, her eyes huge with fright and doing her best to pretend otherwise. Protectiveness rose within him, but he suspected she would repulse any effort on his part to find out what was wrong. And correct it.

Hands behind her back like a child hiding a secret, her head canted to one side, she asked, "H-h-have you f-f-finished your business?"

He nodded, his eyes moving over her expressive face, thinking that he'd like to get his hands on Charles Dashwood for five minutes. Forcing a smile, he said, "*Oui*. It wasn't very important." Running a finger down her cheek, he murmured, "Especially not important enough to keep me from you for very long."

Gillian giggled, as much from nervousness as amusement.

Luc grinned and cocked a brow. "You find my compliments amusing, Madame wife?"

"No. Never," she said quietly, her lips rosy and tempting. His gaze traveled down her curvaceous form—a form that delighted him and that after the past several days he knew as well as his own, the shape of her breast, the slope of her hip, the taste, the texture and scent of her skin. Looking at her, seeing the fragility, knowing how much just the sight of her filled him with pleasure, he couldn't help dwelling with incredulous fury on what Cornelia had related to him this afternoon. Gillian had been Charles's wife, a creature to be loved and treasured, he mused, and that bastard had been willing to toss her, for a night, to cover his debts, into the arms of another man. *Zut!* What he wouldn't give for that five minutes alone with Charles Dashwood. No, he thought savagely, three would be enough to tear him limb from limb.

Something in Luc's expression alarmed her and Gillian stepped near him, one of her hands caressing his cheek. "Luc? What is it?"

He looked down into her troubled face and his rage vanished, his heart expanding with so much love for her that he feared that his body could not contain it. "It is nothing, *ma coeur.*" His arms slid around her and he brushed a kiss against her temple. Astonishing both of them, he said, "You are very dear to me."

Happiness flooded through her. It wasn't, perhaps, the declaration of undying love she yearned for, but it was a step in that direction. A smile curved her lips. "Very dear?" she teased, unabashedly seeking more.

Luc's features softened and he kissed her with a tenderness they had never shared before. When his head lifted, he stared into her eyes. For a long moment, they stayed thus, staring into each other's eyes as if the most important answer in the world were written there. Never breaking the look, Luc shook his head. "No. I misspoke," he murmured. "Very dear is a pale description for what I feel for you." His fingers trembling, he fondled a strand of sable hair. "I love you, Gillian—more than I have ever loved anyone or anything in my life." His lips twisted. "I may be master of my house, but you rule my heart. . . . I adore you, *m'amie*." A whimsical smile crossed his dark face as he finished simply, "My life, my happiness is in your hands."

Gillian thought her heart would stop beating, so powerful was the emotion that filled her. He loved her, she thought stunned. Loved *her*. Joy, bright and shimmering, cascaded through her. "Oh Luc!" she cried, love infusing her face with a luminous glow. Flinging her arms around his neck, she strained against him, her lips caressing his chin, his jaw, any part of him she could reach. "I love you," she breathed against him. "Love you. Love you. *Love you!*"

Laughing, Luc swept her up into his arms and, her skirts flying, whirled her about the room. "No more than I love you, my pet. You could not love me more." With his arms full of warm femininity, Luc sat down in the only chair in the room. Love shining out of his eyes, he stared at her. "I do love you, you know. I have for what seems like forever."

"Oh Luc," she breathed, nestling her face against his neck, her fingers locked within his.

They stayed thus for a long time, tender murmurings the only sound in the room. As lovers have always done, they spoke of things vital to them and them alone, their ramblings broken only by sweet kisses and gentle caresses and quiet laughter.

Gillian could not imagine a happier time, but as the minutes passed, like a serpent slithering from beneath a rock, the items she had kicked under her bed intruded. The urge to tell Luc was overwhelming, but she wanted nothing to taint this moment, and so she pressed nearer to his warm body and held her tongue. Later, she thought, later, after dinner when we are alone for the night. But just as she came to that conclusion, the memory of his private meeting with Cornelia crept into her mind. What had the other woman told him? Whatever it had been, recalling that silent ride home, it had put Luc into a withdrawn, introspective mood. The meeting might not have had anything to do with her, but convincing herself of that was impossible.

Ask him, she told herself. Just ask him. The question trembled on her lips, but just as she had not wanted to sully this magical time with ugly events from the past, she didn't want to risk asking questions that could disrupt their growing rapport.

Luc was thinking about his meeting with Cornelia, too. The first flush of elation fading, the information Cornelia had given him this afternoon droned annoyingly at the back of his mind. Confirmation of Gillian's innocence by Cornelia, via Hugh, had been gratifying, but it hadn't been necessary to him—his heart had long ago concluded that his sprite was no murderess, but the bargain Charles had made with Winthrop . . . He could feel the rage coiling up through him and fought it back. Charles was dead. And Winthrop would escape unscathed, because to go after him would only hurt Gillian. He didn't like it, but he could see no way to get at Winthrop without harming Gillian. A thought occurred to him and he smiled. Not a nice smile. Winthrop was a gambler. . . .

Beyond the friendly game of cards or wager, Luc had sworn that his gambling days were behind him, but he decided, with a cold glint in the azure eyes, that in Winthrop's case, he would make an exception. Yes, sometime during the next year or so, an opportunity would arise. . . .

Gillian stirred in his arms and he glanced down at her, delight and pleasure in the love they had found tumbling through him. His, he thought, dazed. His wife. His darling, dearest sprite. And Charles Dashwood had been willing to defile her for his own ends. His gaze wandered over her soft, relaxed features. Would she tell him? Did she, would she, trust him enough to tell him of that infamous trade?

It would be simple for him to tell her that he knew about it, but perversely, even with her admission of love, he wanted more. He wanted her to feel comfortable enough with him, wanted her to trust him enough to tell him herself. Greedy? Arrogant? Unreasonable? Luc half-smiled. Undeniably.

He frowned. Charles's vowels. They were out there somewhere, and he would have to find them. Find them and destroy them. In the meantime, he thought, pulling Gillian closer to him, there was his enchanting bride to enjoy.

Except for the niggling apprehension about Luc's meeting with Cornelia and the resurfacing of Charles's vowels, the following hours passed in a delirious blur for Gillian. Luc loved her! She'd known it. Sensed it, but to have had him actually say the words . . . Like precious jewels she held those words of love to her, marveling and treasuring them. Luc loved her.

That night when they made love, it was as if for the first time, each one discovering new pleasures, new sensations and new heights, each one reveling in the knowledge that it was love that guided each caress, each kiss.

Lying in Luc's bed, wrapped in his arms, her body sated in ways she had not thought possible, as their heartbeats calmed, Gillian knew that she could not postpone telling him about the note much longer. But not yet, she thought. Just not quite yet.

Behind her joy, thoughts of the note were never far from her mind. After Luc left her room that afternoon, she'd extracted the brooch, note and vowel from beneath her bed and stuffed them in the back of a drawer, wishing she never had to think about them ever again. But she did. Just not yet, she bargained with herself, hoarding the sweetness of the moment. Not yet.

She tried to recapture her happier mood, but failed. The note and Cornelia's private meeting with Luc bedeviling her, she wiggled around, unable to sleep.

Aware of her restlessness, Luc glanced over at her and asked, "What is it?" Her hand lay on his naked chest, and he picked it up and pressed a kiss to the tips of her fingers. "What keeps you awake, *m'amie?*"

Gillian stilled. Tell him. Now. She hesitated, wondering how to begin. Perhaps his conversation with Cornelia would give her an opening? Without thinking she blurted out, "What did you and Cornelia talk about this afternoon?"

In the darkness she couldn't see his features, but she felt his body stiffen, and mixed with guilt from the past, the note, all her anxieties and fears rushed back. But he loves me, she reminded herself. Whatever Cornelia had told him, it hadn't, couldn't have anything to do with what they felt for each other. She was being silly—and nosy. But as the seconds passed and Luc continued to lie stiff and silent beside her, her doubts grew.

After what seemed an age, he said flatly, "It was a private matter." As soon as the words left his mouth, he wanted to call them back. It *was* a private matter, but she was at the center of that private matter. I should tell her, he thought wearily, but wanting her to tell him herself had taken on paramount importance. He couldn't explain his reasons, but he suspected that not telling her had to do with knowing that when she trusted him, trusted him without reservation, she would speak of that night. Until then, he would love her and hope that the day would come when there were no longer any secrets between them.

"Of course, I understand," Gillian said from beside him, hurt and angry by his short answer. Any notion of sharing with him the contents of the note vanished. She forced a yawn. "My goodness, I'm sleepier than I realized."

Luc knew he'd made a misstep. "Gillian, I didn't—"

"Well, I'm for sleep," she interrupted brightly. Yawning again, she said, "Good night." And turned her back on him.

Luc stared impotently into the darkness. He'd handled that badly, and he didn't blame her for being annoyed with him. He sighed. Was he being unreasonable for wanting her to tell him herself? A week, he decided. I'll wait a week and if she has not spoken of what happened at the duke's hunting lodge that night by then, I will tell her what Cornelia related to me.

Despite their best intentions, the next morning, breakfast was a strained affair between the newlyweds. Luc escaped to his office as soon as he could and was relieved when a note from Barnaby arrived at Ramstone a few hours later. Folding the note and placing it in his vest pocket, Luc had gone in search of Gillian. He found her and Mrs. Marsh, the housekeeper, busy mending linens in a small, cozy room on the second floor near the back the house. Luc dropped a kiss on Gillian's cheek and murmured, "Barnaby has some things he'd like to discuss with me. I should be back no later than midafternoon."

She gave him a clear-eyed look. "More private matters?"

Luc had the grace to look uncomfortable. "My dear, I, ah—"

Just as she had last night, she interrupted him, saying, "No matter—I intend to drive into the village to the draper's shop this afternoon. Emily mentioned yesterday that Mrs. Webber, she used to be a fine needlewoman, and her sister, Mrs. Grant, opened the shop only a few months ago. Emily says they have a nice selection of fabrics." She flashed him a smile and added carelessly, "Don't worry if I run late—you know how it is when women shop."

Luc trusted neither her smile nor her words, but he could not say why. He wouldn't say that she was sulking over his refusal to discuss his meeting with Cornelia, but she had certainly put a distance between them. He hadn't meant to hurt her, but he was aware that he probably had with his blunt reply last night. His lips quirked. He wasn't exactly being open and honest with her either, yet he expected her to trust him? He snorted. Perhaps, he thought, as he rode toward

Windmere, a week was too long to wait to explain about Cornelia and his meeting with her.

Shown into Barnaby's study, Luc wasn't surprised to find Lamb, Mathew and Simon already there ahead of him. After offering Luc some punch and seeing him settled like the others around the fire, Barnaby said, "Hugh and the others left this morning for Parkham House. I didn't want to call a meeting between us until they were out of the house." He grimaced. "Hugh is too clever by half, and though there was no love lost between the brothers, I'd just as soon he not learn that Jeffery was so closely aligned with Nolles that he gave our smuggler leader free rein at The Birches."

Luc nodded. After taking a sip of the hot punch, Luc said, "The new moon is tonight, and I've noticed the past day or so that the barometer has dropped. Even after yesterday's rain it's still falling, storm coming in."

"No moon and a storm," observed Lamb. "A perfect set of circumstances for the smugglers."

Barnaby rubbed his chin. "I'm thinking it's time that we bring in our Preventive Officer, Lieutenant Deering."

Over his cup of punch, Mathew regarded him. "Why now?"

"My wife's cousin is dead and her former home is presently no longer holding smuggled goods. She won't have to bear the shame of having the world know just what a bounder Jeffery was or that he was storing contraband in her old home."

"How do you know that?" Luc objected. "It's true the cellars are cleared out now, but that may have been in anticipation of the arrival of new contraband. This time tomorrow the place could be bursting with smuggled goods."

Barnaby smiled and nodded toward Simon. "For the past several days, The Birches' new owner, along with several servants borrowed from Windmere, have been staying in the place to drive home the point to Nolles that things have changed. Drastically. Even if Nolles thought to continue to use the cellars, with Simon and a half-dozen servants bustling about the residence, he'd have to abandon that plan."

"So what is our plan?" Luc asked, frowning.

Barnaby sighed. "I shall have a talk with Deering. Alert him to the fact that we believe that Nolles and his gang are expecting a shipment from France any day."

"And what," inquired Mathew dryly, "causes you to believe that? No matter what sort of a friendly relationship you have with him, Deering's not going to simply take you at your word." He took a long swallow of his punch. A challenge in his gaze, over the rim of his cup, he stared hard at Barnaby. "You may have been able to bamboozle him with that neat and tidy tale of Tom being shot by smugglers, but don't you think Deering will get suspicious about your intimate knowledge of the comings and goings of a smuggler's gang? He may be young, but he is honest and intelligent."

Luc grimaced. "Mathew's right. How would you know with any certainty that Nolles is preparing for a new shipment? You can't mention Townsend's part or the use of The Birches, so what does that leave you with?" Luc grinned. "Intuition?"

"Don't forget his glib tongue," Lamb offered, smiling. "Don't forget, Barnaby was able to get us over some heavy ground with Deering earlier in the year. But unless we have some information that comes from other than Barnaby's 'suspicions' of a run by Nolles, I don't see how we can bring Deering into the situation."

Barnaby glanced at Simon and cocked a brow. Simon shook his head. "No. I've heard nothing. Of course, I didn't go to The Ram's Head for a few nights following Townsend's death, so there is no telling if something significant occurred. Certainly, beyond expressing false sadness over Townsend's death, nothing was said last night in my hearing to make me think that a landing is in the offing."

A scowl marring his handsome features, Barnaby stared into his cup of punch. "Blast it! Nolles must be expecting a shipment, but we have no way of passing that information on to Deering."

"Or where he will store the goods when landed before transporting them to London," Lamb muttered.

"*Vraiment?* You have been unable to find out anything about a new hiding place?" Luc asked.

"It's not something I can ask outright," Lamb replied. "Remember, the villagers aren't opposed to smuggling—not when half of them earn much of their money from the trade and the other half have relatives connected to the smuggling. Add to that they're a closemouthed bunch, and even though I've lived here for a year, I am, after all, to most of them an outsider."

"If Nolles does have somewhere else to hide his goods, what about Stanton's place, Woodhurst?" Simon queried. "It's inland a little farther than The Birches, and if Stanton is one of the investors, why not use it?"

"I should have thought of it myself," Lamb said. "You stayed there a few nights; what do you know of the place?"

"Not a great deal, but there is only a pair of servants, a man and wife, the Archers. Cornelia knows of them and says their reputation is unsavory," Simon replied. A look crossed his face. "They're reputed to be friends of Nolles's."

"Anything else?" asked Lamb, sitting forward in his chair.

Simon hunched a shoulder. "Woodhurst is about five miles from the village and sits in the middle of a woodland park. Stanton mentioned that there's around a hundred and twenty acres with the place." Looking thoughtful, he added, "It is isolated, now that I think about it. There are no near neighbors."

"Cellars?" asked Barnaby.

"That I can't tell you. I was foxed most of the time I stayed there and really only saw a few rooms." He frowned. "Stanton treats the place like a temporary camp of some sort. I don't believe he will be spending much time there."

"Stanton is not known for his love of, er, pastoral

charms," murmured Mathew. "His milieu is London and the hells and whorehouses that abound."

Rising to his impressive height, Lamb said, "Since there is nothing else in the offing, I think I shall ride over to Wood-hurst this afternoon and see what I can spy."

"I'm going with you," said Mathew.

Everyone looked at him, surprised. Mathew scowled and muttered, "I've been at Windmere nearly a fortnight and have done nothing but partake of Barnaby's hospitality—which wasn't the reason I came here in the first place." He shot Simon a look. "I know that you were behind the invitation that brought me here and that Barnaby provided the bait—a chance to get at Nolles." His mouth tightened. "As I said, I've done nothing these past few weeks. Accompanying Lamb will at least give me the feeling that I am doing something to bring about Nolles's downfall."

Lamb wasn't happy about having Mathew following at his heels like a puppy, but a glance from Barnaby stilled the objections on his tongue. With something less than enthusiasm, Lamb said, "There's no need for us to hurry away—at this hour Stanton and Padgett are probably still sleeping off last night's overindulgence." He looked to Simon for confirmation.

Simon frowned. "Perhaps not." He glanced at the clock on the mantel. "It's nearly noon, and while they have no set routine when I stayed there, they were usually up and riding to The Ram's Head for breakfast at this hour. The, ah, comforts of Woodhurst and service of the Archers provide little incentive to linger."

"Very well," Lamb said. Slapping his knees, he stood up. His gaze on Mathew, he asked, "Shall I have our horses saddled?"

With a spark in his eyes that had been missing for a long time, Mathew nodded.

*   *   *

Gillian never considered that a female had written the note, but one thing was certain, a female would have known how difficult it was for a respectable woman of the upper class to go anywhere alone . . . and without anyone knowing her destination. Her comment to Luc about visiting the draper's shop had been brilliant. Since she'd woken that morning, she'd been anxiously thinking *why* she needed to go to the village, knowing her errand had to be something she couldn't send a servant to handle. A visit to the draper's shop to select fabrics for the house settled that problem.

Of course, it was unthinkable that she ordered a horse saddled and rode into the village alone: the rain banished the idea of riding anyway—which meant she had to use a vehicle. One she could drive herself, and the rain made an open vehicle out of the question. While it wasn't ideal, the hooded gig in the stables fitted her purpose. She still had the problem of having an escort to solve, and her choices came down to Mrs. Marsh or Nan. The choice was easy: Mrs. Marsh.

Gillian grimaced. Nan knew her too well and with the familiarity of a longtime servant, Nan wouldn't hesitate to question what her mistress was about. With Mrs. Marsh such was not the case. In the short time of her marriage to Luc, she and the housekeeper had established a cordial relationship, but Mrs. Marsh didn't *know* her. A bit in awe of the new mistress, Mrs. Marsh would follow orders and not object or argue with her when she left her at the draper's shop— as Nan would.

As the hour grew near for their departure for the village, Gillian's greatest fear was that Luc would return and insist upon escorting her. Finally seated in the hooded gig, the brooch nestled inside her velvet and ribbon reticule lying on the seat between her and Mrs. Marsh, Gillian urged the horse forward. Sweeping out of the lane that led to Ramstone, she glanced in the direction that Luc would take on his way home from Windmere and her heart jumped when through the rain, she spied a lone rider in the distance. Praying it wasn't Luc and that if it was she'd be far enough ahead of him to make the idea of following her dubious, she headed the horse in the opposite direction of the rider and drove toward the village. And a meeting that hopefully would finally put Charles's wretched vowels in her hands.

As the horse sloshed down the road toward the village, the rain fell harder, turning the road muddy and making travel cold and uncomfortable—even with a warmed brick at her feet and a heavy wool blanket across her knees. The days were short in early December, and Gillian was uneasy about the hour of the meeting—sunset. Wandering around searching for an abandoned fisherman's cottage in gathering darkness was not something she was looking forward to. The rain and the possibility of a storm blowing ashore didn't make the prospect any more appealing.

Her mind only half on the fabric samples before her, Gillian glanced out the chintz-hung window of the cozy shop, aware of the passing minutes and the creeping gloom brought on as much by the rain as the lateness of hour. How long, she wondered, as she nodded and exclaimed over the samples in front of her, before she could make an excuse and leave?

Occasionally, Gillian asked Mrs. Marsh's opinion about a particular sample, but in her mind a clock was ticking away, aware of time passing second by second, minute by minute. . . . She felt guilty using Mrs. Webber's service to hide the real reason she had come to the village, but once she'd seen the selection offered by the old woman, she soothed her conscience, knowing she'd be making some handsome purchases. The selection was impressive, and Gillian had already decided that the mulberry velvet with a cream strip made into drapes would look stunning in the main salon at Ramstone and the burgundy and gold-flecked damask would be perfect for Luc's bedroom.

A look at the painted china clock on an old bombe chest in the corner of the room told Gillian that she could not linger longer. Rising to her feet, she said to Mrs. Webber, "If you'll excuse me, I have an errand to run." Smiling she added, "I'll leave Mrs. Marsh here to continue to look at your excellent samples, and she can discuss with you the amount of the mulberry velvet and burgundy damask we'll need. I shouldn't be gone very long." Clutching her reticule, Gillian turned away, opened the door to the shop and made her escape.

Chapter 21

Climbing into the gig, Gillian clucked at the horse and drove down the street toward the Coast Road, her mouth dry with fear and her stomach in knots. She glanced at the reticule beside her on the seat and, grabbing it, shoved it to the floor and beneath the blanket. What she was doing was full of risk, perhaps even foolish, she admitted, but she had no intention of skipping into the fisherman's cottage and simply producing the brooch. At least, she reminded herself, I wasn't completely stupid. I *did* leave a note for Luc in case. . . .

Tendrils of fright coursed through her when she considered the "in case." All the horrifying things that could happen to her—murder, rape or abduction—had crossed her mind more than once, and because she wasn't entirely foolish, she'd written a letter to Luc, enclosing the note she'd received along with Charles's vowel. Though determined to handle this alone and hopefully return home without incident, the idea of traipsing off and meeting a stranger in a secluded place with not *one* person knowing where she had gone made no sense to her. If she did not return home by seven o'clock, Nan was to give her letter to Luc.

Nan's eyes narrowed when Gillian handed her the letter and explained what she wanted. Seeing the barrage of questions forming on Nan's lips, Gillian begged, "Just do as I ask,

Nan. Please." Nan hadn't liked it, but she'd nodded, and Gillian took comfort knowing that if she did not return by seven o'clock that once he'd read the note, Luc would be looking for her.

Gillian bit her lip. Mrs. Marsh would raise the alarm before then, she thought with a mixture of dread and relief. If she didn't return to Mrs. Webber's drapery shop within the hour, or less, inquiries would be made and word would spread through the village. She groaned. There was no time to waste.

A stiff wind was blowing, and peering through the sheets of rain, she almost missed the cottage. Seeing it, a forlorn and shabby bundle of wattle and stone near the edge of a cliff in the distance, she drove cautiously forward. Leaving the road, she halted the horse in front of the building and stepped down from the vehicle, leaving her reticule with the brooch inside it concealed under the blanket on the floor.

Keeping the reins in her hand, she stood there indecisively, the wind howling and plucking at her pelisse, the rain lashing with growing ferocity against her. Even to escape the nasty weather, the last thing she wanted was to enter that beastly little hovel, but if there was any chance of retrieving Charles's vowels, she had no choice. After fastening the reins around a stump of driftwood, she resolutely faced the cottage.

It appeared deserted, and she wondered if the writer of the note had decided not to meet her after all. Reluctance in every step, she walked to the gaping door of the cottage. She hesitated, and staring at the yawning black opening before her, her instinct warned her of danger.

Except the danger didn't come from inside the cottage. The storm hid the man's approach, and Gillian's first warning was when her horse threw up its head and shied and snorted. She spun around just as a bulky figure bore down on her.

Gillian had no time to react; a coarse blanket was thrown over her, and trapped in its thick folds, it took but a moment for the man to grab her and prevent escape. She fought wildly, terror galvanizing her, arms and legs flailing in all directions. She kicked and clawed, but engulfed in the blanket, her struggles failed.

"Be still, you tiresome bitch," growled a voice in her ear, "or I may strangle you and throw your body over the cliffs."

Recognizing the voice, ice spurted in her veins. *Stanton.* She wasn't surprised, but if she had been frightened before, remembering his dark, heavy features, his cold, empty eyes, her fright doubled. Never doubting that he'd do as he said, she froze.

"That's better," he said. Shoving her forward, she half-stumbled, half-fell in the direction of the cottage. Unable to see and fueled by momentum, she hit the rear wall with a loud thump. She slammed hard into the wall, and a cry broke from her. Dazed, she fought to get her bearings, but hearing movements behind her, she spun around; the last thing she wanted was Stanton at her back.

Her spine against the wall, trapped in the suffocating folds of the blanket, Gillian heard rustling sounds, the clink of metal and then a faint glow appeared under the blanket near her feet. A lantern?

Hard hands grasped her shoulders and shook her. "Where is it?" Stanton demanded.

Pushing aside her terror, Gillian frantically considered her next move. He shook her again, rattling her teeth. "I don't have it with me," she prevaricated desperately.

Stanton cursed viciously and to her shame, she cowered away.

"Don't play with me! Where is it? You were to bring it with you."

"I, uh, I wanted to m-m-make certain you were going to d-d-deal honestly with me before I brought the b-b-brooch," she lied, hating the quaver in her voice. Gaining courage, she asked brazenly, "How do I know you have the vowels? How do I know you won't give me one or two in exchange for the brooch and then come back and want something more for the rest? It didn't s-s-seem wise to bring it with me today."

"You're lying," guessed Stanton. "I'll wager you have it on you. . . ." An ugly laugh came from him. "If I have to strip you bare as the day you were born to find it, I shall do so."

She sensed him moving toward her and she stumbled back. "Wait!" she cried and struggled free of the blanket.

In the wavering light of a small lantern set on a rickety table, she faced Stanton. "Show me the vowels, and if I am satisfied, I will give you the brooch," she said with more bravado than confidence.

Stanton's eyes narrowed. "I didn't bring them with me."

Her heart sank and she muttered, "You didn't trust me any more than I trusted you."

"Who the devil cares whether you trust me or not," Stanton snarled. "I want that bloody brooch."

Gillian thrust her chin forward. "And I want those vowels. All of them."

"If you don't give me that damned brooch right now, I'll have you peeled out of your clothes before a cat can lick its ear." He smiled nastily. "Then we'll see if you're telling the truth or not."

The thought of his hands on her, ripping her clothes from her body, added to her terror, and throwing out a warning hand as he stepped forward, she cried, "Stop!" Relieved when he stopped, she said hastily, "I don't have it on me, but I can get it in . . . in a matter of minutes." Sticking to her position she muttered, "But I insist upon seeing the vowels."

This wasn't how Stanton had intended their meeting to progress, and frustration ate at him. He didn't want to believe that she didn't have the brooch on her, but he couldn't take the chance that she was telling the truth. Wasting time stripping her down to determine for himself the truth of the matter hadn't been part of his plan. Her assertion that the brooch was nearby, or at least someplace not far away, gave him hope that he still might walk away with the brooch.

Stanton had no intention of allowing her to leave here with the vowels, let alone alive. But he had brought the vowels with him, figuring at some point, he'd have to show them to her. His plan was simple, and Townsend's suicide had given him the idea. Along with the vowels, in his vest pocket was a folded sheet of paper and in the pocket of his greatcoat rested a quill and a small bottle of ink. The bitch was going to write a farewell note to her husband, a note that would be delivered to Ramstone by a street urchin several hours from now. Her body would be found over the cliffs and that would be that. Marry in haste, repent in leisure; the new Mrs. Joslyn had been overcome with repentance and taken her own life. Tidy and simple. His hands closed into fists. But first he needed the brooch.

He studied her small form in the faint light of the lantern, wondering whether she was telling the truth or not. Torture was easy enough, but he didn't think he had the time to waste. He hadn't missed the speculative glint in St. John's eye when he'd shoved away from the table at The Ram's Head. Blast him! St. John wasn't above questioning what he'd been about when he returned, and the longer he was gone from the tavern, the more questions that arrogant bastard would have.

Stanton was wise to worry about St. John. Giving Stanton a few minutes' head start, St. John followed him from the tavern. The rain and deepening gloom simplified the task of tracking Stanton's movements as the other man rode out of the village toward the coast. From a distance he watched as Stanton guided his horse down a narrow draw, dismounted and tied the animal to a piece of brush. When Stanton removed a folded bundle and took it with him when he clambered up the draw, St. John wondered if he was on a fool's errand.

St. John glanced through the rain at the barren landscape, the sound of the surf crashing against the cliffs echoing through the draw. Beyond the decrepit hut fifty yards or so in the distance, he could see nothing that would induce Stanton to leave the comforts of the tavern. Stanton wasn't in the petticoat line, and St. John had trouble believing that it was a woman that had prompted his desertion of The Ram's Head. So why was Stanton here, creeping toward the small building? He had nothing to go on but suspicion and instinct— that and the fact that Stanton had been by turns boisterous and surly all afternoon, fidgeting in his chair until finally Padgett had asked him if something was wrong. Stanton glared at Padgett, snapped a denial and then a few minutes later mumbled an excuse and barged out of the tavern.

Unlike Stanton, St. John double-checked that no one followed *him* and once Stanton reached the hut, he dismounted and secured his horse near the entrance of the draw. Like a wraith St. John drifted through the rain, his keen eyes fastened on Stanton's dark form at the rear of the cottage.

Because of the weather, most sensible folk were inside by the fire, and the sight of a hooded gig traveling slowly toward the front of the hut made St. John's brow rise. So Stanton was meeting someone, but whom? And why such secrecy? When Stanton disappeared around the side of the building, St. John risked climbing out of the draw. There was no place of concealment and shrugging, he hurried toward the cottage, hoping the rain would give him cover and that Stanton would be too preoccupied to notice him.

Seconds later, pressed against the frail walls of the abandoned building, St. John was startled at the sound of an object hitting the wall and a woman's cry. Even above the wind and rain, he heard Stanton's voice and that of the woman. His heart pounded with thick, savage strokes as he realized what he was hearing. He wouldn't have recognized Gillian's voice, but from the exchange between Stanton and the woman, the topic, he knew it had to be her. His hand closed into a fist as the knowledge that he had been right crashed through him. He smiled fiercely; he knew *why* that brooch was so important to Stanton. . . . Reaching into the pocket of his greatcoat he withdrew a pistol and slid around to the side of the cottage, edging toward the front. He'd waited for over two long years for this moment. Vengeance would be his before many minutes passed. . . .

Intent upon what was happening inside the cottage, St. John almost missed the arrival of the horseman who rode up and stopped his horse beside the hooded gig. It was the clink of the bridle as the man dismounted that alerted him to the newcomer.

Knowing it was Gillian Joslyn inside the hut allowed St. John to identify the tall figure that swung out of the saddle. Luc Joslyn. Just what he needed—a jealous husband, come in search of an erring wife. Torn between a curse and a laugh, St. John hesitated, uncertain what to do next. Show himself and pray he could wave Joslyn over without giving away their presence to those inside the cottage? Or let events play out with no help from him?

Luc *had* been the horseman Gillian had spied as she'd turned onto the main road. Seeing the hooded gig come onto the main road from Ramstone's drive, Luc had known it was his wife. More on a whim than any other reason, he'd kicked his horse into a gallop and continued toward the village. It wouldn't hurt to talk to Mrs. Gilbert and learn what gossip she'd heard about a possible run by Nolles and that was excuse enough for his actions. After all, he'd told himself, with no sweet wife waiting for him, returning to Ramstone didn't hold the appeal it would have if Gillian had been there to greet him.

Having the intention to escort her back to Ramstone when she finished at the draper's shop, Luc had not lingered long at

The Crown. Mrs. Gilbert's news had been disappointing in that she'd heard not a whisper of Nolles's plans. "No one has said a thing," she complained as she served Luc a tankard of ale. "Most of the talk has been about the squire's death and speculation about having Mr. Simon Joslyn living at The Birches." She'd shook her head. "Not a breath about Nolles or what he might be up to." Her blue eyes narrowed. "There has been some curiosity about the fine gentlemen from London that have been frequenting Nolles's place, though. Broadhaven isn't exactly Brighton, and people are wondering why they're here. We're a fishing village used to the ways of our local gentry to be sure, but not the likes of them. Drunkards, gamblers and womanizers the lot of them. The feeling is that Mr. Stanton's inheritance of his great-grandmother's place isn't necessarily a good thing." Luc shrugged and, leaving his ale half-finished, said his farewell and headed outside. Mounting his horse, he turned the animal in the direction of the draper's shop.

Luc was over a block away when he spied Gillian's small form dashing out of the draper's shop and entering the gig. He'd thought to hail her, but decided between the wind and the rain she wouldn't have heard him anyway. Expecting her to turn around to drive back to Ramstone, he'd halted his horse to wait for her. To his confusion, she drove off in the opposite direction. Another errand?

More mystified than suspicious, Luc trailed behind her, wishing she'd chosen a more agreeable day to discharge what had to be minor duties—or left it to the servants. His greatcoat and boots kept him warm and dry, but he wouldn't deny he was looking forward to sitting by his own fire and enjoying a brandy . . . with his wife in his lap. If she didn't accomplish her tasks soon, they'd be riding home in the dark. And the rain.

He didn't consciously hang back, but once she left the village and it was obvious she wasn't doing any shopping, he found himself allowing the distance between them to lengthen.

There wasn't, he argued, any need to catch up with her. Let her take care of her business and then he'd make his presence known in time to escort her home.

When she'd turned onto the Coast Road he'd been even more puzzled, knowing only a few fishermen lived out this way. What the devil?

He was far enough back that by the time he'd turned on the Coast Road, her gig was already stopped in front of the fisherman's hut and there was no sign of her. The hut was abandoned, and the first icy trickle of anxiety ran down his spine. Frowning, he halted his horse beside the gig and dismounted.

A sensation of wrongness swept over him and he started forward. The sight of a tall figure garbed in a greatcoat motioning him to the side of the building stopped him in his tracks. Through the rain and deepening shadows, Luc regarded the other man suspiciously. *Sacrebleu!* What was Gillian about?

His hand closing around the pistol in the pocket of his greatcoat, Luc stalked forward. Recognizing St. John, he opened his mouth to demand what was going on, but a finger to St. John's lips stopped him.

St. John shook his head and indicated they step away from the building. A few yards from the cottage, in a low voice, St. John said, "I beg your indulgence. Your wife is safe, but she is meeting with Stanton."

At Luc's expression of angry astonishment, aware that time was precious, St. John added hastily, "It is not an assignation. At least not the kind one would expect. By means I can only guess at, Stanton has gained possession of some vowels signed by her first husband. He got your wife here by promising to exchange them for a brooch Dashwood gave her shortly before he was murdered."

Luc's eyes narrowed. "Why does Stanton want a brooch given to my wife by her first husband?"

"Because it proves that he is a murderer," St. John declared harshly. At Luc's look of incredulity, he hurried on, "I am not mad! That day we met you in the village with the others, I recognized the brooch your wife was wearing as one I had ordered fashioned exclusively for the woman I was going to marry—Elizabeth Soule. It is one of a kind and it was stolen from her home on the night she was murdered. I always suspected that Stanton was behind it—he was suddenly flush with money after her death—but I could never find proof. Until now."

Luc stared from St. John to the cottage. "Stanton murdered the woman you loved," he said in a furious undertone, "and you delay me while my wife is in there with him?" He swung around to charge the cottage, but St. John caught his arm.

Luc turned on him like an enraged tiger, and his blue eyes blazing, he snarled, "Unhand me or I'll kill you where you stand."

"And if you interrupt them, you may destroy the only chance of clearing your wife's name," St. John snapped.

"What do you mean?"

"Only that if we eavesdrop for a moment or two, Stanton may betray himself further." When Luc violently rejected that notion by jerking his arm free and started again for the cottage, St. John said urgently, "It is a chance, perhaps the *only* chance, to prove her innocence. I swear to you that she is unharmed and if she appears in danger we will strike immediately."

Luc paused. Every instinct demanded he whisk Gillian away from Stanton immediately but he had to weigh those feelings against the possibility that St. John was right and her innocence could be proven. If St. John was to be believed, she was in that cottage with a murderer, a man who had murdered twice already. Was clearing her name worth risking her life? He shook his head. *Non!*

St. John caught his arm again. "Please," he begged, his green eyes beseeching. "I've waited over two years for this moment; all I ask is a moment's delay."

Something in the other's man expression moved him, and Luc said thickly, "A moment only. That is all I can give you . . . and if she is harmed, by God I'll kill you."

Their hurried exchange took only moments, and as one the two men crept to the cottage, St. John circling around to the front on one side of the doorway, Luc pressed against the wall on the other side of the door opening. Stanton's and Gillian's voices carried clearly through the doorway to the waiting men.

Inside the cottage, tamping down her terror, Gillian held her own against Stanton. As the minutes passed he'd cursed her, threatened her and demanded that she give him the brooch; she stubbornly refused. In the wavering light of the lantern they stared at each other, at an impasse.

Regarding her balefully, aware of the time flying by, Stanton finally growled, "Suppose I do have the vowels on me. You say you don't have the brooch. Why should I show them to you?"

"Because if you don't show them to me," she responded tightly, "you will never get your hands on the brooch."

His eyes narrowed to slits and his face flushed with rage. "You're a cheating bitch just like that husband of yours."

Gillian's head lifted. "How dare you!" she gasped, furious. "My husband is an honorable man. He may be a gambler, but Luc Joslyn would never *cheat!*"

Stanton laughed unpleasantly. "I'm not talking about Luc Joslyn, you silly little fool, I'm talking about Dashwood, your first husband."

"Charles?"

"Charles?" he mimicked. "Yes, bloody Charles. If not for him, you wouldn't be here and I'd have gotten rid of that damned brooch years ago."

Uneasy at this turn of the conversation, Gillian asked cautiously, "What does Charles have to do with my brooch?"

He flashed her a calculated look, and she had the sensation that he'd made a decision. One she wouldn't like.

"He wouldn't give it back," he said slowly, advancing on her. "He won it from me and when I tried to redeem it at Welbourne's lodge that night, he refused." His hands closed into fists. "Just as you're refusing to do now."

Gillian's eyes widened and her mouth went dry. "You!" she blurted without thinking. "It was *you*. You murdered him."

His lips twitched in a travesty of a smile, and he bowed. "At your service, Madame." His smile fading, he said, "And I'm afraid you're about to meet his fate, but first you're going to write a note for me to Luc." He reached inside his greatcoat for the sheet of paper and a second later had retrieved the quill and ink. Placing them on the table, he said, "It will be a tragedy, your suicide."

"You can't kill me. You don't have the brooch," Gillian argued desperately, her gaze moving from his face to the implements on the table.

"That's true, but I'm willing to wager that you did bring it with you. You said that it wasn't far away, and I'm gambling its hidden in your vehicle."

Her face gave her away and Stanton smiled. She was going to die, she thought, terrified. She'd never see Luc again. Never feel his strong arms around her again. No! She would not accept that her life ended here and now at the hands of this monster.

"Get over here," Stanton growled, "and write the bloody note before I decide to kill you without it. It makes no difference to me. You'll be just as dead."

"Go to hell!" Gillian shouted and, with a strength and determination borne of fear, launched herself at him.

Several things happened at once. Gillian rushed forward, her fists hitting Stanton soundly in the chest, catching him off guard. He stumbled back, and she dashed around him at the same instant Luc came flying into the cottage, his pistol aimed and ready. St. John followed, his pistol leveled on Stanton, both men fanning out on either side of the small room.

Intent upon escape, Gillian screamed with rage and terror as a hard arm grabbed her and pushed her into a corner behind a tall frame. "Hush!" commanded Luc, one lightning glance assuring him that she was unharmed.

Gillian's heart was galloping in her chest, and she was never so grateful to see Luc's lean features in her life. Nothing mattered but that he was here and she would live, she thought on the verge of hysteria. Nothing. The vowels. None of it mattered, and she cursed her pride that had placed her in such danger.

From across the short distance that separated them, Stanton stared at the two men. He was gambler enough to know that he had lost, but he didn't yet know the extent of his loss.

A sickly smile curved his lips. "Gentlemen, this isn't what it looks like," he muttered. He glanced at Luc. "I assure you that your wife has not played you false. We were merely, ah, taking care of some old business." When Luc's glittering blue eyes never moved from him and the pistol remained fixed on him, Stanton said, "There, uh, seemed to be a misunderstanding and I'm afraid I inadvertently frightened her. I apologize."

"He killed Charles," Gillian said from behind Luc. "He told me so and that he planned to murder me."

"We know," Luc answered. "We overheard everything."

Stanton blanched, his gaze going to St. John's face. What he saw there caused him to take a step backward.

"The vowels," Luc said coldly. "Give them to me. Now."

"Of course," Stanton said eagerly. But when his hand went to his greatcoat, Luc snapped, "Slowly. And if there is anything else in your hand when you remove it from your coat, you'll not draw another breath."

Stanton did as ordered, tossing a small pile of papers onto

the table. Luc took a few steps forward, swept them up and, trusting St. John to keep Stanton still, turned around and thrust them into Gillian's hands. Their eyes met. "I would have retrieved them for you," Luc said softly.

"I know," she said huskily. "But it was something I needed to do myself."

Luc swung back to Stanton. "It is you who will be writing a note, but a far different one than you would have forced my wife to write." Nodding to the single sheet of paper, he said, "Write your confession to the murders of both Elizabeth Soule and Charles Dashwood."

Stanton balked. "You're mad! I'll not do it. You can't prove anything."

Grimly, Luc said, "Both St. John and I can testify to what we overheard. And my wife as well. Write it."

"I'll not hang," snarled Stanton, his eyes darting around the room.

"I promise you," drawled St. John, "that you will not hang."

Luc glanced sharply at him.

"You'll let me go," questioned Stanton, his disbelief clear.

"I swear on Elizabeth's grave that you will not hang," said St. John.

With two pistols aimed at his heart, already scheming to find a way to turn the tables, Stanton nodded. Bending forward, he opened the bottle of ink, snatched up the quill and wrote quickly. When done, he picked up the sheet of paper and held it out toward St. John.

His eyes fixed on Stanton, St. John said, "Luc, read it and make certain the bastard wrote the truth."

Luc took the paper and scanned the scrawl. "He did. He admits to killing both Elizabeth Soule and Charles Dashwood."

A queer smile curved St. John's mouth. "Take the confession and your wife and leave us."

Without a word, Luc tucked the confession inside his

greatcoat and swept Gillian out of that small cottage and into the stormy night. They exchanged not a word, until Luc had put away his pistol, tied his horse to the back of the vehicle and, gathering up the reins of the horse harnessed to the gig, joined her on the seat under the protection of the hood.

Inside the cottage, his eyes fierce on Stanton, St. John said, "Knowing you, you did not come here without being armed. Put your weapon on the table in front of you. Slowly."

"Going to kill me in cold blood?" sneered Stanton, withdrawing his pistol and carefully laying it on the table.

Motioning him back, St. John picked up the pistol and threw it outside. "No. I'll leave the cold-blooded killing to you," St. John answered. Placing his own pistol on the table, he stepped an equal distance away from the table.

"I'm giving you more of a chance than you gave Elizabeth," St. John said, his green eyes bright and feral. "If you can reach my pistol before I do, you might live." His teeth gleamed whitely in a tiger's smile. "I promise you one thing—only one of us will leave this miserable hovel alive."

Seated in the gig, her eyes fixed on the doorway, Gillian asked in a fearful tone, "What will happen?"

"St. John will kill him."

Gillian gasped and Luc bent a fierce glance on her. "As I would in the same position. Stanton murdered the woman St. John loved and planned to marry."

"But how do you know that?"

"The brooch. St. John had it made especially for her. It was one of a kind. He recognized it that day we met him and the others in the village when I was escorting you home to High Towers." His eyes fastened on the doorway of the cottage where the light from the lantern danced, Luc added, "There was no time for full explanations, but St. John suspected Stanton killed her. He needed proof. Tonight he got it." His gaze shifted to her. "I'm not certain whether to kiss you or wring your neck," he said dryly.

Gillian looked up in the gloom. "I would much rather you kissed me." When he only stared at her, she said, "Luc, I had to get the vowels. I can't explain it, but it was wrong to expect you to untangle something that Charles had caused." He snorted and she added indignantly, "I did leave a note for you. Along with the note Stanton had sent me. Nan was to give it to you at seven o'clock if I hadn't returned."

Luc's hands closed around her shoulders and he dragged her next to him. "You little fool, you would have been dead by then."

She smiled mistily at him. "But I'm not . . . wouldn't you much rather kiss me than scold me?"

He laughed reluctantly. "Yes, *ma coeur,* I would indeed." His mouth came down on hers and he kissed her, feeling all the rage and terror he'd felt when he knew she was in danger fade away. She was safe. And in his arms and he intended to keep her there forever. Lifting his head a long while later, he murmured, "You ever do anything like this again and I *will* beat you."

Nestled against him, Gillian smiled, not believing a word of it. "Never." Her eyes moved to the cottage and she shivered, knowing a man would die tonight. The wind was howling, the rain lashing against the hooded gig and any sound that might have carried from the cottage was drowned out by storm, but she could not help imagining what was going on inside and she shivered again.

Luc felt her shiver and pulled her even closer. Dropping a kiss on her temple, he said, "It won't be long now."

"What if . . ." She swallowed. "What if St. John fails?"

"That's why we're still here," he answered simply, taking out his pistol again. "If St. John doesn't come out of that cottage and Stanton does . . . I'll kill him. One way or another St. John will have his revenge."

Not even the storm could mute the sound of a shot that came from inside the cottage. Gillian jumped, and her eyes fastened painfully on the doorway.

Luc stiffened, relaxing when he recognized the tall, dark form that appeared in the faint light seeping out from the doorway of the cottage.

In swift strides, St. John closed the distance between them. There was barely enough light to reveal a cut over his right eye and an ugly gash along one cheek. "Poor fellow," St. John said quietly. "He killed himself." He looked expectantly at Luc. "And now if you will be so good as to give me the confession, I will see that it surfaces at the right time and in the right place. The confession will clear your wife's name and explain his suicide."

Luc reached inside his greatcoat and handed it to him. "I'll trust you to do so, *mon ami.*"

St. John nodded. "It will be my pleasure."

Gillian spared no sympathy for Stanton; he had already murdered two people and if events had turned out differently, he would have murdered her. She fumbled around for her reticule and opening it, found the brooch. She handed it to St. John, saying shyly, "I think this is yours."

He held it in his hand for a long moment. His voice thick with emotion, he said, "Thank you, Madame." And then he was gone into the night and the storm.

Luc slapped the reins and turned the horse, then, one arm around his wife, their bodies close together, they slowly drove away into the rainy night.

Epilogue

Christmas at Windmere that year was one of quiet joy. Sitting cozily ensconced in a tall wingback chair of blue velvet by the fire roaring in the fireplace, Cornelia sighed with pleasure, enjoying the warmth.

Silas, sitting in the twin to Cornelia's chair on the other side of the fireplace, said, "That's precisely how I feel." His eyes twinkled in his little gnome face. "It has been a most exciting and enjoyable day, but I find that this quiet time by the fire is my favorite part."

Cornelia nodded. Silas was right. After partaking of the rich meal of chestnut soup, oysters, roast goose, haunch of venison and sirloin, new peas from the greenhouses of Windmere, creamed cauliflower, mincemeat, apple pies and a damson dumpling, to name a few items served, it was pleasant to doze by the fire.

The scent of evergreens wafted in the air; archways, mantels and banisters dripped with branches of evergreen and holly; mistletoe hung in strategic places throughout the grand house; and silver bells with scarlet ribbons festooned either side of doorways. Even the weather had cooperated for Christmas, and while drifts of new-fallen snow blanketed the countryside, it hadn't prevented guests from traveling to Windmere to share the holiday with Lord and Lady Joslyn and their firstborn child.

Ten days previously Emily had given birth to a daughter, Noel, named for the season of her birth. If Barnaby had been disappointed at not having sired an heir, no one could tell from his demeanor or manner. He doted on Emily and his daughter. Girls, he explained proudly to anyone who would listen, didn't run in the Joslyn family; his sister, Bethany, was the only girl in over three generations, yet he was lucky enough to be the father of what had to be the most beautiful female born in all of England. Next to her mother, he added, his dark eyes, warm and loving, gazing upon Emily's face.

At present, Noel's eyes were the solemn blue of a newborn, but Cornelia suspected that in time they would be the same brilliant azure for which the Joslyn family was famous. Right now pale downy fuzz covered the baby's head and would, no doubt, grow out to be the same silvery-fair color of her mother's hair. Of Barnaby's swarthy coloring there was no sign, but Cornelia and the rest of the family had already recognized the confident curve in the tiny jaw and the willful jut of her chin as having been inherited from her father. It was fortunate, Cornelia admitted, that Noel had inherited many of Emily's far more feminine and lovely features than her father's bolder facial characteristics.

A laugh broke into her reverie, and she looked across the room at the group gathered around a table littered with plates of sweetmeats, sugared plums, delicate lemon biscuits and bowls of punch and hot cider.

Barnaby and Emily stood side by side, Luc and Gillian next to them, Luc's arm possessively around Gillian's waist. Mathew and Simon were nearby, as were Sophia and Stanley. Cornelia was sorry that dear, sweet Anne and Hugh and Althea hadn't been able to be here, but she understood. Jeffery may have made himself thoroughly disliked, but he had been Althea's son and Hugh's brother and the wound of his death was too raw to allow for a celebration.

Watching Luc smile at something Barnaby said, she nodded to herself. They all had much to smile about these days, especially, she thought, after the shocking events at the end of November and early December. She shook her head. Canfield, an accidental death. Townsend, dead by his own hand. And Stanton shooting himself in that abandoned cottage by the cliffs. Three such sudden, shocking deaths, each in close proximity to the other, had set the tongues in the neighborhood wagging.

The discovery of Stanton's body by an itinerant ragman the morning after the storm had sent a firestorm of horror over the area, but that was nothing compared to the uproar that erupted when Stanton's confession to the murder of Elizabeth Soule and Charles Dashwood had been discovered. Padgett and St. John, as friends of the deceased, had been helping the constable and a local attorney go through Stanton's belongings at Woodhurst, when St. John discovered the incriminating evidence the next day in a desk downstairs.

Once the confession was made public, it was amusing, Cornelia thought, the many members of the *ton* who exclaimed and declared that they had known all along that Gillian couldn't possibly have had anything to do with her first husband's death. To think otherwise was ridiculous! These days Gillian was hailed as a respectable, charming young woman who had been unfairly vilified, and she and Luc had been bombarded with invitations to visit some of the most illustrious families in the *ton*. Gillian took her sudden return to the bosom of the *ton* with aplomb, but Cornelia was convinced that the young woman didn't care a fig for the opinion of the *ton*. The only opinion that mattered to Gillian, Cornelia thought with a smile, was Luc's.

Cornelia's gaze rested on Gillian's vivacious face as she smiled up at Luc. Luc's bride was a vivacious little thing, and it was as plain as the nose on your face that the pair was deeply in love. It was there in the way their eyes clung, in the soft, secret smiles they shared and the way neither was ever far apart from the other. Luc hadn't cared what the gossip had said about his wife, but it was a good thing, Cornelia decided, that Stanton had so considerately killed himself and then thoughtfully left a confession that St. John had so conveniently "discovered," which absolved Gillian of any connection to Charles Dashwood's death. Cornelia snorted. She might be an old woman, but she knew when she was being bamboozled.

The events fit together neatly, but she'd wager next quarter's generous allowance provided by Barnaby that there was far more to the tale than the authorities or the public knew. Luc had been determined to clear his wife's name. . . . Her gaze fastened on Luc's face, and she snorted again. One of these days, she'd have a word with that young scamp and badger him until he told her the truth, because she didn't doubt for a moment that he'd had a hand in Stanton's fate.

At that moment, the group around the table split apart. Stanley and Sophia came over to see if Silas was ready for the journey to High Tower. He was, and the next several minutes were spent in farewells. Mathew was visiting with Simon at The Birches until after the new year, and a half hour later, the two brothers, after another round of feminine hugs and masculine handshakes and all around good wishes, prepared to depart. The women wandered back toward the fire, but Barnaby and Luc followed the other two men outside in the sharp night air.

Simon hesitated a moment, then flashing Barnaby a speaking look, said, "Matt and I are stopping by The Ram's Head for a few hours before returning home."

Barnaby cocked a brow. "Be careful," he said quietly, his eyes following Mathew, who was already swinging into the saddle. "Your brother is ripe for mischief. This cat-and-mouse game with Nolles we're playing is wearing his patience thin."

Simon's eyes darkened. "I know. He needs Nolles either caught or killed. I think only then can he forgive himself for what happened with Tom."

Barnaby nodded and, once the men disappeared into the darkness, along with Luc returned to the warmth of the house.

The ladies had not lingered in the salon and had disappeared into the upper reaches of the house. Unable to resist, a moment later, as if drawn by magic, the women were on their way to the nursery. After dismissing the nurse dozing in a rocking chair by the crib, much like a trio of fairy godmothers, they hovered around the crib, admiring and murmuring over the sleeping Noel.

Barnaby and Luc retreated to Barnaby's study, where Lamb joined them. The three men sprawled around the room, now drinking snifters of brandy.

"Simon and Mathew are going to The Ram's Head before returning home," Barnaby reported.

"Not very wise," responded Lamb. "With Padgett and St. John no longer in the area, there's little excuse to frequent Nolles's place."

Luc shrugged. "I wouldn't say that—one can always find a game of cards or dice, and Nolles provides privacy and willing wenches. Neither Mathew nor Simon are monks."

"If I thought it was because of women and gambling they were visiting the place, I'd feel less uneasy about it," Barnaby admitted. He looked at Luc. "You know that they're both hoping to catch Nolles out or learn something that will enable us to bring him down?"

"I know," agreed Luc, "but Nolles is a slippery bastard. We've been after him for what? Nearly a year now, and we are no closer to bringing him to justice than we were in the days following Tom's death."

"I was certain," Lamb said, "that there would have been a run or two by now, but it's as if he knows we're watching him and isn't willing to take any chances."

Barnaby grunted. "He'd be a fool if he didn't know we're watching him. We've made our hostility toward him plain."

Barnaby scowled. "And he has to know that we're not going to let his attack on Luc go by without retaliation—even with Lamb's, ah, message to him."

Lamb smiled into his brandy. "Well, yes, there is that."

Luc snorted and glared at Lamb. "I was the one who endured the beating, and you'd think that *some* people would have the decency to let me fight my own battles."

"It appears we were wrong about Nolles having cleared out The Birches in anticipation of a run," Barnaby said hastily. "If that had been the case, there'd have been one by now."

"Mathew and I haunted the vicinity of Stanton's place, even after his death," Lamb grumbled, "but we never saw any sign of Nolles or his men at Woodhurst."

Luc frowned. "I'm of the opinion that Townsend's death caught Nolles by surprise, and with Simon in residence and a far different kettle of fish that poor drunk Townsend, he dare not try to use the cellars to store his goods. Nolles might be lying low for a while, considering his options." Luc glanced at Barnaby. "Don't forget, if Canfield and Stanton were a pair of his investors, their deaths must have been a blow to Nolles's operation. Certainly it would have meant less money to buy contraband."

Barnaby stared at his snifter, as if the answer he sought were there. "Which leaves him with only Lord Padgett. . . ." He made a face. "Padgett certainly cleared out as soon as he could after Stanton's death."

"And St. John right along with him," murmured Lamb.

Luc shifted in his chair. What had happened the night Stanton died was a secret shared by only himself, Gillian and St. John and he saw no reason for anybody else to know about it. The possibility that St. John had been an investor in Nolles's smuggling operation had occurred to him but, he reminded himself, it had been revenge that had brought St. John to Padgett and Stanton's circle, *not* greed. "St. John isn't part of it," Luc said abruptly.

Lamb cocked a brow and looked skeptical.

"I agree," said Barnaby. "Although his association with that group arouses suspicion."

"I'll wager that you'll not see St. John rubbing shoulders with Padgett in the future," Luc muttered. "His reason for having been in the company of those licentious rakes doesn't exist anymore."

Both Lamb and Barnaby stared at him, but when Luc remained silent, they exchanged looks and shrugged.

Barnaby finished off his own brandy and said, "We shall have to hope that the new year will bring us better luck at ending Nolles's smuggling career than we have had so far."

Luc lifted his snifter and said, "I propose a toast: to the downfall of Nolles within the year."

The three men drank and dispersed, Luc going in search of Gillian. She was descending the stairs with Emily, Cornelia having sought out her bed, and at the sight of Luc crossing the hall, her breath caught and her knees nearly buckled at the wave of love that washed over her.

Taking her hand in his and dropping a kiss, Luc said, "Shall we go home, *m'amie?*"

Gillian agreed, and not long after that, wrapped in an ermine-lined cloak with a hood that framed her face, mittens and muff to keep her hands warm and a hot brick at her feet, she was seated beside her husband in the hooded gig as they drove away from Windmere. Carriage lamps on either side of the gig cut through the darkness, lighting their way as they drove toward Ramstone.

Her head resting on his broad shoulder as he drove, Gillian could not remember a time when she'd been so happy and contented. She had a husband she loved and one who loved her; what more could she want? The image of tiny Noel, looking like a sleeping angel, flitted across her mind and a secret smile curved her lips. She sighed blissfully.

Hearing her sigh, Luc took his eyes off the horse and asked, "What is it?"

Gillian snuggled closer. "I was thinking of your niece—she is quite adorable, isn't she?"

"*Oui,*" he answered. Grinning down at her, he added, "But not as adorable as our own children will be."

Gillian smiled shyly up at him. "I agree . . . and sometime next summer, the end of August, I think, you shall see for yourself."

It took Luc a second. But when he realized what she was saying, he jerked the horse to a stop and turned to stare at her, an expression of joyous incredulity on his face. "Do you mean. . . . ?"

She giggled and threw her arms around his neck. "Yes, my love, I am going to have your baby next summer."

Heedless of the horse, the gig, the road, Luc dropped the reins and, his arms closing around her, kissed her. "A father," he said, dazed, several moments later. "I shall be a father."

Nestled against him, Gillian murmured, "Yes. You shall be a father and a very good one, too."

Luc's eyes caressed her. "But I shall always be a husband first. A husband who adores you."

"Oh Luc," she cried, "I *do* love you."

What could he do but kiss her again? After several minutes, the horse snorted and moved restlessly, reminding them where they were. Breaking apart, they laughed, and picking up the reins, Luc urged the horse forward. Her head leaning against his shoulder, they drove slowly home, the future beckoning bright and glorious before them.